COVER STORIES

Richard Easter

8 Classic Songs Covered and Remixed as Short Stories

Volume 1: Sinners & Beginners

TO BE READ AT MAXIMUM VOLUME

THE VIVID PRESS

This edition first published in Great Britain in 2019 by The Vivid Press.

thevividpress.co.uk

© The Vivid Press / Richard Easter, 2019

Richard Easter has asserted his rights under the Copyright, Design and Patents Act, 1988, to be identified as the author of this work.

Paperback ISBN 978-1-9162169-0-7
Ebook ISBN   978-1-9162169-1-4

"Any true pop fan with romance in their soul has surely wondered now and again about the real story of the characters in their favourite songs by David Bowie, The Stones, The Beatles and others. Not the minutiae of the actual writing of a song, but what's actually going on with, say, Major Tom. Richard Easter's brilliantly conceived, witty and loving book offers some of the answers. Read it at maximum volume."

- Kevin Bourke, Rock & Reel Magazine.

"The style is great, the creativity is off the scale, and I thoroughly enjoyed it. For music lovers this book is a must."

- Lauren Cinderey, Amazon.

"I love music almost as much as I love reading, and with a heavy dose of artists I grew up on (Bowie, the Stones and Lou Reed) I had to try this intriguing mash-up. I wasn't disappointed, as each story is creative and clever. I particularly loved the haunting Space Oddity, the wonderful A Team and the heartbreaking couplet of Caroline Says (II) and Hey Joe."

- Sarah U, Amazon.

"A great concept and one that's been executed to absolute perfection. If you're a music lover and want to delve even deeper into songs you've listened to for years then there's no doubt in my mind you'll love giving this a read."

- Charlie Latham.

OK, ready? *Let's do it.*

To hear the songs COVER STORIES has remixed, use the QR code below to access the entire playlist via the website.

For Tom Binns, who filled a room with music
and let us all share it.

INTRO

Volume up, needle down, hey, ho, let's go.

First, these pages are immensely grateful you've picked them up. Books are almost completely pointless if not being read, so the fact you're reading *these words, right now*, has given this particular copy a purpose. So on its behalf, I thank you.

This is a book inspired by, and in love with, music.

We are surrounded by music, but often never stop to consider its rather strange and wonderful properties.

For example, at a certain time in your life, one song can make you dance like a loon, but at another, that exact same track leaves you weeping like a child. Something once joyous has become unbearable, without changing a single note.

And we've all experienced the curious emotion of hearing a piece of music for the very first time, then discovering we've somehow instantly connected with it, possibly even been reduced to tears. Even though we've had no previous relationship to the track, we're still strangely moved for reasons unknown.

A song can mean the world to me whilst being possibly abhorrent or even invisible to you. Because songs are like people - they have personalities, don't they? And we are either attracted, interested, repulsed, or usually, simply indifferent to them.

How can the movement of air, clattering tiny bones in our ears, transform us from happy to sad, still to movement, despairing to hopeful and every emotion in between?

Well, I can only assume it's magic, obviously. That's a nice, vague catch-all term that saves me any serious research. I'm sure there are theses and papers on it, but life is short and we all have other things to do.

OK, let's add another piece of fantastic to music's properties.

It's also time travel.

Apparently, smell is the sense most linked to memory, but I'll bet you have *way* more memories attached to music than smells. I know I do.

It gives our lives a through line - a multitude of way points, some good, some terrible, but markers, none the less. Play a song that means something to you and see what it conjures up. Those recollections aren't just shades or flickers, are they? No, you're there, *right back there*, instantaneously. And if that's not time travel, then what is?

That's why older people tend to re-visit songs from their youth - not just through nostalgia, but because the grooves flip them back to a precious space and time.

So don't begrudge Grandad asking for Elvis at the Wedding Disco, because when he hears The King, *he's not a pensioner any more.* By the way, that will happen to you, if it hasn't already.

So here's a loaded question; what was the first single you ever bought? Your first single is usually super-dense with memories. Of course, if you're under a certain age, *what was the first single you ever bought?* may present a semantic problem. *Single*? Single *what, exactly?*

Long ago, when both the world and I were young, there were over-made-up New Romantics, smoking on tube trains, and phones kept leashed to walls by wires, thank God. In those far-off days, "buying a single" only ever referred to the purchase of a seven inch piece of vinyl. When rotated at forty-five revolutions per minute and connected to a needle, these black discs would play a *single* song.

These days, of course, Vinyl Is Back, so the need for a description is probably redundant, but one never knows. There may be sixteen year olds nostalgically hanging on to their MP3's, unaware of this ridiculous new vinyl fad.

Since you haven't asked, my first single was, "Automatic Lover," a 1978 one-hit wonder by the criminally under-rated Dee Dee Jackson. Why? Simple; I was obsessed with Star Wars, and the song featured backing vocals from a rubbish robot. So, in my C3PO-fixated brain, the presence of a slightly threatening vocoder relentlessly intoning, "*I. Am. Your. Automatic. Lover. Automatic. Lover,*" made it a must-buy.

I know we're only a few paragraphs in, but Google it, watch and weep as poor Dee Dee is uncomfortably seduced by a cardboard android. It's fine, I'll wait.

OK, you're back. What did you think? Wonderfully odd, isn't it?

But it remains My First Single, and like yours, whenever I hear it, I am *back there.* In my case, sat on the worn carpet in Mum and Dad's house, watching Top Of The Pops.

I am kneeling in front of my Dad's black ash Hi-Fi, putting the needle down over and over again.

I am hearing that flirty cardboard android on a crappy Dansette player in my first solo bedroom.

So everybody's First Single, even if sonically dubious, still has power.

We never forget it, even if sometimes we really want to.

My next few purchases saw a marked improvement in quality, depending on your musical stance. After Dee Dee came, "Silly Thing," by The Sex Pistols, which of course, was actually by Paul Cook & Steve Jones, drummer and guitarist of the band, who'd split by then. I didn't know that, I just thought I was being seriously punk - I seriously wasn't.

Mind you, by that point, neither were they.

Then came, "Are 'Friends' Electric?" by Gary Numan, which changed my life and led me into electronic music and synthesisers, which I still bore people with today. However, at the time, I didn't just like "Friends" because of the monumental synths, but also because it made me think beyond the grooves.

Numan was sat in a room with walls of peeling paint, while out in the cold, a man watched, with a long coat and cigarette. Was this man Numan's 'friend'? What's the significance of 'little deals and S.U's'? Why were his 'friends' always mentioned in quotation marks?

Numan had his answers, I had mine.

One song can mean a million different things to a million different people. How? Because music is magic.

So even back then, I wondered what was going on *outside* the tracks. In many songs, the composer takes the listener so far, then leaves them hanging. We all know Major Tom ends up lost in space, but why – and who was he?

Who wanted "Dear" Prudence to come out and play in that bright blue sky?

What does it take to join Ed Sheeran's "A Team"?

Some songs spell out their stories quite clearly, but many have mysteries to uncover. And that's where this book comes in.

I've taken eight songs and "remixed" them as short stories. In other words, I've listened to what the track's given us, then expanded it out, beyond the lyrics.

Now, these "remixes" are, of course, purely my take on some classics, concocted from where I'm sitting when the needle hits the vinyl, or the MP3 does whatever it is an MP3 does. For example, Lou Reed has already given us his version of Caroline's life (in "Caroline Says II") but in this volume, I have another angle.

David Bowie is my musical hero, so you'll notice he bookends both "sides" of this collection. As far as I'm concerned, that's only right and proper. Bowie's all over popular culture from '69 – '16, so he's all over this volume, too. If you have a problem with that, take it up with the rest of the world. To be honest, I could have written a whole book based on his songs, but let's be sensible.

OK, the intro's nearly done and the first verse is on the way, but here's a piece of advice before the needle moves on.

You *can* read these stories in any order you wish, but don't. As with any LP, the "tracks" are sequenced in a specific order, so you might want to stick with that. Trust me, everything will make more sense if you do.

Put it this way, some riffs re-appear. Like any album, my various "tracks," are up, down and mid tempo. Some are raucous sing-a-longs, others more introspective late-nighters.

Oh, and one last thing; each "side" comes with a run-out groove, which is a cryptic clue to a song. Solve the two grooves and there's a bonus track in it for you. A hand typed, one-off Cover Story of your choice.

Do let me know when you've worked them out.

Anyway, forget Britpop, this is Litpop, written in enhanced stereo. So put on your literary headphones, set the pages to thirty-three rpm, run the original tracks in your mind and READ. LOUD.

R Easter, 2019

TRACK LISTING
PARENTAL ADVISORY; EXPLICIT CONTENT

SIDE ONE

1/ "Space Oddity" (*David Bowie*)
Duration;   54
2/ "Dear Prudence" (*The Beatles*)
Duration;   19
3/"Sympathy For The Devil" (*The Rolling Stones*)
Duration;   33
4/ "Caroline Says (II)" (*Lou Reed*)
Duration;   35

Run Out Groove 1

SIDE TWO

1/ "Calling Occupants Of Interplanetary Craft" (*Klaatu / The Carpenters*)
Duration   35
2/ "Hey Joe" (*Billy Roberts / Jimi Hendrix*)
Duration;   23
3/ "The A Team" (*Ed Sheeran*)
Duration;   30
4/ "Station To Station" (*David Bowie*)
Duration;   39

Run Out Groove 2

SIDE ONE

David Bowie, The Beatles, The Rolling Stones, Lou Reed.

You can never truly experience the same thing twice.
Because even if the thing *hasn't changed,* you *have.*

Needle…*down.*
Crackle.
Crackle.
Crackle.

"SPACE ODDITY"

(David Bowie, 1969, from the album, David Bowie *)*

8th January 1947, Heathrow Space Dock

This was it. Showtime. And what a show it was going to be, courtesy
of the world's greatest circus. The spotlights were glowing, the
audience looked upwards, rapt, the drumroll had begun and now he
waited, higher than any trapeze act.

No-one could stop the show now. He'd been checked and re-
checked, taken protein pills and given cardiograms. He'd put his
helmet on, ready to be waved off. David Jones felt like he'd prepared
for this moment forever, but now Major Tom was ready. Ready for
what, though, he still didn't know.

8th January 1947, B.S.N. Ground Control, Brixton.

The children obediently filed into Observation Room Six.

O.R.6 resembled a large, white classroom. Painted across the back
wall was the logo of the British Space Navy, a stylised rocket with a
Union Jack nosecone. Underneath, three italicised letters, *B.S.N.*

The floor was set at a slight angle, so everyone had a clear view
through a thick window on the far wall. To the right stood a large
televisual screen.

A man in his mid thirties wearing a tweed suit stood at the front.
He bounced on the spot, clearly excited, eager to begin.

"That's it, children, that's it. Chop chop, find a desk, quick as you
can. Twenty-five minutes until launch!" He clapped his hands
together, impatiently. "Quick sharp. Any desk will do, they're all the
same." There were thirty children in all, aged between six and fifteen.
Some wore school uniforms; others, what was clearly their Sunday

best. The younger children looked about in wonder, as if they'd stepped through a wardrobe and found another world. The teenagers mostly gave off an air of studied nonchalance.

"Older children at the back, if you can, please. The floor is raked, but the little ones can't see, so the biggers, please help them out and sit toward the back, if you would."

A metallic voice suddenly grated from the speakers and made some of the children jump.

"Launch in twenty-four minutes and counting," it barked. "Launch in twenty-four minutes and counting."

"Sorry about that," the man in the suit adjusted a dial on a panel nearby. "Shouldn't be quite so shocking next time. So, are we all comfortable? Good."

He gestured at the room below. "Welcome, welcome. Look. Down there, children, are the men – and a few women, yes! – who are about to launch the first ever human being into space. This is Brixton, Ground Control, today is 8th January, 1947 and you are here as witnesses to history. This is your job today and for the rest of your lives, so pay attention to everything. For the many years to come, you will say, "*I was there*," because others will want to know what it was like. Today is your job, children. You will be emissaries of this day for future generations. When everyone else here," he swept his arm toward the control room, "has gone, you will remain the world's first-hand memory of this momentous occasion. Mark it well."

The children knew their task. They had been specially picked as part of Britain's "Future Legend" programme. Brought from all over the Empire, they represented a cross-section of King George VI's subjects.

"Future Legend," was a project that ensured major events were witnessed by the very young, who would then pass on those experiences over their many decades to come. Since the '30s, British children had been invited to watch most of the Empire's epoch-defining events, to mythologise them into legends for the future. Since time began, empires had been built on such stories. Those in charge wanted to ensure Britain's past was more than just dry facts - they wanted it to have heroic status. Observation Room Six, therefore, was a room full of little future storytellers, ready to be filled with an epic poem written by the Empire, for the Empire.

"What are Future Legend's three R's? What is your job today?" asked the man.

"Record, remember, recall!" The children shouted with varying degrees of enthusiasm.

"Right. You'll find paper and pencils on your desks, but this isn't a lesson. They are only there if you feel the need to note down something factual. Today is about living in the moment as it happens. You are the recorders here, not the paper. Today is about how you feel, how you react, what you experience."

He tried to look them all in the eye, to impart the gravity of this moment.

"As I say, this is Observation Room Six. Six of twelve, all circling the Control Room down there. In the other Observation Rooms, we have all kinds of important visitors. Journalists - lots of journalists from around the world – dignitaries, presidents, kings, princes, queens, celebrities, movie and radio stars…Children, today, you have – how do they describe it? – yes, the 'hottest ticket in town'. In the world, actually. You are where everybody wants to be today. To see *that*." Like a ringmaster, he waved his hands again, to the room below.

Most of the people in Ground Control sat behind ugly control panels comprising equally unwieldy dials and switches. Many had tiny televisual screens and spoke to each other through curved microphones attached to Bakelite headphones. It was very British down there. Dials were politely turned, switches carefully thrown, slide rules consulted, the occasional cup of tea sipped and biscuits nibbled.

"Busy, isn't it?" asked the man. "That's Ground Control. But I'm getting ahead of myself. I haven't even told you my name. I am Terence Jones. Terry. I am the brother of David Jones, soon to be the first man in space." He knew that would get their attention. There were a few gasps and a couple of uncontrolled whoops of excitement. Hands shot up to ask questions.

"Yes. A few miles to the west, at Heathrow Space Dock One, my brother is sitting atop a Jupiter Eight rocket, ready to be the first person in history to leave this planet and journey into the space between worlds."

Terry had just jumped several hundred places in the children's estimation. One young Indian boy couldn't help himself. He jittered in his seat and his hand fluttered like a caged bird.

"There will be plenty of time for questions, all the questions you could ever ask. But since you seem so keen…er…?"

"Darpad, sir."

"Darpad. From…?"

"Kangra, Sir. The Punjab."

"Well then, Darpad from Kangra. One question. What is it to be?"

"Your brother, sir? He is your *brother*? He is Major *David Jones*?"

Terry groaned internally. He knew where this was going. "Yes, he is my brother. Major David Jones."

"So why does everyone…the papers, all, why do they call him Major Tom?"

Terry took a moment.

"Major Tom is the nickname my brother had since…a while back. He is not a Major any more, he is, as you know, a Starman, but the nickname stuck." Terry hoped that would be enough for Darpad. It wasn't.

"But why, Sir, why Major Tom when his name is David?"

Terry sighed. He'd known this question was probably going to be asked, so gave the sanitised answer he'd already prepared.

"There is a character from literature, Darpad, called Tom Jones, from a book by an author called Henry Fielding. It's called *The History Of Tom Jones, A Foundling*. In his younger days, my brother, David Jones, reminded people of this character, so, instead of David, they started calling him Major Tom Jones, you see? And everyone still does to this day. So…"

But Darpad wasn't quite finished.

"How did your brother remind everyone of this literature man, Tom Jones?"

"Ah. My brother was…adventurous, like Tom Jones. He liked, er, meeting interesting people. He was very popular, with men and, er, women. So David Jones became Tom Jones became Major Tom. So that is why."

"Twenty-two minutes until Launch," ground the speakers, which saved Terry from further explanation. "Twenty-two minutes until launch."

"So, everyone, I said this wouldn't be a lesson, as such, but we do need some context. I'm sure you've all been swotting up before today, so let's just have a quick recap of how we got from there…" he gestured with his thumb over his shoulder, to the past.

"To here…" he pointed at the door of O.R.6, then the B.S.N. logo on the back wall.

"To the British Space Navy. That is why we are here today. Britain leads the entire world in rocket and space technology. We are, simply put, decades ahead of our nearest competition, the United States, who, if I may be cheeky, are still playing with sparklers whilst we are launching entire firework displays. Speaking of which, who can tell me who first had the idea for the B.S.N. and when?"

Quite a few hands went up again.

"Girl at the back there?"

"Winston Churchill, sir."

"Indeed. Our prime minister. And which day gave him the idea that has led to my brother's historic trip into space?"

"Firework night, sir."

"Firework night," confirmed Terry. "Guy Fawkes Night, if you prefer. Funny to think, isn't it, that the 5th of November should have become such an auspicious date for Britain not once, but twice? You all know the story, I'm sure. "Action This Day" and all that."

*

Chartwell House, Kent, 1928.

The fifty-four year old Winston Churchill stood on the stone steps of his garden at Chartwell House, looking back toward London. It was 5th November,1928, and the fireworks that filled the sky from there to the capital were both a welcome diversion from his current problems and an awful reminder of the war that had ended just one decade previously, almost to the day.

Churchill drew on his cigar and looked up at the playful flashes that cracked the sky.

This aerial entertainment reminded him of his more mortal experience at Flanders. His battalion never saw direct battle, but the war had been ever present on that Belgian horizon.

These explosions over the south of England were almost like those of ten years before in Belgium, except tonight, no-one was taking cover.

There was a rapping sound behind him. He looked round to see his wife Clementine at a window on the ground floor. She waved a mock-angry finger at him.

"At least put on a hat, dear. A scarf?" with her other hand, she pulled up a gruesome multicoloured scarf. "You'll catch your death and then where will I be? I simply don't have time to organise a funeral this month, and then there'll be Christmas…"

"Another few minutes, Clemmy," he grunted over his shoulder. "Just looking at the fireworks."

"Really?" she said in mock surprise. "Oh yes, the fireworks. You do realise we own these glass objects called windows? They keep the cold out. You could easily use one of these 'windows' to sit behind and watch from there. In the warm. I would have thought you'd have seen enough fireworks to last a lifetime, dearest."

"A few more minutes!" he snapped. Clementine huffed and closed the window.

It had not been a good few years for Churchill. He'd rejoined the Conservative Party in 1924 and become Chancellor of the Exchequer, but his tenure so far had been disastrous. He'd re-introduced the Gold Standard and pre-war exchange rates in good faith, only to see massive unemployment which led directly to a General Strike in 1926. He privately called that time his "Economic Gallipoli" – a spectacular mis-reading and mis-handling of the situation. What was supposed to make things better had made them much worse.

Churchill watched the rockets that flashed across the night sky. Something stirred in his mind. He felt it coming. Something good, or something bad? His ideas always seemed good on paper, but often fell apart when they collided with reality.

Churchill's Great War had involved some terrible decisions and a few innovations. Just before the conflict, he'd been appointed First Lord of the Admiralty. There, he'd seen the potential of aeroplanes as weapons and so had keenly supported the creation of a dedicated Flying Corps.

Then, as the war stagnated in trenches across France, he'd pushed for the development of tanks to break the deadlock. Those tanks may not have won the conflict, but they'd hastened its end and saved lives.

Churchill watched the sky explode and thought of his tanks. *Technology can take lives and save lives*, he thought. *But it never saves enough.*

Every day he offered up a silent prayer for the souls lost through his decisions. So many of them at Gallipoli, the one-sided battle he'd instigated that killed thousands of men.

Never again. That thought had haunted his mind for the last ten years. *Never again. I will atone for Gallipoli. The men that lost their lives must know their sacrifice meant sons, grandsons, great grandsons and on, for eternity, will never be called to fight again.*

Technology is the key.

By the time the guns fell silent in 1918, some had already described the bloodshed as the "War to End all Wars" but Churchill knew that was a fantasy. As long as there were men, borders, politics and religions, there would be war.

If we'd had a better equipped Air Corps, more pilots…tanks from the very first day, it would have been a skirmish, not a war. We would have packed the battle up and sent it home, tied up with string, in a couple of months. We need to think ahead. Because there will *be another war. Someday, someday soon, another little man with big plans will rise. The politicians will try to placate him. They will have the choice between war and dishonour. They will choose dishonour, they will have war. We need to stop that little man before even one of his soldiers puts on a uniform. Stop him with a display of such devastating force he won't be able to fight. End his plans without a single one of our men even leaving these shores. End them from a distance, with technology. But how?*

Churchill looked up at the rockets. Launched from a garden in Kent, one could streak into the air and be seen from a home in London. A big enough rocket could be seen from Manchester! Why not even Glasgow? Why, with a big enough rocket you could…

Churchill flicked the stub of his cigar into the air. It wheeled, spun sparks then landed on the lawn.

If I were an ant in that grass, I wouldn't have even known where my death had come from, he thought. *Only that the world is burning. With a big enough rocket…*

"Clemmy!" he shouted. "Clemmy!" Churchill turned and marched back toward his home. "Action this day, Clemmy, action this day!"

*

Heathrow Space Dock, 8th January, 1947.

David Jones, "Major Tom", sat in his tin can. There were many voices in his ear, millions more around the world listening on the radio, even a few thousands lucky enough to watch on the televisual, but despite all that attention, he was alone.

He could only see two small circles of sky through the windows of his capsule. *If something were to go wrong,* he thought, *this would be my last ever view of Planet Earth. Just blue. No trees, no seas, no people. Just this endless blue sky.*

Funny how something you see every day becomes the only thing in your mind when you realise you may never see it again, he thought. *Happy bloody birthday to me.* It was an unusually blue sky for a January day. Normally, London skies in winter were slate grey and sulky, but today, it was open to him and his tin can. The sky welcomed Major Tom to the heavens.

Maybe when I get up there I'll see what eternity looks like, he thought. *Maybe that's where the Angels live, on an ever circling dance in the stars. I am Odysseus, off onto the wine-dark sea of forever.*

No.

Do shut up, David. Pretension doesn't suit you.

He shook his head inside his helmet. Those kinds of thoughts wouldn't do. He often drifted like this, away from the moment, into other realities.

He frowned at himself. The world saw him as the *Starman.* The cool, analytic adventurer, rider of rockets, eyes fixed to the beyond.

But then there was this other, strange side to him which few ever saw.

It's almost as if there is another David Jones somewhere and we meet in our dreams. David thought. *I chose to enter the military, but in other universes, maybe many different David Jones exist. Perhaps, somewhere, I am a great leader of men, on a dais, dressed in black, saluting a fanatical crowd, or in another reality I'm a simple troubadour, guitar across my back, serenading the ladies from station to station. Or maybe elsewhere I'm just a clown.*

Perhaps. Probably not. If there are other versions of me, I hope they *are happy.*

But there was only this world, this universe and this David Jones. He had one face and it had served him well. Wasn't his face the reason he was up here, strapped to a tank full of high explosive, whilst his brother waited on the ground?

It could have been Terry. Maybe it should have been Terry, who was always, ironically, the more grounded of the brothers, therefore the one better qualified to fly. Yes, Terry was stable while David felt the ground beneath him shake. His sanity had been leeching away for some years now, not enough for anyone to notice, but there was a whispering madness waiting in the corners of his thoughts. Perhaps that's where these weird drifts into poetry came from?

No, put them aside.

I am a Starman. A steely-eyed, cool as ice Starman. There is no place in my mind for wonder, just the business at hand. It's showtime and I am the only one on stage.

"Twenty minutes until launch, Major Tom," said a voice in his headset. It was Pitt, flight director, and the only person at Brixton Ground Control allowed to call him "Major Tom," over the airwaves.

At first, the British Space Navy had baulked at that nickname. *"Major Tom?"* they'd puffed in various memos. Knowing its provenance, they hadn't considered it "gentlemanly", but when the public got wind of the name, they embraced it enthusiastically. The British people got the joke immediately. Nobody said it out loud, but everyone knew "Major Tom Jones" had once been quite the womaniser. It gave him a dashing, pin-up quality. Mind you, his good looks, boy-next-door South London accent and taste for well-cut suits also helped.

The B.S.N. quickly realised that "Major Tom" was an asset. He resembled a movie star, but unlike Hollywood leading men, David wasn't playing a brave, death-defying adventurer, he was the real thing; a Starman.

The B.S.N. had played with various names for their rocket pilots. "Rocketeers", "Space Riders", even dabbling with Greek – "Astronauts" (but that was considered a little too esoteric); "Starman" said it all.

David was designated SM3, "Starman Three".

Terry was SM1, Captain Mark Feld, God rest his soul, had been SM2.

Captain Feld died when his J4 capsule ignited during training. Afterward, the B.S.N. moved away from highly flammable capsule oxygen, but that was too late for Feld. Perhaps if the stars had aligned differently, Mark would have lifted off whilst David stayed put, wondering what may have been.

"Pulse is in range, oxygen good. Flight is go across the board. Anything you want to get off your chest, Major T?" David could hear the smile in Pitt's voice.

"No, everything is across the board here. Slight drop in air pressure, nothing in red range. You seeing that?"

"Osterberg is across that and he's…yes, he's go. Weather holding. If I went up to the roof, I'd be able to see you. It's a beautiful day."

"I think everyone in the South East will see me."

"That's true. What was it Sir Winston said?"

They spoke together as one; "*If you build a big enough rocket…*"

"Oh, Sir Winston's decided to watch from the viewing platform at Heathrow One. You could give him a wave. He's the reason we're all here."

"In more ways than one," agreed David.

"Temperature holding green and steady, Tom. All in the E's. Mild for January. God's given everyone a lovely public holiday."

Originally the B.S.N. had planned a summer launch, but there had been whispers that the U.S. was planning to steal the Empire's thunder and attempt a potentially suicidal manned mission. According to rumour, the Americans were going to put a man inside one of their primitive A4V2 units, blast him off, take him to the edge of space then have him parachute back down in the nose cone.

It was a disaster waiting to happen, but nobody doubted the U.S. would be willing to sacrifice one man in order to fly into the history books first. So the B.S.N. had brought their mission forward.

"Your wife is here," said Pitt.

David silently carried on with his checklist.

"Ground Control. Major Tom, do we still have comms?" asked Pitt, concerned.

"We still have comms. Just running eights to fifteens. All green."

"She's ready."

David's headset went dead for a moment. There was a crackling noise and squeal of feedback before Pitt's voice came back on line.

"We were on public comms, David. I've switched to private, but I can't do it for long. I know. *I know*. But you know what the B.S.N. think about this. Just talk to Angela. You only need sixty seconds; thirty seconds private, thirty on open comms. That's the deal. The press want to hear the Starman talk to his wife. The B.S.N. want the world to hear you talk with Angie. It's part of the story, you know it is. Everyone knows, David. It's theatre."

"But I'm not an actor."

"At Launch minus ten, you speak with her. Thirty seconds so the world can hear. That's an order."

David said nothing.

"That's an order. Going back onto public comms now."

There was another crackling sound before Pitt came through clearly.

"Sorry about that. Comms re-route. Lost you for a moment. You can speak to Angela at minus ten."

David closed his eyes. " I look forward to it."

"We're starting main pumps. Please engage. Oh, Kemp would like to speak with you about the One-One-Ten roll."

"Good old Lindsay. Go ahead, Flight."

David Jones, Major Tom, sat in his tin can and prepared to be the first man in space. He felt more alone than ever. *Happy 37th birthday*, he thought. *One hell of a candle I'm sitting on. What should I wish for?*

*

"Yes," said Terry to the enraptured children. "Sir Winston stood in his back garden and saved the world from further wars thanks to a few fireworks. And now here we are. Well, there were a few other little

events that took place before today, naturally. We all know what they
were, don't we?"

Darpad waved his arm about frantically.

"Darpad, there will be time for questions later. All the questions
you wish. But for now, *I* ask the questions and you answer them."

"But sir, but sir," squeaked the boy. "Just one more, sir."

"Very well, one only."

"What's he really like, your brother, sir? I bet he doesn't really talk
the way the B.S.N. make him, sir, does he? I bet he's more fun, sir, is
he?"

Darpad had seen through the B.S.N.'s rather dry charm offensive,
which was to make David into some kind of Stiff-Upper-Lipped
British Hero character, a real-life Biggles. His wife Angela had helped
with that. David often protested he was no actor, but slipped into the
role easily. Terry had no doubt his brother would have made a fine
thespian.

"That, Darpad, is a rather big question that would take a rather big
answer I am afraid."

Darpad waited for the rather big answer with rather big eyes.

But who was David Jones, really? The rebel, the dreamer or the
Starman, with his jolly-good-show act? Or perhaps the silent, empty
David who Terry saw more than he cared to? The fact was, he didn't
know. His brother was all of them and yet none. Maybe even David
didn't know who he was. So much had changed over the last few years
and the boy he'd grown up with had become a man Terry barely knew.

No-one else could spot those changes. It took a brother to see them.

No, David wasn't the man he'd been a decade previously; a light
had gone out. Of course, he'd passed all the psych evaluations. The
doctors and headshrinkers had pronounced him both physically and
mentally ready for launch, but Terry knew better. His brother hadn't
been right since 1943.

There was no outward evidence of this crumbling, nothing he could
go to Pitt with and say, "I don't believe David is right for this mission,
sir. I think he is unstable." If he had gone to the Chief, Pitt would

have put it down to brotherly jealousy. David was going up, while Terry stayed on the ground. SM3 was flying, SM1 was watching. That was how it had turned out. On the toss of a coin, no less.

*

B.S.N. Headquarters, Bromley, 1946.

Both Terry and David were equally qualified to pilot the J8 rocket. As far as the B.S.N. were concerned, there was nothing between them. Terry was the only one with doubts about his brother's mental health, but that's all they were; doubts, not facts. So, two months ago, in December 1946, they'd been summoned to Chief Pitt's office and a coin had decided for them all.

"One, three," Pitt had said while the brothers stood to attention in front of his desk. "Here's the thing. Here's the thing. At ease, chaps."

Terry and David had relaxed their posture, but their minds were far from calm. They both had an inkling as to where this was going.

"Got some flapping tongues coming out of America, chaps, regarding their A4V2 programme."

"Flies about as well as a skier going up a hill backwards, by all accounts," David had said.

"Indeed. But you know the yanks. They'll keep throwing money at the A4 until it'll end up in orbit simply by standing on a huge pile of dollars. But here's the thing. This tongue of ours out there – yes, we have people in their programme, deep – this tongue says the yanks are planning on sticking a chap in the A4 nosecone and blasting him off."

Terry and David must have looked shocked. "Yes, I pulled the same face when I found out. They may as well take one of their Starmen, sorry, *Astronauts*, and stick a bullet in his head. It would be quicker for all concerned. But that crowd-pleasing idiot Lindbergh is determined, as far as we can tell, that the first man in space should be one of his chaps, even if the flight kills them."

"President Lindbergh needs to get over his Paris jaunt, sir. He thinks just because he risked his life once, everyone else should do the same."

"Well, whatever his mad thought processes, that's where we are. We know their offensive rocket programme has completely stalled. So their Roswell Rocket Proving Ground is a base without a purpose. Lindbergh wants to galvanise the people, "Make America Great," you know, his tiresome phrase. He seems to think sending some poor sod on a death trip would do it. The A4 can't hit another country, but space is rather difficult to miss. Just aim upwards and keep going."

"That's insane."

"Succinct appraisal, SM1. Well, America can make its own mistakes, but they're not going to do it while we have the Jupiter Eight and you two. This is Above Top Secret, you understand. What I'm about tell you is known by myself, Churchill, Ferry, Eno, Schneider and that's it. We're bringing the launch forward. Provisionally it's slated for January 8th."

"My birthday?" David had exclaimed.

"Pure coincidence. Don't read anything into it."

"My *birthday*?"

"The Jupiter Eight is mission ready. You're both ready and equal. There's nothing in it. Had a chat with the other four chiefs and no-one could really decide between you. So we're letting the King make the decision."

"The King?"

"No, SM3, not in person," Pitt had laughed, reached into his trouser pocket and pulled out a sixpence.

"You're going to throw a coin?" David had said, shocked. "A *coin* to decide the first man in space?"

"Do you have a better idea, SM3?"

Neither of them did. Pitt handed the coin to David. "Your throw, Major Tom. Heads or tails, what's it to be?"

"Heads."

David had flipped the coin but missed the catch so it rolled under Pitt's desk. He'd fumbled on the floor and brought up the sixpence, king-side up.

"Well, that's that, then. SM3, you're off on a trip in a Jupiter spaceship. Congratulations."

"Well done," Terry had said and put out his hand. David shook it, but couldn't look his brother in the eye. "Sorry," he'd said. "Just, you know, luck."

"Could have been the other way round, old chap. Not a single problem."

"Keep it under your hats, obviously. We announce the flight on New Year's Eve. Give people something else to celebrate, won't it? On the day, Terry, you'll be with me at Ground Control. For now, David, please report to Ferry, he has more for you. That will be all."

The brothers left the room silently. Terry went to congratulate David again, but his brother had simply walked off in the direction of Chief Engineer Ferry's office.

*

O.R.6, B.S.N. Ground Control. 8th January, 1947.

In Observation Room Six, Terry realised he must have lost himself for a moment. Darpad was politely waiting for an answer.

He's not suitable, Terry thought. *That's the true answer, my brother should not be in that machine, less than twenty minutes from history. This isn't jealousy, it's fear. Because if David cracks, then this will be the time. I just hope it happens before the engines engage. Because a cracked Major Tom in space would be disastrous.*

Of course, Terry said none of this. "What's my brother like?" he mused and pretended to think. "In short, he is a very funny, warm, caring man. You don't see or hear his wit in interviews. He's *very* 'British Space Navy' when he's on show. But in private he can be one of the funniest men you will ever meet."

But he hasn't been funny for years. Nowadays, Terry thought, *David's humour can be very odd indeed. Yes, that's the best word for him, but one I could never say. My brother is an oddity.*

"Please. No further questions until after lift off. So, everyone, back to the matter in hand. Churchill initiated the British Space Navy, but it wasn't called that at first, was it? Anyone know its original name and where it's based?"

A girl put up her hand. "Jura, sir."

"Jura, correct, the Inner Hebrides. Close enough to reach, far enough away from prying eyes. And what was the Rocket Project called?"

"The Postal Service?" she offered.

"Correct again. Why?"

The girl didn't know. "The Postal Service," was one of Churchill's jokes.

*

Jura, the Inner Hebrides, 1932.

"'The Postal Service'?" asked Sir Frederick Field, Admiral of the Fleet. "You want to call all this,'The Postal Service'? Why?"

Churchill and Field stood on a hill on Jura, looking down at what was known – by those with a need to know – as the First Rocket Research Establishment, or F.R.R.E., pronounced "Free."

In 1932, F.R.R.E. was just a collection of simple concrete buildings. Some were several stories in height, the fabrication units, where the rockets were to be assembled. Several miles away were test stands, where the machines would be put through their paces. It presented a bleak sight. Trucks bounced along newly made roads. Soldiers and WRENS mingled with plain clothed scientists. It was, by a long way, the most secret place in the entire Empire.

"Yes, we should call this place The Postal Service." Churchill waved his umbrella at the establishment below them. "For a start, calling it the bloody First Rocket Research Establishment is a damned foolish idea. Who gave that the thumbs up?"

"I believe it was Worthington Evans," said Field, who stamped his feet to keep warm. Jura was bitterly cold, even at the height of summer.

"Bloody Worthington Evans," huffed Churchill. "Why doesn't he take out posters on the Underground while he's at it. *"Don't Tell Anyone, But We're Building Rockets To Destroy Our Enemies."* Damned fool. One wrong person sees a memo, or whatever, and the cat is very much out of the bag."

"I agree, Winston. But The Postal Service? Why?"

"Well, for starters, it's indescribably dull. No-one is going to pay the slightest bit of notice to any document headed, 'Postal Service'. Second, it is a very special delivery we are planning here, is it not?"

Field laughed. "Oh, I see, Winston. One of your jokes. Very good, yes. Postal Service, yes, that is what it should be. So why are we up here? I'm freezing."

"This," said Churchill, who waved his umbrella at the buildings again. "This is now. But think about the future. We want to put explosives on top of our rockets. Explosives big enough, one day, to level cities."

"That is the point of this place. And?"

"We need a better future than that. We cannot prepare for war alone. What kind of society would we be if that were the case? We need more. We must also be preparing for men. Men atop our rockets. An Empire of the stars, Frederick." He pointed his umbrella straight up. "Give the people the serenity to sleep well at night knowing they are protected, but also give them hope. Humans have looked up at the sky since we first walked this earth. We now have the potential to unlock that sky. Hope, Frederick. Our rockets will strike fear. Let them also bring hope."

"I agree, of course. We can't be just an Empire of war. The people need more. It is the next obvious step. But the Cabinet will never agree to it. This is a military establishment."

"Indeed it is. So we must play a clever game. Let us train up some rocket-riders, space-men, without the cabinet realising that is what they are."

"How?"

"That is what I want to show you, to help you imagine. Look down there. Imagine if there were runways with sleek, silver, arrow-nosed rocket planes. Let's not just build missiles here, but aircraft too. Use all this research to also create planes faster than any other."

Field looked down at the buildings and pictured the scene Churchill had just painted in his mind.

"Let us find pilots, Fred. Find men willing to dare. First, we train them in our planes, then send them to the stars. Let Britain put the first man into space and make history – again! What do you say? Do I have your support?"

Admiral Field thought for a moment. He too was a visionary. "Yes. Of course. Action this day," he replied. "I'll talk to the people that matter. The ones with the purse strings. If they think they're getting another weapon, they may agree to it. But we must keep our true intentions hidden. The powers that be must be assured this remains a military operation, until we reveal our other, more peaceful mission. So let's put your rocket planes under the auspices of the Navy. But a new kind of Navy. A British Space Navy."

"British *Space Navy*," repeated Churchill with child like wonder. "Yes, that is what it should be. Ships amongst the stars! Action this day!" he yelled and slapped Field on the back. "Let us send a Briton into the forever!"

*

O.R.6, B.S.N. 8th January, 1947.

"A very special delivery," said Terry, who hoped it might raise a titter. Nothing. He pushed on.

"But of course, it wasn't as easy as writing a letter. At first, The Postal Service was a rather shaky endeavour. Our scientists were making it up as they went along. Creating giant missiles, loaded with explosive, deadly accurate? That's a tall order. Naturally, there were a few false steps along the way…"

Terry threw a couple of switches on the panel nearby and the televisual screen lit up. A black and white film showed a stubby silver rocket on a test stand. Smoke collected around the its fins. Despite the passing of the years, its stillness remained menacing.

"This was a Mercury 1, the first test rocket out of Jura. Not a great success…"

On screen, the rocket billowed out flame and slowly began to rise. Although the film was silent, the camera shook. But then, only a few feet off the ground, the rocket tipped over, cracked in two and a massive explosion filled the picture. A few of the younger children squeaked, either with fear or excitement, Terry couldn't tell.

"That happened a lot. The guidance problem wasn't solved until a way down the line, the Mercury 5. But it took a lot of time and money before that."

There followed a compilation of disasters. Rockets tipped over like drunk men. Engines exploded before they'd even left the ground. They took off but then threw tantrums and span out of control once in the sky. Terry still winced at the footage, even now.

"Unbelievably, no-one was killed or hurt in any of those events, but damage was being done – to the reputation of the programme. Prime minister Ramsay McDonald was ready to scrap the entire secret project. Each time we lost a rocket, we lost thousands of pounds and more goodwill. We'd had the War to End all Wars, hadn't we? What possible use was a squadron of rockets, standing idly about in this wonderful world of peace and prosperity? The Postal Service came this close…," he held his thumb and forefinger together, "…to being packed away and forgotten about. But then three things happened that gave it a much needed shot in the arm. Anyone have any idea what those three things were?"

Darpad was first to put his hand in the air.

"The Mars One?"

"Very good, Darpad. The Mars One."

Terry flicked another couple of switches and the picture on screen changed. Now it showed a much bigger rocket waiting on a test stand. Engineers scuttled around it, dwarfed into toy soldiers by the machine's height. This film was in colour and the missile shone bright red.

"Mars, the bringer of war," said Terry. "They painted it red, so it could be tracked by the eye as well as radar. But red's rather appropriate don't you think? Mars, the red planet, bringer of war, Mars One, the blood-red war rocket. There was a certain theatricality about it. But the M1 was The Postal Service's last gasp. If it failed, that would have meant goodbye and toodle-oo to Jura. Waiting in the sea fifteen miles away was H.M.S. Dreadnought, decommissioned from the Great War. It was empty, a target."

On screen, the picture cut to footage of a battleship, floating imperiously amongst the waves. The image cut back to the Mars, which lifted off, straight and true. After a few seconds, the machine adjusted its course, levelled off, then hurtled away.

"It was the first manmade object to travel faster than the speed of sound, which meant it arrived on target before the noise of its engines, which totally confused observers out in the Atlantic when this happened…"

On screen, H.M.S. Dreadnought erupted in flame. Its twenty-thousand tonne body actually rose out of the water, then split in two. The two ends began to sink from the centre. The picture cut to show the stern and bow as they slipped beneath the waves. It was an undignified death.

"Such accuracy! Hitting a battleship in the middle of an ocean! Wow! Radar-guided, with enough explosive to…well, you saw what. When Whitehall saw this film, any doubts as to the validity of a rocket offence disappeared. However, there was still concern that it would ever be needed. The P.O. wasn't out of the woods just yet. But then what happened?"

"The jets!" shouted a boy. "The Jet Men! You!"

"Exactly. Before the Starmen, there were the Jet Men. The rockets were top secret, but Frank Whittle's jets were way out in the open. And, even though I say it myself, we were treated like Hollywood stars. I still have some of the old posters: myself, David and Mark Feld in our silver jet suits, like we'd just flown in from the future. In some ways, I suppose we had."

Footage appeared of a sleek silver Spitfire jet rolling down a runway toward the camera. As it got closer, a plummy BBC announcer spoke up. "The Jet Men are coming! Yes, coming to keep our shores safe! Britain's skies will be patrolled by aircraft faster than a bullet! And here's one of our boys now! It's Flight Captain David Jones!"

As the jet came to a standstill, the canopy was pulled back and David waved from inside, removing his face mask and helmet. His blonde hair tumbled down his forehead, longer than regulation length. He looked every inch the superstar pilot. "This beauty 'as an angel's push!" he said, pure London, then gave a crooked grin.

Wouldn't smile properly though, would you, David? Thought Terry. *Not with those tombstone teeth of yours.* He looked at his brother smiling and a sadness crossed him. He wouldn't smile like that again. That grin was old news, quite literally.

Terry thought back to that day on Jura in 1934. He remembered it clearly, because soon after the film had stopped rolling, David had met Angie.

Dave's professional life was to climb on a constant upward trajectory, but from that moment, his personal life was to slide in the opposite direction.

*

B.S.N. F.R.R.E. Jura, 1934.

On Jura in 1934, David Jones unzipped his silver flight suit while scientists fussed about him, examining paper read-outs of his heart rate and breathing patterns from the flight. He'd just landed and, of course, the cameras had been there, as always. He'd waved, smiled and said a few words, some nonsense about an "angel's push", then gone for his usual debrief and check up. The Jet Men – David, Terry and Mark Feld – were explorers at the very edge of human achievement. Their every twitch was important. While David's body was poked and prodded, in a hangar across the way the Spitfire jet was also being carefully examined. The human and machine were extensions of each other. Neither knew their real purpose, but one was about to find out.

Eventually, David was let go and padded back down the hallway to his boxy little room. Back in the army, he'd shared a dorm with twenty-five other men, but was now, "an asset". He was one of the few public faces of Jura, so had been given a slightly more luxurious home.

David and Terry had discussed this strange assignment at length, into the long nights. They'd both left the army after displaying aptitude in flight. Mirroring each other's careers, they'd been taken into the Navy's secret Test Pilot programme. Bigger, faster aircraft were needed in this bigger, faster world. The Sopwith biplanes had been cutting edge in the Great War, but had found themselves rapidly out-dated. Now, even the most cutting-edge modern planes would soon be in the junkyard, once the jets went into full production. Britain would lead the way.

David knew about the rockets, of course. While they were secret to the world, it was rather difficult to keep them hidden or, indeed, quiet on Jura. Every few months, a new model would blast off into the Atlantic and everyone on the island would stop and watch, awed again by their own classified firework displays.

But there was something about the place and about the jets that bothered him.

It hadn't escaped David, Terry and Mark's notice that they seemed to spend more time in front of cameras and microphones than the cockpits of the machines they were testing. Up until now, every aircraft they were assigned to had been kept behind closed doors, strictly need-to-know. But the *jets* were firmly in the spotlight and had been since the very first day.

That made David uneasy.

"What are we doing here?" David had asked Terry within the first week of arrival in Jura. They'd been in the almost empty mess hall late one night, both nursing a well-earned beer. There were a couple of WREN's on a nearby table and a few engineers playing darts. The hall was otherwise quiet.

"We're testing jets," Terry said, monotone.

"But doesn't it feel like that it's all just…a sideshow? Every time the jets are rolled out, the cameras are rolling too. Everyone knows our faces. They've made us famous. I bet next time we're back in London, we'll be recognised. We're just test pilots. We're not supposed to be known. We're being treated like Spencer Tracy or something. Don't you think it's odd?"

"Yes," Terry conceded. "It is odd."

"You'd think the jets would be top secret, like the rockets. Why are we telling the world we have them? It doesn't make any sense. What strategic benefit could there possibly be in announcing their existence to our enemies?"

"It feels like a bluff, yes," Terry had agreed. "Perhaps, Dave, perhaps the jets are just that – a sideshow. Everyone's so busy looking at them and us, that no-one's even thinking about what's really happening on Jura. Maybe the jets are misdirection, like a magician's trick. We're just, I don't know, a little bit of camouflage, flimflam."

David had looked up at his brother angrily. "Flimflam? Is that what we are? We're risking our lives up there so the rockets can stay in the shadows? Is that what you're saying?"

"Calm down. I don't know that. It was just a thought. I'm trying to make sense of it. The Spitfires are a cover story perhaps? To explain the noise, the money, all these people on Jura? I don't know. And anyway, even if that's the case, we're Navy, as you say. We follow orders. Ours is not to reason why. Whatever's going on, we just have to trust it's for the good of the country. Whatever we are in this, we must have faith that it's the right thing."

David had fallen silent. Terry regretted mentioning the idea immediately. He knew David didn't like to be kept in the dark about anything. If they were a sideshow, his brother would find it insulting, infuriating, even.

"There has to be more to it than that," he growled. "Otherwise, orders or not, I'm gone. I'm not going to be anyone's performing monkey. I'm a fucking organ grinder. There has to be more to it or I'm walking away. I mean it. "

He was right. There *was* more to it.

*

David had sat in his boxy little room on Jura and stared into the mirror. The Spitfire flight had gone as well as could be expected, but there had been those infuriating, ever present cameras and his stupid phrase *"this beauty 'as an angel's push!"* Ridiculous. But now what? More flights and tests, repeat, repeat, *repeat* and for how long?

He didn't even know what day it was, so checked a calendar on the wall. Ah, Tuesday. It seemed like it was *always* Tuesday. Not the start, end or even the middle of the week. Just a characterless day. Tuesday suited Jura. Let it always be Tuesday out here at The Postal Service.

Over and over, it went. Sometimes he felt he was playing at being a pilot. Here, he was just an actor who happened to have fully working, life-sized props.

"There has to be more than this," he said to his reflection. It had become his mantra. Terry didn't seem to mind the grind. Mark Feld was a natural in front of the camera and played up to it. One day, when this was all over, David didn't doubt that Mark would still be famous, but probably not for flying.

There was a knock at the door.

"Come," said David, quietly.

What happened next surprised him.

The door opened slowly and a pretty girl stuck her head round the frame. Blonde hair frothed out from under her WREN's cap and, David noticed, she wore slightly more make-up than was allowed. She had a nice face – slightly androgynous, but androgyny was always interesting to David. He didn't like to think about why he sometimes liked girls that looked like boys. He wasn't sure if he'd even like to know.

"Sorry. Flight Captain Jones?" Yes, her lips were definitely too red for regulation. And the mascara was a little too thick as well.

She's dressed up, he thought, *she's put on the old slap, got dolled up. For me? Wait. Do I know her?*

"Well, obviously I know you're Flight Captain Jones. I mean, everybody does. You're not hard to miss. So yes, of course you're Flight Captain Jones. I knew that already. I don't know why I even said that. I know who you are. You're Flight Captain Jones."

She's gabbling like a schoolgirl, he thought. *What on earth does she want?*

"Come in," he said. She stepped in and snapped to attention.

"Am I supposed to salute you? Er, Sir?"

"I don't believe so."

"Oh, OK." She relaxed her posture a little and then David noticed she was holding a file of papers in a shaky hand.

"I'm a WREN," she said, looking down at herself. "Well, obviously I'm a WREN. That was a stupid thing to say. I wouldn't be wearing this if I wasn't. Sorry. Ha."

David smiled. "Do you have a name, Miss WREN?"

"Oh, yes, I do. Yes. Ha. I do. Angela. My friends call me Angie."

"Can *I* call you Angie?" David attempted a mild flirt. Whoever this girl was, he was instantly very interested.

"Oh. Yes. Ha. Yes, you can."

"Hello Angie. You can call me David. Dave, if you like."

"Hello David, *Dave*," she giggled.

"Now, I'm pretty sure you're not here so we can just call each other by our first names." He nodded down at the folder.

"Oh yes. Yes." She looked over her shoulder with a guilty expression. "May I shut the door?"

David nodded. She shut it quietly, like a burglar.

"May I sit down?"

David held a hand out to the chair. She sat and placed the file on her lap.

Nobody said anything for a few seconds.

"I shouldn't be here." She stood up again, flustered. David motioned for her to sit back down. "Well, you are here, aren't you, and you have something for me, I'm guessing. So why shouldn't you be here?"

"I'm Admiral Field's, er, secretary. You know Admiral Field?"

"I do. He is somewhat of the Gaffer round here, so it would be rather rude of me not to know him. Only met him a few times, but yes, I know who he is."

"Of course you do. Of course. You're Flight Captain Jones. He's the boss. Of course you know him. Oh, I'm sorry. I should *not* be here."

"Angela. Angie. Calm down and just tell me what's going on."

She closed her eyes and took a deep breath.

"Promise you won't tell anyone?"

"I can't promise something if I don't know what it is."

"I know why you're here," she blurted, then put a hand to her mouth as if she could take it back.

"I'm here to test the Spitfire jets, Angela."

"Yes. You are. Of course, yes, but that's not it. No, not really," she looked about the room and chewed her lip. "I heard you."

"Heard me?"

"In the Mess, the first week you were here. You were talking with your brother. Wasn't spying. Just overheard. You were wondering why you were here, said you thought it was more than just the jets. You sounded angry, sad. Listen, I know why you're here."

Aha, so that's why I sort-of know her, he thought. *I clocked her in the Mess that night. Hard not to clock her, really.* He nodded again at the file on her lap.

"Is that file why I'm here?"

"Aha. Oh, I really shouldn't. But you sounded so sad and upset. And you were going to find out anyway, so I'm not exactly breaking a confidence, just bringing it forward a little. No, I shouldn't."

David gently took the file off Angela's lap and looked at the cover. CLASSIFIED A3+ ONLY it read, SM PROJECT OVERVIEW.

"SM Project? What's that? You're A3 cleared?"

"I have to be, all the stuff I have to type up for the admiral."

David glanced through the file but nothing jumped out.

"You're not testing jets. They're testing you."

"I know they are. They're finding out what the speeds do to the body, the manoeuvres."

"Ah-ah, no. Not quite. They're testing you for the next stage. For the next flights."

"I'm sorry, you're going to have to be a bit clearer. Next flights? What? New jets?"

"No, er, David. No. For the rockets. They want to find men to fly the *rockets.* 'SM' stands for Starman. That's what you could be. The rockets aren't just for war, they're for exploration. They want to put a man in space within the next ten years. They're testing you, to see if the human body can take it. To see if *you* can take it. That's why you're here. The jets are testing you. "

David stared at this girl who'd just managed to turn his world upside down in just a few moments. She looked back at the door and seemed very eager to leave.

"I'm sorry. I've gone to knock on your door so many times and turned away. They were going to tell you and soon. But you were talking about walking away. I didn't want that to happen. You would have been walking away from the...greatest flight any man will ever take. And you wouldn't have known. You'd have just thrown away that chance. You don't seem like the kind who would turn up his nose at that kind of challenge. I wanted you to know, before you did anything silly and walked away. If you want it, you could be a Starman. You can do this. If the tests check out, you could be up there one day." She pointed to the ceiling. "Not the next floor, ha. *Space.* That's what I wanted to tell you. Please don't tell anyone I came."

"But…" David couldn't take it in. Rockets? Space? Starmen? "…if anyone finds out, you'll face a court martial for telling me this. Why? Why risk it?"

"Because," she stood and held her hand for the file. "Because I like you. I don't know you, but I like you and I want you to stay, so I can see you. Because I like you."

She blushed and, before David could say anything else, swept from the room without looking back.

David watched the door close and, at that moment, knew she would be back in this room, hell, on her *back* in this room very soon and to hell with the consequences. What he didn't know is that this one meeting would change his life.

Not for the better.

*

O.R.6, Brixton Ground Control, 8th January, 1947.

In Observation Room Six, the speakers grated again. "Fourteen minutes to launch." The closer lift-off was, the more concerned Terry became. That was natural, but he'd never worried about David in this way before.

Yes, he'd been scared for his brother's life, terrified every time a Jupiter flew, even when they were unmanned. They were full of terrible possibilities, loaded with potential disasters. But this was a different kind of fear. Terry was sure David's body wouldn't fail. No, not his body.

Was his brother's mind truly ready? And was the Jupiter Eight ready? Men are fragile, they have a habit of dying when things go wrong, and everything about space wanted to kill you.

Today, that fear wouldn't stop circling Terry's mind. Physically, David was more than capable, but physicality wasn't the problem. The danger came from his off-kilter mental condition. It had always been lurking but had become worse four years ago.

No-one saw it. David was an exceptional actor, even though he denied any interest in make-believe. But Terry knew David had been playing dressing-up games, perhaps without even knowing.

For a start, he'd been dressing up as a happily married husband and that continued to be an award- winning act. He'd been playing the happy human being, the contented brother. He'd dressed up as a heroic, steely-eyed Jet Man, then topped even that performance with a crowd-pleasing rendition of David Jones, Star Man.

But David's ever-growing list of characters were painted with broad brush-strokes. There was no subtlety in them, but that's why they fooled most people. Yes, they were facets of his personality but none touched the core of the man.

So who's up there in the Jupiter Eight today? Terry wondered. *Which David has his hands on the controls? The Star Man, or another version with feet of clay, earth locked and going no-where?*

Terry willed himself back into the room, but it was hard. That was his brother out there, waiting at Heathrow, Space Dock One.

If this flight fails, the Empire loses a race, but I lose David. The Empire would shrug and start the race again, but I will never see him until the angels come for me.

"Well, we are getting near," he said, finally. "But let us not forget the day the rockets flew. When was that?" All the children put up their hands. Terry picked one of the youngest, a black girl in the front row.

"Yes, dear? Your name?"

"Imani, sir. From Port Elizabeth, Sir. It was the Five Day War."

"Excellent, Imani. The Five Day War. Who would have ever thought we'd have a war that lasted just five days? Does that even count as a war?" he mused, more to himself than the children. "The historians don't really like the name, 'the Five Day War' – it's inaccurate. They prefer, 'the Polish Event' or, 'the Rocket

Deployment'. I suppose a war is when two sides fight. 1939 definitely did not count as two sides fighting."

He turned another dial and the voice of Churchill filled the room. "People of Britain," Winston began, a speech every child knew by heart. Spoken on 3rd September, 1939 at 11:15 a.m., it went down in history even as the words were spoken. Terry pressed a button and the recording paused.

"I remember looking out of a window when this was being broadcast. I was in Regent Street at the time and the entire place was deserted. The whole of the Empire were gathered around their radios. Churchill had finally become prime minister after Baldwin, although it was a close thing between him and Chamberlain. I wonder if old Neville would have played things differently? Backed away from the inevitable? Who can say? But on 1st September, 1939, Adolf Hitler's Wehrmacht raced into Poland. He'd already stolen Austria and parts of Czechoslovakia. Baldwin let him do it. But Churchill was and is a different beast altogether. He'd seen the threat. The more Hitler ranted and raved in the '30s, the more money went to Jura. The rockets were pointing his way and the *Führer* didn't even know. Listen to Winston, children. Listen again and hear how *excited* he is. He had been waiting for this moment all his life. This was his chance to…put things right. To atone for the Great War, for Gallipoli. This is history."

Terry pressed a button and Churchill's voice began again, slow, measured and, yes, excited.

"This morning the British Ambassador in Berlin handed the German government a final note stating that, unless we heard from them by 11 o'clock that they were prepared to withdraw their troops from Poland, a state of war would exist between us. I have to tell you that no such undertaking has been received, and that consequently this country is at war with Germany."

Terry paused the recording.

"Some of you may just about remember this, but you would have been very young. But for many of us, well, I'm not being over dramatic, it was the end of the world. War, terrible war, again. In

Regent Street you could hear a collective wail rise, like a despairing orchestra tuning up."

Terry realised he was getting a bit purple. These were just children and he was no Wilfred Owen.

"But as I say, Churchill didn't sound upset. Because he – and a few thousand others, including myself – knew that Britain had something up our sleeve. Listen again, knowing that fact…"

Terry switched the speech back on. Churchill knew exactly what he was doing, playing to his audience, both here and in Berlin.

"Yes, war," the prime minister went on. "That is not a word any of us wished to hear again in our lifetimes, but what other word is there? The German government have ignored our ultimatum. Their forces continue to rage through Poland. We have pledged to come to their aid. What else do we have but war? But let me say this, to you, the people of the Empire and yes, to you, Herr Hitler and your gang of bandits. There will be no war. No British soldier will fall before your guns or beneath your shells and bombs. No British pilot, no sailor, no civilian. There will be no war, Herr Hitler.

But do not think that statement means we are running from this conflict. I simply mean the *British Empire* will have no war. If you do not end your attack on Poland, Germany will have war. Germany will have all the war and destruction it seems to desire. Know this, Herr Hitler. You have until 11 a.m. tomorrow to end your attack, turn your forces about and remove them from Polish soil.

If this fails to happen, you will be given a warning. Just one. Let me repeat that. There will be just one warning. If you still fail to remove your army, then you, Herr Hitler, *you* will be responsible for what will happen next. You alone. Then let the German people judge as they will. You will not bring this war to the The British Empire. The British Empire will bring it to your land. Now, Germany, may God bless you. We will not need God's blessings. We already have his vengeance on our side. Remember Bismarck, Herr Hitler."

The recording ended. Every subject of the Empire could recite the speech by rote.

"Of course, we were all a bit confused by those last four words. *'Remember Bismarck, Herr Hitler.'* A strange reference to bring up. But we all know why Churchill gave Hitler that warning now, don't we?"

The children all nodded. *"Remember Bismarck,"* had become one of the most quoted – and shortest –moments of the English language.

"Hitler, of course, didn't pull his troops out of Poland. The following day, at 11:15 – or as near as damn it – all of Germany, all the world, knew what Churchill was talking about."

Terry pushed a button and the televisual screen lit up once more. Black and white footage showed fire and smoke dancing into the sky. The footage cut between shots of fire crews dousing buildings and a massive, blackened metal structure listing low in dark water. Other shots showed crowds silently watching the burning horizon.

"This is German footage taken on 4th September at the Blohm & Voss Shipyard and surrounding area in Hamburg. Around an hour before this was filmed, the battleship Bismarck had been docked there for final fittings. Now, as you can see, it had become twisted metal and flames. At first, they thought it was an accident. One moment the ship was there, the next, the sky had fallen in and it had died, along with around one thousand five hundred people. Churchill went back on the air that afternoon with a direct message to the German Government and their citizens. It was another very short message. But long enough to make his point."

Terry flicked another switch and Churchill's voice boomed into O.R.6 again.

"I am now speaking to the people of Germany," Churchill had said calmly, like he was about to read them a bedtime story. "Yesterday I gave your Führer, Herr Hitler, a warning to withdraw from Poland. I also told him to 'remember Bismarck'. He failed to heed my warning. Now he will remember Bismarck. The world will remember Bismarck. The British Empire now has the power to reach anywhere into Germany. You cannot defend against this power. You cannot predict it. Your battleship Bismarck is dead. Remember it. By 11:15

a.m. tomorrow, if the troops are not withdrawn, we will begin an attack of such ferocity the gods themselves will quake in fear. That is all."

"They didn't withdraw," said Terry, quietly. The picture on the screen changed to broken buildings and roads paved with rubble. Shell-shocked survivors picked their way through what was once the heart of a city. A torn swastika hung from a shattered wall.

"The following day, the end of the five day 'war', Churchill gave the order to deploy 'Red Five'. *Five* Mars One rockets. One for the Reich Chancellery in Berlin. One for the Nuremberg Stadium, one for Templehof Airport, another for the Prussian Cadet Academy and the last for the Anhalter Station. Hitler was killed at the Reich Chancellery, along with many of his strange gang. They never saw it coming. How could they? And so, the Five Day War ended with a bang and not a whimper. The Nazi government collapsed soon after. Without Hitler, they seemed to lose their, I don't know, sense of purpose. It was like a magic spell had been lifted. *Remember Bismarck.*"

"Ten minutes to launch," squealed the voice. "Opening comms to the Jupiter Eight capsule in fifty seconds."

"My brother," said Terry, softly. "It's time to hear my brother say au revoir."

*

David Jones, Major Tom, sat in his capsule as history whirled about him.

Every communication between his Jupiter Eight and Ground Control was recorded for future generations. David thought it might be possible there were more camera crews in London than bystanders.

There are more people watching this moment than any before, he thought.

It was not a pleasant thought.

If something goes wrong, this will be the most public execution ever carried out. For the rest of time, my last moments will be played on repeat. Stories will be told of my misguided heroism. Songs will be

sung of Major Tom and his lost, doomed capsule. I will live on as a
sacrifice to the gods of progress. I may even get a statue or two.

He smiled to himself.

That would be a glorious end to an inglorious life.

Pitt's voice burst into his ear.

"David. Angela's ready. Thirty seconds on pubic transmission, then off comms, private, for thirty seconds only. That includes visual, as we discussed?"

Major Tom's expression didn't change.

"Copy that. Thirty seconds then off public comms and visual for further thirty seconds."

It had been agreed that the First Man In Space should have a few moments "alone*"*, as it were, with his wife, before lift off. A half-minute window in which no-one else in the world could peek before mankind's greatest achievement. The B.S.N. meant well by the gesture. They believed, like everyone else, that David and Angie's marriage was strong. It had survived. They needed each other and their love had overcome their life.

But the world had been fooled. David's marriage, like so much else, went no deeper than the surface. It was as flimsy as the piece of paper they'd both signed in the registrar's office.

But first, he had that thirty second transmission with Angie that the world *would* hear. He knew somewhere in Ground Control, she was sitting alone in front of a microphone. She knew the deal, too. Angie could act with the best of them.

Curtain up, thought David, *eyes and teeth, this is the real showtime. Planet Earth is listening.*

"Darling, " she said, breathlessly. She sounded like she was flirting. David knew she was, with the entire world.

"Hello, darling," he answered, equally aware of the millions of strangers listening.

"I just wanted to say God speed and how everyone is proud of you. None prouder than me."

"I just pray I live up to everyone's hopes."

"You will."

"I'll be back on earth before anyone knows. This is just the first small step. After this, in the years to come, all mankind will be part of our Empire of the stars."

That was one of Churchill's lines. Winston would appreciate him appropriating it.

"Remember, David, this may be one small flight for you, but it is a giant leap for all mankind."

Oh, bravo, David tried not to wince. *That'll be Angie, staking her claim on the history books. She must have sat up late for nights on end thinking of that. Unless the B.S.N. provided it, of course. No more or less than I expected. I need to top that.*

"I am just one man," he improvised, wildly. "But through me, Man*kind* will fly. To the stars!"

Now fuck off, Angie, thought David. *I timed that perfectly.*

Sure enough, a tiny light above him blinked twice and went out. The camera was blind.

A crackling in his ear told David that the radio frequency had changed. Now the rest of the world was deaf for thirty seconds.

Oh yes, it was a well-meaning gesture by the B.S.N. to let man and wife speak in private.

But David knew how the Empire worked. This next thirty seconds were yet more mythologising on their part. It was all about creating a mystery for future generations to ponder – what *did* Major Tom and his wife speak about in that half minute, before he blasted into infinity? What truths were exchanged? What can be said in a few seconds that could possibly be enough? David knew this moment was actually part of the Empire's bigger story. He was a bit player in his own drama. The script and the stage had been provided. He just had to hit his marks. This was one of them.

Whatever the outcome of this mission, no-one would ever know what was said. In this way, myths are created. Legends grow best in the absence of facts; they do not enjoy light shone upon them.

David waited for his wife to speak again. He was in no rush. Let the seconds tick away until the world came back into his capsule.

"Well done, David, good line." Her voice was suddenly tinny and small in the headphones. For a moment, his heart fell away from him, aching, beating for what could have been.

"You too, Angie. *One giant leap.* Take you long?"

"Not really."

David watched the clock count away.

"Where are you watching from?"

Part of David's brain was busy commenting on this exchange as it happened. *The planet will be wondering which words of love and beauty we are sharing now,* it said. *If they could actually hear us, their dreams would be lost. The silence from this capsule will speak more truth than we ever could. The people will fill the silence with their own versions of this conversation and it will mean more to them than anything we* actually *say.*

"I won't be watching. David. You know that. I still have no wish to see you die."

"Really? That surprises me."

He knew that now was not the time, but couldn't help himself. He thought he could have this last talk with Angie and be a bigger man, but also knew this really was the last conversation they'd ever have. Successful mission or not, this was it. Goodbye, in thirty seconds.

He had too much to say, and had tried to say it for some time now. But it was never right.

"Enjoy your life, Angie."

"I will. Whatever happens, you know I will."

"You always did."

"I tried."

"You tried for you."

She sighed, a long, whooshing sound, a lost wave crashing on a distant shore.

"Ash would be proud."

"Goodbye Angie."

"David..."

The comms line crackled again and there was a brief hum before Pitt came back into David's ear.

"Jupiter Eight, we're now back on public comms, back on *public* comms, Jupiter Eight."

David shut his eyes just for a moment and found himself again. Or rather, he found Major Tom, the steely-eyed Rocket Man. With fate's blessing, soon to become the First Man In Space.

"Hello Ground Control. Hello to everyone watching and listening. This is, er..." *Yes*, David decided. *Do it. Give the people what they want.* "This is Starman Three, *Major Tom*. Everything checking out across the board, I'm all go here."

"We're all go here. Green one hundred. Looking good."

"We're about eight minutes from launch. Final checks."

"Final checks. Aha, there'll never be enough final checks for me, Flight."

Pitt laughed. "Well, we can't hang around all day; seven minutes fifty-two seconds."

"Just enough time to pop out for a pint. Fancy one, Flight?"

Yes, that's it, thought Major Tom. *That's the character the world's been waiting for. Upper lip, stiff. Check. Righty-ho, chaps. Check. Cheeky bonhomie. Check. Yes, I can be a hero, just for today. British Hero Model 1B ready to go.*

"Perhaps a swift one after you land, er, Tom."

"I'll hold you to that."

David looked over the instruments above him. There wasn't much to do now except sit and wait for around seven million pounds of thrust to kick him off Earth.

He wished he could have said something, anything to Angie, to the girl he'd first met back on Jura. The one who made him laugh so much. The cheeky, authority-snubbing rebel who never quite did what she was told but managed to charm her way past generals and security guards with equal ease. It wasn't supposed to have ended this way. But then, whose love stories are ever supposed to end?

David knew he'd fallen for an idea and so had Angie. He'd been captivated by the WREN who was captivated by him. Hero worship is only an attractive feature when *you* are the hero. He now knew she'd played to his ego. That hadn't been difficult since his ego – amongst other things – was bigger than most men's, so anyone who wanted to stroke it was most welcome.

He had to admit Angie was exactly what he'd needed. That day, when she'd "reluctantly" entered his room (and now he knew that "reluctance" was sheer pretence) he'd been ready to leave the project.

But she'd steered him, kept his eyes on the prize. When his confidence wavered, she was always ready with a pep talk. David wondered if she'd practised them ahead of time and had a collection of YOU CAN DO IT speeches memorised, ready to bring out for every occasion. He wouldn't have put it past her. Then again, he wouldn't have put anything past her.

"David, LOOK AT ME. YOU have the skills. YOU have the drive. YOU have the looks, the personality, hell, the BRAVERY to do this! YOU are number one! How DARE they give you designation SM3? THREE? NOBODY else should be up there except YOU. YOU are the STARMAN, David. YOU are NUMBER ONE!"

She'd re-worked his wardrobe, coached him on interview techniques, posed him for the cameras, even taught him how to "WALK LIKE A STAR". How did she know all that stuff? She acted like both a Hollywood drama coach and a cut-throat agent. Before Angie, he'd achieved much, but wasn't NUMBER ONE. Angie had cleverly remoulded him into Major Tom, version two. Before David knew it, he'd become Angie's creation, and to his surprise, he'd liked it.

They'd married at Bromley Registry Office. The B.S.N. had been dismissive of the relationship at first; a WREN marrying a Starman? But the British public loved the Cinderella story – they adored a plucky underdog and Angie knew it. The B.S.N. had pushed for a more sumptuous, public and, most importantly, *Christian* wedding in keeping with the Empire's obsession with image, but Angie knew her audience. She'd put her foot down and insisted on the Registry Office. "We are just ORDINARY guys, like everyone else," she'd screeched to the press, without believing it for one second. "Just a boy and a girl in LOVE. Why should the BRITISH TAXPAYER shell out for a wedding for US TWO KIDS? We just need two small rings and two BIG hearts!"

People had adored it.

But that first crazy merry-go-round ride hadn't lasted. In fact, the crazy part had soon overtaken the merry-go-round. David admitted he was partly to blame. Angie had made him a Starman and a star. Inevitably, that led to temptation. There'd been lots of girls, but Angie wasn't squeaky clean, either. She hadn't been averse to assignations with photographers, engineers, soldiers, possibly, David suspected, even other WRENS... She'd become almost as famous as her Starman, which had been the whole point of her exercise, from the moment she'd crept into his room with a Top Secret File and a little-girl-lost pout.

The truth was, they were too similar. They were almost a male and female version of the same person. Both driven, ruthless and consumed with a need to be number one.

Although all good relationships are equal, David and Angie's was based on constant competition and his wife was never going to win. She was married to a Starman. In life's game of trumps, he'd been handed the winning card. If they both walked into a room, David would instantly become the focal point. He wouldn't have to try – with women, men, all ages, all classes, they'd flutter about him, leaving Angie seething in a corner with another large glass of something strong and flammable.

The rows became more vicious, to the point of violence. She flaunted her lovers, but he didn't care. He had enough of his own lined up and lying down to keep him happy for the rest of time.

Divorce was out of the question. This was not the way the Empire's society worked and certainly not how the B.S.N. wanted their Starmen to behave. The idea of divorce, the B.S.N. had carefully said to David one day, *was not compatible with our standards and ethics and would certainly lead to a "downgrading of mission status",* which none-too-subtly equated to, *leave your wife and you will never leave this planet, Tommy boy.*

So they were caught in a terminally loveless marriage with no escape. It wore them both down but they had to keep the performance up.

After a while, it was clear she needed him but he no longer needed her. She'd played her hand, given him all the chips and had nothing left to put on the table.

Except one thing.

One thing David wanted, but could never provide for himself.

*

The final minutes before lift off passed very quickly. In O.R.6, Terry wrapped up his brief history of the space programme, neglecting to mention Captain Feld's tragic death. Mark had lived for two minutes, hammering at the capsule window to escape the flames, but the engineers couldn't get the hatch open in time. Nobody knew about Feld.

The Starman project was still classified at that point, so the family were told his Spitfire had spun out of control. No statues for Mark, just a footnote in the history books. One day, Terry knew the truth would out, but at this point, the official story was that Britain's space race had progressed without a single life being lost. *Once we have won this race, and keep winning it, Mark Feld will be mythologised too,* Terry thought. *Welcomed into the legend as a fallen hero. But now, he is another dirty secret in the B.S.N.'s files. He deserved better. The Empire guards its secrets well. All those newsreels of smiling faces across the globe, under the Empire's kindly protection? Propaganda, like Hitler used on his own people, but infinitely more subtle. Our Empire is no munificent uncle, but a bullying, jealous God. Mark Feld was just one sacrifice amongst millions. And yet, we all play the game and wave at the camera. We are slaves. We are slaves who believe we are free.*

Terry also failed to mention Barker, who had been the *real* First In Space.

Did people really believe that David was the trailblazer? That the B.S.N. would risk everything on just one flight?

No, Barker was the original, but nobody except a few high-ranking B.S.N. members knew about him and they would take his secret to their graves. David's flight was for all the world to see. Barker's had been confined to Jura. Even many of the Ground Control operators hadn't known he was in the capsule.

Truth was, Barker wasn't expected to survive. Surviving would have been a bonus. He was just up there to be tested, like they all were. Tested to see if life could endure up there and if it couldn't, how to put that right.

Barker had burned up during re-entry. Few tears had been shed – how could they have been, when nobody knew of his sacrifice?

The B.S.N. sent him up there and he would be given no statues, either.

Terry had liked Barker. He'd been a good dog, a smiling, excitable Labrador. But it wasn't considered "British", to send an animal up to be killed by space. As the old saying went, the Brits preferred pets to people and there would have been an outcry if they'd known that poor Barker had fried in the atmosphere, alone. So he and all the other Barkers that followed remained dirty secrets, too.

Instead Terry told them about how they'd tossed a coin to decide who would be First Man. He'd told them about "Ziggy", the dummy who'd been sent up to mimic the effects of G-Forces on the human body and who now stood in the Mess on Jura, dressed in a cape like a superhero. But all the while, he felt his own heart rate increasing and palms become sweaty.

A WREN had arrived pushing a trolley and now the children feasted on sandwiches, cake and crisps as if this were a jolly birthday

party rather than an epoch-defining event. But then again, it was a
strange kind of birthday party, wasn't it? Happy birthday, Major Tom.

Then, too suddenly, Pitt's voice broke from the P.A.

"This is Flight Director Pitt, B.S.N. Ground Control Brixton to
Heathrow Space Dock One. Read?"

The voice of Space Dock Controller Visconti filled the room.

"Reading Ground Control. This is Visconti, Heathrow Space Dock
One."

Both men knew the ears of the world were listening. Everyone
could feel history encircling them.

"Final SysDef checks rolling here, in the pipe, five, five, five. We
are green one hundred. What is your status?"

"Green one hundred go here at Heathrow. Five, five, five. Picking
up some hull ionisation."

"Got it. Pitt to SM3, J8. Read?"

Terry's heart went into overdrive. These would be David's last
words on Earth. His next would come from the heavens.

"SM3, read. Primary couplers released. Hit the internals. Green one
hundred here on J8. Switch to DCS ranging. That's a blue, an electric
blue sky up there. Let's find out if the Earth is as blue from above."

"You'll know soon enough. Pressure stable. C02 in range. Lift off
in thirty seconds. God speed, SM3."

"I'll have all the speed God will give me. I am go."

"Gentlemen, Ladies, green, red. Go no go poll. What do we have?"
There was a pause.

"Green on go," Pitt said. "Repeat, green on go across Control."

"Excellent," replied David. "Let's not keep the sky waiting. Light
this candle. "

Terry realised his hands were shaking. Some of the children were
barely paying attention, more focused on their food. Some "future
legends" they'd be telling. He wanted to shout, grab them by the
shoulders and shake them, turn their faces to the televisual. Instead, as
calmly as he could possibly manage, he simply said, "Children. This is

the moment. Put down your food, look at the screen and please watch. Watch and remember."

The children did as they were told, as Terry thought, *I hope this will be a glorious memory for them. Not a bad dream we will all be waking from, shaking and crying, for the rest of time.*

*

David appeared calm. He knew his face was being watched by the camera above and wasn't prepared to reveal even the slightest trace of what crackled inside his mind. He tried to push those thoughts down, back to where he'd tried to keep them for four years already. Now was not the time. He closed his eyes briefly and took a deep breath. He'd taken years to prepare for this moment, physically and mentally. There was nothing else he could do now. Whatever would happen, would happen. *My spaceship knows. It knows where to go.* His eyes flicked back and forth over the read-outs across the control panel, searching for any deviation from the expected. All was well. But all was not well.

She had to mention Ash, didn't she? Why did she do that? It was a rule between them that the unspoken remained unspoken, but she mentioned Ash's name anyway. Did she hate him so much she wanted to re-plant that terrible seed in his head *now*?

Ashley, oh, Ashley.

Time seemed to stand still for Major Tom. He looked at the clock counting down, from *TO - 10* but the read-out seemed to be faulty. The seconds were taking much longer than they should. But then, sometimes that happens. David knew time is not constant. He realised that terrible fact four years ago. Time could bend and twist depending on where you were standing. Occasionally, it was a White Rabbit that raced past, always late. Then, there were the other moments, like this, when the seconds passed by languidly, in no rush to go where they needed to be.

The capsule seemed much smaller, too. Did Angie mention Ashley because she knew it would crack him at the moment he needed to be unbreakable? He tried to push away the many thoughts that crowded about his mind, but they jostled and pushed, trying to get his attention.

It had been a stupid idea, David knew that now. A stupid idea that led to a wonderful, magical reality. A too short reality, as it turned out.

David and Angie's marriage had fallen to pieces. The public hadn't known, of course. The B.S.N's edifice of respectability remained untainted by rumour. He hadn't wanted to admit it, but David was more than prepared to endure the daily emotional minefields that were laid. Yes, he could weather it all if it meant he still had a chance to fly to the stars.

Nothing else mattered and Angie felt the same. Being married to a Starman overcame any and all objections for her. It opened doors for both partners and those doors were too good to have shut in their faces. So they grit their teeth and played their roles beautifully.

They hadn't planned on becoming pregnant. Mutual loathing is a very effective form of contraception, so it was never going to be a problem, but there had been a brief clearing of the storm clouds eight years ago. For an all-too-brief moment, their planets had aligned again. The scowls had turned to smiles, the slammed doors remained open and crockery stayed on the shelves. Neither of them knew why this had happened. Perhaps they just needed a ceasefire to retain their sanity. Maybe they simultaneously remembered why they'd fallen in love. Neither of them spoke about it. Perhaps they should have done.

They'd begun to connect again. They went to parties and actually stood with each other rather than scanning the room for someone, *anyone* rather than their spouse to talk with. They laughed, a lot. Angie could be very funny when she wasn't snarling. David had forgotten that.

There had been some party in London. Before the détente, they would have arrived together, split, circled each other like animals staking out their territory, then left to go back to their separate rooms. But that particular night, they'd stood, giggled and drank together – they'd drunk a lot. They kept catching each other with an expression neither had formed for a long time: attraction.

That night, without any discussion, they'd stayed in the same room.

Perhaps that one event was what shattered the renaissance of their relationship. Perhaps re-consummating it was the worst thing they could have done, as when an object you once coveted immediately loses lustre the moment you own it. The thrill of the chase, the *desire* recedes and you find yourself looking for a new object to pursue. Whatever the reason, the warmth between them began to cool. By the time Angie announced she'd missed her period, they were back in separate rooms again.

There was never any question of an abortion, just as there was never the possibility of a divorce. They'd made a mistake but that wasn't the unborn child's fault. They never said it out loud, but both thought that maybe, just maybe, the gravitational power of the baby's need might actually pull them together again.

It hadn't, of course.

When people have a child as a relationship repair-kit, it never works. You just end up with two enemies forced to shake hands in no-man's land. The opposing sides both still want to kill each other, but their guns are resentfully holstered.

Angie had named the boy Ashley. David hadn't argued. It was only later that he realised she could have been making a sick joke. Their life together was ash. Their life together was Ash. David never asked if that had been her intention; she'd have denied it anyway, but again, he wouldn't have put it past her.

The husband and wife came together for the baby, but not as partners – more like two rival businesses with a common investment. Obviously, the B.S.N.'s public relations department loved it, so there had been plenty of pictures of the boy sitting on Daddy's lap in his Spitfire jet, plenty of "candid" shots of the adoring new parents going about their new lives *just like everyone else*, but that's all those moments were, photographs: staged, developed, printed, published, thrown away.

Although David and Angie had gone back to icy tolerance with each other, they both loved the boy more than they could have ever expected. As fine actors, they never allowed their child to see anything but a happy home. The rows took place out of his earshot.

Neither of them realised their behaviour meant Ashley was growing up inside a piece of theatre and when the stage was revealed to him – as it inevitably would be- then his reality would crumble. They were too busy keeping the act going to consider its consequences. But that day never came. Ashley remained blissfully unaware his parents were not what they seemed, right until the end.

David tried to keep his expression neutral, but he felt his eyes becoming wet. He'd managed to perform his way through the last few years, convinced no-one had seen how he was hollow inside. There had been no David Jones, not really, since 1943.

The clock had started again. David hadn't noticed.

"T.O – ten seconds. Good luck, Major Tom."

The countdown began.

10...

Ten seconds could be a very long time. Ten seconds could be a lifetime. David had gone over it in his head, on awful replay, over and over again. He'd spent nights drinking, pushing his hands against his temples, howling to keep the memories out, but they'd infiltrated him, traitorously. Ten seconds was all it had taken. He'd timed it, moaning and shaking on those long, terrible, endless nights.

9...

It happened when Ashley was four. Those four years were another example of time playing tricks. One moment, Ash had been a newborn in the hospital. David had looked down into his son's electric blue eyes and said, "hello there, Kookie." He hadn't known where the word had come from. His boy just looked like a "Kookie". Angie hated the nickname, but it had felt right to David. "Come on, Kooks!" "Kick the ball, Kookie Woo!" "Run to me, Kook! Run to me!"

8...

The B.S.N. had sat David down and gave him a serious talk about being a parent. They weren't concerned about his skills with nappies or nursery rhymes, no – as always, the Navy were concerned about their investment. They were worried that now David had "other responsibilities", his position as a Starman might suffer. The B.S.N. knew his priorities had changed – of course they had and having a child is a wonderful God-given gift – but the project must continue, with or without him. They couldn't have Major Tom taking his eye off the ball. They needed total commitment. There wouldn't be any special treatment. Terry and Mark Feld were both single, they had as much right as the others to be the First Man. David assured them that the B.S.N. was his only priority and hated himself as he'd said it.

7...

David conceded that Angie had been a good mother, even though at first her version of motherhood involved a nanny doing most of the heavy lifting. Angie would rise, as usual, between nine and ten in the morning, then pad through to Ashley's nursery, where Nanny could be found dozing in a rocking chair. Ange would then spend around an hour reading and cooing to her son, before the help did the walking and feeding. Consequently, when David was around, he spent every possible moment with his boy. Each second was precious before the car came to take him back to Jura, so David hoarded them. He was jealous of Angie's time with their son, resentful she had access to him every day but chose not to be at his side. That had led to rows, like everything else. Angie always won, though. She had the winning argument, every time: "If YOU want to be with HIM so much, you know what to do! It's Space or your Son, Dave, Space or your SON!" David had chosen space. He hated himself for that, too.

6...

On Jura, nothing was ever completed. Training was never done, there was always something new the scientists had come up with, some scenario or other to mock up, a new piece of kit that may or may not work, and if it didn't, *why not and how could they put it right*? The

B.S.N. were in a strange, slow hurry to get into space. They couldn't
wait to blast off, but had so much to put into place first. They'd get
one shot at this and if even a single nut or bolt wasn't right, it could
spell disaster. So the Navy rushed, whilst standing still. Launching
Mars rockets at Berlin was one thing, sending one into orbit with a
man strapped to the top was of a different order altogether. David was
OK with waiting. He didn't fancy immolating himself for the glory of
the Empire. If that happened, he'd never see his son grow up.

5...

Since it happened, David had lost himself. All he had was Jura and
the B.S.N. If his relationship with Angie had been normal, they could
have collapsed into each other. They would have retreated into their
marriage, he'd have turned his back on the space programme and
disappeared, forever. He still wished he could. But there had been no
"relationship".

After Ash died, all David could do was fixate on the programme. It
kept him sane. Or rather, it kept his insanity hidden. The B.S.N. had
given him compassionate leave, of course, and the British people had
been supportive. But how many times can a man hear the words, "I'm
sorry"; how many times can he see a stranger pulling a sad,
understanding face; how often could he walk into somewhere,
anywhere, everywhere and know that people were watching the
grieving father, thanking God they didn't walk that awful path? The
B.S.N. made sense. It had purpose where David had none. It couldn't
fill the nothing inside him, but gave a semblance of meaning. That
was its function, nothing more.

4...

Ten seconds. Father and son had been walking one Saturday. David
had two days leave and, as always, every possible moment was spent
with his boy. Even when Ash slept, David would stay in his son's
room on the rocking chair, waking occasionally to watch, awed, as
Ashley breathed and dreamed.

That Saturday, Ash had been carrying a bright yellow ball. David
had bought him a selection of different coloured and sized balls to

represent the planets of the solar system. Ash's favourite had been the big yellow one, the Sun. "Will you take your tin can all the way to the Sun?" he'd asked that day. Ash always called it Daddy's Tin Can after David had demonstrated how the capsule worked using a tin of beans. He'd laughed and picked up the blue ball. "No Ash," he'd replied, "*this* one is Earth, our planet. I'll only be going…here," and he'd pointed to a spot just above the ball's surface. "Not that far." Ash had frowned. "Far enough, Kooksy!" David had picked up his boy, made a whooshing sound then lifted him to the sky, as Ash laughed fit to burst.

3…

They'd stopped by a newsagent David was friendly with. This particular newsagent didn't seem to know who his customer was, despite the amount of times his face had appeared in the papers. That was refreshing. Perhaps the man did know and was giving David a break from the relentless attention. But David didn't think so. To this day, he couldn't remember what they'd spoken about – football results? Unlikely. Politics? Probably not. David didn't know and that made him angry, as if somehow that was letting Ash down. He should remember every moment of those ten seconds, but that conversation was lost to him. David had been looking at the racks for just a few seconds while the man had been talking about – *talking about what?* - but then, the strangest thing, the newsagent suddenly *shouted* where he had just been *speaking* and his face contorted into a look somewhere between horror, panic and disbelief. It was the oddest thing, yes, because it had come from nowhere. But then, there had been a squeal and a small thud, like someone dropping a bag of flour. Nothing more than that, just a tiny thud, not big enough to change anything. Huge enough to change the world.

2…

The driver of the car hadn't been able to stop. He'd seen the bright yellow ball roll in front of his vehicle, then he'd seen the child, but it was too late and would always be too late. A stupid ball, rolling into the path of a car, like a hundred Road Safety Films. David had

replayed that moment again and again, trying to find an iteration that
didn't end with that ridiculous little thud, but he couldn't. *If I hadn't
bought him the ball if I hadn't bought him the ball if I hadn't bought
him the ball*, went round and round, but he had bought him the ball,
the ball had fallen and his son had fallen and it would always be too
late.

1...

"Engines engaged," said Pitt in David's ear. "Running green one
hundred thrust. Jupiter Eight, you are go, go, go! Lift off, we have lift
off. Jupiter Eight has lift off." David stared out at the blue, blue sky
and wondered if, any moment, the J8 would buckle, then there would
be blackness, his life would be over and he would be with Ash forever.
He welcomed it.

Surely there has never been a noise like this before, he thought.
*Surely nothing has ever shook and roared this way, not even since the
gods themselves fought, splintering the sky with their thunderbolts and
clashing swords the size of trees. No, stop, what are you thinking?* He
grimaced. *Gods and thunderbolts? Concentrate. Don't lose this. Who
are you? Where are you? You are SM3, on J8 and you have a job. Do
what you are here to do.*

"Green one hundred," he managed over the screaming of his ship.
He could already feel gravity trying to pull him back to earth. He
knew it would not relax its grip without a fight. "Green one hundred
across the board."

"Flight tower cleared," informed Pitt. "J8, you have cleared the
tower."

David knew that fanning out across London, then across the world,
people would be cheering, waving, crying. But all he could see was
the sky. Had it ever been this blue before?

The ship juddered and bucked. He'd heard the Rolls Royce S15
engine up close many times, of course. But now more than seven
million pounds of thrust was beneath him and that could never be
trained for. He thought that perhaps the J8 would simply shake itself to

pieces before it got anywhere near the atmosphere. Surely there were no rivets or bolts that could keep this raging animal together.

"Looking good, Major Tom," crackled Pitt in his ear. "How are you feeling?"

"Feeling the Gs," managed David. "Earth doesn't want me to leave, I think. Looking good here. Goodness, got a lot of shake and shimmy. Is that in range?"

"In range," confirmed Pitt. "My goodness. I wish you could see this. It is the most incredible sight."

"I'm going to get a better view soon enough."

"Fourteen seconds. Pitch and roll."

"Copy."

The ship started to roll on its axis and pitch toward the east, to use the Earth's rotation for a more effective escape. Sometimes, straight up is not the most efficient direction.

Crowds across London looked up at the plume of smoke that acted as a giant arrow pointing to the position of the J8. The rumbling of the machine crashed over the entire southeast of England. Up, up, UP it went, faster than anything mankind had ever created. Another crash signified the cracking of the sound barrier, just one minute into the flight. The last time these crowds had witnessed something of this magnitude had been the surprise launch of the five Mars One rockets at Berlin in '39. Then, only a few people had known the truth of that event. It had created panic in the streets as engines thundered and the rockets pierced the sky. As Churchill's attack headed for Berlin, he'd addressed the nation to calm them. He told Britain that these angels of death were on our side and doing our bidding. Today, the Jupiter Eight had been anticipated with fervour, but even the cheers of millions would never reach Major Tom's ears.

David simply sat motionless as gravity pushed at him. He could feel his face flattening; his body, despite the pressure suit, protested as the weight of the world pulled him back into his seat.

"Roll good. Pitch good," said Pitt.

David said nothing. Mankind's greatest flight would also remain one of its shortest. Just three minutes to change everything. One hundred and eighty seconds to place one man into space and history.

It doesn't feel long enough, thought David, as the sky began to darken and he approached the lower Earth atmosphere. *Three minutes? To go from there to here? The culmination of man's evolution so far takes just three minutes? Ironically, that doesn't have enough gravitas, ha. It should be a mighty journey, like Scott or Columbus. An adventure that demands time to complete. Not three minutes. Not even enough time to hard boil an egg. History doesn't feel heavy enough today, not long enough. You don't earn history in* three minutes.

Stages fell away, fuel exhausted, purpose fulfilled.

Then.

He.

Was.

There.

No fanfares, nor dancing girls, just utter silence and total darkness. David looked out of the tiny round windows either side of the capsule. *So this is what space looks like* was his first thought. *Just as we imagined. No, wait, no, not at all. This is black, blacker than the darkest darkness. An infinity of black, as old as time. Darkness, forever and after.*

David tried to shrug the words out of his mind. Somewhere, that other David, the poet, the *troubadour*, was whispering to him, saying, *See this for what it truly is. See yourself for what you are. A Starman. You are of the stars now, where you should always have been. You aren't a test pilot. You are not a man made of equations, thrust ratios, pitches and rolls. You are not disconnected from this universe. You are this universe. All of us. All humanity down there is up here. We are made of the universe. You are all Starmen and Starwomen.*

Pitt hissed and popped in his ear. "SM3, this is Ground Control. David. Happy birthday. You are now the first man in space." In the background, through the whooshing of the transmission, David could hear cheering and shouting, possibly even champagne corks popping, but it was difficult to tell through the carrier noise.

"Read that," David managed.

"The prime minister is on the line," Pitt continued. Major Tom knew that Churchill had been waiting at Space Dock One with a specially adapted telephone, patched into the B.S.N. transmitters at Alexandra Palace. Winston had been offered a Navy headset and microphone, but preferred the telephone for all communications, including this one. He also knew it would make a great photo opportunity, telling Pitt, "First we needed a teles*cope* to reach space, but I'll use a tele*phone*." Churchill liked his jokes.

The King had been offered the first call, but had deferred to the P.M. It had been Winston's idea, his Highness had explained, Churchill's baby. The King wanted "the Father Of The Rocket" to be first to speak to his child in space.

"SM3," growled Churchill, in his most imperious voice. "The thoughts and thanks of the entire Empire, the whole world, are with you in your capsule today. At this moment, you have taken humanity on its first step to a greater Empire than any one country could have imagined or created. An Empire of mankind, all mankind; our grasp exceeding our reach, our grasp holding the stars themselves."

David waited. He was about to thank his prime minister, but held himself. It wouldn't do to interrupt Churchill while he was busy adding himself to yet another page of history.

"David, SM3," continued Churchill. *Phew, thought Major Tom, nearly trod on the P.M.'s moment there.*

"David, you have achieved what we all set out to do. You will be welcomed back as our new Odysseus. You will have such tales to tell. We shall see you here on *terra firma* very soon. This is the Prime Minister, Winston Churchill, over and out."

The line went dead. *Ah, so I was never supposed to speak*, David realised. *That was Winston's solo performance.*

Pitt returned. "SM3, G.C. We're guessing – or rather, we know – that your view is somewhat limited at the moment. So is everything looking good for Earth Roll?"

David checked his instrumentation. "Good for E.R. Tell me when."

"You have control. On your mark."

"On my mark. Rolling ninety."

David reached up and pressed one of the many buttons above his head. Outside the capsule, a small propulsor emitted a jet of carbon dioxide. In space, that was all you needed to change or correct your direction. His capsule turned slowly and Earth rose in his windows. If he was further out, he'd be able to see his entire home planet, but at this low orbit, it now revealed itself to him in small circular pieces, through the windows.

"Roll ninety confirmed," said David, monotone.

"How are we looking?"

David looked down at his home. It was blue, so blue. There were patches of green, white and yellow, but they were just intermissions between that blue. He was higher than any man had ever been. This was the view the Gods had when they opened their curtains first thing in the morning. He'd thought he was alone back there on the ground, but he'd had no idea – this was lonelier, the loneliest. David craned his neck and could just make out the curvature of the Earth and beyond that, the blackness, waiting.

His planet was alone out here, too. The stars were alone. The blackness swallowed even the universe's giants. Jupiter was less than nothing. The great boiling suns that dominated their own systems were simply motes of dust. Nothing mattered out here, not least one frail man in one tiny tin can, no matter what history might declare.

David looked at his home and thought, *My planet is blue. It will be blue until the sun dies and eats its young. Blue, blue. I am here above it, standing on history and I can do nothing. I can change nothing. I pass through and there's not one thing I can do.* David looked at his home and realised with hollow horror that it meant nothing to him, none of it. From here, this eternal perspective, he knew even the entire planet was ephemeral. As disposable as a child's ball. Once again, these thoughts felt like they came from another mind inside his own.

"How are we looking?" asked Pitt again, concerned his comms were faulty.

"Blue," said David. "We look very blue."

Pitt laughed. " I knew we should have sent a poet. Lucky we have your onboard cameras to let us share your view."

David attempted a laugh and pulled off something akin to the real thing. He knew he had to give the millions listening something else, even if he didn't believe it himself for one moment.

"From here, Ground Control, you see how fragile this little world of ours is." David let the *troubadour* take over for a moment, giving in to this strange, lyrical romantic who walked alongside him, within him. "You can't see borders from up here. You can't see flags or the colour of a man's skin." *Good, troubadour*, he thought, *this is good, keep it up. You have control now.* "All I can see is one single word: *home*. Floating here in the blackness of eternal space is Earth, the only home we have. I wish everyone, from world leaders to the children who will be our future, I wish they could all see through my eyes now. Because all I see is our home. I do not see division, hatred or conflict. I see home."

If only I thought that were true, he thought. *But sometimes, people need the troubadour, the actor, the mask. Sometimes you have to hide the truth to see the beauty.*

There was a silence from down below at G.C.

"That was…" David could hear Pitt trying to formulate a response that history would judge appropriate. "This is…Home to Major Tom, we thank you."

Yes, that would do just fine, thought David. *You've made the grade, Pitt.*

Three minutes to get up here, thought David. *Another one hundred and two minutes in orbit. Then I fire the return engines and streak back down to Earth, a comet with a man inside. What a thought. What a birthday present.*

Pitt left a respectful pause, to isolate the meaningful from the dutiful before giving the next order.

"Very well, SM3, we'll be expecting updates as you have them, Let us know what you see, what you feel. There are a lot of people down here wondering what their homes look like from up there. You'll be passing over many of them. Give them a wave."

"I will," replied David, giving a little wave to the camera. "Hello, Norway. What's 'hello' in Norwegian?"

"Hallo," said Pitt, droll.

"Hallo, Norway."

"Just some housekeeping, SM3. We're seeing the Earth Roll Propulsor still has 15% C02 in the tank. Isolate the Roll Propulsor, please, and vent off the C02, vectoring to keep present position. We recommend a vent of six seconds, rear."

"Six seconds, rear, read."

In English, this was a simple enough instruction. The small propulsion engine David had used to orient his capsule toward Earth hadn't used all the C02 planned for that roll. To prevent any possible leakage, the remaining 15% in the tank had to be vented out, to the rear of the craft. It wouldn't make any difference to the overall speed and would keep the J8 on its current trajectory.

"Isolating Propulsor…" David flicked a switch. "Venting remaining C02, vectoring for current, rear."

David flicked another switch.

At that moment, everything went horribly wrong, horribly quickly.

There was an unmistakeable pop from behind the cramped walls of his capsule. Not much louder than a balloon exploding, but then the J8 suddenly lurched "downwards", nosecone facing toward Earth. It began to roll wildly and tumble. One after another, red warning lights began to blink for David's attention. He felt like he was trapped in a washing machine.

"SM3, SM3," said Pitt. He didn't raise his voice or give the slightest hint of worry, or fear. That was protocol. The world was listening.

David did his best to reply in the same manner.

"Read. Slight shimmy up here. May have had C02 burst ahead of venting. What can you see?"

"Aha, yes. Here's the thing," replied Pitt, in the same emotionless tone of voice one would use to give directions to the nearest shop.

"Yes, we're seeing Red Fifty-Five."

Red Fifty Five. That meant that fifty five percent of all the B.S.N.'s flight analyser circuits were screaming that something was very wrong.

"Red Fifty Five, aha, read," said David. He tried not to look out of the windows, because the Earth now appeared to spin around his tiny craft. He'd been taught how to avoid disorientation, but lessons in a simulator were a very different proposition to pulling it off for real, one hundred and seventy seven nautical miles above the surface of home.

"SM3, we're having trouble hearing you on this frequency. Could you try switching to Channel Two?"

Channel Two was the frequency that would remain silent to everyone else listening on Earth. It was only to be used in "life-threatening emergencies." Giving the order to use it was all the confirmation David needed that he was in mortal danger.

"Channel Two, read," he said, trying to keep fear out of his voice.

"Apologies, everyone," said Pitt, jovially. "Just sorting out a minor comms glitch. Normal service will be resumed as soon as possible," he added in a silly plummy voice.

"Normal service" was a phrase the BBC used whenever one of their transmitters started acting up. Everyone listening would have heard it as a joke, nothing to be concerned about.

David turned a dial switching from Channel One (written in green) to Channel Two (so there could be no misunderstanding, written in red.)

"Here's what we see, David," said Pitt, and now he sounded grave. "The analytics are suggesting that the rear left C02 tank has…it's gone. We don't know how, we'll deal with that when we need to. What's the J8 doing?"

"Spinning all over the place, pitch and roll. The instruments can't track it, everything's haywire. I'm tumbling, Ken. I'm tumbling."

"Yes, yes. The explosion – and it's only a small one, the tank is only three inches in length, remember, just three inches – the explosion has vented what's left out in several directions at once. That's what's causing the tumble."

David shut his eyes for a moment. *Explosion* was not a word you wanted to hear on the ground, let alone in space. A tank three inches long could still do a lot of damage and there were no life rafts up here.

"Read. So…"

He tried to think. They'd practised so many emergency routines on Jura to cover every contingency, or so they'd hoped. He went through the options in his mind. Venting. Explosion. Loss of Control. Pages and pages of contingencies flickered in his mind. Pitt got there first.

"We allowed for this, remember? Remember David?" David knew that Pitt was busy flicking through one of the many operational manuals that sat on the shelf beside his station. Some were also coloured red. David would bet good money Pitt was holding a *red* manual right now.

"Aha. Vent Control Protocol. Remember? VCP…" he was clearly turning pages. "VCP Six. David. The C02 has all vented. That's not the problem any more. The tank has burst for reasons unknown, but that's gone. That's over. Your first problem is bringing the J8 back under control and ensuring you are on exactly the right trajectory for re-entry. First, we need to bring the pitch into line…"

Together, David and Ground Control worked the problem. It was a case of a push one way whilst pulling with another, delicately manipulating the remaining propulsors, tiny degrees at a time, to correct the wayward, tumbling J8. First, the craft's chaotic roll had to be slowed, stopped and re-calibrated back to the original position and trajectory. Then the capsule had to be brought into the correct re-entry attitude, heat-shield first.

Meanwhile, the world waited. Observers and commentators out of the loop tried to both re-assure the people whilst indulging in many dramatic *possibly*'s and *perhaps*'s as to what might be going on up there. With every second of radio silence from both Ground Control and the capsule, the crowds fell ever more silent, staring at their radios or public address systems as if that might make them clatter back into life.

Eventually, after a few minutes, there was just the singing of the uncaring birds and a low, worried mutter from the people. The commentators were also reduced to fitful, hushed tones.

In G.C., a grey telephone on Pitt's station buzzed into angry life. Pitt knew the phone sounded like the man on the other end. Whilst his flight engineers slowly coaxed the J8 back, he closed his eyes and picked up the receiver .

"Prime minister," said Pitt. It wasn't a question.

"Pitt? What the hell is happening? We have total silence here on the radio. Total silence! You cannot black out the entire bloody planet and you cannot black out the bloody Prime Minister!"

"Well, er, Heathrow, we have a problem."

"A problem? Is our Starman alive?"

"Yes, Sir, but his craft is out of control. Tumbling. We are attempting to bring it back."

"Can you?"

"Sir?"

"Can you bring it back under control?"

"We believe we are doing so. But…"

"Then resume transmission, man! Resume transmission! This is the greatest day in the history of humanity and you give the people silence?"

"But we could still lose him. This could be our…" Pitt struggled for the right words. Not too defeatist, but not too wildly optimistic. Churchill got there first.

"This could be our finest hour!" he thundered. "Resume transmission! Tell the world what is happening! Do it now! That is an order!" With that, the line went dead. Pitt looked at his mission clock. They'd now been silent for over three minutes. He didn't have long. Churchill expected the transmission to return, but he couldn't do that, not yet.

He pulled up his headset and microphone. What he was about to say would be shared with Ground Control, David and no other. But he had to be quick.

"David?"

"Ken. I'm back in the pipe. Five, five, five. We're good. Got Green one hundred across the board." David sounded relieved.

"Listen. I don't have long. Churchill wants us to go back onto Channel One. Now. David, remember, I said your first problem was to get the ship back under control..."

"Yes, and that's..." Major Tom paused as the words sunk in. "Wait. First problem, Ken? First?"

"See, we don't know, but the explosion could have damaged your heat shield. If that's the case..." He left that thought hanging. If the heat shield were damaged, David would burn up on re-entry, just like poor Barker. No life raft, no Plan B, just around one thousand six hundred degrees C and an unscheduled cremation.

"I see."

"So here's what we do. You space walk."

"Space walk? But that wasn't scheduled until Saturn Two."

"Forget schedules. You leave your capsule. You visually check your heat shield. You come home."

"And if it's damaged? I don't come home. I burn. What's the point if it's damaged? All I'll achieve is knowing I'm going to die."

"And if it's not damaged, then you'll know you won't die. Listen, David, it could be nothing. It could be minimal and you'll still have more than a fighting chance. But better to know, old man, hm? Better to know?"

David thought. Time was running out in so many ways.

"Read that. I walk."

"Let me handle the announcement this end. Get ready. Just as we practised, just as we planned. You can do this. But you can't let anyone down here know it's an emergency. Act, David. Can you act?"

Act? Oh yes, I think I can, thought David. Grimly, he began pre-checks. *I'm Major Tom, I'm playing a role. I'm leaving my capsule*, he thought. *Showtime. Again. But no script. Do I dare? Do I have a choice?*

*

The children, unlike the rest of the world, had not fallen silent. They hadn't even been aware that anything was wrong. The Ground Control room below them showed no signs of panic and, if truth were told, some of the children were a little bored, as they'd expected more.

Internally, Terry was rolling and tumbling like David's craft, but like everyone else, had no idea what was happening.

Transmissions were dead and that meant his brother could be, too. He desperately scanned the faces of the flight team below. They were up to something, he could tell – they were all talking too much. At this point of the mission, they should have silently monitored progress, but instead stood in bunches, pointed at their stations, held up notes and slide rules.

He's not dead, thought Terry. *If he were, it would be a very different scenario playing out in G.C. No, he's hit some trouble. Nothing fatal. Not yet,* his mind added. *They're fixing something, but what?*

At that moment, the speakers crackled back into life. It was Pitt.

"This is Ground Control, this is Ground Control. Apologies for the problem with our radio broadcast. We're aware that our silence has been a cause for concern, but can I just assure you the mission is continuing and David Jones, SM3, is alive and well. The problem concerned our transmission channel and the receiver onboard the Jupiter Eight Capsule…"

Terry turned to look over at Pitt. The flight director didn't look relieved or calm. His forehead glistened with sweat and his eyes darted about G.C. at the various operatives on their stations.

Something's dreadfully wrong, realised Terry and the fear that had been circling now dug its claws into him. There were no problems with the transmission. They'd cut it. Other frequencies could have been used, that was standard operating procedure. You don't rely on one channel, not ever. They'd gone to Red, Terry knew. They'd gone to Red and that was very bad.

Pitt continued. "But we do have some good news. The flight is progressing perfectly to plan. So perfectly, in fact, that we now intend to make history twice today."

That made the children sit up. Terry knew that the entire world outside had done the same.

"We have put the first man into space. We had scheduled further advances to our mission on the next flights, but it has been decided at the highest level that today, we will also be making history by sending David Jones, SM3, on the very first walk in space…"

At that moment, the picture on the televisual returned, showing David in his capsule. You still couldn't see much from this angle, but it was obvious he was preparing. He removed pipes from his suit and clicked new ones into the valves. He was methodical, dials were turned and switches flicked as he cross referenced a checklist. The children gasped and whooped. Terry nearly fainted.

"Within the next few minutes, SM3 will leave his capsule and, tethered to his craft, float above Earth. From this incredible vantage point, he will be able to take further photographs of our home planet. External cameras will be able to show us live pictures of this event. SM3 has ascertained the very minor risks and concurred that he is ready to undertake this next incredible step into history…"

Very minor risks? Terry thought. *A space walk wasn't scheduled until the Saturn programme! This is totally off mission. They're making this up as they go along. There is no need for David to take the risk, no need whatsoever. He's done what was required. He's become the first man in space. Bring him home. Why would they do this? It could kill him. Why?*

But then Terry realised something else and this time he really did become light headed. Tunnel vision closed in and he had to steady himself against the wall as a wave of nausea crashed over him.

They're taking the risk because they have no choice. Whatever has happened, a space walk is the lesser of two evils. Because this isn't a space walk. No, this is a life belt.

He pulled himself up straight, weaved a little and made his way to the door as Pitt continued to speak about the mechanics of the upcoming walk. He sounded like this was all routine, but the bustle below gave the lie to that.

Terry opened the door where he knew the WREN would be waiting for any further requests from O.R.6.

"Excuse me," he stuttered. "I need to go to G.C. for a minute. You'll need to oversee the children."

The WREN looked confused. "But Sir, you're not scheduled to leave until 1600 hours."

"I know. This is an order. Oversee the children."

"Yes, Sir."

Terry ran for the stairs.

*

In his capsule, David completed the checks. Yes, they'd practised for a space walk, but it had never been remotely considered a viable option. An entire mission had been earmarked for that event. Now he was about to perform an ad hoc version to confirm or deny his death.

He flicked the last few switches that would re-route his oxygen and power to the external supply pipes. He felt the internal ones shut down and removed them from his suit. Then, he carefully wound out the pipes and attached them to the same valves. This system had never been intended for a space walk. On re-entry, David's capsule was due to land in the Atlantic, to be picked up by HMS *Ark Royal*. But if something went wrong and his ship sank into the waters, the external life system was to have been used to keep David alive as he made his escape. It was designed to keep him alive in water, not a vacuum.

But what was the alternative? If the heat shield had been damaged, he was dead anyway. *Do I even want to know?* He wondered. *Isn't ignorance bliss?*

But he knew that this walk wasn't for him. It was for the *B.S.N.* to give them advance warning of tragedy and prepare whatever story or coverage they needed to. If Major Tom wasn't coming back to earth, the Navy could at least play it their way with no further nasty surprises. How very British.

This is insane, he thought. *No,* they *are insane. I am the only sane person in the universe right now.*

He knew the world was back watching and listening. So not only was he performing a potentially mortal manoeuvre, but was also having to pretend it was all completely normal. Few people went to the gallows with a script in their hand.

He looked down at the comms line that would also attach to his suit. It would allow him to talk to G.C. from outside the capsule, but he could just unplug the line and give the acting a rest. He couldn't do anything about the external cameras, but at least he wouldn't have to talk to anyone if he saw the hangman's noose. He fiddled with the comms line for a moment, but then decided against going silent, at least for now.

"It's time," said Pitt, back before the ears of the world, giving them a show. "Are you ready to leave the capsule?"

"This is SM3." *Of course it is,* thought David, *there's no-one else up here.* "I'm preparing to open the hatch."

"Good luck."

David turned the two opposing handles that fastened the capsule's hatch shut. He glanced about his instrumentation one more time. It wouldn't do to have forgotten to switch his oxygen on, or vent the air from inside the capsule first to prevent explosive decompression. All the switches were in the correct positions. He took a deep breath and opened the hatch.

It was no more dramatic or strenuous than opening the trap door that had led to his parents' cellar. But this was darker and went on forever. Now there was just David and infinity.

Slowly, he pushed himself out. The feeling was like swimming underwater, just as he'd trained on Jura. But unlike water, which surrounded you with pressure, here there was none. This was as close to flying as any human had ever come. He grabbed hold of one of the external handles. David knew the tethers would keep him close to his ship, but instinct over-rode training. Sometimes, despite yourself, all you can do is hang on for dear life.

He remembered to speak.

"Ground Control," he breathed heavily. "Major Tom." He didn't know why he'd chosen his alter ego at that moment. Perhaps if it was happening to Major Tom it wasn't happening to him. Perhaps he could hide behind this character, safe from reality. "I'm, er, leaving the capsule. I'm floating for the first time. It's a very peculiar feeling."

He looked up and around. Earth was on the other side of the capsule, but it still filled his vision around the little tin can. He stared around up at the stars. He could see them properly now, away from the confines of his ship.

No-one has seen the stars like this before, he thought. *They've always been filtered through our atmosphere. My God, they twinkle. They really do. It's my own private audience of stars. They're watching this strange little object float about a tin can. Perhaps the twinkling is laughing?*

"The stars," he said out loud. "They're so…different. They're not like I expected. More vivid. They sparkle up here."

"We have visual from your externals. Wish we could see what you can. From here, they're just dots of light. We're watching in black and white, of course."

"Yes," David remembered. Those on earth could only see the stark contrasts. They didn't know, couldn't imagine. Up here, the stars were a jewellery box of colours. He slowly turned, grabbed on to the handles and made his way toward what was now the "front" of his ship, the heat shield. He crabbed along its hull and looked toward the Earth, finally saw it stretch out beneath him. Before, he'd only seen fractions of its blue brilliance through the capsule windows, but now it sat below him as he fell, twisting, above his home.

"Oh, God," he said. "I see Earth now for the first time, properly." Again, David realised no-one else had ever seen this sight. It truly was a day of firsts, but only for him. The rest of the human race could only live through their Starman vicariously. "It's huge, but so tiny. Our home. My home. Everything we love, everything we hold, is there, below me. We are children and this is just our nursery." He realised the *troubadour* had taken over again, when there were more mortally pressing concerns, but he didn't care. This was the *troubadour's* element. He knew that now. This roaming musician was the true Starman. "Like any nursery, there's a big world out there. We just need to take those tiny steps and go to find it."

David didn't care about the thousands of machines recording his every word. History meant nothing to him. Posterity was an illusion. *For all of us*, he thought, *there is only this precious now.*

"SM3," said Pitt and there was a trace of concern in his voice that he couldn't hide. Perhaps he thought this troubadour may be too much. David didn't care. He didn't care about anything. "SM3, we see Earth through the externals and yes, it is a sight we thank God and you for. We have already taken some giant steps from the nursery you talk about. How is your capsule looking?"

Well, that was a non sequitur, thought David, as a wry grin scuttled over his lips. *From the grandeur of God's creation to my tin can. Very poetic of you, Pitt. But I get it. I know what I'm out here for.*

"My capsule…"

He pulled himself forward over the hull and looked down at the circular heat shield.

He stared at it for what felt like ages, but that may have been time playing another game.

A large crack zig-zagged from around two o'clock on the heat shield to seven o'clock. It looked like a lightning bolt.

David put out a hand and traced the crack as far as he could reach. He rubbed a finger along it, felt the shape of his death.

Shouldn't have faked the coin toss, he thought, sadly. When the Starman for this flight had been decided by the toss of a coin, David had *deliberately* dropped the shilling, then, on retrieving it from beneath Pitt's desk, pulled a deft roll on the coin to reveal the king, heads.

He'd tricked Pitt and his brother, made them believe fate had chosen him to become the First Man. David had chosen himself. *If Terry had been up here, would the accident have happened?* He wondered, unable to tear his gaze from that crack. *Was this fate, punishing me for my vanity?*

"How's the capsule looking?" asked Pitt again, the only question that counted.

David touched the crack again. If he attempted re-entry, within seconds, the heat would reach into this fissure and split it apart. Moments after that, the fires would engulf his entire capsule, incinerating it from the shield up. *How much would I know, would I feel?* Major Tom wondered. *Would I have time to recognise my death when it stares me in the face? Would there be a moment to be formally introduced before my body became ash?*

Ash.

Before he could think about his response, the troubadour answered. "Capsule Green One Hundred. Everything is fine."

"That's great, SM3," Pitt exhaled as if he'd been holding his breath for some time. "That's…" David could hear him remember he was live to the world. "That's all to be expected. Thank you. You've made history twice in just…twenty five minutes. I think that's another first."

"Returning to the capsule," David said. He took one more look at the crack in the shield and made up his mind. *No, I made up my mind a long time ago. I cemented my decision the moment I faked the coin toss in Pitt's office. I knew where I was going from the second I heard that small thump from the street behind me.*

Major Tom pulled himself back into the capsule and closed the hatch.

*

In G.C., Terry rushed up to Pitt. From another door, Angie had been brought into the room, looking confused and a little scared.

"What's happening?" Terry whispered to Pitt.

"Nothing," said Pitt who took off his headphones. "We thought we may have had a problem, but it's fine."

He looked over at the WREN who accompanied Angie and shook his head. *We don't need her here.*

Angie, however, spotted the move and strode over to the flight director.

"What's going on? Why have I been brought down here? They said I needed to come. Why? What?"

Pitt held up his hands to the Starman's brother and wife.

"Sorry. Sorry, we thought there could have been a slight problem with re-entry. David's performed a visual. That's what the space walk was for. Some subterfuge, apologies for that. All is well. I'm sorry to have worried you, to have worried everyone."

"You never said anything on the broadcast," said Terry, who looked round the control room and took in the expressions of the team. They looked like they had been through the wringer.

"No, because we didn't want to panic anyone. Anyone, of course, being the entire world."

"So is he in danger or not?" asked Angie. She may not have loved her husband, but still had some residual care.

"No. In around thirty minutes, he'll begin re-entry. Everything is fine. Honest. I would tell you if it wasn't."

Pitt looked like he wanted the wife and brother to leave. Neither of them looked like they wanted to move.

*

Major Tom sat in his doomed capsule.

Thoughts he'd repressed now came, fully focused, with joyous clarity.

He didn't care about Earth or anyone on it.

He'd stopped caring four years ago, the moment he'd heard that tiny thud and then seen life as he knew it was over.

He'd pursued this mission not to be first man in space, but to be the first man to leave Earth behind; he knew that now. He'd always known it, he supposed, but managed to hide that truth behind his many elaborate masks and costumes. Behind Major Tom.

Now he would never see Earth again. That was not so bad a price to pay.

Where was Ash?

Well, Ash was where everyone had said he was, of course. All the kindly strangers, the holy men, the poets, books, friends, colleagues, story tellers, the loved and the lost.

They all said Ash was up there. Ash was *up here*. He was in *Heaven*. He was *free*. He *flew*. He was *with the stars now*.

I can go back to a world that has nothing for me and burn as I try to reach it, he thought. *Or I can go to my son. I can go to him.*

Major Tom reached for the switches that would engage the starboard propulsor. The tiny engine that would push his capsule out of this decaying orbit, out of this decaying life, away from this decaying planet with its decaying people. He reached for the switch that would send his capsule out there, into that forever blackness where the stars laughed and his son surely played.

His finger stopped above the two ENGAGE switches. He reached for the TRANSMIT button.

There was one last thing he had to do before he went on this grand, great adventure.

One last wrong to make right.

"Major Tom to G.C.," he said.

"G.C. reading."

"Tell my wife. Tell my wife I love her. I love her very much. She may not believe me, but she knows."

Major Tom pulled the transmit lead out from his helmet. Now he was alone. Truly alone, at last.

With no further thought, he pushed the ENGAGE switches. There was a slight judder as his capsule shrugged off Earth's gravity and headed out, away to forever.

"Major Tom?" Pitt asked. "Your transmit circuit has gone dead. Repeat, your transmit circuit is dead. Can you hear me? Major Tom, can you hear me?"

Major Tom switched Earth off, for good.

"Ash," he whispered and smiled.

"DEAR PRUDENCE"

(The Beatles, 1968, from the album, The Beatles *)*

Remember this; time neither respects, nor notices you.

But *timing* is everything.

James waited on her doorstep. It felt like he'd been there for a lifetime.

He raised his hand to knock, but it rebelled mid air, and went nowhere. He looked at his motionless fist, which then slowly returned to his side, ashamed.

James was sweating and not just from this situation. He looked up and down the empty street. The sun had scalded the grass to a light brown and above blasted lawns, trees hung down, jaded.

A few insects buzzed listlessly from flower to flower, but even the flowers looked exhausted. James felt shattered too. It had taken a lot of effort to get this far.

Because now he was here, really here on her doorstep, what could he say?

His first thought had been, "Would you like to come out to play?" but quickly realised that was an atrocious line.

They were both fifteen, for heaven's sake. "Come out to play?" Where had that come from? James realised it was nerves. He'd always said that at friends' doors, but back when he was eight or so. It wouldn't work talking to a fifteen year old girl. Especially not her.

No, he thought. *This is what I'll do. Stick to the plan.* He would smile and casually mention he *happened* to be passing and since it was such a lovely day, perhaps she might like to, *perhaps maybe* come out for a little stroll? Nothing much, just a little walk around the fields that surrounded the village. And if she didn't want to come, then nothing ventured, nothing gained, as his Dad always said. Yes, he would play it casual.

But he wasn't dressed casually. He'd put on a shirt, for starters. When did he ever wear a shirt, especially on a sweltering July day like this? His trousers were ironed, too, with a crease, as if he were going for a job.

He pulled at his collar and imagined steam rise from inside. It certainly felt like he'd brewed up quite a sweat. He raised his arm again and sniffed his armpit, but only smelled fresh cotton. Good.

Down the street, an elderly couple walked arm in arm. Otherwise, there was no-one else about. It seemed like almost everyone had taken shelter indoors from the heat. The name "Sunday" had never seemed more appropriate. Yes, this was the sun's day alright. English rain was not welcome.

James listened, turned his head this way and that. Nothing. Even the birds were too hot to sing. No dogs barked, no music spilled from the open windows, not even the leaves of the trees whispered, since the breeze was too lethargic to be bothered.

It was possible there was just him and that old married couple in the world. Maybe everyone else in Great Wakering had simply evaporated. If he looked inside any of the houses, he would just find piles of clothes, with a fog of moisture above them.

Great Wakering is a village at the very tip of South Essex, one of the driest places in Britain, apparently, a fact that gave the residents an odd sense of pride that their quiet, tiny home had achieved something of note. There was no drought, not yet, but the fields that surrounded Wakering were parched, the mud had cracked into mosaics, and the duck pond was dangerously low. It surely wouldn't be long before the taps dried up too.

Thirty-something miles up the road, James knew London would be hot as hell. If there was no breeze here on the open plains of Essex, then London would be infernal. The buildings would trap the heat between them and reflect it out again, like giant radiators. He imagined most people would simply, limply, lie on their sofas indoors, like lions draped themselves over trees.

Four miles west was Southend-on-Sea, which wasn't "on sea" at all, but *Southend-on-the-Thames-Estuary* didn't sound so grand. Many Londoners would have escaped their seared city today to seek respite at Southend seafront. Trains from Fenchurch Street and Liverpool Street would be packed with hopeful day-trippers, who'd then march down the High Street toward the famous pier and then on to the arcades and pubs.

Some would paddle or even swim in the dirty estuary water, while others would simply sit and happily burn their skin. Southend would be busy today, but Great Wakering was deserted. No day trippers ever came. The village's only claim to fame was its record-breaking dryness – hardly a tourist attraction.

James raised his fist again to knock, but again, it wouldn't move. He stared at his hand, frowned and tried to push it toward the door. It stayed put.

*

She'd arrived from East London four months ago.

Old Man Marsh the butcher had dropped dead over some pork sausages at his shop. "It was how he'd have wanted to go," the villagers had muttered. James had thought that was probably untrue. Old Man Marsh had almost certainly not wanted to keel over whilst he filled a skin with minced pig. On his list of Things To Do In Life, he'd absolutely not written, "Die Whilst Making Sausages." The villagers, however, seemed to equate Dying Whilst Doing Your Job with being a poetic, perhaps even heroic, act.

But Old Man Marsh had popped his clogs and there had been a teary farewell at the church. It seemed like everyone had turned up, since, of course, everyone liked meat. James was at the funeral with his Dad, who'd been a genuine friend to the butcher.

James' father ran the local fruit and veg shop, so of course, the Meat and Veg Man were two sides of the same coin. They sent customers between themselves in a mutually beneficial arrangement: "You know what would go lovely with that pork? Some nice braised carrots!" "I tell you what works with cabbage – bacon!" It helped there was no competition for either of them – Great Wakering only had a few shops anyway, so if people wanted something more exotic than, say, *food*, they had to go into Southend.

So James and his Dad had gone to the funeral and that's when he'd first seen her standing there, albeit from behind.

She was stood at the front with a tall man. James had noticed a glorious sunburst of red hair that fell from a black hat. There were no other redheaded girls his age in the village, so that was new.

New was good in Great Wakering. Different was good. Anything that broke the monotony was to be welcomed. James had closed his eyes and made two wishes:

1/ Whoever she is, I wish she's staying.

2/ Whoever she is, I wish she's pretty.

He'd admitted that wish had been rather shallow, but it mattered.

New was good, different was good, but when you are a fifteen year old boy, pretty was even better.

Once the service finished, the front rows filed out first, as was right and traditional. James had tried not to make his gaze too obvious, but as she passed he'd glanced over and his heart had beat out of his chest, because she was *very* pretty.

That afternoon, in the shop, he'd nonchalantly asked Dad who the other people were at the funeral. Of course he knew the villagers, but what about those at the front?

His Dad hadn't seen the real point of the question and replied, "Oh, that was Stan's family from London. He wasn't from round here originally, like us. He arrived about twenty years ago. Heaven knows why he wanted to swap London for Great Wakering, but there's no telling with some people, is there? He came from somewhere in East London. Where was it? Bow, I think. Yes, Bow. That made him a proper Cockney. So yes, that was his family. They were straight back on the train, I suppose. Couldn't get out of the village fast enough. Don't blame them."

But, James had asked, what about the tall man?

"Oh, him? Peter. Mr Marsh's son. I hear he's coming to take over the business. Did you see the girl with him?"

James had made a play of thinking. *Oh, was she the one with red hair?* he'd offered.

"Aha, his daughter. She's coming too, I hear. His wife – her Mum – died last year, poor people. So they're leaving the East End and coming here to deal with sausages. That means, I hope, they'll be dealing with me, too. Continue the old tradition, eh?"

James had nodded when he'd actually wanted to jump into the air.

"Your age, she is, I think." Dad had finally seen the real motive behind this conversation. His son wasn't a great actor. "Perhaps you two could be friends, you know? You're at that age where you should start having girl friends."

James's mouth had gone into an O of shock.

"Not a *girlfriend*, girlfriend. I mean a friend who is a girl. Your, er, male friends can be a bit single minded. It would be good to get a female, er, perspective sometimes."

At that, Dad had gone silent and thoughtful. He'd lost his wife, too, four years before. She'd also died suddenly, in her sleep. The doctors said something had gone wrong with her brain and a blood vessel had popped like a balloon. One tiny vessel, such huge damage. She hadn't suffered, which was a small consolation and realistically made no difference. She was gone and that was that. Trying to hunt for pointless positives was a waste of time.

So there they were; the newly arrived butcher and the resident fruit and veg man – two widowers with one child each. There was no doubt that their paths would collide.

*

So, a few weeks after the funeral, the new butcher and his daughter had moved into Great Wakering. Their shop was on the High Street and their home was here, on Alexandra Road, where James now stood, and tried to summon up the courage to knock on her door in this oppressive heat.

He'd seen them both going about their business around the village. Dad had made his introductions and Peter, the other father, had been pleased to meet him.

Finally, James had discovered her name: *Prudence.*

It surprised him because *Prudence* sounded so…old fashioned. It also resembled, "prune", which was a trifle off putting, but he dealt with it.

Dad had explained. "Very popular in Victorian times, apparently. But although it's uncommon now, her parents chose it because *Prudence* means someone with good judgement, intelligent. They just liked it."

James had said it many times after, out loud in front of the bathroom mirror, in practice for the day when he'd meet her properly. "Prudence," he'd raised his eyebrow like an actor. "Pleased to meet you. Would you like some carrots, you know, on the house?" "Prudence. I'm James. Call me Jim, if you like." "Prudence, I have tickets for a concert in Southend, would you like to come?"

He'd played out so many scenarios in his mind, but when she'd finally walked into their shop one Saturday morning, all preparation had failed him and he'd just camply spluttered, "Oooh, hello, we've got beetroot on offer."

She'd looked at him quizzically and her first, historic words had been, "Yes, I can see. Very good price, too. But I'm just dropping off some steak for your Dad." She'd held up a paper bag, smiled and raised an amused eyebrow.

She'd worn a black coat buttoned up to the neck with a little beret perched on the back of her head. Her skirt had come down below her knees, and her feet were encased in flat black shoes. All this should have made her look incredibly sensible and stodgy, but James thought she was the most stylish girl he'd ever seen.

"Oh, steak, yes," James had managed to reply and then, bizarrely, held out his hand for her to shake.

She'd looked down at the hand and grinned. "Ooh, you're proper posh ain't yer?" But she hadn't taken up the offer. Instead, she'd pushed the bagged up steak at him. "Oh, I'm Prudence," she added. James had managed *not* to say, "I know," but just replied, as per the practice run, "I'm James. But you can call me Jim if you like," then smiled in what he'd imagined was a charming, rakish way.

"I'll stick to James, if that's alright, since I don't know you, well, anyway, right, ta-ta." She'd given an odd little uncomfortable curtsey then quickly left the shop. The doorbell laughed in her wake.

James had stood silently for a moment and looked down at the bag of meat in his hand as if it were a holy relic. This angel had come down from heaven and bequeathed him steak.

"I'm *proper* posh," he'd whispered to himself. Her accent was so thick, so East End. The Essex accent was similar – it was a gift from the Cockneys who'd visited and stayed – but hers was of a different order. It twanged, climbed and swooped. She drew *aaaaaaht* the vowels, dropped the *consonaaaan's*. On her tongue, a phrase like, "I'm droppin' off saaaam steak fer yer Daaaayd," was like a foreign language. It made her seem incredibly exotic, even though she'd come from just up the road, comparatively.

He'd tried out her Cockney accent in private, in the hope it might endear her to him, but it had sounded ridiculous, music hall, and sometimes veered more toward Welsh. He'd given up and stuck to Essex. It was close enough, if you stuck your fingers in your ears.

*

After that first rather awkward meeting, James hadn't stopped thinking about her.

He'd go out of his way to walk past Prudence's house and hoped she'd appear at the door. He'd always volunteer to visit the butchers in case she was there, but no luck. To be fair, hanging around the hung-up rabbits and other assorted carcasses probably wasn't her idea of fun.

His second meeting with Prudence had taken place in equally inauspicious circumstances. James was kicking a ball in the recreation ground when he'd seen her in the distance, alone, hands in the pockets of her black coat, face up to the cloudy sky, lost in thought.

For some reason (and how he berated himself every time he played the scene back in his mind) he thought she'd really, *really* like someone to kick a ball her way. Yes – that was exactly what every lonely girl wanted, to have some idiot lob a ball at her and then ask if she fancied a kick about.

Before his sensible side could scream, *No, you fool!* He'd taken a kick and then watched in horror as the ball arced beautifully toward her. The one time he'd actually managed to place a ball with pin-point accuracy was the one time he really shouldn't have. It had flown toward Prudence and James realised she hadn't even noticed. She'd managed to look up at exactly the moment the ball hit her square in the face. Then she'd fallen backwards into the grass and lain there, motionless.

Oh my God, I've killed her, was James' first thought. He'd pictured the inevitable arrest, trial and surely public execution that would follow. He didn't know if "Murder By Football" would even be recognised as a crime, but murder, per se, certainly was.

She'd lain flat out, arms by her sides. Her eyes had stared blankly up at the blue sky and then he really had thought she'd popped her clogs.

"I'm sorry, I'm so sorry," he'd groaned and held out his hand to help her. She'd looked at it disdainfully then slowly picked herself up from the floor. He'd withdrawn it quickly. That had been the second time he'd offered a hand and she'd ignored it, *again.*

Oh, please, please smile and hold my hand, he'd thought. *If you hold my hand, just once, everything in the world will be perfect.*

"I'll get myself up, ta very much," she'd scowled at him, touched her nose and winced. "Ow. *Ow.* What was that about? James, isn't it?"

Despite the circumstances, his heart skipped a beat because she'd remembered.

"Yes, but you can call me Jim."

"James. So explain that to me. Ball in the dial, why?"

"I thought…" *Don't say, "I thought you might want a kick about"* flashed through his mind.

"I thought you might want a kick about," his treacherous mouth had offered.

"A kick about?" She'd looked down at herself in her black coat, skirt and flat shoes. "Do I look like I'm trying for West Ham?"

Prudence had dusted herself down and frowned. "I've only been in this bloody boring village for ten boring minutes and someone tries to knock my bloody block off."

James had never heard anyone actually say, *"knock my block off"* before. From her it was strangely charming.

"I'm sorry. I'm really sorry."

The briefest of smiles had fluttered across her lips. If James had blinked he'd have missed it. "I bet I looked proper funny. Did I?"

He hadn't known the correct answer. Did girls ever want to look "proper funny?" So he'd shrugged and hoped that would do as a response.

"Of course, now, you have to let me kick the ball back at you." She'd thoughtfully stroked her chin and considered the proposal. "Yes. Right in the knackers. That would be fair. Tit for tat."

"Well, er, I, er…"

"Mm, yes. You stand there…" She'd pointed to the ground, like a referee awarding a free kick. "And I'll stand here…Since I'm not as good an aim as you, and then I'll wallop it right in your meat and two veg. After all, you have mutilated my face, for life."

"Oh, well, er…" James had stepped over to the spot. "Yes, that's fair, I suppose."

She'd looked at him, open mouthed. "I didn't mean it!"

"Oh, er, yes, ha ha," he'd managed to laugh, totally confused. "Kick it in my, er… Ha, that's funny."

"I did mean it! I was joking about *not* meaning it. So go on, striker. Take your position. No hands over yourself, neither."

So James, totally lost, went back to the spot.

"Nooooo! I was joking about meaning it!" She collapsed into an odd, high-pitched tittering. "Blimey, are all the boys round here this stupid, or did you win a competition, or something? Did you forget to wear your "I'm Stupid" crown today, or what? Is it an Essex thing?"

He'd laughed again, nervously. This girl was wild and he'd liked it, a lot. The other girls round the village were so – what was the word? Ah yes, parochial. But she was from the city. The capital city none the less. She was sophisticated and brought a bigger, wider, wilder world to Great Wakering. At that point, James thought he might already be a little in love with Prudence Marsh.

But how he wished she'd just smile and take his hand.

*

After that near disaster, they'd had a common bond of sorts. If she saw him across the street, she'd run in the opposite direction, hold her face and shout, "Keep him away! He wants to knacker me beautiful boat!"

Sometimes he'd pretend to kick a ball, she'd mime a strike, then run in a circle, hands above her head like a champion. "Prudence Marsh gets the winning goal for West Ham! The fans are crying! The title goes to the Hammers!"

He adored the fact there was this private joke between them. He saw other boys stare her way, but never saw her look back. It seemed she wasn't interested. Having said that, she didn't seem interested in *him* other than as something amusing, a novelty, nothing more.

One day, after another pretend ball-attack incident, he'd walked over and held out his hand, mock seriously. "Let's make a deal. I promise never to kick a ball in your...," he'd been about to say *"pretty"* but stopped himself, "...your... face again and you promise you'll never tell your Dad about it. I don't want him stringing me up in his shop. Promise?"

But once again, she looked at his outstretched hand and smirked. "I've already told me Dad and he says he has a place for you in the window, on a hook, next to the pheasants. Nah, the *peasants*." Then as she'd walked away, Prudence whistled a song James recognised but couldn't place at first. He'd identified it later; "Two Lovely Black Eyes", a Cockney standard which he'd often heard boom from pubs. But she'd still not taken his hand. He'd just wanted one touch, which was hardly a marriage proposal.

He hadn't been able to tell anyone and it ate him up. Dad and Mr Peter Marsh had been getting on like the proverbial house on fire, like two old friends who'd met up again after years of estrangement. That had made things worse. It appeared that the Dads were made for each other, but their children were on separate paths.

James imagined what would happen if he asked Prudence for dinner. They'd sit around the table and then he'd catch her gaze his way. She would redden, but he'd hold her stare. Then he'd look into Prudence's grey / green eyes and talk about precious things. He'd read her poetry, fetch his guitar and play her favourite songs. She'd have no choice but to fall madly, desperately in love with him. Then they would get married.

Madness, yes, but wishful thinking never hurt anyone.

But he couldn't ask. He didn't want anyone to know how his feelings for Prudence grew every day, scared they'd laugh, especially her. She was from *That London*, but he was born and bred in a place the rest of the country had never even heard of.

It seemed she was out of his and everyone else's league. While she was polite to all and had made some friends, he never actually saw her with anyone. He'd see her in the distance and make up his mind to stride up and say, "You're walking, I'm walking, perhaps we should walk together," but never could. He felt it as a physical ache, like growing pains. Maybe that's what it really was; his body was growing, but so was his heart. They both ached.

*

Today, however, was different. He'd woken on this blue-skied blistered July morning and decided if he didn't do something, then she'd always be in the distance. At this rate, she'd never rush at him, grab his hand and pull him into some adventure. She'd always be walking away.

"Be a man" had been his first thought on waking. Those three words had written themselves like a headline across his mind: "Be a man."

In that moment, he knew what he must do; go to her home, pull that rakish grin, hold out his hand and ask her to come walking. Nothing more.

It was a perfect day. Shining sun, bluest sky, daisies ready to make chains, poppies in the field near the Old Farm...wait, yes, that was the place. They'd go to the Old Farm, the dilapidated broken sheds where the poppies grew.

Be a Man. That's all he had to do. Be a Man.

He was absolutely terrified.

At midday, Dad had gone to Southend with some friends, to drink cold beer in a hot pub, and so, alone in the house, James had walked about like an actor side stage, tried out various lines and waited for the spotlight to hit and his performance to commence.

He'd laid out shirts and trousers on his bed, then, as he'd held them up against himself in the mirror, attempted to work out the perfect combination that looked both casually thrown on, yet respectfully thought out. In the end, he'd chosen a simple white cotton shirt and plain brown trousers. He'd toyed with a tie, but that was just stupid.

Then he'd sat on his bed as the heat played about him and stared out of the window. It felt like it could be the beginning of everything. It also felt like it might be the end.

All it would take was Prudence to say, "Naaaah, bit *hot*, ain't it?" and he would agree, smile, turn, walk away and burst into tears. He realised in just a few short weeks, he'd invested all his hopes in a girl he didn't even know. All he had was a football in her face and that wonderful, dirty, beautiful sense of humour.

Then, like a condemned man on his way to the noose, he'd simply stood and walked to his front door, eyes front, face blank. The first moment he'd stepped out into the ferocious day the heat had hit him like boiled plate-glass. He'd actually taken deep, shocked breaths at its brutality.

Indoors, the temperature had sat alongside him like part of the furniture, but out here, in the open, it buffeted him from all sides simultaneously. His sweat began to trickle seconds from the door and it felt like the day had wrapped itself about him, a layer of molten clothing.

Prudence's house was exactly eight minutes from his own. He'd timed it, of course.

The walk through a deserted, searing Great Wakering seemed to take both no time at all and forever. Then, to his surprise, he was there, on her doorstep, reluctant fist by his side, not knocking.

He closed his eyes, like he was about to have a tooth pulled. You know it's about to happen, *must* happen for the best, but you want to delay the moment, to live in the second between seconds, before you commit to something you can never take back.

He knocked.

*

There was no sound of footsteps, no shout of "'ang on!" The heat waited on the doorstep with him. James formed a few different expressions.

A smile. No, too much.

A hand to his chin, thoughtful. No, too weird.

Neutral. No, too neutral.

He raised his eyes to the heavens, hoping perhaps God might intervene. But God was obviously lying in a back room somewhere, being fanned with palm leaves by bored and twitchy saints.

She obviously wasn't in. That was both a relief and a massive disappointment. When you have worked yourself up into a state of fevered expectation, there is nowhere to go but down and James' shoulders slumped. The gamble had failed. He would go back to miming kicking balls at her, nodding across the street, offering her cheap beetroot because it was on sale, and she'd continue to giggle and walk alone across the fields, close, but an eternity from him.

He turned away.

But then the door opened and Prudence was there. Without a sound, she'd simply appeared, like a magician's assistant. He turned back and tried not to look too eager, scared, hopeful or shocked but mainly not too hopelessly in love.

"Oh." She rested one hand on the doorframe, the other on her hip. She looked past and around him, as if he'd come with company, like he couldn't possibly be here alone on her doorstep, on this ridiculous, roasting day.

"Oh," he'd muttered, because he couldn't think of anything else to say.

She'd looked up and down the street. "Yes?"

"Oh, yes."

"Yes what?"

"It's a lovely day."

"Nah, it's not 'lovely'. It's a hot day. It's bloody hot actually. Not sure if 'lovely' is the word. I'm sweating my hair off."

Her pale skin wasn't sweating at all.

She looked down at his hands, as if he must be here to deliver something, surely not to just stand there, for no reason, on this deliriously hot afternoon.

"So…?" She shrugged and raised her hands, palms open.

"So, yes, so…"

"So…?"

James tried to smile again, the devil-may-care grin he'd practised in front of the mirror.

"What are you smiling at?" She looked back up her hallway in case she'd missed a clown or performing dog, who surely must be behind her to make this idiot smile for no reason.

"Oh, I'm just, you know, smiling." He realised that sounded insane.

"Smiling's good, but...So?" she asked again. The first two times hadn't worked.

Time was running out for James. He had to leap into his fantasy now, run up, jump, do it, ask and to hell with the consequences. The only other option was to walk away silently and never, ever see her again, exiled in his shame.

"I was wondering...I was passing...and I was, I thought, I saw your house and I wondered...would you like to come out..." (*to play?* asked his mind and he managed to slap it down) "...for a walk, or something?"

She looked up and around him again, to that eternally blue cloudless sky.

"It is a nice day," she agreed.

For the first time, he saw her. Up until now, she'd just been Prudence, a set of girl-shaped objects on a doorstep. But now he *really* saw her, red hair up in a careless band, wearing a simple short-sleeved white cotton dress, bunched in at the waist. Her feet were bare. James swooned, internally.

"Me Dad's out."

"So's mine. That's why I was just around, walking."

"Yes."

Yes? Yes to what? Had she agreed to his statement, or his proposal? James didn't know, so went for the neutral expression again.

"Yes, James, let's go out for a walk." Without further comment, she bent down, picked up some shoes, sat on her stairs and began to fasten the buckles. "You're the first person to ask me out to do anything round here. So, er, thanks."

"Oh, er, yes."

"It's boring. Sorry, I don't mean to be rude but back in Bow, we had shops. Lots of them. We had parties, music, we could go to the West End, you know, Oxford Circus, Regent's Street? I had lots of friends. This might sound pathetic, but you're the only friend I have here."

She thinks of me as a friend, thought James and although he wanted to spin on the spot with joy, he admirably restrained himself. He put out a hand to help her up, but she didn't even notice. She stood, smoothed down her simple dress, then picked up some keys from the window sill.

"Come on then. Show me the sights. I think I may have seen all of them already, but I'm prepared to be amazed. Do you have an Egyptian temple knocking about I've missed? A battlefield, *strewn* with guns and armour? Or anything of interest, at all?"

"No," James answered, truthfully. She laughed.

"At least you're honest. Shall we make sandwiches? Have a picnic?"

Once again, James managed not to jump several hundred feet into the air, but made a show of thinking about it.

"Yes, why not? Yes." He shrugged, as if this wasn't the single best thing that had ever happened, or would ever happen to him.

"Come in then; don't make the doorstep look scruffy."

James walked into the hallowed hall of Prudence. She cocked her head at him to follow and walked through into the kitchen.

"We've got ham. We've got chicken, pork, steak, bacon…Let's be honest, me Dad's the butcher, we've got all the meat. Or cheese? Egg? You an egg man?"

"Ham?"

"Ham it is. Ham for the man!"

She sliced up some bread, spread on a thick slab of butter, then added an equally large slice of ham. Prudence grabbed a couple of apples from a cupboard and filled a bottle of water, then put everything in a knitted woollen bag. "There. A proper old-fashioned picnic. So come on then, Mr Grace, show me around Great Wakering. Give me a reason to stay."

She held out the bag for James to carry. Obviously, she expected to be treated like a lady and he was happy to oblige.

They stepped out of Prudence's house and looked up and down the road.

"Quiet." She fanned herself with a hand. "Quiet and bloody, bloody hot. Perhaps we should have an indoor picnic."

"No, we'll find some shade." James waved his hand over her face. It was the closest he could get.

"Aaah, nice. Thanks for knocking on. Ya know, I was just sitting about. Didn't know what to do with meself. Too hot even to read a book. Do you like books?"

Books, marvelled James. *She likes books. She really is like some Victorian lady, in her drawing room, enjoying books.*

"Yes, I like books."

"I love books. They're all I have *raand* here. Just open them up and lose yerself. I like the old books mostly. You know, Jane Austen, the Brontës, so romantic!"

She put her hand to her forehead and pretended to swoon. James laughed.

"You're funny."

"Never tell a girl she's funny," she said, sternly. "Tell her she's beautiful, interesting, fascinating, but never funny. Funny will make her think she's the odd one out and all the other girls are the ones who are beautiful, interesting, fascinating…" She blinked her eyes rapidly and framed her face with her hands, pouted like an actress in the spotlight, then collapsed into giggles that tinkled like bells.

But you are beautiful, interesting and fascinating, thought James. *And you're funny.* He still couldn't believe it had been this easy to walk with her. All those nights when he'd wondered, hoped and fretted had been a waste of time. All he'd really had to do was wait for an infernal Sunday, knock on and there she'd be.

"But funny is alright, too, I suppose," she shrugged. "I'd rather be funny than dull."

They walked on toward the dirt lanes that would take them out to the fields.

"So. What about you, James?" She reached into the bag and pulled out an apple. "Sorry, famished. Let's call it a walking picnic."

Me? He thought. *You want to know about me? Well then, how about this? I adore you. I saw you at your Grandfather's funeral and at that moment, I couldn't stop thinking about you. I kicked a ball in your face and was overjoyed, because it meant I could actually talk to you. Every night I've been wondering how to make this happen, this, which is happening, just you and me and the sun and the blue sky and a bag full of ham sandwiches and you, Prudence, asking, "What about you, James?"*

But instead, he said, "I was born here…"

"Blimey," she laughed. "I didn't want the full life story! We don't have all day. Oh actually, I suppose we do. Nothing else to do, is there?"

"Well, ha. I was born here and I've lived here ever since. That's me."

"Oh. I didn't expect it to be quite that short. Nothing else? No adventures? No life or death experiences? No girls?"

He glanced over at her, but she simply looked out over the parched fields and munched on her apple.

"No, Prudence. This is Great Wakering. It's lovely, but it's not London. You must have realised that by now."

"I realised the moment I came here for Grandad's funeral. Yep, the second we got here, I thought to myself, 'I would hate to live in this village, I'm so glad I don't', and then, ha ha, what fun, a few weeks later I'm here and London may as well be the moon."

"It's not that far away."

"It is. It's a lifetime away. But…"

She stopped and looked about again. A few crickets chirruped in the grass and waited.

"But…you know, it's not that bad. Sometimes it's good just to stop and not think about things. London is London. I know, that's an obvious, stupid thing to say, but what I mean is, you can't get away from it. Wherever you are, there it is. You go to, I don't know, Hyde Park, and it looks like the countryside and smells like the countryside and has all the plants, flowers and animals, but it's just pretending.

You walk and walk and eventually, you reach a metal fence and realise it's all play acting, a city, pretending to be the countryside. The countryside has been brought in and forced into this little bit of land surrounded by bricks. Look. Look, James – what do you see?"

He looked and saw nothing.

"Er, just fields?"

"Exactly. Fields, on and on. No fences. This *is* the the countryside. It hasn't been made to up sticks and park itself in the middle of a city; it is what it is, just gets on with being itself. Sometimes, you know, we need to be away from something to see it for what it truly is. You've never been away from Wakering, so you've never seen it. I see it. Yes, it's flat and dry and hot, bloody hot, but it's real. It gets on with it. You could live and die here, like my Grandad, but I suppose when you accept something for what it is, you can be at peace with it. Actually, that might be the most any of us can hope for – that one day we'll be at peace with whoever we are and wherever we are. Yeah, 'at peace' – that's what I'm hoping for."

She took another large bite of her apple as James looked on, astonished. Yes, this was a girl who read books, alright. He'd never heard anyone speak with such clarity and wisdom before. This fifteen year old had just put his entire life into context and hadn't even realised.

"Sorry. Went on a bit there." She threw the core of her apple out into the dried, ashen field. "So where are we going, then? What have you got to show me?"

"Well, as you just said, there's not much here. But I thought we could go to the Old Farm."

"Aha, let me guess. It's a farm…but it's old. Am I right?"

"Got it in one."

"I *am* Sherlock Holmes. So what's at the Old Farm? I guess it's capital 'O' and capital 'F'?"

James hadn't thought about that before but had to admit that, yes, it was.

"Not much. A few broken-up old sheds. Owls nest in them. We might find some pellets."

"Pellets?"

"Owls eat mice whole. Then they sick up the bones in little pellets."

"Oh, James, you know how to treat a lady."

"Poppies grow there. It's pretty."

"So just because I'm a girl you think I like pretty things?"

"No, No, I was just…"

She smiled, then punched him lightly on the arm. It felt like heaven.

"Well, I do. Everyone should like pretty things. There's too much ugly in this world. Pretty is good. Beautiful is even better. Oh, I don't mean people. People are only pretty or beautiful if someone else says so. I've known some terribly ugly 'pretty' people and some absolutely beautiful 'ugly' people, so none of that counts. No, I mean beauty that just gets on with it. Beauty that doesn't even know it's beautiful, the best kind."

Like you, he thought, but kept silent.

"So where is it? This Old Farm of yours?"

"We have to go off the path, over that way."

"Off the beaten track? Excellent."

There was a ditch by the side of this dried-out dusty path. James tried to jump it, but fell backwards. He held out his hand for her to help him up, but she folded her arms and just watched.

Please take my hand, just this once, he thought.

"You got into it, you get out of it."

He scrambled up, his white shirt now streaked with dirt. "You could have helped."

"*You* could have not tried to show off like some big man." She daintily stepped her way down into the ditch and up the other side. "See? Just walk it."

They walked side by side across the lumpen, scorched field. Across the way were a row of trees. After a while, Prudence took the lead and

James watched. She looked totally at home here, in her simple white dress. He realised she could have come here from any time in the last few hundred years. In Great Wakering's past, there had always been a girl like Prudence picking her way over this field. He watched her unselfconsciously swing her arms and raise her face to the sky. *She's always been here,* he thought. *Prudence is the forever girl.*

As they reached the tree line she stopped and leaned against a beech, in the shade.

"Aaah. That feels good. You only realise how hot it is when you're out of it. Well, sort-of out of it. Thank you, tree," she turned and kissed the trunk. James was slightly jealous of the beech for that.

"Where's the Old Farm?"

"Through here. You can see the poppies."

"Laaaavely," she Cockneyed, "but let's enjoy the shade a bit."

She slid down the tree trunk and sat against it. James sat opposite and offered her the picnic bag.

"Nah, not quite yet. I think we need a picnic in the poppies."

She bent down and started to pick daisies. She didn't look up but said, "I'm sorry about your Mum."

James picked some daisies of his own. Together, they started to make chains, but didn't look at each other.

"I'm sorry about yours."

"Mm. It just happened. That's the thing, isn't it? Things just happen. You start a day as one thing and end it as another and things just happen. I still can't quite believe she's not here. But I suppose if she was here, I wouldn't be here. I'm not sure Mum would have wanted to leave Bow. But Dad… Dad ran away. Bow reminded him of her too much. Every street, every shop; she was all over the place. I'd walk to a park and see her in the distance. I'd go home and she'd have just left the kitchen. I loved her. I love her. I miss her."

"I miss mine too. I was eleven. It was the same. She just went to sleep and stayed asleep. I remember Dad shouting when he realised. He was just screaming, *no, no, no, no, no.* I was downstairs. I'd got up early that day, I don't know why. But then he was wailing, *no, no, no-*

no, no. I knew. Dads aren't supposed to wail, are they? When somebody shouts like that, you just know. I cried even before he told me. I still cry."

He'd never spoken this way before, not even to his Dad. Prudence delicately weaved her daisies into each other.

"Daisy chains." She looked up at him, finally. "That's all this is, life. Daisy chains. Fragile, barely holding together, but while it does, it's lovely, ain't it? Life is a daisy chain. You just hope it stays together, but you know it will fall apart. You just have to admire it while you can."

James nodded. Prudence was fifteen, but ancient, it seemed. She really was the forever girl.

"Come on." She stood. He willed her to hold out a hand, but she pulled on the daisy chain and set off toward the poppies.

The tree line was thin and suddenly the sun was back to greet them as they stepped into the overgrown poppy field. At one end stood the dilapidated barns of the Old Farm. Prudence stopped amongst the flowers, looked down at them, then smiled at James.

"You said there was nothing here in Wakering," she admonished, and waggled a finger at him like a teacher. "You lied, James Grace! Look at this! None of this in Hyde Park, Regent's Park, Greenwich... This, look, this has just happened. No gardeners, no planners, no blokes in suits deciding what goes where. These poppies have just grown, without permission. They don't care if we see or don't see them. They just get on with it. There could be no human beings on the entire planet and they'd still be here, being lovely."

She spun, arms wide, in the sunshine.

"We're lucky, you know. We are the only people here, at this moment. London is full of hot and bothered Londoners, Southend is full of hot and bothered...what do you even call them? Southenders? Seasiders? Anyway, they're hot and bothered, too. We're hot yes, but we're not bothered. We're here, we are alone, we have these poppies and...I love it. Thank you, James. I was just planning on sitting about being prickly Prudence today but now I have this. That's all thanks to you."

She bent down to pick a poppy, but stopped herself.

"Nah. Let it grow, It's not my right to stop it. Too many people are busy stopping things these days. Too much arguing, too many opinions, too much judgement. We should just let things be. The poppy is happy where it is. I feel guilty about the daisies now."

She held up her wrist with its daisy chain.

"But I'm sure the daisies would be happy there. They look lovely." His brain nearly stopped him, but his heart got there first. "*You* look lovely. They're beautiful and so are...they suit you."

She looked him square in the eye and smiled.

"Thank you." She glanced down at her chain. "They look lovelier, I'm sure, but thanks for saying it. Sometimes we all just need to be told we're doing alright. Not brilliant, not exceptional, just alright."

James didn't push it any further, but sat down amongst the poppies and held up the bag to her.

"Picnic? Poppy picnic?"

"That sounds like a very good idea," she smiled and sat next to him.

They pulled out the sandwiches and shared the bottle of water, which was no longer cool. But even lukewarm it was still refreshing.

"So. Is this it?" she asked.

"It? What do you mean?"

"Great Wakering. Will you stay here, like your Dad? Take over the carrots and potatoes? Or will you spread your wings and fly?"

"I don't know. I'm fifteen."

"So am I. But you know, we'll open our eyes one day and be fifty and wonder how that happened. I don't intend to stay in one place too long. It's too big a world for all that nonsense."

"I'd like to see the world, I suppose."

"You suppose? You need to grab life by the knackers, James."

It continued to amuse and thrill him whenever she spoke like a docker.

Tiny flies danced about them. Heat has its own noises. A winter's day doesn't sound like one in summer. A rolling, baked day has a heavy, soporific atmosphere, a dense, languid hum. They sat in it and ate their sandwiches.

"You know," she said, thoughtfully. "I like you."

James tried not to squeal with happiness. He managed to pull an expression resembling a smile.

"Well, er, I like you, too."

"Because I'm funny?"

"Because you're funny."

She slapped him on the arm again.

"Because you're funny and clever and you say things no-one else does. You're not like the other girls."

"Thank heavens for that," she sighed.

"I'm sorry I hit you with that ball."

"Oh, give that one a rest. I don't care. Actually, I'm glad you did. It got us talking, even though my face is now totally ruined."

"Your face is beautiful."

There. He'd said it.

She reached up unconsciously and rubbed her mouth. "Thank you. I don't think anyone has ever said that."

She thought for a moment. "Nope, I just checked. No-one has. So that's a first. You're a man of surprises, James."

I'm a man, he thought. *I started today promising to Be A Man and now she's confirmed it.* He felt himself flushing.

"I liked you the moment I met you, actually," she went on. "When you went to shake my hand in your shop. When I brought the steak. Do you remember?"

James pretended to think, but of course every moment with her was chiselled into his memory. "Yes, I do."

"I thought to myself; that's funny. Funny but nice. Going to shake a girl's hand. Most boys just stare and mumble, but you were like a businessman, or something. I didn't know what to do. I might have seemed rude, but didn't mean to be. I was just a bit taken aback."

"That's alright."

"You're not like other boys. I'm not like other girls! Oh, listen to us! What I mean is, I wanted to get to know you. But you were always on the other side of the field or the street. I didn't think you wanted to know me."

James wanted to smack himself on the forehead. All that time, he could have just gone over. She'd been waiting and he'd been an idiot, too weighed down by his own doubts to just, in her words, *"get on with it"*.

"Well, ha, er, I did. I saw you the same way. I didn't think you wanted to know me."

"Couple of idiots, aren't we? So when you knocked today, I was…" She considered for a second. "Happy. Yes, I was really happy. You weren't 'just passing', were you?

He held up his hands in surrender. "No. I wasn't just passing."

"Hence the Sunday Best?" She picked at his shirt sleeve.

"Er, yes."

"You dressed up to take me for a walk?" she asked in disbelief. "In this heat?"

"I did. Because I like you."

"Well, that's all worked out very nicely for both of us, then, hasn't it? We are now officially friends."

They sat for a while. Prudence raised her pale face to the sky, eyes closed. James watched, lost in her hair, which blazed like the sun above.

"I know what we should do next." Her eyes snapped open and she turned back to face him.

"What should we do?" he asked.

"We should see what happens, that's what we should do."

"What do you mean?"

"Well, let's see what happens. With us. Friends should stick together. We have the future, don't we, and whatever it holds. We should take it, go on adventures, don't you think? We should see the world, find fields like this and have picnics, share books, dance, help each other out, cry on each other's shoulders. You're my only friend here and I have a feeling I might be your only one, too. Certainly I'm the only one you can go on picnics with and talk about grabbing life by the knackers. Ha. Yes, we should see what happens next."

"Yes, that's what we should do."

"And then, we can get married, have children, get old and wake up one day when we're fifty and be glad it happened."

James looked at her and she beamed.

"Well, one thing at a time, perhaps. We're only fifteen. Well, then. How about five years time? In five years time we'll be twenty. In five years time I want to be…I want to be happy, first, and then I want to be, oh, I don't know, a dress maker. Oh, is that really bloody female of me?"

"Nothing wrong with making dresses."

"There isn't. So what about you? Where will you be in five years time? In 1918?

"Oh, lying in a field just like this, among the poppies, I think," he said. "At peace."

"Yes. At peace," she smiled and reached for his hand.

"SYMPATHY FOR THE DEVIL"

(The Rolling Stones, 1968, from the album Beggars Banquet *)*

It's said that history repeats itself; first as tragedy, then as comedy. But that rather *depends on where you're standing, doesn't it?*

Berlin, 30th April, 1945.

As he sat in his airless bunker beneath the ruins of his dead Reich, next to the body of his dead wife, Adolf Hitler was finally forced to concede it had been a generally unsuccessful war and a totally unsuccessful marriage.

Most marriages, he thought, looking over at his wife of just twenty four hours, *most marriages start with a party, speeches, some nice gifts, then, a romantic honeymoon somewhere.*

Most marriages *don't* end with the groom holding a Walther pistol in one hand and a cyanide capsule in the other, whilst his lovely bride lay poisoned next to him. Most marriages don't have 99% of the world trying to kill the newlyweds. Then again, most happy couples don't take their honeymoon thirty feet below ground while up top, the entire Red Army played hide and seek with them.

Yes, it has been a generally unsuccessful war and a totally pointless marriage, thought the Führer, then corrected himself. *Führer of what, now, exactly?*

Above, Berlin was falling, Germany, rubble. The thousand-year Reich had only managed twelve, which was a bit of a disappointment. The *Volk* had let him down, quite badly. They hadn't displayed the iron hearts and molten blood demanded of their leader. They kept getting killed and losing battles. They'd been, in conclusion, a whining, weak, *kindisch Volk*, undeserving of the name "master race". He knew his pathetic *Wehrmacht* were up there, learning Russian as quickly as they could, surrendering in their masses... *well*, he thought, *they deserved this defeat. Good riddance to them.*

But there had been so many good times over the years. The Nuremberg rallies had made him feel like a film star, albeit one with a very captive audience. The early successes were so exciting, the Rhineland, Austria, Czechoslovakia, Poland, France – ah, when the world was at his feet and everything went his way. He had the magic touch, back then. It was hard to believe that it had all gone so very, very wrong, so very, very quickly. But obviously, he wasn't to blame, that much was obvious.

He mentally made a list of the guilty parties.

Right, he stuck out his tongue in concentration. *I'll write it down, leave it for my S.S. guards outside to find.* He'd already dictated his Last Will & Testament to Traudl, his secretary, but now realised he really should have put a postscript on there: *P.S. these are all the people who didn't try hard enough and should be very shot.*

He scrabbled about in his uniform and managed to find one of many orders that hadn't gone out. In his top pocket there was the stub of a pencil. But what to put?

I need this to be perfect. When the Reich is reborn, as it surely will be, when Germany realises National Socialism and I were the one true path, people will want to know who not *to trust.*

At the top, I'll put, "The Following Are Responsible For All This. Have Them Killed, By Order Of Me, Adolf Hitler, Currently The Führer." *Yes, then I'll make a list, THE definitive list of who messed up what should have been a pretty simple, quick war. But oh no, certain people didn't pull their weight.*

They were, in no particular order;

The German Volk. *Well, I can't have* all *the German people shot,* he admitted, *but we can make inroads.*

Himmler. *Damn Himmler, trying to make peace behind my back. I'm extremely vexed about that.*

The Luftwaffe, the Wehrmacht, Kriegsmarine, the S.S. *Well, some of the S.S.*

Göring, Speer, Funk, Ribbentrop… In fact, all of them, apart from Goebbels, who'd absolutely 100% promised he was going to kill himself plus his wife and children, which was quite a generous gesture, really.

The British, Americans, Russians and Italians, who kept getting in the way. Then there were the Jews, of course, whom Hitler was convinced had done *something* to lose him the war, but still wasn't quite sure what.

It turned out there were a lot of people to blame.

Hitler scowled at the tiny scrap of paper. There wasn't enough room for all the guilty parties, so he crumpled it up, then attempted to hit a bin in the corner, but missed. The Führer stared at that bin for a while and tried to make sense of it.

Wait, what? They provided my glorious death room with a bin? *Why did the S.S. put that in here? There's a bench, a door and a* bin? *What did they think I needed to tidy up?*

But that bit of paper now lying on the floor aggravated him. He sighed and rose to pick it up, *oh, I'm so* German. *The Russian Army is above my head, Berlin is in ruins, I'm about to kill myself and I'm now bothered about one piece of paper that hasn't gone in a bin?* Hitler picked up the rubbish and primly disposed of it, thinking, *I wouldn't want history to assume I'd got messy in my last moments.* He sat back down and picked up the gun. Eva, slumped next to him, didn't care about the wayward paper, or anything else for that matter.

They'd been married yesterday, here in the gay confines of the bunker whilst artillery, rather than bells, clanged above their heads.

He'd kept Eva secret from the people throughout his career, promised them that he was "married to Germany", but in the end, the country had been unfaithful. So yesterday, he'd thumbed his nose at Germany and married Eva. That would serve *Deutschland* right.

He supposed it must have been a bit of a weird wedding for the guests, knowing that within a day or so, the happy couple would be doused in petrol and set alight in the garden above. That knowledge had made the reception a little dour, if he were honest.

Eva had agreed to the wedding knowing full well the, *"til death us do part,"* bit of the contract would have to be fulfilled rather quicker than most marriages.

After twenty-four joyous hours of wedlock they'd stepped into this room, knowing they wouldn't leave again under their own steam. Vain Eva hadn't taken up her husband's offer of a gun because, *"I don't vant to mess up my hair,"* which Hitler thought was missing the point somewhat. Soon enough, her hair would be on fire; what difference would a bullet hole make?

Ah, women, he smiled to himself, ruefully. *Will I ever truly know their minds? No, actually, no, I won't and never will. The only woman I was ever close to is dead and I didn't even know her that well.*

Eva's expression wasn't peaceful. If anything, she looked a bit surprised. Hitler didn't blame her.

We were all a "bit surprised" it had come to this, he realised. *We were all a "bit surprised" by Stalingrad, Africa, D-Day, the Ardennes Offensive...To be brutally honest, since 1942, we've all looked a bit like dear Eva. How did that happen?*

He wanted to close her eyes, but was suddenly a bit squeamish around dead things. The irony wasn't lost on him. She stared over toward the door. Perhaps, as the poison hit, she'd thought about finally making a break for it. But cyanide is a one-way trip and now all she could do was stare blankly at an exit she would never take.

Hitler knew two S.S. men waited outside, looking at their watches and shrugging at each other. They had things to do and he was tying them up out there. They were probably making circular motions with their fingers at the door, as if to say, "hurry it along, Führer, skip to the end."

He scowled. Adolf had done a lot of scowling these last three years. They could wait. He was still their leader and was going to take his time. History demanded it. He shouldn't rush into this final act, his thunderous *Führerdammerung*.

Hitler fiddled with the Walther pistol for a while, then realised that during the entire war, he hadn't actually killed anyone personally. Oh yes, he'd given orders that had annihilated entire cities, an entire race, for Heaven's sake. His Army, Navy and Luftwaffe had wiped out men, women and children mercilessly, but he, Adolf Hitler, hadn't fired a single shot in anger. And now, the only bullet he'd shoot at a human being in this whole conflict would be at himself.

Now that *is grimly ironic*, he thought.

Yesterday, Goebbels had asked how the Führer wanted his death reported to the German people. The scenario they'd agreed on was heroic, Wagnerian and totally untrue, which was very Goebbels.

Soon, the people would be told that Hitler had fallen, fighting to his last breath against Bolshevism at his command post in Berlin.

Adolf supposed he *was* fighting to his last breath, it was just this final bullet wasn't being aimed at any Russians.

He looked at the door again. Should there be some final words as he pulled the trigger and bit down on the capsule? Something for the guards to hear, then report breathlessly to the rest of the bunker and from there, into history? But what?

His mind was completely blank. *Come on, one last push. How about…*

The Reich will rise again!

Death to Bolshevism!

For Deutschland!

No. None of them sound historic, they just sound pathetic. Petulant. Hitler sighed. He was the greatest orator that had ever lived, who'd changed the world with words - admittedly, lots of guns and bombs had also helped - but couldn't even come up with an unforgettable final statement.

Well, this is it. I can't sit around here all day. The time has come. The Reich is over. Eva's dead – quite a few people are dead – and Zhukov will be knocking at the door any moment, but not to bring flowers.

Hitler unclipped the magazine of his little Walther PPK pistol and looked inside. One bullet. Yes, that's all he needed.

No, wait a moment.

He frowned and pushed out the round. There was another one
beneath and another, and another…hold on, this was a full clip. Seven
bullets.

   Enraged, he intended to throw open the door, indignantly wave the
gun in the S.S's faces and shout;

   "SEVEN BULLETS? Did you think I'd miss? I know I haven't
actually handled a gun during the last few years, but I did get an IRON
CROSS in the Great War! I am familiar with shooting!"

   Adolf looked down at the gun and then really saw it for the first
time. *Whoah, hold on, a WALTHER? It's tiny. It's like a toy gun. They
should have given me a LUGER at least. Something with a bit of heft
to it. No, wait, I'm the Führer! Get me a STURMGESCHUTZ in here!*
Hitler gnashed his teeth.

   The fact the magazine contained seven bullets had really touched a
nerve. The inference that somebody out there in the bunker now had
so little faith in their Führer they thought they'd *better give him a few
goes at blowing his brains out* made the soon-to-be-shot veins in
Adolf's temples pulse with fury.

   Hitler strode up and down the tiny room. He silently clenched his
fists and pulled some of the old classic Nuremberg moves that used to
drive his adoring audience crazy. He gesticulated madly and threw a
full on Führer temper tantrum, but was unable to shout in case the S.S.
out there thought he was having a moment of cowardice. He hopped
about, pulled his hair, waved the gun in the air, then pushed it at Eva's
dead eyes, so she could see the ignominy of the situation.

   SEVEN…BULLETS.

   At this rate, he thought, *maybe I should do what Goebbels had
suggested, run up there with my little girl's pistol and let the Red Army
have all SEVEN bullets, fall whilst fighting Bolshevism to my last
breath.*

   But of course, he'd never be taken alive or worse, allow his corpse
to be used as some kind of Hitler puppet to entertain Stalin with. He'd
heard Stalin was extremely weird. He wouldn't put it past his arch
enemy to display his cold, stuffed corpse in a museum, or worse, as

some kind of odd trophy in the Kremlin. The thought was enough to stick his courage to the sticking post.

He sat back down next to dear Eva, placed the cyanide capsule in his mouth, the Walther PPK to his temple and without any final words, bit down and pulled the trigger.

There was a crack in his mouth and a bang in his ear, but other than that, nothing happened.

He was still alive.

Hitler spat the capsule out, confused.

Oh. A faulty batch of cyanide pills. And I gave them out to everyone, too, so they could all *go down with the Reich. They're going to think I'm totally unreliable now.*

But that wasn't all, was it? Because it also meant he had a faulty Walther PPK, too. He'd pulled the trigger and yes, there had definitely been one hell of a bang, but he was still here. Eva was *still* staring at the door, *still* wondering if it wasn't too late to make a run for it, the piece of paper was *still* in the bin and the gun was *still* smoking in his hand.

What do I do now? Adolf wondered. *Its going to be a bit awkward when the S.S. come in any second and see me sitting here with a sheepish grin on my face. But what choice do I have? The Red Army are breathing down my neck and time's not on my side.*

He sat, put down the gun, folded his hands primly across his lap and waited for the door to open, then embarrassment to enter, dressed in black and silver uniforms.

The door stayed shut. Perhaps they'd gone for a cup of tea since he was taking so long. *Noooo*, surely not. They must have heard the pistol's retort. He knew there was a lot of noise going on, what with Berlin falling and all that, but the shot should have been their cue to enter and then, in an ideal world, find him dead before carefully removing his body, respectfully drenching it in petrol and then reverentially setting it alight.

Nothing.

Hitler was in a quandary. He couldn't possibly open the door and stick his head out. For starters, it would look ridiculous, secondly, the men outside would probably scream on seeing their supposedly dead Führer lurch back into life. It would be farcical. But then, he couldn't just sit there and wait for someone, anyone, to enter and discover him Not Dead, as that would make him a failure who couldn't even do one simple, suicidal job properly.

Perhaps, he thought, *I should have another go. They have, after all, kindly provided enough bullets for a second attempt and I hate, hate, HATE them for that.*

He felt his right temple to find the best spot but then – the queerest thing. It was wet.

Hitler gasped when he saw his finger was red with blood.

So I've injured myself, but not managed to actually <u>die.</u> He looked at his finger with disbelief. *When they eventually find my corpse, when they can be* bothered, *I'll have two injuries, then everyone will know, without any single shadow of a doubt, that I messed it up first time.*

He felt his temple again. Yes, there was quite a lot of blood. *How on earth did I not die?*

Hitler whimpered as his finger found a hole there. *What? A hole?* Cautiously, he pressed the digit into his head and grimaced as it sank in, about a centimetre.

Oh-oh. So, the bullet managed to make a hole, but still not kill me, he thought, dismayed.

That's a first, surely. Hitler pressed a little harder and his finger sunk in a little more. He gave out a quiet yelp of disgust but kept on pushing. Now theF finger was in his head, actually *inside his head*, past the knuckle and still going when it stopped on something hard.

Hitler knew his brain didn't have a bone in the middle which meant this something hard could only be...*no, no way*...but yes, what else? The bullet.

I have a hole in my head and a bullet in my brain and I am still alive, he gasped.

Throughout his ghastly career, Hitler believed Providence had steered him to become Germany's Führer. He'd only served nine months in prison after the failed Munich Beer Hall Putsch, risen to Chancellor against the odds, survived a bomb by minutes at the same beer hall, conquered Europe, saw off yet another bomb attempt by that traitor Stauffenberg, and now this. He'd actually survived his own suicide attempt.

Perhaps, yes, this was fate telling him the war was not yet over. There was still a chance. He should leave the bunker, show everyone his miraculous, Christ-like wound and lead his army to victory against the accursed Russians! *Ja!*

Poor Eva, of course, was not part of this miracle, but he'd build a statue on this very spot to remember her sacrifice. He made a note to depict her picking edelweiss rather than lying crumpled in a heap with cyanide round her mouth.

Right now, however, he had a war to win. He had just beaten death itself, so thrashing Stalin should be as easy as a walk in the Tiergarten.

Without hesitation, he strode the full three feet to the door and banged on it. Hitler thought he'd better alert the guards before just marching out. But what should he say?

I know, he thought, how about, *"Guards! I live!"* It was straight to the point and would sound great in the history books. *That's it – "Your Führer lives! Fate has spared me once again! The fight for Germany continues!"* He smoothed down his jacket and turned the door handle, but it wouldn't move.

Typical. I've just gone into history again and the door needs oiling, he groaned, internally. He rattled the handle but it was stuck stiff. He knocked again, remembering not to say anything too stupid. History was still rolling.

"Open the door and let the fight continue! Guards!"

There was still no answer.

I was in here, playing out the final act of my story, he ground his teeth. *While the S.S. were sitting somewhere out there, planning their escape. I will have them executed, yes, that'll show them.*

He hammered on the door, a perfect fusillade of blows. "Your
Führer is speaking!"

Where on earth were they? Taking a stroll up there in Broken
Berlin, where the Sturmoviks flocked?

"Hey!" Hitler finally screamed. Sometimes, posterity has to wait.

*

"Oh, do sit down and shut up, you idiot," a voice sounded from behind
him.

Adolf turned, slowly. This room had but one door. The only other
person here was Eva and she'd been dead for a few minutes already,
unless her poison was also faulty and she'd been playing possum until
he shot himself.

But Eva's voice had been as light and fresh as a Tyrollean morning.
That other voice, the one that had just called him, the *Führer of
Deutschland*, an "idiot" – that had sounded like it was coming from
the end of a very long hall, far away, but simultaneously, very close. It
echoed as if the ceiling was as high as a cavern, but also whispered
like whoever-it-was had been stood right by his ear.

Hitler looked and - *not possible* - there was a figure in the corner,
wrapped in darkness. The one light bulb in this tiny room couldn't
reach into that black. The stranger wore the darkness of an awful
forever, but how had they got in? The door was still jammed shut.

Hitler found that, most unusually, he was unable to speak.
Speaking was his party trick – literally, his Party trick – but now his
jaw was locked and tongue frozen. He looked into the dark and tried
to make sense of what was happening.

He could make out the figure wore a very smart suit. White cuffs
extended *just so* from the jacket sleeves and the triangle of a perfectly
folded handkerchief poked from the breast pocket. The shoes were
clearly expensive. The suit warped and weaved amongst the darkness
and its face could not be seen at all. As Hitler's gaze took in the
neckline, he saw just above it was the shape of a head and nothing
else. No features nor hair, just this awful hole in the dark, cocked to
one side as if amused.

One white hand emerged from the black and a long-nailed finger pointed directly at Hitler, who realised the temperature in this room had dropped quite substantially.

"No-one can hear you, Adolf," the figure smirked. "No-one will come. We are outside of time, outside of the universe. There is just us now – out there, beyond that door, there is eternal nothing. If you could open it, and see, you would be sent mad within moments. Nobody could look into that infinite nothing without cracking – not even you, who has made a career of being empty. But the door is locked and so…," the figure shrugged, "…there is just you, me and Eva. And a bin?" The figure's blank head looked down at it. "Why did they give you a bin? No mind. Poor Eva. Poor, stupid Eva. She didn't deserve you and I mean that in a negative way. Germany didn't deserve you, again, in a negative sense. But there are no victims, only volunteers…," the figure sighed, "…and so many volunteered to walk behind your dreadful flute. What a Pied Piper you turned out to be, eh? You played your horrible little tune and led all the children into the dark caves and now there are no more children, are there? You cannot have any children when this world is so awfully grown up, can you?"

Hitler still couldn't speak. He realised he was shaking and not just from the cold.

"Mmm, poooooor dear Eva," the figure swooned, like a cabaret actress. "Poor Germany, poor world. You poisoned everyone, didn't you? Eva, at least, had the semblance of choice in the matter – oh, but she didn't, *noooo*, not really, did she? – but what about all the rest? Many Germans voted for you, yes, but did they know where you were going to take them? Piece by piece they found out, though, didn't they? Note by note you played your tune and it was like St Vitus' Dance; the *Volk* found themselves jigging along and they couldn't stop. But many of them liked it, didn't they? They liked the permission you gave them. That is what a 'leader' does, do they not? I have seen it many times. Leaders give their people permission to act. Act well, or act badly? Well…," the figure huffed, "…that depends both on the 'leader' and their people. All a 'leader' really does is give their people permission. And if that is permission to act badly, then just watch how many people grab it with both hands. It's said bad things happen when good people do nothing, but the truth is, bad things happen when awful people are given permission to act just as they please. Yesssss," the figure hissed.

Hitler, having become strangely paralysed by this visitor, finally found his voice again.

"Guards!" he screeched and realised he was screaming like he'd never done before. This was a new sound, sheer terror. He battered against the door and wailed, "Guards! Guards! GUARDS!"

The figure folded its arms and yawned, loudly.

"Excuse me?" it asked politely over the Fuhrer's hysterics. "Did you hear anything I just said? All that poetic stuff about eternity and nothing? It took me quite a while to work up, show some respect."

Hitler continued to bash and yell.

The figure held up one slim-fingered, long-nailed hand and suddenly Hitler fell silent. His mouth opened and closed like a goldfish. From that darkness opposite came the sound of *tut-tutting*.

"Tch, tch, tch. I just did a rather brilliant speech, did you hear any of it? Don't make me say it all again. I'm rather a good speaker. You learn to be when you have my job. You and I, we know all about public speaking. So – quick quiz. What's the really annoying bit about doing a speech? It's when no one listens and you have to repeat yourself. Now, obviously I know a lot of your technique was repetition," he shouted then, mimicking Hitler's own voice exactly. "Say SIMPLE STUFF LOUDLY, A LOT. SEE? I'M DOING IT NOW, SAYING VERY SIMPLE THINGS A LOT, VERY LOUDLY. Oldest trick in the orator's book, but I really don't like repeating myself. So. Sit down. Sit."

Hitler mechanically went back over to the bench and sat next to Eva, holding his throat. He was white with fear.

"In precis – and do NOT make me do this again – this room is now out of time and space. You could shout forever with an infinite megaphone and no-one would hear. So, give it a rest. Can I give you your voice back yet or are you going to have another huff?"

Hitler nodded weakly. As the figure raised its hand again from the darkness he felt his vocal cords return.

"So. Tra-la-la, here we are. Now, let's have a chat, shall we?"

"Who are you?" asked Hitler, and his voice cracked a little.

"Seriously?" replied the figure. "This? The blackness? The suit, my horror hands?" It held up those awful white hands in the light again. "I don't always do the horror hands, but I thought they seemed appropriate. Honestly, I turn up in a locked room inside an underground bunker at the end of what, for you and most of the world, has been a frankly dreadful few years and you ask who I am?"

Truth was, Hitler did think he knew who this was, but didn't want to say it out loud. He felt madness sizzle about him, and not for the first time.

"Very well. Let's take this in easy-to-follow steps shall we? You're dead. Not only are you full of cyanide, but you have a bullet hole in your head so – it follows, do try and keep up – as your friends in London say, you're brown bread."

Hitler unconsciously felt up to his temple and grimaced when his finger still came away bloody.

"Aha. The red stuff is supposed to stay inside. That's one of the rules. So; you're dead, you've been responsible for misery on an up-until-now unknown scale and still you ask who I am? Go on. Have a go. Guess who I am. Go on. Guess."

Adolf just stared balefully up into the shadows.

"We do have forever, you know. I'm really in no hurry. Well then, it's not a fairy story, so don't try Rumpelstiltskin. Any ideas?"

Hitler sulked and looked back at the door, wondering if he should try and make a run for it.

"Still locked, Addie. Alright. I shall introduce myself, since you're not going to play my rather fun guessing game. Honestly, the people I've played it with over the years. I LOVE it when the penny drops. When they suddenly realise who I am and try to bolt, fall to their knees or wet themselves. Or, in the case of Vlad the Impaler, bolt, fall to his knees *and* wet himself at the same time. True story. So... I've had many names over the years. Let's try a few you might know. By the way, I'm extremely pleased to meet you, finally. I am the Dark One –obviously. Daylight bores me. I am Baphomet. Old Scratch, Old Nick, Voland, Hob, Lucifer. Or maybe...Satan? The Devil?"

The figure held out his hands wide as if accepting applause.

"Thank you; you're too kind. None of them are my real name, *noooo*, not the name I call myself when no-one's around, but they'll do. As introductions go, they'll do."

"This is madness," croaked Hitler.

"Oh it is, it really is,' said the figure agreeably. "The last five years have been the maddest of the mad, wouldn't you say? What have you done? Do you know the phrase, 'The road to hell is paved with good intentions'? You didn't even have good intentions, did you? You just went straight for the bad intentions, from day one."

Hitler thought he may have actually shot himself, bungled it and now lay in a coma as his dying brain conjured this Faustian piece of fantasy.

"No, you shot yourself, you're dead and this isn't Faust, you moron," said the Devil. "You never made a deal with me. Come on, surely you know your Goethe? If you'd come to me in '33 and said 'Give me the world and I'll give you my soul', that would have been Faustian, but not this. There has to be a deal, you utter imbecile. That's the story."

Hitler shot the Devil a look of his most blazing hatred and went to rise. "I am the Führer of the German people!" he attempted to thunder. "You will treat me with the respect I deserve!"

"Sit down, Adolf," said Old Nick, calmly. "This *is* the respect you deserve. Calling you an imbecile is much more respect than you deserve, actually. Ooh, look at you," Lucifer cooed. "I was exactly like you once. All shouty and intolerant, thinking I ruled the world. I tell you now, mein Führer, once you've spent as many years walking the earth as I have, you'll have seen them all come and go. Puffed up little men with big egos and a quite frightening amount of Oedipal complexes. Your Oedipus complex wasn't your mother, per se, but your father, or rather, your Fatherland. What was all that tosh about being "married to Germany?" Marrying your own Fatherland? Eeoo. Boy, Addie, you are one seriously unstable Austrian. Not even a German, you halfwit. Freud would have had a field day. Shame he was Jewish, you could have done with his help. A few sessions on the couch might have stopped all this..." Satan waved his hand around the room as if it were the entire world. "But probably not. The trouble with you, Führer, is you think people are different when they are all the same. Believe me, I know, I've seen enough of them. *Führers* always find a group of people to blame for their own problems and never realise that everyone is the same. Every time. You identify so strongly with your homeland, politics, race, colour of your skin or *whatever*, you just don't see it. People are identical everywhere, you total dunce. Get on a train with a load of *volk* from every different country and you'll be sat with a bunch of thick, genius, creative, dumb, wonderful, horrible, selfish, selfless people. Not one country, not one so-called race has the monopoly on any of those traits. Ah, I'm wasting my time. You won't see it. That's the trouble with you *Führers* and all your little lapdogs. You never see it."

The Devil stood quiet for a moment. That darkness where a head should have been peered into Hitler. The abyss looked at him and he could not hold its gaze.

"Well, that was a speech I've delivered many times over the many years and you know – it's never once changed a single person. Mind you, by the time I usually deliver it, everyone's at this kind of point. Metaphorically, my friends are all in their bunkers, with a bullet in their heads. Bit late in the day. But you, Adolf, I know you might listen. In fact, you will listen, you don't have any choice."

Hitler closed his eyes and willed the insanity, this hallucination, to stop.

"Not going to work, I'm afraid. This is happening. Stop feeling sorry for yourself. You put yourself in this bunker. You were marching to this door with gun and poison from the moment you stood up at Drexler's meeting in 1919. Get over it. You should be feeling sorry for me. I've lived forever. Well, not forever, but near enough. For as long as people have been around. I deserve a little sympathy round here. So open your eyes, look at me and listen. It will be instructive. Are you sitting comfortably? Let me begin. I was born in a hurricane, a long, long time ago. I was once King of Hell. I became King of Nothing."

Hitler couldn't help himself. He did as he was told as he had no choice – the Devil was talking. Lucifer began to tell his life story. It started like this.

*

The Devil woke up. Well, no, that wasn't right. It wasn't coming to, more of a slow clarifying, as if he were an object in the distance being brought into focus. He felt his consciousness return in the same way, like a dial on the radio being turned, picking up fragments of broadcasts that made no sense until one was tuned in. His memory was fractured and visions flashed about his mind of so many events, places, people, all unfamiliar but strangely known to him. He was cold, wet and lay on the ground, but didn't open his eyes yet. Part of him didn't want to.

Where had he come from, who had he been before this weird "re-focussing"? He kept his eyes closed and tried to remember.

Satan frowned because thinking was difficult. Thoughts careered about his mind that felt alien to him, like another person with an entirely different way of thinking had taken up residence in his brain, uninvited.

Hell. The word suddenly appeared, monolithic. **HELL**.

He rolled it about in his head for a bit, looking at it from all angles, trying to seek out any other words or images that lurked in its massive shadow. He'd just been down there in Hell, yes. Hell was his land. He saw flames and so many people writhing and grasping to escape his fires. He saw avenging demons from the skies, flinging thunderbolts at those people as they tried to run. Yes, there had been fiends capering through his kingdom, tearing at the damned, and there, in the middle, down, deep in the seventh circle, he'd sat on his throne, surveying it all with a strange glee.

Hold on, he thought, eyes still clamped shut. Wait a moment. If I was king of that place, if I was ruler of Hell, then that must mean...

I'm the Devil.

His eyes flew open, pupils dilated with excitement.

He knew the fact of his devilishness as incontrovertibly as he knew he was being rained on, hard.

But after that, he didn't know or remember much. He had been King of Hell, but been cast out of his own kingdom for some reason and thrown down (or was it up?) here, lying in a hurricane, being rained on like a common serf with no roof to call his own.

He lay and looked up at the rain which spattered over his face.

Who had cast him here and why?

God? Asked his mind, although he wasn't sure what or who God was, or even if there had ever been a God. Surely no God would have allowed a Hell to exist – but oh, it had, and he'd gladly stomped about it once upon a time. He'd once ruled Hell, but now his rightful kingdom had been denied to him.

It was important he remembered why he was no longer in his land of fire and fury. He tried to conjure up more memories and while there were many – thousands, millions of faces and places it seemed, whirring about him – he couldn't bring any into focus. But one fact remained: where once he had been Maker Of All Pain, he was now a long way down the pecking order. Whoever he'd been then, he was nobody now.

No, I'm not nobody, he thought, whilst also not thinking at all.

There it was again, an alien mind alongside his own, thinking dumb thoughts like an animal. This other mind took in the moment, but didn't analyse it, just lived within it, stupidly.

He became aware he was simultaneously dumbly primitive but also aware and intelligent.

The rain didn't care who he'd once been, before his casting out. It continued to splash his face, unimpressed.

The sky above was grey. No individual clouds rushed up there, just one giant dome of ugly, moody dreariness, full of water, which ran into his eyes. The Devil needed to do something about that.

He raised his hands to his face to see what he was wearing and a weird situation became even weirder. For some reason, he wore sleeves and gloves made of coarse black hair. Lucifer stared at them for a while, trying to work out why he'd chosen this particular outfit to sling on before being thrown out of Hell.

I thought I had taste once upon a time, he mused. *I was always smartly turned out, but now look at me. I've lost all sense of style.*

He went to pull off those hairy gloves, but it hurt when he grabbed the hair because it was attached. He felt up to his chest, which was also covered, then to his face, which bristled with the stuff.

Obviously, he thought, before panic set in, *I wasn't allowed to bring my travel kit, razor, comb…*

He felt upward and was surprised to discover his forehead was a little ridged. No, it was a lot ridged. It stuck out like a shelf over his eyes. Now the Devil was becoming quite twitchy. At first, he'd been simply confused, maybe in shock, but now, with this hairy naked body…

This hairy naked body? He was surprised, but that other animal mind in his head didn't think or register any shock at all. That other brain just got on with it, as if all this were totally natural.

My hairy naked body? I have a hairy naked body? I'm in the nude?

He sat up and began to breathe faster as panic set in. Yes, there he was, naked, shrunken and ashamed for all the world to see.

But what was this world?

The Devil knew he wasn't a scaredy cat. He'd once been overlord of Hell, a place that rather prided itself on its ability to be terrifying. It wouldn't have done at all for the King Of Darkness to be a bit of a whimpering cry baby when it came to fear. But now, yes, he was experiencing genuine horror. Satan lurched up (which was tricky; his body didn't obey him like it used to) and looked about his new setting. He saw an open plain, which stretched away forever, dotted with twisted trees that appeared to be contorted in suffering.

Where am I? He thought. *What* am I?

He was in the middle of a group of large stones and now saw there were other hairy naked people lying and sitting about him. Some slept. There were a few women, too, but nothing to write home about. Just these big-breasted – no, big hairy-breasted – hunched, staring harridans who gazed at him blankly. Beelzebub remembered he'd once been quite a catch, back there in Hell. His female furies had always looked at him with adoration and barely disguised lust, but these awful specimens weren't interested in the slightest. They just picked at their hairy bodies or each other.

The Devil looked about and that other animal brain painted pictures in his mind. But that's all they were, pictures, not thoughts, just images that loosely translated to: *family. Mine. Friend. Safe. Hunt. Eat.. Eat. Sit. Hunt. Safe;* they went, round and round.

These are my tribe, he realised. *My little collection of subhumans. Where once I owned Hell and everyone in it, now I've been reduced to this, a ghastly collection of hairy, shelf-foreheaded morons lying in the open, scratching themselves, unable to think of anything except* family, safe, eat, sit, eat, hunt, *over and over in their stupid hairy brains.*

The Devil tried to speak to them, to say, "I don't care who you are, I'm off. I'm going to have a word with whoever's in charge and put this right. Enjoy your evolutionary cul de sac, but I'm gone, ta-ta."

But instead it came out as, "WHOO WHOO! WHOO WHOO! WHOO WHOO! WHOO WHOO!"

The Devil stopped and put his black hairy hands to his mouth. That hadn't come out right at all.

He looked down at those hands again, at his stooped, way-too-hirsute body, at this bleak, empty new world and at the equally shaggy companions who watched him silently.

Satan was rather surprised it had taken him this long to figure out.

I'm a *Neanderthal* now. He thought, wildly. *I'm a Neanderthal.*
Oh, the injustice. I'm a stupid, tottering, fur-covered, near brainless
excuse *for a human being because... I'm not even a* human being. *I'm*
several thousand years off. I'm way back on the evolutionary ladder.
No, I'm not even on the ladder, I'm footing *the ladder while humans,*
actual humans, will climb up it.

He shouted then, loud and clear, OH, NO NO NO NO THIS
CANNOT BE!

But of course, it came out, WHOO WHOO! WHOO WHOO!
WHOO WHOO!

The other Neanderthals watched him, barely interested.

*

The Devil chuckled in that grey, airless room outside of time.

"As you can imagine, I wasn't very happy about the situation.
Actually, yes, you of all people should imagine it. One moment you
are Emperor of All That Is Awful, and the next you have literally
found yourself amongst the *Untermenschen.* But you can't imagine it,
can you? I can see it in your eyes; this is all unimaginable. Well, try. It
is instructive, as I say."

Hitler stared into the giggling darkness and picked up his gun
again.

"Ooh, what's the big, brave Führer going to do?" asked Satan.
"Kill himself? Spare himself having to hear Lucifer's sad and sorry
tale?"

Hitler pointed the gun into that place beyond black.

"Oh, please. He's actually going to try and shoot the Devil. Whoo
whoo, that's clever. I knew that was coming, by the way. Go ahead, if
you like, if it will make you feel better."

The Führer pulled the trigger. A bullet exploded from the nozzle
but then slowed to a dead stop in front of Beelzebub. One long-nailed
hand took it from the air. The black shape of the head looked down at
the shell.

"Feeling any better?" Old Nick asked. "Got that off your chest, did you?"

Hitler slumped back against the wall, all fight gone.

"Where was I?" continued Lucifer, as if nothing had happened. "So yes, there I am, cast out of my kingdom, covered in hair, unable to talk, surrounded by – let's face it, they weren't exactly blonde-haired blue-eyed members of the master race, *noooo* – idiotic non-humans, thinking to myself, *where did it all go wrong?*"

He tittered. "I'm sure you can identify with that. You haven't exactly ended your career showered in glory have you?"

"Whatever you have to do, do it," barked Hitler.

"What, rush the punchline? Race to the denouement? 'Denouement,' that's French, by the way. Remember the French? One of your many temporary conquests. 'Denouement,' you see, means 'unravelling" and by the time I'm done, Mr King Of *Kampf*, you will be most unravelled. No, I'm going to take my time with this story. You may have sprinted to your own Twilight of the Gods but I've been waiting years for this. Literally years and endless years, more than you could possibly begin to imagine. No, you have to hear. Not the whole sorry tale, that would take forever, and although we do have eternity, it would bore me senseless. I lived it, after all. So. There I am, the once mighty Diablo, reduced to a hooting near-chimp. And so, as I started my new life amongst the beautiful people - ha- one thought kept going around my mind. Do you know what that was?"

Hitler crossed his arms and looked sullen.

"Oh, there's the face. The face that launched a thousand years. Except it didn't, did it? How about you, Eva? Any ideas?"

Eva didn't, but Old Nick appropriated her coquettish Bavarian voice. It made the Führer jump when he heard it. "I don't know, Mr Devil, sir. Ooh, you are such *im nacken*. Do tell me your story. My husband here was *zuch* a bore. He'd go on and on, every night with his monologues, his awful breath like green smoke making us all choke. You are zo, *zo* much more entertaining!"

Satan pretended to tip a hat to the corpse. "Thank you, Eva, you're right of course. Oh, by the way, in case you're wondering, she's in her own private hell now. Do you know what that is?"

Hitler stared ahead and refused to play the Dark One's games.

"She's underneath you for infinity. Well, an exact simulacrum of you, obviously – indistinguishable from the real thing, as far as she's concerned. *Ja*, for the rest of time, she'll see your sweaty, handsome, *Aryan* face leering down at her. No getting away from your awful breath or your pasty sex expression, for always and ever, amen. Nothing more than she deserved, poor sweet Eva. In Hell, you get what you deserve. I have nothing to do with the actual form of punishment, that's the wonderful thing. Your punishment fits your crime. Her crime was falling in love with you and now she has you, squawking dreadful erotic Teutonic scenarios in her darling little ear in your deep brown Bavarian voice, for eternity. Oh, you have a frankly awful record with women, don't you? You've had *two* girlfriends, count them, two - and they both killed themselves. That's a pretty sad achievement. Two out of two, a clean sweep. First there was your half-niece, Geli, wasn't there? Shot herself with your Walther pistol in '31. *Busy* little pistol, isn't it?"

"Leave Geli out of this!" Squawked Hitler.

"Ah, but *you* wouldn't leave Geli out of anything, would you? You kept her virtually a prisoner. I sometimes wonder if she was a trial run for the German people, to see how much control and manipulation you could use before anyone cracked. The more I think about it, the more I believe that was the case. Shot herself in the chest, didn't she? Was she aiming for her heart? Or her *womb,* hmm? Oh, and talking of sex…"

Satan made a play of checking his watch. "No, we're good for time. Sex was my first…achievement, if you like. Not inventing it, no, I wish. Sex was around way before I woke up in my new hairy suit. You see, I knew where I was and what I was, but I didn't know *why* I was, *who* I was. I'd forgotten. Does that make sense? It will. What was my new purpose? I didn't know. Why had I been cast out and placed here? Not a clue. But I had my first vague inkling of an idea with *Ug, Og* and *Ig*. Only an inkling, mind…"

*

Out there on that empty, rainy, grey plain, in his itchy, lice-ridden, ape-like body, the Devil began to piece things together as much as he could. He'd been given no clues, no instruction manual. He knew who he was, knew he'd been King of Hell once, was pretty sure someone (*God?, no, not God*) had told him his purpose in all this, but everything was blurred. He felt like reasons would present themselves to him in time and knew he was going to have a lot of it.

His new undeveloped family seemed to accept him, which made Satan believe that perhaps he was just hitching a ride in this body. He'd been placed in here to fit in, right at the start of humanity. But why he needed to fit in was a mystery.

The Devil became interested in three Neanderthals called Ig ,Og and Ug.

Of course, Ug wasn't actually called Ug; these idiots didn't have the first clue about giving each other names and it drove Lucifer crazy that such a simple concept was beyond them. So he'd named them internally, just to save his sanity.

Ug was what would be called the Alpha Male of the group, the pin-up boy. The girls (all four of them) loved Ug.

He named one of those girls Ig. Ig was a looker, if dribbling, shelf-foreheaded, hairy ape-creatures were your thing. The Devil supposed it took all sorts. Ig knew how to work the boys and Satan had called one of those boys Og.

Og adored Ig.

Og was not the Alpha Male, he was down there at Omega. Og, even by his species' standards, was extremely dim. He would bump into things that were right in front of him, then look surprised they were there. He was a very, *very* stupid Neanderthal.

Oh, Og worshipped Ig, but his love wasn't interested because she adored the Alpha Male, Ug.

The Devil had watched this sad little love-triangle unfold and wondered how he might help. He liked Og. He was harmless, like a puppy. Occasionally, Satan would see a boiling fury in Og's face, a raging temper he recognised. *Well, let's see what I can do about that,* he thought, making a tiny step toward whatever his purpose here on Earth might be.

The moment came one night. Sundown on Earth back then was darker than anything Satan had ever known, but then again, he'd come from a place where there was no night, just endless fires, which crackled the darkness away whenever it came close.

It was so quiet on Earth. He'd come from a land made of screams and cries, but here at night the silence lay over you like a thick blanket. The Devil could have done with a blanket, actually. It was freezing and he was rather used to flames.

Is this how it's going to be? He'd wondered. *Will I just live here, in this dreadful stinky body, until I reach the grand old age of, ooh, I don't know,* seventeen *and then die and go back to my own kingdom? Will I have learned whatever lesson I'm* supposed *to be learning by then?*

Somehow, the Devil doubted it. He felt this was only the beginning and he was in this for a very, very long haul.

But then, there was movement in his peripheral vision.

It was Og and he was sneaking.

Yes, that was it. Stupid, dim-witted Og was sneaking. It looked hilarious. A Neanderthal trying to tiptoe was never going to be a particularly impressive sight, but when it was Og, who fell over his own toes if he wasn't looking at them, the image was stupefyingly funny. But why was he sneaking?

It's lovely Ig, the Devil realised. *Og gets up at night when everyone's asleep and goes over to look at Ig. It's almost sweet – the unrequited love of an undeveloped near-human.*

Satan watched. If he could have smiled using this face, he would have, but all he could do was stare through hooded eyes. Poor Og, poor, devoted Og, stood over his one true love, adoring her, whilst he furiously rubbed his crotch.

The Devil waited patiently for Og to finish his one-way relationship with Ig, which didn't take long, and thankfully the object of his desire never knew.

Og then padded over to Ug, who snored and grunted, slept sat up against a rock. Og stood in front of his love rival for some time, turned his head this way and that. He stared at Ug like a boxer sizing up an opponent, seeing where his strong and weak points were.

Og squatted down alongside the much larger Neanderthal and studied his thick arms and huge hands. He got as close as he dared to Ug's fearsome face, which, even in sleep, looked ready to cause severe damage to anything it didn't like the look of. Og then looked back over his shoulder at Ig.

He's *thinking*, thought the Devil. *Well I never. So there is a brain in Og's thick skull and he's finally using it. Og does have ideas, but they're different. The rest of them see everything through those simple thought-images, eat, sleep, hide, hunt...but it looks like Og's just come up with a brand new emotion. Yes, come quick! Roll up, roll up, this is the dawning of one of mankind's most selfish and destructive feelings. Damen und Herren Mesdames et Messieurs, Ladies and Gentlemen, I give you, for the very first time on Earth...put your hands together for the premiere of...Jealousy!*

Lucifer watched. Og didn't know this as jealousy of course. He felt it as:

Og want Ig.
<u>*Ug*</u> *have Ig.*
Og want Ig.

It was a rolling, repeating cycle, which confused poor Og because now he was at the outer limits, a brave explorer who has set foot on the terrible land of *jealousy* for the very first time.

But if Ug had woken...

If Ug had woken...

The Devil considered that fact. An awake Ug was unbeatable, but while he slept, he was vulnerable as a child. Og hadn't made that connection. Satan would do it for him.

Lucifer quietly rose and picked up a large rock. Og saw him immediately, but did nothing.

The Devil crept over. He wasn't sure how he could get this other new idea across in a world without language and particularly to this particular Neanderthal.

So Satan held out the rock to Og, who blinked down at it, baffled. The Prince of Darkness then held the stone above the sleeping Ug's head and mimed bringing it down. All this took place in silence. Og watched, dumbly.

Oh come on, thought the Devil. Slowly, he repeated the actions. Rock. Head. Rock. Head. Rock. Head. Then, in a Eureka moment, he took Og's head and guided it toward his lady love, Ig.

Rock. Ug. Head.

Og have Ig

Rock. Ug. Head.

Og have Ig.

He gently placed the rock in Og's hand, who would either get it or not. The Devil couldn't be bothered to play matchmaker any more.

Og looked at his love rival, then something odd happened. He didn't smile – that was yet to come in evolutionary terms – but his face definitely gave off an impression of happiness and realisation. His expression didn't change, but when the Devil looked into Og's eyes, a spark of feral, wicked intelligence had ignited there.

With no further thought, Og, the dumbest member of humanity's aborted evolutionary line, brought the rock down on Ug's head, again and again. He did it silently, mechanically. He'd had a problem, but now was fixing it.

The Devil watched, strangely proud.

Og has made history today and in just a few short minutes, he marvelled. *First he discovered jealousy, then, moments later, with a little help from me, he committed the first ever murder. Yes,*

Neanderthals had killed each other before, for food or territory, but this was the first actual killing for any reason other than pure survival.

Og wanted something. Og was jealous. Og did something about it.

That's my boy, thought Lucifer. *Together, Og and I, we've just brought* murder *into the world.*

*

Inside that airless bunker room, the Devil once again acted out receiving applause.

"Thank you, thank you, flowers? For me? No, no. I was just a small part of the cast. An actor / director, if you please. I'd like to thank Og, of course, without whom that particular act in this epic production of 'Humanity' wouldn't have hit the stage. I'd like to thank my agent, manager, costume, lighting, props – who provided the rock…"

He stopped. "Too much?"

Hitler still stared straight ahead, silently.

"You think if you ignore me, I'll just go away? Not going to happen, *mein Führer*. I've never told anyone my story, and if I have an audience of just one, then so be it. But what an audience you are! You have the Royal Box, Adolf, the best seat in the house for the best story in the world. Enjoy it. It is instructional, as I may have mentioned. So, there I was. Born in a hurricane, into a body not my own, sharing a brain with a mainly unfathomable intelligence, introducing the idea of murder. Why did I do that, you might wonder? Is Hitler wondering that?"

Hitler stuck out his bottom lip.

"Very grown up of you. Well, yes, why did I place a rock in Og's hand and show him how to murder? I didn't have to do that, did I? But that was the funny thing. Somewhere in my mind, I knew I *did* have to do it. That was exactly what I had to do. Now, don't think for one moment I knew my real purpose. I was still confused to why I'd been cast out of Hell and sent to earth, but…do you ever have an idea that doesn't seem to be your own? That's what it felt like, an idea that had been placed there in my mind and I just acted upon it. I needed Og to commit the first murder. I did it for me, not for him, but I didn't know why. Not then. Dry in here, isn't it? Would you like a drink?"

Hitler looked back and saw those two white hands now held crystal goblets of red wine.

"Château Mouton Rothschild, 1923. Very good year. Oops, not a good year for you, obviously. 1923 set you on the slippery slope that led you here, with a bullet lodged in your brain. How uncouth of me. But in terms of wine, it's a good one. I do have excellent taste. Mind you, it's taken me long enough to develop. Back when I was King of Hell, I was very uptight, serious, exactly like you. But over the millennia, I've learned to enjoy the finer things in life and to laugh. My personality developed a sense of humour. You should do the same. Go on, have a glass."

"I don't drink," Hitler spat.

"Oh, you don't do you? That'll be that uptight and serious thing I was talking about. You should. Perhaps if you'd imbibed once in a while you might have relaxed a little. Stopped blaming everyone else for your own faults. Very well then…"

One goblet disappeared and was instantly replaced by a glass of water.

"Good old Adam's ale for the Führer," the Devil held it out to Hitler, who reluctantly took it. Satan's goblet disappeared into the darkness about his head, followed by the sound of drinking.

"That is a very fine wine. Costs a fortune. I got it on my business account; I can write it off as a justifiable expense. You know, 'entertaining'."

Hitler sipped at his water and whispered, "are you finished?"

"What do you think? That was hardly my life story, now was it? Aren't you intrigued to know what I've done, where I've been, what my game is?"

Hitler retreated back into sullen silence.

"Well, you're going to, like it or not. So, there was me, a Murder-Introducing-Neanderthal. Murder really caught on, you know. It remains popular, even today – one of the few fashions to endure. Murder was very *'this season'* wasn't it, in Germany? Everyone was wearing it. You were one of the top designers working that particular catwalk, were you not? How many outfits from Hitler's Murder Label did you put out there? You measured up six million Jews for starters, didn't you?"

"They were enemies of the Aryan race," Hitler stuck out his chin, petulantly.

"Oh, there he goes again. Of course they were. *The Aryan race*," Satan scoffed. "You didn't look at that tawdry concept too hard, did you? Your whole *weltanschauung* was based on the vague, weird and totally discredited ideas of a bunch of freaks, with all respect. Nobody could define what the Aryan race was, just as the S.S. tied themselves in knots trying to define a Jew. Compared to Himmler, you were positively stable. *The Aryan race*, honestly," the Devil repeated, scornfully. "After all these years, I now know there is just the human race, in all its wonderful, awful, beautiful, ugly manifestations. As I said, the country of your birth has as much to do with your innate goodness or badness as the colour of your hair."

"The Jews are the enemy of the people," Hitler repeated and tried to look the Devil in the eye, which was difficult, since there was only that whirling darkness.

"Aha, yes, you keep on telling yourself that. You can tell yourself that for the rest of time, but repetition doesn't make truth out of a falsehood. You'll learn. So, anyway, enough about you; back to me. I thought for some time that I was going to live in that ghastly Neanderthal body forever, but, like all bodies, it gave up and fell apart. Dust to dust, ashes to ashes and all that. For a moment, I thought my strange ordeal was over, but then, I was suddenly in another body. Then, of course eventually, that body died and along came another and so on and on and *on*. With every person I occupied, there were always two minds in each brain, except their mind had no idea mine was alongside, renting out space. It was so strange; I could make these

bodies do whatever I wanted and those other minds always thought
my decisions were their ideas.

But I still didn't know my point, my purpose in all this. I just
moved from body to body through history. I was only Neanderthal
once. After that, I became human, both men and women. Very
interesting. Very confusing, when you don't know if you're a boy or a
girl. But I was never a child. I don't know why. Perhaps adults have
more influence. They can get more done. Oh and believe me, I got a
lot done. It wasn't always hijinks and party favours, though. Most of
the time, it was deathly dull, but I always managed to cause some
mischief, whoever and wherever I was.

I rarely became a main player in history, either, one of the truly
famous or infamous. No, most of the time, I was more in an 'advisory
capacity'. You could call my job *'putting temptation in their way'*, if
you like. Temptation was one of the most useful tools I kept in my kit.
It worked wonders and never seemed to wear out.

Mainly it was enough for me to be in the shadows, you know, just a
whisper here and a suggestion there, to keep things interesting. But it
was hard. Do you have any idea what it's like to live forever? To jump
from body to body, to keep feeling the pain of cancer, torture, disease,
execution, murder, to feel your body decay, to sense your heart
stopping, over and over, never able to get off the merry-go-round and,
worst of all, not knowing why?

But it hasn't all been bad. I've had fun, if you can call it that. Well,
maybe not fun, then, but a curious sense of achievement. I seemed to
have often found myself at important waypoints in human history, as
if I was needed to just jog things along a bit. But why, again, why? I
didn't know. Oh, *oh!*"

The Devil bounced up and down on the spot a little, excited. "I
must tell you about the time I met Jesus."

Hitler looked up and into that pulsing dark. "Jesus Christ?"

"No, Jesus Hitler. Yes, Jesus Christ, which other Jesus is there?"

"You met Jesus Christ?" For the first time, the Führer sounded
awed.

"Yes, yes," said the Devil, who waved a hand as if this were nothing, just a trifle. "Seemed quite nice at first; bit confused the next time. *Had* to die, of course."

*

The Devil had been very busy these last few thousand years. He'd been jumping about body to body, but in those times, when BC became AD, life was short and cheap, so he was getting through quite a few.

Mainly, he'd hung around in the area of what would become known as the Middle East, particularly in the part called Palestine.

As with all his previous incarnations throughout history, Lucifer didn't know exactly what was going to happen, but always knew something would, and he was going to be part of it. Life was like having massive déjà vu, all the time.

So he knew his presence here in the Middle East was part of a bigger story and he'd only be given his role when he started playing it. That was the most delicious part. It was like an actor stepping onto a stage with absolutely no clues as to the nature of the performance, but when the spotlight hit, knowing exactly where to stand and what to say, fully dressed for the role of a lifetime.

Except the King Of Hell had already enjoyed many roles of many lifetimes and didn't know when the curtain would come down, if ever.

Something was happening here in this scorched part of the world. You could feel it in the air, a fevered anticipation. Many had blabbed on about these being the "last days", but the Devil knew that wasn't the case. He knew he had some way to go before his last days. There had been many Messiahs popping up to celebrate the End of All Times. You couldn't move for Messiahs in Palestine. They were on every corner, all being painfully messianic – a deeply unattractive trait.

This plague of Messiahs knew all the right things to say. They'd studied their prophecies, knew what was required, so could all lay claim to being the one true saviour.

However, one thing none of them could pull off were miracles, a prerequisite for the post of Messiah. They could talk the talk, but couldn't walk any particular miraculous walk. Many of them ended up being stoned to death and the Devil couldn't really feel too sorry for them.

But these many Messiahs really fuelled the apocalyptic hysteria. They whipped people up about it, promising fiery death from above, then, after their febrile lectures, they'd ask their terrified audience if they had any loose change. It was an excellent act. *I'll save you if you give me some money.* Same old story. Same new story, actually.

However, the name of one "Saviour" kept coming up. That name was Jesus Christ and he'd already earned quite a reputation. But the problem back then was that news travelled extremely slowly and was often totally distorted in the telling.

For example, a few thousand years after fighting in the Trojan Wars, Satan was surprised to finally hear the *"official, authorised"* account of the conflict called *The Iliad*, knocked up by some homeless poet opportunist named Homer.

It was a mess. What had been a relatively minor skirmish over six months had evolved in Homer's fevered mind into a ten year epic battle, populated by people that Lucifer had never heard of, like *Odysseus* and *Achilles.*

Allegedly, many gods had been involved (none had actually showed up) and it had started over some woman called Helen, which not one person had mentioned during the entire rigmarole. Then, there had been a wooden horse, which people still talked about to this day but had unequivocally not existed. The Devil wanted to shake people by the neck and scream, "It never happened! No wooden horse! Get it through your head, no wooden horse!" but of course, he couldn't. He felt he had to pick his targets carefully. He couldn't damn people just because they were gullible.

So Satan took all these whispers and rumours about Jesus with more than a pinch of salt. Saviours were coming and going every day and he couldn't keep up.

But that name was everywhere. Even the Romans were talking about Jesus. Not in any meaningful way, no, not yet – but the fact they'd noticed him amongst all the righteous noise was interesting to the Devil. The Romans had their own belief / propaganda system and were very happy with it. Their deities seemed to be producing results – that massive Roman Empire, for starters – so the pantheon wasn't threatened by one man and a few hangers-on claiming yet another direct lineage from yet another god. But still, they'd taken notice.

The Devil asked around and received the usual mix of confusion, lies and supposition.

Jesus had been born in a stable, they said. Well, that made sense, because the Persian Mithras, another son of *a* god, had been born in a stable, too. Plenty of gods had humble beginnings, nothing special there. Christ's mother was a virgin, they said. Again, par for the course: the Egyptians and Greeks had claimed loads of virgin births.

But there was something about this Christ that pulled at Lucifer. His name felt loaded with potential. It had weight. None of the other Messiahs' names had rung any bells with His Dark Holiness, but Jesus Christ…*Jesus Christ!*

He'd rolled it around his tongue many times and it felt right. The Devil thought it was high time he met this Christ figure, to see how he fitted into the story.

But just at the moment he'd made up his mind to seek him out, The Man Who Would Be King disappeared. Lucifer had asked around again and discovered that Jesus had gone to be baptised by a man called - wait for it - John the Baptist. He obviously hadn't wasted time thinking up a clever name for his business.

According to some of the Devil's contacts, this John the Baptist had become convinced Jesus was the Son of God. John had seen quite a few wannabes, so had some experience in that field.

After the baptism, Jesus had walked out into the Judaean desert to fast for forty days and nights, to spend time with his God and try to get some answers.

Jesus' very human reaction to the news he was the progeny of a deity intrigued the Devil.

Most "Messiahs" would have gone straight to the market and shouted this exciting development to the shoppers, but not Jesus. He'd done the opposite. Christ had gone away to consider his potential messiahship.

Oh, I think we should meet, Satan had thought. *Out there, in the desert, alone. Just me and thee, the Emperor of Hate and the Possible Prince of Peace, yes, just to see what happens.*

It hadn't taken long to find Jesus. The Devil felt he'd been led there, as had happened on many other occasions throughout his long history.

Jesus had been sitting in the shade of a rocky outcrop, wearing a simple off-white robe.

As he'd ploughed through the sand toward this possible Messiah, the Devil thought Jesus was a scrawny, ill-looking specimen. Mind you, malnutrition had probably contributed to that. But this Christ had given off a hypnotic serenity. The other Messiahs looked mad, desperate or violent (mainly all three at once), but Jesus appeared at peace. His eyes had been closed as the Dark One approached and he spoke without opening them.

"So. You came?"

Lucifer was somewhat taken aback by that. In all his years, no-one had expected him. You weren't meant to expect the Devil. *Very well, then*, Satan thought, *so* this *is how we're going to play it.*

"Of course. I felt we should meet. Didn't you?"

"Not really; you weren't top of my list," smiled Jesus and finally opened his eyes. "Oh. That's a disappointment. You're not like I imagined."

"What did you imagine?"

"Well, scarier, I suppose. Like the priests describe. Not of this earth. Scales, fur, wings, like a beast, many beasts forced together. You just look like someone I'd forget in a crowd."

"Oh, well, thank you," the Devil had replied haughtily. "That's one of my talents, you know. Blending in. If people knew Satan actually walked amongst them, they might be ready to do something about it."

"Yes, I suppose. A disguise, then?"

"No. This is what I happen to look like at this moment. And you? The robes, the beard, the saintly expression – a disguise?"

"I don't believe so. This is what I happen to look like...," Christ laughed then, a little giggle lost in the dunes. "...*at this moment.*"

"Mind if I sit down?"

Jesus held out a hand and indicated Satan should sit at his side. "There's plenty of room. But not, I fear, for both of us. There isn't enough room in all creation for us two, wouldn't you say?"

Satan looked at this strange, still man, who stared at the rolling dunes in front of him, unafraid.

"Well then, er, Jesus Christ. Let's get straight to it. It's hot, I'm hungry and I have plenty of people to see. Are you the Son of God?" he asked and for the first time, realised this may be a viable question.

Jesus continued to stare at the shifting sands.

"Are you who I think you are?" he asked.

"Yes. I believe I am."

"You believe?"

"Have some patience, Jesus. We're both making this up as we go along. I don't know, you don't know. I haven't even been told what my purpose is. I just know when bad things happen, there I am."

"So is something bad going to happen to me now?"

"Ooh, not now, no. But you do know you're going to die, yes?"

"We all die. But not you, I think. You go on and on and on, Satan, don't you? So yes, I'll die and be reborn, I think."

"Don't get too excited about the whole rebirth thing. It's dreadful."

"Not the way I'll do it. I won't be reborn here."

"But you could live forever, here, Christ. Why wouldn't you take that option?"

"Mm, I will live forever, but not as I am. Not in this flesh." Jesus held up his hands and looked at them. He held a palm up to his eyes and studied the centre of it. "What would be the fun living like this? Why are you here then? What do you want to know?"

The Devil didn't have an answer. But then he remembered his toolbox. He remembered temptation.

"You're just a man, Jesus. That's all."

"I am. As are you...*at this moment.*"

They both shared a wry laugh and their eyes met for a moment, just two guys in a desert, talking obliquely about the fate of humanity.

"Christ, I don't know that you really are the Son of God. I've seen many mad Messiahs. You could be another one. Calmer on the outside, I admit, but inside you could be dribbling insane, in which case, I shouldn't waste any time on you."

"Don't you have forever? You could waste as much time as there will ever be."

"I could, true, but if you're mad, what's the point? So..." Lucifer looked about this empty sandscape, picked up a stone and turned it about in his hand, thinking.

"If you're the Son of God, Jesus, let's see it. Prove your power to me. Rise to the occasion. You've been fasting, I respect that, but surely you are starving. I am. So go on, turn this rock into bread. Do that and I'll know who you are."

Jesus took another stone and also turned it over in his hand. He smiled.

"Man cannot live by bread alone. But by every word that proceeds from the mouth of God."

The Devil looked at Jesus, eyes wide. "Seriously, you just said that? I asked you to turn this rock into bread and you say that? Goodness me, that was weak."

"If I turn it into bread then I have failed in my fast. You have given me a simple, lazy, temptation. I expected better."

"Well, do it for me, then. I'm not fasting. I'm famished. Just one. Make a roll or something."

"If you're who I think you are, make your own."

"Oh, whoo-hoo, that was really poor," said Satan, quietly impressed. No bluster, no theatrics; this Jesus had just out manoeuvred him. "Well, then. Try this. let's say we go to the temple in town…"

"Which one?"

"Does it matter? Jesus, there are loads of them. A temple. Any temple. You go to the pinnacle and throw yourself off. Then, if you're God's own, some angels will swoop down and stop you breaking your serene little neck on the ground, right? Let's do it. Right now."

Jesus shook his head. "If you have faith in God, you do not test God."

"Oh, that was even worse than the first temptation!" cried the Devil and slapped his forehead. "What does that even mean?"

"It is better to have faith than certainty," answered Jesus and then pretended to take a bite out of a rock. He winced and held his jaw. "Ow," he said, sarcastically. "I really should have made myself a nice loaf of bread. And rustled up a few hundred fishes."

"Oh, don't mock," growled Jesus' nemesis. "If I was jumping off a temple I'd prefer to know my people would come to the rescue."

"Well, be my guest," said Christ. "Go on, go jump off a temple. Your army of demons will come. Help yourself. There are loads of temples. Can't move for temples these days. There's a lot of money in the temple business. Too much, now I come to think about it."

This man's absolute tranquility unnerved Lucifer.

"Right, Jesus. You're just some guy in a dirty robe in a frankly dreadful part of the world – and I've seen a few. You have literally no proof in your divinity. You can't even turn a rock into bread…"

Jesus took another pretend bite from the stone and said, "Mmmm, tasty."

"Stop. It wasn't funny the first time. So I'm taking a bit of a gamble here. I am who you think I am. You know it. I know it. So here's the deal. It's a one off, never to be repeated offer. You will die. You know that. You will die with only your *faith* to tell you there will be everlasting life and your kingdom of loveliness and wonder to sit around in, being…smug. But I'm offering you this. One time, one

shot. Get down on your knees, just for one second, worship me and
I'll make you my number two. Guaranteed. That's a promise. You
either have a very, very tiny chance that you are related to God –
which is doubtful, considering the whole bread/ rock, temple/angel
reluctance, or you can have it, right now. Dominion over the Earth.
What do you say?"

Jesus threw the rock into the distance, a surprisingly long throw.
Satan couldn't even see it disappear into the sand.

"Oh, get thee behind me, Satan," he sighed. "There's just God, the
one God, whatever name you use for him, just the one. The God of
kindness and compassion, of love. Do you really think I'd turn my
back on Him for all this?" He spread his hand across the expanse of
nothing. "So, no. No to bread and rocks, no to angels and temples, no
to a pathetic slice of your Kingdom of Hate."

The Devil grimaced at this man, with his serene expression and
absolute certainty, built on faith and nothing more. It shouldn't make
any sense, but yet, here he was, this Jesus Christ, who beatifically
smiled out at the eternal, rolling dunes.

"Well, you can't say I didn't try," said the Devil.

Christ shrugged. "Oh, you did. Now, please, fuck off."

*

"Jesus said that?" asked Hitler, who now seemed interested. Talk of
Neanderthals and original sin hadn't appeared to get through to the
Führer, but Christ swearing had hit a nerve.

"Well, yes, I suppose, but it was in Aramaic," replied the Devil. "It
doesn't quite have the same violent disdain. But it does translate to the
same thing; go forth and multiply, if you like. He was a cheeky one,
Jesus. Very good sense of humour. He could be devastatingly witty. At
the Last Supper, after he said, 'One of you will betray me', he gave
this really camp wink to Judas and everyone laughed, even Judas. It
wasn't reported, but then Christ said, 'But at least you got some bread
and wine out of it. Remember, though, there's no such thing as a free
lunch.'"

Hitler didn't know what to make of that. The Devil sighed.

"You really are simply the most humourless fun vacuum, aren't you?"

"You are talking about our Lord Jesus Christ," said the Führer, piously.

"Oh yes, the King of The Jews. The Jews, Adolf. Whom you murdered, along with all the others." Satan's hand emerged from the dark and pointed at Hitler again. It shook with fury. "I created murder. Or did I? I don't know. Then it was industrialised, for the first and only time under your leadership. If I could have stopped that, I would have, but I let it happen. Because I had to. Because I wanted it to happen. Because I am…" he sighed. "I am Old Nick, Lucifer, the Cloven One. That's what I do. That, my dreadful friend, is what I have to do."

"Where is the point in this?" wheezed Hitler, barely able to speak now. The cold, the airless forever in this bunker had finally reached him.

The Devil ignored the Führer's question.

"Jesus really annoyed me, that day. The serenity, his… dismissiveness. Oh and his righteousness, yes. I didn't know if he was the Son of God. I still don't. There have been many contenders for that position over the years. But he had such conviction. You know when somebody angers you to the point that you can't let it go?"

Hitler had to internally admit the entire Second World War had been a product of exactly that.

"Mmm, you do. I hated Jesus. So, I kept an eye on the man. I was never there at any of the miracles, which was a pain. It would have helped to know, for sure. But, almost at the end, I went and found him again, at the Garden. I tempted him, gave the same choices, tested his faith and doubts but the fool – or the Messiah, my jury is out – ignored me; he walked away. I hated him. I whispered in Pilate's ear, made sure, damn sure, he'd wash his hands and seal the Christ's fate. And then, there he was, on Golgotha, hung next to criminals, in his ecstasy. Nine inch nails through his palms. I saw. He died, Adolf, he died. Like any man. He didn't roll away any stones. I was there. I stood with the legionnaire Longinus as he pierced the Christ's side. Longinus wasn't blind; he wasn't healed. Jesus died. He never came back. I was there. So. That was the moment the world changed forever. I made it happen. You killed the Jews because Jesus existed. And I made it happen. You made it happen. And look what happened. Jesus thought he was there to save the world. But look how many have died in his name."

Hitler tried to answer, but couldn't.

"Well, after that, I died, lived, died, lived, repeat, repeat, repeat. I walked the earth, always finding trouble, but still never knowing why. I know why now, of course. It's taken until this moment to truly realise. I've been everywhere, seen everything. I have witnessed the depravity that man can sink to and seen the glory he can achieve. But glory is in short supply on this planet. People think they are so advanced, so cultured, but they are no better than those Neanderthals. You still think in images, really; *eat, kill, take, destroy, burn.* Oh, I know there is love out there, lots of it, but it has to fight through the stupidity. Love is a delicate thing, easily crushed, unlike stupidity, which is a rampaging, colossal beast. Love takes effort. Stupidity is airborne. Love needs nurturing. Stupidity breeds like rabbits. I have seen so much stupidity, Adolf. I've been responsible for most of it."

The Devil reached out a hand to the Führer and pointed again. Images filled Hitler's head – whirring, immersive movies in full technicolour, but he couldn't leave this cinema. It was inside him.

*

There was Lucifer - he looked different again, but the Führer knew – leading a charge at the Crusades, slicing at the heathens with his sword, laughing as he did so. Around him, the bodies of women and children were hacked apart and, at Satan's side, the other Crusaders righteously went about their business of cleansing in the name of God. They felt no remorse or guilt. This had to be done to protect Christianity, to protect their *race* from the subhumans that worshipped false idols. When this was over, their people would rise, untainted by the scourge of Islam. They would be the master race.

*

"Familiar, isn't it?" asked the Devil. "So sadly, predictably, stupidly familiar." He clicked his fingers and the reel changed.

*

Armies marched. So many armies, of so many kings and queens, filled with the virtuous sense of their always blameless causes. Satan was always amongst them somewhere. Not always at the front, but Hitler could always spot him in the ranks and knew he was goading them on, pushing for greater atrocities in the name of their flags, countries, religions and leaders. There were many battlefields, but in the end, it was the same one. The weapons changed and became more efficient at their dreadful function, but ultimately, they were the same weapons, too. It doesn't really matter if you are on the business end of a *Panzerfaust* or a scimitar, the result was still death.

*

"You see? But don't fixate on just the mighty battles of days gone by and days so close. I wasn't just about the wars that get immortalised in the plays and poems and songs. I micromanaged, too. Always busy, Adolf. Always busy. Most of the time, I just whisper to the little people, to see what happens. You know, go and sit in a random New York bar, meet a pimp, get chatting about his girls, maybe suggest they don't respect him and he needs to beat that respect into them. Maybe go to another bar in the middle of no-where and give a broken-hearted guy a gun, just for fun. Tell a minor, hate-filled politician how to become a major one. From little acorns…Tiny whispers, big results. Yes, I put weapons into people's hands, but most of the time, I put weapons into their minds. Mischief. Temptation. Revenge. Honour. All wonderful tools. I'm always busy."

*

Flickering pictures, edited together at breakneck speed. Satan was everywhere. Not just in moments that had gone down in history, but yes, on the street corners, in the drinking dens, bars and back rooms, the places history had forgotten, but whose impact lived on, even in tiny ways. The Devil's work was cumulative. A little badness goes a long way. It ripples out from the point of origin, affecting people who were never even there, at ground zero. You do not have to fight on the battlefield to feel its roar. One death can have many victims. He was there, muttering to the jealous husbands, suspicious wives. He encouraged the deluded, put knives in the hands of the furious, whipped up the paranoia, stoked up the hatred. He capered through the calendar, popped up wherever he could to upset apple carts, unhinge, break, turn things sour. If people were ruined, Hitler knew Lucifer had passed through. Sometimes he was just an ill wind, at others, a tsunami, but it didn't matter. Whether his touch destroyed one person or one thousand, his job was done. The work was cumulative. The Devil always found work for his idle hands to do.

*

"Quite a CV, isn't it?" asked the Devil. "Oooh, I have many references. I am *experienced*. Are you? But what was I doing, in those dark rooms, bedrooms, backrooms and war rooms? What was I really doing? What was my game? Oh, my game. I now know it was a game of exquisite complexity. I was putting together a series of events that suited my ultimate purpose. Each piece of the puzzle contributed to the whole, but I couldn't see the jigsaw's true picture. I had to put it together for myself, to know my name."

*

The picture changed again. Satan was ransacking a palace, along with others like him. Slavs, Hitler realised. Subhumans from the East. They hollered and hooted as they tore down curtains, ripped paintings, smashed statues. They were tearing apart their past, creating a new utopia from the destruction.

The image flickered. Pushed up against a wall was a family, cowering. Hitler recognised the man who stood in their middle, trying to protect them. He was Czar Nicholas II. Next to him, his crying wife and five children were huddled together. Anastasia screamed as men approached, with guns, bayonets and clubs.

*

"The Russian Revolution led to the Bolsheviks, which led to the rise of your nasty little NSDAP. It led to Stalin, to Barbarossa, which led to everything going so very, very wrong for Mr Self-Destruct sitting there. It led to Stalingrad, which, as you are well aware, caused the destruction of your Sixth Army, reversal of fortunes and the Reich fighting a defensive war for the first time. It led to this, Adolf. I was at Stalingrad, too. You had to throw *two hundred and fifty thousand* men into the mincer just because a city had your enemy's name. *My* name for that particular act was Richard Stempel. I was a *Generalleutnant*. Rode a tank and everything. Even despite the snow, the stench of the bodies was appalling. You let an entire army die there, because of some stupid spat with a man who was just like you. Bravo."

The Devil did a slow hand clap, which reverberated about the room. "That's what you did to your own people. Of course you had no problem with everyone else. As Herr Stempel, I killed myself, rather than be taken prisoner by the Soviets, but there was no honour in it. I just died another inglorious death. But still, but still...Well. It's time. Time for you to know my name. Have you guessed it yet? Time to reveal the purpose of my game, which has taken millennia."

The Devil stepped forward, out of his darkness.

Hitler stared and tried to scrabble backward, away from the figure who had emerged into the light, but he had nowhere to go. He now knew there'd never been anywhere to go. He would always be trapped here.

Satan smoothed down a black fringe that fell diagonally across his forehead. A smile appeared beneath his ridiculous little toothbrush moustache.

"My name is Adolf Hitler," said Lucifer. "It was always Adolf
Hitler, from the moment I was born in that hurricane, in the emptiness
that was once planet Earth. I couldn't quite remember who I'd been,
back then. I knew I was once the ruler of Hell, a place full of
screaming people and flames…" he waved his hands about the room
and up at the ceiling. "But Hell was here, wasn't it? I was the King of
Hell on Earth. My demons rampaged, throwing men, women and
children into the ovens; they flew and unleashed thunderbolts. I was
once the overlord of palaces made of fire, but ultimately I reigned over
just this one room, down deep, deep in the seventh circle, my only
Fury by my side, dead."

Lucifer, or rather Hitler, looked down at his other self and Eva,
slumped there.

"I told you the punishment fits the crime. I am, *you* are, *we* are and
always will be the Devil. Cursed to walk the earth, causing trouble,
whipping up hate, trying to find or make someone *worse* than we are.

Because if we can find someone, just one person, more evil than
us, then this curse will be lifted and we can just – poof! – disappear.
So, over and over, we travel back in time, to start again, hunting the
globe for one more wicked to take our place. But we never do. We
cause wars, misery, pain; we push people to do terrible things, hoping
they will become badder than we were, but it never happens. Nobody
tops us in the Great League of Evil. So we always end up back here,
facing our other self about to put a bullet in our heads, telling
ourselves this story, preparing ourselves for the eternity we will face.
Because we are Satan, Lucifer, Old Nick, Hobb, The Devil…and we
always will be. It is, you have to admit, a great cosmic joke."

Satan / Hitler clapped his hands again. "Encore! Encore! It will
always be encore for us. We are *made* of encore. So. Perhaps you will
have better luck than I, even though I am you and you are me. Perhaps
this time round, you will put the bullet in your brain, wake up as
Neanderthal – again – and then eventually create someone who is
more black hearted than us, and then we can become nothing. Good
luck. There – that is our story, that is our game, this is our name. Live

it again. Come back here and tell it again. Round and round. You will put a bullet in your head, go to the start of time and try to find a new Devil. I hope you do, but you won't. You have my sympathy."

Adolf Hitler, once Führer of Germany and King of Hell, sat on that bench next to his dead wife and picked up the gun. He looked his other self in the eye and that other him gave a little wave. "I still don't know why they put a bin in here, though," said Satan. "Odd, isn't it? Auf wiedersehen." Hitler closed his eyes, put the Walther to his temple and pulled the trigger.

It worked.

*

Adolf Hitler, the Devil, woke up. Well, no, that wasn't right. It wasn't coming to – more of a slow clarifying, as if he were an object in the distance being brought into focus. He felt his consciousness return in the same way, like a dial on the radio being turned, picking up fragments of broadcasts that made no sense until one tuned in. His memory was fractured, visions flashed about his mind of so many things, places, people, all unfamiliar but strangely known to him. He was cold, wet and lay on the ground, but didn't open his eyes yet. Part of him didn't want to.

"CAROLINE SAYS (II)"

(Lou Reed, 1973, from the album, Berlin)

"Apartment 2!!!"
517 Lexington Avenue,
New York, NY
10017
7 / 26 / 1973

Dear Tony,

It was so *so* good to hear from you.

Sorry I've taken a while to write. I've read your letter so many times but didn't know where to start.

It's funny hearing your voice again as I read your words. I guess two years isn't that long, but it feels a whole other life away.

So you're *"Anthony"* now, are you? You're all grown up! No, no, you'll always be Tony to me. Always.

I'm so glad you wrote back.

I thought California was hot. I knew nothing. New York freezes you solid in winter, then cooks you alive in summer. There's a little breeze through the hole in my window, but that's all. I can't open it anyway. The window's broken, like everything else.

You said you were "surprised" and "happy" to get my letter. I'm happy you were happy. I suppose it would have been a big surprise though. I can't believe Mom told you I'd moved to England. No, that's not true, I CAN believe it. I'll get on to Mom soon enough, when I can deal with her.

I'm glad your Mom and Dad are still there in SB and passed my first letter on. I'm also happy you finally moved out and found a girl – about time, Tony. It's good you enjoy your job. You deserve it. We were such good friends, weren't we? I guess we still are. You stay good friends even when you don't see each other, right? I know I should have written before, but I didn't know what to say.

I do now. I'm writing because now I know exactly what to say.

I'm sorry you were worried about me. I know I just disappeared, but I couldn't risk Mom finding out where I was. It's good you didn't trust what she said – NEVER TRUST ANYTHING SHE SAYS – but you don't have the first idea.

But I'm getting ahead of myself and yourself a little. You have a lot of questions, and tho I'm not sure I can give you all the answers, I'll try, but it's going to be difficult. Hey, remember whenever we got in your Dad's crappy old pickup he used to say, "Careful, guys, it's going to get bumpy!?"

Well, careful, Tony, it's going to get bumpy.

Whatever I write in this letter, forgive me and don't hate me. I'm writing because I have to.

You see my address there, at the top? *"Apartment 2?"* That makes me laugh every time. It actually says that on my door, on a cracked old sign. It sounds so fancy, doesn't it, like I'm sitting here in my "apartment" sipping champagne with little bibbity-bobbity dogs yapping away at my ankles as if it's the Dakota building or something. The truth is not fancy at all.

Sorry, I'm not making any sense. Except for you, I haven't written anyone for a long time and that last one wasn't a *letter*, letter, was it?

This is a real *letter*, letter, aha.

I'm out of practice. I tried to remember last time I really wrote to someone and it was in high school. A *"Love Letter,"* yeah. Ha ha. Do you remember Charles Stokes? Sure you do. He was an asshole. But I bet you didn't know I dated him for a whole two weeks, did you? Nobody did. Well, we weren't dating. I was his dirty secret. Dating is when you hold hands in parks and stare into each other's eyes, kiss and tell each other you love them. But I didn't do any of that. For two weeks Charlie just took me to his Mom and Dad's garage and I went along with it because I didn't know any different.

I didn't mean to put all that, it just came out of the pen. Sorry if I offended you, Tony, I just started writing and it all came out, boom, straight from my head, into the ink and onto the paper.

Why did I write you that first letter? I guess I just wanted to know there was someone, anyone out there, you know, from before. Before New York, before I ended up here, in "Apartment 2."

I know it was only a quick, "Hi, how are you, let's stay in touch," thing, but I couldn't think of anything else to say. I didn't even know if you were still there or would even want to write back. I didn't want to hope too much, that was the real reason, to hope there might be someone out there who'd actually listen.

You know, I even had to ask Mike the Doorman for paper and a pen to write that first little note to you. I don't even have paper or a pen anymore, Tony. I had to beg a doorman for them.

Well, we call him the doorman, like he wears a uniform and tips his hat while he carries bags to your "apartment" but he doesn't do any of that. He's mean.

It takes a lot not to become mean in New York.

You have to keep smiling, or the city gets inside you. You see them everywhere, the people who have become New York. That's right, they're not human any more, they're the city itself, walking around in clothes. You look in their eyes and it's like looking into the windows of the blocks. You see nothing in there, only yourself, reflected back.

You know, your letter was the first one I ever got here in NY actually addressed to me. The others are always just addressed to *"the occupant."* New York sees us all like that. We just occupy the city, none of us have names. Just "the occupant," until another one comes along and the city doesn't care about them, either.

Sorry, I lost myself there for a moment. If I had more paper, I'd tear this page up and start again, but I don't and people have to know. You have to know, Tony. You have to know why I came and what's happened since. I have so much I want to tell you, so it's all coming out at the same time. It's like the thoughts are flying in from everywhere, all trying to get into the pen. I have to slow down.

I knew it was you from the writing on the envelope.

But even if I hadn't recognized that, I would still know it was you. How?

Because of your lists!

You always made lists, to make sure everything was written down, organized, ready to go. I'm the total opposite, remember. I still am. Just look at this letter! I can't finish a thought without another one taking over.

So I'm going to follow your example, I'm going to reply to your list of questions. I bet that's why you made it, right? Because you knew I'd just ramble all over the place and never get to the point. Ha. That's been my life, really. I never get to the point. I always go around or past it. It's like I've been avoiding the point all this time.

You listed me seven questions to answer, so I'll try to do it without missing, going around, under, over, or past the point! Wish me luck, it's not very me, but I'll try. I'm so glad you wrote, Tony, so glad.

You ask, 1/ *Where are you living?*

I'm living in an "apartment," as you now know, the fourth I've had since I ran here to New York. Can you believe that? Four "homes" in two years.

But then, it's no hardship, not really. I don't need a removal van whenever I leave, just me and my bag – and not much in that bag, either.

I've got it right here, by the bed. Inside there's a brush, my Dad's old copy of *The Great Gatsby*, a few dollars, and a purse with my stuff in it. They're my possessions, Tony. A brush, a book, and a purse. I have a few clothes piled in the "closet", too. Well, it <u>was</u> a closet once, but now it's just a shell with a bar and no hangers, so my clothes are on the floor.

Not having any clothes is hell. I always liked to dress up but now it's just one pair of jeans, two skirts, three blouses, and some underwear. I try my best with them, but it's no good for a girl like me, no good for <u>any</u> girl to be without her clothes. But guess what I can see through my broken window? A clothes store. It's called Carter

Hall, right opposite. So close, but so far, Tony. Ha, the story of my life.

So here in my "apartment", there's a broken window, bust-up closet, an old, shaky table, and my single bed, which gets changed maybe once a week. I have to wash in a bathroom down the hall, but I always feel dirtier afterwards. Can you imagine that? A bathroom that leaves you dirtier than when you went in. I'd laugh if it was funny.

Tony, I hate this place. I've hated all of them, they've all been variations on the same room. I once had a TV, my own bathroom and shower, but that was before my money run out – ha, no, Caroline – *Mom's* money ran out. Now I live with whatever I can afford.

I'm hungry all the time.

So I can't stay here and I can't go back. This room is home, for now.

That's another thing I keep thinking: "This is all just for now," but *"now"* just keeps going. It's always now. The next time never comes. I live in "now." I can't escape from "now."

Sorry, Tony. You asked and I told you. So this is where I live. Up on Lexington, a long way from Santa Barbara, but, I guess, still not far enough from Mom, not far enough from SB.

You ask, *2/ Do you have lots of friends?*

I think I already answered that question. At first, New York is very good at welcoming you.

Oh yes, at first, I thought New York was welcoming me with open arms. I had money and that helps, oh that really helps. Money helps everywhere – you'd be surprised how welcoming arms can be when they know they can hug up to some cash.

So when I first arrived I was the big cliché, the wide-eyed new girl in town, holding my one-way ticket to JFK. Yes, I got a one-way ticket. That should tell you a lot, Tony. It wasn't a money thing, I could afford to come back, but there I was, Santa Barbara Municipal to LAX, to New York, one way, baby. No looking back. You know how the song goes, if you can make it in New York, you can make it anywhere…Ha.

Why New York? Look at the map! It's the other side of the country! It's about as far as I could get from Santa Barbara without a passport. So I wonder, when Mom tells you I went to England, how did I do that with no passport? I didn't even think about it at the time, I just knew I wanted to go far, far away.

I thought New York was the furthest <u>and</u> most likely place to hand me a new life.

I wonder how many people that song has trapped here? Did New York whisper those words in Frank Sinatra's ear one night, to make a deal with him? " Hey Frank, I'll give you Madison Square Garden, you give me your tired, your poor, your huddled masses." I wouldn't put anything past this city. Ah, listen to me. I just read that back, I'm making no sense. It's hot, I'm tired, there's a hole in my window, and I wish you were here now, instead at the end of this pen.

I thought I had friends at first, but they all turned out to be New York, wearing different clothes, different disguises. All the Janes and the Candys, Hollys, Edies… they were all New York, made flesh. I thought people back home were the primitives and these were the sophisticates, but I was wrong. I rented a nice enough room over on Bleecker, OK, kind of funky. Bars and a few clubs, music, exciting people. That's how it seemed, anyhow. I got to know a few guys and girls, all very cosmopolitan, I thought.

I hung out there, went to their rooms, sorry, their "apartments," but they weren't interested in me, not really. To New York, you are either a threat, of use, or you don't exist. Everyone is just one of those three options, I know that now.

A threat, of use, nonexistent.

Was I going to be of use to these new "friends?" No. I was another 18-year-old who wanted to make it as a dancer in New York. Those people also wanted to be dancers, actors, and producers, so once they found out I was of no use, I must be competition and that made me a threat. So after that, I became nonexistent. *Threat, of use, nonexistent.* That's New York's attitude to "friends." It's not the only city that

167

thinks like that, but at least LA smiles while it stabs you. New York doesn't even bother with a smile.

I honestly believe some people here think they have genuine friends. I'd love to be like them, happy in my ignorance. I've seen too much, though, Tony. I'm so sorry. You ask a little question like, "Do I have friends?" and you get that answer. But you have to know, Tony, you have to know why things happen.

3/ Did you join the circus?

Oh, three questions in and he asks if I joined the circus! I laughed at that and got a bit tearful, too. Oh, the circus. Our circus.

How old were we? About nine or ten, wasn't it? I don't even remember how we first met. At school, of course, I know that, but how? Who said what to who? What did we talk about, in our very first conversation? TV? Food? Movies? Or did we talk about the circus?

But we did start talking didn't we? Then we were friends, just like that. Do you remember, the other kids thought we were KISSING? Ha! The girls would make little pucker-up noises behind our backs when we walked together, even though we never held hands and never kissed. Noooo, we never kissed – did you know that? Friends don't *kiss*, kiss, of course, but I don't remember even laying a little peck on your cheek. Not once. But we were friends through and through and friends don't kiss. So the others made noises and sang little songs and we just ignored them, didn't we?

But yes, we had a plan. We were going to join the circus and had it all figured out. Remember? When the show people came to town, we'd pack our carpetbags, hide in the elephant's straw, and by the time the circus reached the next place, it would be too late to send us back. They'd see how talented we were and HAVE to let us join.

"Hide in the Elephant's Straw!" Ha! I still remember that one. We had this vision of a "Dumbo" circus rolling into town with a brightly colored elephant wagon, full of straw. Our Grand Plan was to hide underneath it! Boy, was that scheme totally full of holes. Do you know, we never talked about why we wanted to run away. What was your reason? I knew mine, so I guess I kind-of assumed yours was

similar. I assumed all other kid's lives were like mine. That was reason enough.

We trained so hard for our imaginary circus career, didn't we?

I wanted to be the tightrope walker, "Caroline the Bird Girl." I was going to wear feathers all over my leotard, walk over the audience's heads on my wire, jump to the trapeze, then swoop through the air as the crowd shouted, "Caroline, Caroline, Caroline!" Nobody calls me the Bird Girl here.

Do you remember how I trained for my tightrope act? Of course you do. It was on your Mom and Dad's front wall. That wall was a whole brick wide and in my mind, I picture it being 50 feet tall, but I bet it was only as tall as we were, right? I'd scramble up there and I was so scared, but I'd close my eyes, take a deep breath and just step out onto my brick tightrope. You know, Tony, I could actually hear the audience, far below in our imaginary circus, calling my name. I'd pretend to wave at them and you, way down there. You'd be pratfalling and rolling in your clown costume. Of course the Traveling People would take us in and now where would we be? I'd be in a leotard somewhere making a crowd gasp and you'd be looking up at me, smiling, rolling, and tumbling. Then I'd fly!

But we never filled our carpetbags and no "Dumbo" circus ever came to Santa Barbara. When did we stop searching the walls for the posters, ready for our great escape? We must have at some point, but maybe our dream faded instead of us waking up. Sometimes dreams do that, don't they? They fade into the distance. You were never going to be a *juggler* anyway, were you? The circus never came and we never left. Well, *I* left, eventually, but not in the way I had once hoped. I miss that circus. That's funny, isn't it? I miss something I never had.

4/ *Did you become a dancer?*

The circus was our little fantasy, but you always knew dancing was what I really wanted.

Did you bite your lip as you wrote, *"Did you become a dancer?"*

Did you cross your fingers (sorry!) and hope it wasn't the wrong thing to ask?

169

I now think my little tightrope act was just a rehearsal for what I really wanted to do, but the young me hadn't realized. I never stopped dancing. Whatever music came on the radio, I'd be jiving. I didn't care. Martha and the Vandellas, Beach Boys, even Peter, Paul And Mary – I was always moving. Look at me now. I danced right out of Santa Barbara, kept right on moving, and didn't stop until New York took away my dancing shoes.

So, I think you probably guessed I'm not gracing the stage of the State Theater, or any theater.

I was so naive. I thought I could just arrive, audition, blow them all away, and then move straight into my whirlwind life of dance, champagne, and little, yappy, bibbity-bobbity dogs. No, that's not right. I wasn't naive, I was stupid – more stupid than I could have imagined.

People train for years to even get near those auditions. There's no such thing as "raw talent" in New York. Nobody takes a chance on "raw talent" here. No-one takes a chance on anything. You don't just turn up to those auditions, you're carried into them on a wave of certificates and medals. No, you do NOT stumble in, like I did, then stand transfixed as New York stared back and said, "whaddayagot?"

No, no, fucking no. Remember how this city works.

Was I a *threat, of use, or nonexistent*?

New York watched my pathetic little auditions and I wasn't of use or even a threat. I was nothing. I faded away from New York's sight every time I stepped into one of those auditions. I ceased to exist.

So no, Tony, I'm not a dancer. I never was. I was just some girl who dressed up as a dancer once.

5/ If not dancing...what do you do now?

So you covered your back with the next question, which you carefully phrased in case I never became a dancer. "If not...what do you do now?" So polite, as always.

What do I do?

That's very difficult to answer truthfully, but what else do I have now apart from the truth?

I just wrote about how dreams fade out, but sometimes reality can fade in.

You rarely wake up one morning and realize your life has changed, because in reality it's shifted by little steps, tiny moments. It's like the old fairy tales. You know, one night elves come in to a shoemakers and at first, they change a little. They sew a button on here, make a stitch there...nothing the shoemaker actually notices. And then, they paint a little here, fix a shelf there, and slowly the store begins to change, and still the shoemaker never sees. Eventually, the whole place is completely different, but it happened with such subtlety the shoemaker never saw. He's living in a different place, but never realized it was even changing.

That's what happened to me and, I think, lots of people. There's no earthquake or thunderbolt. It's more like waves. We just wake up and see one life has receded while another has quietly lapped up.

I didn't realize the auditions were all over until one day there weren't any more. They got further and further apart – New York whispers to itself, trust me – but nobody said, "Just drop it." The doors didn't suddenly slam in my face at once – they gradually shut until nobody was answering.

So, I was taking little jobs here and there, but not because the dream was over. No, just to keep myself afloat until the dream came true, because that's what happens in life, right?

When you're young like us, failure only happens to other people. You are bulletproof. Your dreams are guaranteed or there's a full refund. So, these little jobs were "just for now" except, "now" wasn't shifting. I kept waking up and it was always *"now."*

So I waitressed – New York loves waitresses, its little army of the lost – I ushered at the movie theater, which was difficult. It's hard being so close to that big screen, seeing people living out their dreams while you hand over popcorn and nobody even notices your face in the darkness. That was tough.

I was a cleaner and that was the worst, because then you really are invisible. No-one's supposed to see the cleaners. If we're seen, it shatters the magic, like seeing elves in the shoemakers. Your room miraculously cleans itself. All your nasty, vile little stains disappear from the sheets because the cleaning elves came.

So I worked, but I wasn't working, really. I was in a holding pattern over New York, waiting for it to give me permission to land, but my fuel was running out.

I met a guy. He seemed nice, ha, they all do, at first, but of course he was just New York on the prowl. That day, the city was dressed in a leather jacket, studs, sharp pants, slick hair.

That day, this city, I now realize, had dressed itself up *as* New York – no disguises, that was what NY really looked like.

He was staying at the hotel I worked in. He said he'd noticed me – of course he had. I'd been upgraded, from nonexistent. I was clearly not a threat, but I was of use.

He said I was too pretty to be cleaning rooms and that he had contacts in the modeling business.

Once he'd seen through me – which didn't take long – he claimed he knew a dance company that was looking to hire. Of course he saw through me. He knew me. He was New York, after all, and his streets had been whispering about me for months. We just hadn't got acquainted.

He took me for a drink and a meal. I was 18, Tony, don't hate me, please don't hate me. I hate myself enough. I was cabbage-green off the plane at JFK, a Santa Barbara girl who didn't know where she was going. Yes, I guess I finally met New York that night. He wanted to show me a club and even though it was restricted, he could get me in. He knew people. Of course he did, he knew everyone and everyone knew him. I was tired though. I'd been up since 5 am, cleaning the hotel kitchen, getting my stuff together for the rooms, the linen, the towels, the *everything* that just doesn't stop. Hotels are never clean.

So I was tired and he wanted me to dance, but I couldn't, I was dead on my feet. This guy, he called himself Frank, but I think I knew his real name, even then. His real name was New York.

Frank got a little mean in the eye and said, "I got something to help you dance." He gave me this powder, said it was OK, everyone at the club was using it and look, weren't they having a good time? They did look like they were having a good time, that was true, but they were just acting. Their eyes were wild, they were jerking, slipping, laughing and I saw they weren't having a good time, they were dancing to get away from themselves. Their minds weren't there, just their bodies. But Tony, <u>please</u> don't hate me, I took the powder and I danced, too.

That powder was speed. Do you know it? Somehow I don't think so. I hope not. Frank – New York – welcomes *allllll* the new people with speed eventually. The drug's like the Brooklyn Bridge, it gets you into the city, fast, so you can try what else is on offer.

Speed is like sniffing harsh white light. Your nose burns, then your brain burns and suddenly, the world is white hot. White heat, white light, all around you, inside you. You feel your heart skipping and jumping and you reach for your chest because it feels like that poor heart of yours is going to fly out and start dancing all by itself. So you try to dance for your heart, to do what it wants, to try and keep up with its beats. Your head is pounding but everything about you is suddenly fine tuned, ready to go, vroom, vroom, vroom. You've got this screeching, metal machine music inside you. You're racing full throttle down this dirty boulevard and the lights are so bright in your eyes, but it's not exhilarating, it's a muddy, demeaning feeling.

So I danced and that night the city finally owned me. Once the speed came, the bridge was open and there were other powders and pills. They all came my way. Don't hate me, Tony. I was already damaged before I fell to New York.

That's how it works.

Those kinds of people, the Franks, the Jim-Jims, the New Yorks, they make you think you're special because you're given this gift, joined the gang, you know the code words, you're hip, but you're not. You're just another customer, or worse, an employee. Or even worse, both.

Here's the thing. I became an *employee* to afford to become a *customer*.

I know that doesn't make any sense. I'm trying to educate you, Tony, to let you know how things happen around here.

OK, imagine this. You go to the pizza place, you know the one downtown, on Anacapa Street? If it's still there, ha. Now imagine that's the <u>only</u> place you can get pizza. You're hungry, but you're broke, so they give you a free slice. The next day, you're hungry again, and that slice tasted so good, right? But you're still broke. So they make you a deal – you work for them, you get to eat. You get paid in pizza, 'cos you need it. Then they start making you work longer hours and dirtier jobs, for the same slice of pizza. But by that point, you're so hungry, you'll do anything, you know – clean the john, unblock the pipes, whatever it takes to get that little slice of pizza every day, because you need it.

That's how it works around here. I guess that's how it works around every city where the Franks and the Jim-Jims walk.

So I took the pizza but I was still hungry and that's how it happens.

So what do I do now?

Oh, Tony, I do whatever Frank tells me to, so I can get my slice. Do you understand what I'm saying? Don't make me spell it out. I do whatever it takes now, because Frank makes sure I need it. He got me hungry for something I didn't even want and now I'm starving for it all the time.

Mike the Non-Doorman knows. Hey, everyone knows, this is Lexington. No angels fly here to come and save us. Just New York, eating everyone alive.

So I sit and wait for Frank – and that's another thing – you always wait. If Frank says he's coming for 7, don't expect him 'til 10, "hey baby, so sorry, got tied up you know how it is, busy, going to get your stuff, promise, got a friend here, hey, spend some time with my friend while I go and get your stuff, baby, yeah?"

So you're climbing the walls because you're hungry, you're ravenous, but first you have to meet Frank's friend because that's the deal and how it works.

Frank has lots of girlfriends all over town and we all work to be his customers.

We work *for* him to buy *from* him. How about that? You want a vicious circle? This is as vicious as it gets.

I want to leave, but I can't, because Frank's made it clear that once you're his girlfriend, you stay his girlfriend. And I don't know where else I can get fed. If I go just a day without it I'm hollow again and it's a hunger you can't imagine. So I sit here on this bed, next to this table and broken window. I've gone from one trap to another and I don't know how to get out.

Don't hate me, Tony.

6/ Do you have a boyfriend!?

*

I had to leave writing this letter for a while.

"Work" to do for Frank. I don't know if it was writing to you that did it, maybe I got bold, maybe it was just seeing my dumb life all laid out on paper, but I was stupid. I got brave, I got "smart" with him. Frank thinks anyone who stands up to him is "smart". I knew he was coming, see? He said he'd be here for 6 so of course, he didn't turn up 'til 8.

It's 10 now.

I've had my stuff, ha, I've had my *slice*, so forgive me if I lose the thread. It's OK, though,

I'm used to it

now. All it does is make me

feel normal That's all.

can't focus on the page.

its OK

It just wraps me up and makes everything

else just GO AWAY go
away. go. Away. Nice. It feels nice and warm.
its OK its always OK
do you know what Frank's other girls call me? When I was little I
wanted to be "Caroline the Bird Girl," but now
I'm just *"Alaska."*
how do you like that? I finally
got my nickname. and
it's "Alaska."
I don't
know who thought of it first
Jane, maybe, she's "smart." Jane's got a smart mouth alright.
Sweet Jane's one of Frank's favorite girls and she's always asking
what I'm thinking about. She's always hungry too – Frank feeds all of
us.

My head's everywhere. My pen is everywhere. The stuff does that.
I have to concentrate it's very important I concentrate Concentrate
Caroline.

OK. I've got some control back. That's good. Control's in short
supply here, too.

I think Jane's fascinated with my mind. "Hey Alaska," she'll say as
she walks in looking around my "apartment" to see if there's anything
she can steal and there isn't. "Hey Alaska, what's in your head today?"

She looks at me like I'm some zoo exhibit even though she doesn't
realize she's one too. It's like the bears laughing at the penguins and
not realizing they're also behind bars.

I don't know why she asks about my mind. Maybe because there's
nothing in <u>her</u> mind and she needs to fill it. But yes, that's who I am
now. "Alaska."

I guess they call me that because I don't seem to care.

I'm just frozen out. That's OK, I like freezing myself out. I'm a
glacier. I just sit here, I'm ice, and nothing can touch me. If Jane came
up with the name "Alaska" it may be the smartest idea she ever had.

But so, yes. Couple hours ago Frank shows up and as usual, he's got a friend coming and doesn't have what I need. So maybe it was writing this letter made me brave, made me remember who I was, God help me, I stood up to him.

"Where's my stuff?" I screamed in his face. "You always make me wait, I always wait, why do I have to wait?" Right into his face, over and over, like I was vomiting up all this rage.

Then he hit me, again.

He never used to get really violent, but a couple months ago Frank got talking to some random guy in a bar. This guy really fired Frank up, said he needed to <u>beat</u> some manners into his girls otherwise we wouldn't respect him. That's what the world is like.

Random guys in random bars, spreading their shit.

So Frank started taking random guy's poisonous advice and enjoying it, as if he needed to get any more cruel.

I fell, of course. But it didn't hurt 'cos none of it hurts any more and hasn't for a long time, not even since before I left Santa Barbara. I just lay on that dirty floor, looked up at him and laughed, because I wasn't afraid.

He could do whatever he wanted, and it wouldn't ever matter again because I am Alaska and I am so cold and I am not afraid.

When you can stare fear down and it looks away, you know you are invincible, Tony.

I didn't know how to stare down fear in Santa Barbara and didn't know how to when I first met New York. NY stared me out every time and I always looked away. But not any more.

Frank could see that power in my eyes and for the very first time, he looked away. But I know he'll be back and he'll win. While I'm hungry and he has the food I need, he'll always win.

But for that moment, I had him, and it felt good.

"Go on, hit me again," I yelled. "Hit me as much as you want, if that helps. I'm not your girlfriend, I don't love you. I know what I am, but you don't even know what you are."

Then I turned my face up to him, because I didn't care.

He walked out without saying another word. But he'll be back. Frank doesn't like it when anyone gets "smart." I'll pay for it. Frank always makes you wait and he always makes you pay.

So now I wait for the door to be hammered again and I'll know it's Frank, back to teach me a lesson. Quite the teacher, Frank, always with another class.

*

7/ Why did you go?

I lay on my shitty bed for a while. I've got my head back. Not completely, but enough.

Why did I go, you ask.

Well, that's the million dollar question, isn't it? Why did I just up and leave in the night, with my one-way ticket, just running for Municipal to LAX, to New York, to this room, waiting for Frank to come back? What was so bad that I traded *that* for *this*?

Do you remember my Dad, Tony? I don't think you do, not really. He left when I was nine and since you hardly ever came to my house, I don't know when you could have met. My Dad was a good guy, but he had no willpower, no strength. Whatever Mom said, he did.

You definitely don't remember Todd, my little brother. He died when I was seven and he was just three. I never mentioned him, none of us did. It was forbidden. Todd was of no use, so became nonexistent.

My little brother fell down the stairs into our basement. He'd opened a door which was supposed to be locked and stepped out, 'cos he forgot there were concrete stairs waiting there and he bashed his poor little brains out.

Well, that was the "official" story. That was what weeping Mom told the police. She is a great actress.

Did Todd fall? I don't know that either. But I <u>do</u> know that he infuriated Mom with crying, questions and mess. He hadn't learned to keep away, like I had. I tried to teach him, but he was only tiny and as soon as I cleaned up after him, he made everything messy again. Mom hated that. So one day he fell down the stairs, died and Mom didn't cry once. Oh, she cried in company but never alone in the house. Take that as you want.

Like me, Dad left in the night. One night I went to bed and he kissed me goodnight. The next morning he was gone, like he'd never been there. Every photo of him had disappeared, too. All his clothes in the closet, vanished. Shoes under the stairs, missing. He became nonexistent too. It's easy.

Did Mom know he was leaving? Or did she throw him out and then remove all trace of him from our lives, overnight, like a reverse Santa Claus, taking stuff away rather than leaving it behind? I never asked. I never asked anything, Tony.

Whether she knew he was leaving or not (and I don't think she did) by the morning, he was gone. Not even history. He drank, he gambled, he did anything, it seemed, to be out of the house. Why did he marry Mom? I often wonder that. Maybe, like Frank and his "girlfriends," Mom sucked him in and, before he realized, he was trapped. I don't know. Love is blind, they say, and Dad was so blind to everything.

Mom was – and is – capable of anything.

Frank's easy to read. Frank just has his stuff and his "Man," a roll of money, his girls and that's all he is. But Mom…You didn't know what you'd get from one moment to the next. Like I said, Tony, never trust her. Not a word, not a deed that Mom says or does is true.

So Dad was gone, which meant the little money he did bring in was kaputt, too. That's when things got really bad. Dad was useless, but he was kind. While he was here, he sometimes took the edge off Mom, just enough. But after he evaporated that night, there was nothing to stop her.

Before Frank, there was Mom. I just went in one big circle, from one shitty place to another. I know that now.

They say you're always drawn to what you know. Maybe I was, maybe I wasn't. Maybe I went to Frank because I'd been with Mom, maybe not. Maybe things just happen and there is no great plan behind it.

You see, Tony, Mom had *"friends,"* too. She let them stay, they'd drink and I was scared because she didn't care. Some stayed with Mom, others found different ways to spend the night. I'm not going to spell it out again. You know what I'm saying.

Why didn't I speak up? Because you don't, Tony. You just *don't*.

You're scared, alone, ashamed, because you think it's your fault, that you made it happen somehow, so you stay quiet, sit in the corner and wait for the next time. Remember, you try to look fear in the eye, but fear stares you down every time. Fear is power. You think no-one will believe you, that you deserved it. You think that this is how all families work. You know it's not right, but Mom let it happen and your parents are your *world* and what they say goes, so it must be normal.

You find all kinds of reasons to explain what's happening but mainly, you're so frightened. Then they come back. They always come back.

So Dad left and, as soon as I was 18, I waited until one night when Mom had medicated herself with vodka, then took all the money she had – she had a roll, too, stuffed in her underwear drawer. I knew she wouldn't call the police, because if one solitary cop took me in, she knew I'd name names, talk and talk and talk until every single *party person* was taken in, too.

But New York wasn't freedom, Tony. That's why I wrote. I wanted you to know, and if not you, anyone. I would have written this letter even if you hadn't replied and just, I don't know, given it to the nearest stranger who looked kind. But I'm so glad it's you that's reading this.

I punched a hole in my window pane a few days ago. That's why it's broken. I punched a hole and the feeling was so…funny. Yes, that's it. The pain came later, but at first, I just laughed, because I knew if I could do that, I could do anything. I wasn't afraid of the pain or what would happen after. That was the first time I'd dared stare at Fear and it blinked. Just one blink, mind, but Fear blinked. I felt the power of that, and it was a funny feeling. Having power.

I am Alaska.

I am Alaska and I'm not afraid any more.

Frank will be back soon enough, so I'm going to mail this letter.

I wish you all the best, Tony, with your life.

Once I've mailed this, I'm going to take the fire escape up to the roof. It's flat up there, and there's a little wall around the edge. Only one brick wide.

I'm going to scramble up onto the wall, and I know I'll be scared, but I'm going to stare Fear down.

I'm going to take a deep breath and just step out onto my brick tightrope and, you know, Tony, I'll hear the audience, far below in the circus, calling my name.

I'll pretend to wave at them, and at you, way, way down there. You'll be doing pratfalls and rolls in your clown costume. You'll be looking up at me, smiling, rolling and tumbling. Then I'll fly.

I love you, Tony.

SIDE ONE; RUN OUT GROOVE

An off-their-face singer and a paradise lost...which song?

Needle…*up*.

SIDE TWO

The Carpenters, Jimi Hendrix, Ed Sheeran, David Bowie.

The world's most effective epitaph is, "well, that *just happened."*

Needle...*down.*
Crackle.
Crackle.
Crackle.

"CALLING OCCUPANTS OF INTERPLANETARY CRAFT"

(By Klaatu, 1976 from the album, 3:47 EST. Covered by The Carpenters, 1977, from the album, Passage)

Somewhere in extremely *deep space, sometime in what is laughingly perceived as "The Future."*

Gff, newly elected Supreme Miasma of the Confederation of the Majestic 12 Interplanetary Overwatch Systems, was furious. He was also ravenous, but mainly, he was furious.

He sat at a news screen and watched the galaxy's reaction to his recent victory. It was fair to say not everyone was entirely happy about it.

Gff should have been overjoyed. After all, he'd just been made Leader of the entire Universe, which surely was cause for celebration, but already whingers and moaners had started to bleat, attacking him and his policies. Many said he didn't have any.

He angrily tapped one of his tentacles on the famous desk of the Dodecahedronal Office and mentally made a note of everyone on screen who'd been critical. Oooh, he'd make them all pay. Gff took every slight, real or imagined, extremely personally.

During his leadership campaign he'd promised to "Make The Whole Entire Total Universe Really Great Again", but hadn't actually known what that meant.

It sounded good, looked great on the banners and hats (MTWETURGA was *such* a good acronym) and meant he could point a tentacle in the air then do his trademark circular motion that said, *hey, that's right; Make The Whole Entire Universe Really Great Again, huh? Huh? I really mean business, you guys,* but what did that business really mean?

Perhaps the critics had a point.

Yes, he'd promised more jobs and fewer species from other stellar systems coming in (he'd even mooted a Hyper Wall around the entire galaxy, extending out into the eighteen known dimensions, but knew damn well that would never happen), he'd stood in front of the flag of the Majestic Twelve and vowed to cut taxes, but underneath the bluster, he didn't have any actual, thought-out, workable policies.

Gff had risen from a well-known business leader to a well-known but divisive System Leader in just a few short par-months and the whole thing had started as a bit of a joke.

He'd mentioned it one night while out with a few friends and buds of his family. Gff was a Temeron, which meant he could reproduce alone, so had budded a family of fourteen.

He enjoyed the process of budding and performed the initial stages a lot, in private, whilst watching his favourite Temeron porn channel, but every time, the offspring turned out to be disappointing versions of his own greatness. They hovered about him, asked for money, made stupid suggestions and tried to bask in his brilliant light. Of course he'd given them all jobs in his business empire, but generally they screwed things up and he constantly made excuses for them.

So this one evening, 8.7 par-months before, Gff had been out on a proper old drunken tentacle-waving night with friends and family, when he'd suddenly said, "Guys, guys, shut up. Listen. Does anyone know what I'd be brilliant at?"

One of his buds – he couldn't remember which, they all looked disappointingly similar and none were nearly as handsome as him – had said, "Ooh, father, you're good at everything!" which was true of course, but typical of the obsequiousness he'd come to expect.

"Yes, yes, I am," he'd agreed. "But do you know what I'd be really good at?"

Everyone had fallen silent. They literally had no opinions of their own, so had looked at each other shiftily and waited for someone to speak up. Naturally, none of them had.

"Anyone? Does anyone round this table know what I'd be extremely brilliant at?"

"Painting?" offered a colleague.

Gff hadn't thought of that. "Yes," he'd mused. "I suppose I would be good at painting. As you know, my great grand-bud was an excellent painter, so it follows that I would be one, too, but no, that's not the answer I was after."

Once one of them had an opinion, it was permission for all to follow suit. "Ooh, ooh, I know, you'd be great at dancing!?" "Eating stuff?" "Pretending to wave, but not actually waving?" "Being a genius? But a modest one? "Green? No, red?" on and on and on. Gff had silently fumed and wished them all dead.

"Shut up, again," he'd sighed. "I would be excellent in the role of Supreme Miasma of the Confederation of the Majestic Twelve Interplanetary Overwatch Systems."

Then he'd sat back with a smug grin on both of his mouths.

For a moment, no-one had spoken, but then, once their tiny brains had processed the concept, they'd all raised their bowls and agreed that yes, that was a brilliant idea, but then again, he was full of amazing plans, so it was hardly likely he'd suddenly go insane and have a rubbish one *now*.

Gff had let them all froth about this potential new business manoeuvre. Because at first, that's all it had been – business. Gff thought running for the top job would raise his profile and attract new investors, but never believed he'd actually win.

That would have been deranged.

Gff's chequered history was full of embarrassing mis-steps and outright disasters. He'd lost his fortune six times already. One of his excommunicated buds had released a kiss-and-tell memoir that detailed his rather *outré* bedroom techniques. Footage had emerged of him making off-colour jokes about another species, the Thargs of

Quaxxann, whom he described as "loving a quick feel of the mohawk, they gag for it, all of them."

With so much against him, there was no way Gff could ever become Supreme Miasma of the Confederation of the Majestic Twelve Interplanetary Overwatch Systems, but…it might be fun to run. The election would only take a few nano-months, then he could get back to making lots of money.

Gff had looked around the table and thought, not for the first time, "Do these people only hang around with me because I am rich, popular and handsome? Do they really like me?"

But he didn't harbour those thoughts for long. He wasn't the kind of Temeron to be plagued by feelings of doubt. Gff was made of self-belief. He genuinely believed himself the smartest creature in any room.

The leadership campaign had been tough. News anchors and satirists treated him like some kind of sideshow to the real politics going on, a comedy interlude while the actual candidates made their proper speeches and unveiled their *real* policies.

But slowly, something odd started to happen. He kept winning the primary elections. The analysts had dismissed these little victories as "blips", decrying the planets that had voted for Gff as "backwaters" and "deplorables". But his undemanding messages began to get through.

He realised that if you said SIMPLE THINGS LOUDLY, A LOT, you'd scoop up loads of voters who couldn't understand anything more complex than, JOBS! HOORAY! OUTSIDERS, BOO! MONEY, HOORAY!

During the campaign, he utilised all his business skills. If nothing else, he was a master salesman, so did what he'd always done, but writ large – he sold himself.

Slowly, Gff saw off the other candidates and no-one could quite believe it. Despite all the sniggering, he kept winning. Planet by planet came to Gff's side.

Of course, the liberal, intellectual, creative planets went no-where near him – they'd always looked down on Gff as nothing more than a cultural footnote, but with every victory, his grins became wider and smugger. He lived by the rule of "having the last laugh". Every night he'd go to bed and giggle at his enemies' shocked expressions. Gff wasn't running to win, he was doing it to get even with all the people who'd ever mocked, undermined or beaten him. Whatever may happen, he'd proved he could take on the establishment at their own game and earn the support of decent, common, working inhabitants of the galaxy, the ones who really mattered.

Naturally, he hated the decent common, working inhabitants of the galaxy, despised the ground they walked on and considered them all freeloading scum.

Why should he work for them? He'd never once held any office or stood up for anyone but himself. The common people were only there to put money in his wallet.

But he was also a great actor. At the rallies, he'd told the crowds he was just like them, an ordinary working guy who wanted to drain the gravitational swamp and get things done. And they'd actually believed it! In his private moments, Gff couldn't quite get his head round how stupid they were.

He was nothing like the people. He was a tetra-billionaire, had his own fleet of luxury Hyper Transporters, mixed with the rich, famous and beautiful, owned homes in the most exclusive parts of the System... He was light years from the sludge that made up most of the population, who'd stunk out his rallies as they screeched and dribbled his name.

However, along with fooling others, Gff was highly skilled in the art of self-delusion.

He began to believe he was a real statesman, a genuine politician. What had started as a joke became deadly serious. Somehow, he'd persuaded both himself and the electorate that he could be a great leader, the *bestest ever*. Gff only dealt in superlatives. If he were to become Supreme Miasma of the Confederation of the Majestic Twelve

Interplanetary Overwatch Systems, then he would be the *greatest, most amazing big-win* Supreme Miasma of the Confederation of the Majestic Twelve Interplanetary Overwatch Systems.

Then, what the holy *fack*?

He won.

When the results came in, the campaign staff had acted like they'd suffered a massive defeat. People had sat around, ashen faced. Despite his own exuberant self-confidence, deep down, even Gff never thought it would really happen. But it had.

By a slim margin, that mud-thick electorate had only gone and done it. They'd actually put their X's next to his name and now he had to actually do this dumb job. It was so unfair. He had Zero Gravity Golf games to play, parties to attend, bullying his subordinates to get on with. But now, because of those idiotic voters, he had to spend the next four neb-years as the Supreme Miasma, which would take up valuable time he could use to do nothing.

Despite his fury, for the first few weeks Gff really threw himself into this new role. He supposed it was mildly interesting at first, but not what he expected.

Once Supreme Miasma, he'd expected to click his tentacles and get whatever he wanted. Gff assumed he'd suddenly be treated with respect, even awe, but that hadn't happened. Joke shops had started selling stupid masks of his face and impressionists mocked him with endless unfunny, *sad* sketches he still couldn't stop himself watching on MeTube.

Gff was eaten up by the knowledge he had no real power and received very little respect.

Surely there was something only he could do? Perhaps one decision that only the Supreme Miasma could take, without having to answer to anyone?

As he tapped his tentacle on the desk, he muttered, "I really facking hate my job."

At that moment, his secretary popped one of her heads round the door. Gff employed her because she was pretty, dim and wouldn't sue him every time he took an opportunist feel.

"Ooh, ooh, there are a lot of people outside to see you," she sashayed over to his desk and bent low, which meant he could see straight down her blouse at six wonderful breasts, six of the seven reasons he'd hired her. "I've put all their names down on this piece of paper, so you can see them and read them. They are these names, here," she pointed at a list. "I've written them down, you see, so you can read them. Those are the names, oh yeah, uh-huh."

God, she is terminally stupid, he thought. *I imagine she probably voted for me, she's that dumb. But would you just look at the possibilities? Swings and roundabouts, Gff, swings and roundabouts.*

"It's these names, here," she went on, but Gff had tuned her out. "Starting here, and going down to here. These are the names."

Gff scanned the note. He liked his reports to take up one side of paper, as anything longer lost his attention. But this *was* interesting. Out of nowhere, unannounced, five rather important people waited in the ante room. That wasn't how things worked. Visitors didn't just turn up uninvited and then demand an audience with the Boss.

I could have been very busy, he mused. *I could have been in the middle of something. I'm not, obviously, but I* could *have been.*

He looked at the list of names as his secretary prattled on. On it were two five-star generals, the head of the Universe's entire Science Division, the Chief of Staff and finally, someone he'd never heard of called Vaag, who was the boss of an office called "Above Intelligence".

Gff had never heard of Vaag, or "Above Intelligence". As Leader, he was slightly affronted by that. How could there be an entire department he didn't know about? He made a mental note to fire someone. He loved to randomly point at people and shout "you're fired", since unplanned sackings kept the whole place on its toes.

"Please stop putting random words together, Kelly," he interrupted his secretary's stream of consciousness. "What do they want?"

"I dunno," she shrugged. "I just wrote their names down on this piece of paper, here, see? They said they were here to see you and I just, you know, assumed you knew about it. But they weren't in the diary. It has your appointments in it. So I looked and would you know? Would you just *know*? Huh? There was no mention of their names in it! That's funny isn't it? So…"

Her voice became a noise again and Gff made no effort to hide the fact he was staring at her busy chest.

"Aah. Nice. Well done. Send them in."

"Righty ho, Big G."

She click-clacked back out of the door. Gff watched her arse and wondered if that alone made her presence worthwhile. He concluded it did. That backside was, after all, the seventh reason she'd got the job.

Five people trooped in.

Gff recognised four of them, so by a process of elimination, the fellow who led the party must be the mysterious Vaag of "Above Intelligence".

Vaag was a Quadra-Terran which meant, hilariously, he only had two legs, two arms and one head.

The Quadra-Terrans were the System's joke species. Spectacularly un-evolved, they were a very basic form of life. Gff supposed it was a bit racist to smear an entire species as stupid just by virtue of their genetic makeup, but they did look *so* funny.

However, Vaag didn't have the scared, snivelling, please-love-me expression most gave when they entered this hallowed ground. In fact, he looked somewhat disdainful.

He didn't vote for me, Gff thought, with absolute certainty. *No, he thinks I'm an idiot. I can always tell. I'm the smartest person in the room. I'm a genius actually. A modest one, but still… I can see straight through you, Vaag, whoever you are. I'm in charge here.*

One of the generals saluted. "Oh, Supreme Miasma of the Confederation of the Majestic Twelve Interplanetary Overwatch Systems…"

Gff held up a tentacle. "Whoah, listen, can we just drop that?"

The general stopped, shocked.

"It's so…" Gff searched for the right description. "It's so science-fiction-y. It's like something from the movies. *Supreme Miasma of the Confederation of the Majestic Twelve Interplanetary Overwatch Systems*. Urgh. Why does it have to be so long? It's like that everywhere round here. All stupid, *sad*, way-too-long names for everything. "His Uber Eminence, the Veiled Guardian of the Ultra Tectones", "The Gilded Emissary of Light and All Urns Of Darkness", "The Crimson King", "Zinc Alloy and the Hidden Riders Of Tomorrow", "The Throne Of Topographic Oceans". It makes my head hurt. How did that happen? Who decided we should sound like we're from some stupid sci-fi story? So here's the thing. I'm in charge, I make the rules." He knew that wasn't actually the case, but pushed on, anyway. "From now on, just call me…Sir. Yes, that'll do. Or Mr Miasma. That's fine, too. It'll save us all a lot of time. Once you've said my entire title, entire solar systems have died. It's that long."

The general looked to his colleagues for support, but everyone stared straight ahead, apart from this Vaag chap, who looked about the room, uninterested. His attitude was really winding Gff up now.

"*Mr Miasma?*" asked the general. "But…that's overturning *millennia* of tradition. *Supreme Miasma of the Confederation of the Majestic Twelve Interplanetary Overwatch Systems*. That's your title, the way it's always been, right back to Pres-Lee, hail him, First Miasma of the Planetary Confederation and League of Systems All Praise His Name."

Four of the party shouted, "Pres-Lee! All praise his name!" Gff rolled his eyes. As far as he was concerned, there was no-one else to be praised around here. He hated anyone else being celebrated, even if they were dead.

"Yes, whoo-hoo, Pres-Lee, all praise his name, uh-huh," Gff said, monotone. "But from now on, guys, call me Mr Miasma, or Sir. It's modern. It's modern presidential. Ordinary people don't have any truck with fancy names. I'm an ordinary person, too. Why should I be treated as some kind of god, just because I sit at this universally important desk?"

"Very well, then, *Sir*," said Vaag, who ladled sarcasm all over the word. "We shall call you Sir, or Mr Miasma, or Jumping Jack Flash Gordon or the laughing facking gnome, whatever you require, if we can just get on."

Gff gave Vaag his very best hard stare, which had reduced many to quivering wrecks, but Vaag stared back, unafraid.

"You do know I'm the boss round here? I demand respect. How dare you speak to me like that?"

Vaag raised one of his side-splitting "eyebrows" at Gff, who tried not to giggle. *A stupid line of hair over each eye? Really?*

Vaag went on, un-moved. "I apologise. But you are just an… incumbent. Soon enough, another dotard will be sitting in that chair and they can call themselves whatever they want, too. Your position is transitory. We, however…" He swept his hand about the other members of his party. "We go on. Our roles continue, no matter who gives the supposed orders. We answer to ourselves. We can't have…" Now he gestured at Gff with a little, contemptuous flick of the hand. "…caretakers getting in the way. Do you honestly think you run the Universe? Seriously?"

Gff finally stood and pointed a quivering, furious, tentacle at the door.

"I don't know what this is, or who you are, but there's the exit. I suggest, no I order, that you take it and leave."

Neither Vaag nor the others moved.

"And who is going to make us?" he asked. "You? You're a big man, but you're out of shape. Your security? Noooo. You have zero experience in office. You've never represented a single member of any system except yourself. You played a clever game, by which I mean a stupid game. You appealed to the basest instincts of the basest voters because you knew there were a lot of them. Stupidity, alas, is the defining force in this universe, as you will come to realise. So do you really think we would allow someone like *you* to have any real power?"

Gff could not believe what he was hearing and picked up his telereceiver. "Secretary! Get the Guard in here, now!"

She replied, tinny in his ear. "Who is it? Is that you? It's me, Kelly. Oh, it's you. Hi. The gentlemen said you'd do that, so they stood the Guard down. They had a piece of paper with a crest on it or something. Anyway, they stood the Guard down. La-de-dah, I've got to go and get some lunch, I'm having soup, I think…"

"Oh shut up." Spectacular body or not, Gff decided he was going to sack her.

"Are we done?" Vaag asked. "Yes, we stood down the Guard, because we can. So please listen, 'Sir', as Leader, you now have to be made aware of certain secrets."

"Secrets?" asked Gff, interested. He liked secrets, they gave him power. He had boxes of secrets on his business and political rivals. Gff dampened down his fury for a moment. He would hear this Vaag out and then find some way to sack him.

"Go on. What are you saying? Why are you here?"

"I am head of Above Intelligence, a department you've never heard of."

"Ah, yes, I'm glad you mentioned that. Why haven't I heard of it? As Miasma, I should have been informed of all departments under my watch."

"You had no need to know of its existence," Vaag continued, calmly. "Sadly, now you do have a need to know, since, as you say, you're - ha - *in charge*. You see, as of this moment, you now have one particular power that nobody else in the universe wields. Every new incumbent of your chair is given this little talk and given this particular power."

"What power?" asked Gff, intrigued. This was more like it.

"In time." Vaag airily waved a hand. "You now have a great responsibility. We hand it to you and do so gratefully. We would not wish to have that power."

Gff rubbed his tentacles together with glee. A power no-one else wants? A responsibility nobody else has? This had turned into a brilliant day.

"Oooh, go on, tell me, what power?" He bounced in his chair like an excited toddler.

"Ah ah, no no, not yet. First, you have things to see. We are today representing a place known as... " Vaag paused and said the next words with great portent. "Area 62."

The group looked at Gff with anticipation.

Gff thought for a moment, then waved his tentacles in the air with a huge belly laugh.

"Oh. Now I get it!" He mimicked Vaag's dramatic delivery. "Area 62! Whhhooooo! Oh, very good. Whoah, fack you! Is this like some kind of initiation joke? Some prank?" He looked about the room and giggled. "Hidden cameras, is it? Do you do this to all the new Miasmas?"

But the group didn't laugh. They patiently waited for "Sir" to stop talking.

"Brilliant!" Gff tried to carry on, but was somewhat unsettled. "I was totally fooled. 'Standing the Guard down.' I should have known. No-one can stand the Guard down apart from me. Guard!" He shouted. "You can come in now, joke's over. Guard! Area 62, ha. Guard? Guard?"

The door remained shut. Gff trailed off.

"Yes, Area 62," said Vaag, seriously.

"But...Area 62," floundered Gff. "Area 62 is a myth, right? It's just a story. It's where you keep all the weird shit that doesn't exist, you know, out on some planet by the..." He tried to remember what he'd read in the trash mags. "...by the Tannhauser Gate? But it's just, you know, science fiction, right? Just for the movies and that."

Vaag shook his head. "Well, it suits everyone for people to believe it's just a bit of conspiracy theory nonsense, yes. We encourage it, actually. The whole area around the Tannhauser Gate, as you know, is dangerously radioactive from the T-Beams explosion back in '22.

Nothing can live there. Except…that explosion never happened. It was a lie, to keep people away. Area 62 is totally locked down. We surrounded it with a fake asteroid field and each rock has a gun emplacement. Nobody gets in who shouldn't be there."

"Area 62 actually exists?" Gff tried to keep up. "What's it for?"

"Well, that's the big question, isn't it? The question that keeps all the conspiracy nutters guessing. But none of them even come close. In part, it is, as you say, where we keep the *'weird shit that doesn't exist'* but it has a greater purpose than that. The greatest purpose in all the universe. And now, Mr Miasma, you have sole responsibility for that one, awesome purpose."

"What is it? What responsibility?"

"We have a CS80 Space Shifter waiting at Oberheim Base. Your diary has been cleared. You are coming to Area 62, to see for yourself, then handed your ultimate task."

"Oh come on," huffed Gff. "Stop being so dramatic. Just give me a clue at least."

"Well, Area 62 is funded by defence so I suppose ultimately, your great responsibility is all about, yes, why not, defence."

Vaag stood, and the others followed. "Mr Miasma, would you please accompany us? We have much to show you."

Gff did as he was asked. For the first time in this job, he actually felt important. He liked it.

*

An armoured Hover-Limo was waiting, accompanied by a phalanx of security guards. Gff loved the sheer theatre of the Supreme Miasma travelling, adored how there were people who would throw themselves in front of a particle beam to save his life. He found the whole operation strangely arousing and often had to sit with his tentacles crossed in case anyone saw he was in a state of some excitement.

The Guards, male and female, did look very sexy in their black uniforms, so Gff did his best to look sexy too and so snapped out little salutes. He'd never actually served in the military as his stiff posterior tentacles prevented him from marching for long periods of time. Well, that's what he'd paid the doctor to say.

Sure enough, a CS80 Space Shifter waited on the ground at Oberheim Base.

The CS80 was a fabulously expensive piece of kit. There were only six in the entire Universe and this one was all for him. That made Gff tumescently excited, too.

The CS80s were top-grade military vehicles, only ever used by Very, VERY Important Persons and now, Gff was definitely one of those. He tried not to laugh out loud.

More Guards waited on the steps leading up to the ship, so Gff saluted them, too. "You're doing a great job, the Universe thanks you," he said meaningfully to one, who looked a little confused, as he was only standing on some stairs.

Gff stepped through the hatch.

Female Squadron Auxiliaries fussed about him as he eyed up the many different lady-alien curves that filled their sky blue uniforms. They were all over the ship at various stations and Gff realised the entire crew were women, of all species.

"They're all girls," he whispered, delighted, to Vaag. "Why is that?"

"Because they look sooooo good," replied Vaag.

"Really?"

"No, of course not. Tests have proved female brains are so much better at picturing trans-dimensional space, which is helpful when flying a craft that flits in and out of dimensions like the CS80. You wouldn't want to end up with your head in one universe while your tentacles are in another time and space entirely. Males just can't operate in multi-frame networks. We're just too stupid, sadly. But women find it a breeze. Very impressive. Oh and they do look *soooo* good, too, if that helps, which for you, clearly, it does."

An imposing eight-foot-tall woman in a dark blue uniform came from the forward deck and saluted.

As she spoke, Gff stared at the tail which curled round her left leg.
He wondered what that fur would feel like wrapped around his
budding tentacle.

The woman followed his gaze, tutted loudly, then clicked her
fingers in his face.

"Oy. Wandering Eyes. Look at me. Welcome to the CS80, Supreme
Miasma of the Confederation of the Majestic Twelve Interplanetary
Overwatch Systems."

"That's me. But today, I've decided I prefer 'Sir' or 'Mr Miasma' if
it's alright with you."

"Fine by me, er, 'Sir'. The other shit's a bit long winded, isn't it?
I'm Group Captain Mazura, I'm in charge. I don't have time for the
full lecture, but are you familiar with the process?"

"Er, I assume it takes off, flies, goes very fast and lands?"

"No. None of that. This is a Space Shifter, It doesn't 'fly'
anywhere. It *can* fly, naturally, but generally, it doesn't. It shifts,
literally shifts space. The Dimension Generators on board, they, ah –
how can I describe it – they pinch and bend space about us. We don't
move anywhere, space moves to us. You're confused, I can see."

Gff hadn't realised he'd looked quite so blank.

She picked up a serviette from the table nearby. "I'll take it slowly.
Aright, this is our ship…" She placed a finger dead centre in the
serviette. "By the way, this isn't actually our ship. It's a serviette. And
we want to go here…" She placed another finger at one corner.
"Normally, we'd have to go in a straight line from there to there, but
not in a CS80. We just…" She pinched the edge of the serviette
toward its middle. "…bring the destination to us. Easy. Well, not easy,
actually. Shifting space is a delicate operation that involves the power
of sixteen different suns. But we channel that power using the same
system. We bring that power to the ship in a self-closing loop,
naturally."

"Aha, yes. Self-closing loop, yes, of course," nodded Gff, utterly
lost.

"Great to talk to a civilian who actually gets it," she smirked. "So, when we engage the generators, it'll feel like you've been pulled into your constituent atoms. Actually, it'll feel exactly like that, because you *will* be pulled into your constituent atoms. If I'm honest, it's not completely pleasant, but it's quick. You'll only be dead for less than a parti-second."

"OK. Phew. Good. Wait, what? Dead?"

"Well, yes. Since you're being pulled into your constituent atoms, that will involve dying. Basic biology, really. But then we're reassembled at the 'other end' if you like, so no harm done. Any questions?"

Gff wanted to say, "Are you free tonight for a drink?" as there was something devastatingly sexy about a cat-woman in uniform talking about his constituent atoms, but held his tongues.

"No, that all makes perfect sense."

"Really? Good. We engage in…" She looked at her watch. "Eighty pro-secs from…now. Enjoy the flight." She wiggled her whiskers at him and winked.

Another female operative walked past. She held a portal-screen and was ticking off important things.

"Oh, Gentlemen," she leaned over and drawled in a Southern Universe accent. "Don't y'all go forgetting the in-flight snacks and do be sure to familiarise y'self fully with the emergency instructions, won't you?"

She motioned to pouches fitted to their seats. Sure enough, each contained a laminated sheet.

"Excuse me." Gff waved a confused tentacle in the air. The operative turned back to him. "Er, Ma'am? This emergency sheet?"

"Mmm?" she replied, uninterested.

"Well, there don't seem to be any instructions for exits, safety drills, life belts, or…anything, for that matter. It just has pictures of people dying in…" He counted up the images. "…twelve different ways?"

"That's why they're laminated," she yawned.

Gff ploughed on. "They also seem to be dying in quite a lot of pain. For example, this person here…," he indicated one drawing in particular, "…is screaming and appears to have voided one of their bladders."

"Oh, aha." She raised one eyebrow, as if to say *yes and your point is what, exactly?*

"So, er, in the event of an emergency, what do we actually do?"

"*Do?*" she asked, confused. "Well, I'd have thought the sheet makes that perfectly clear. If there is an emergency, we'll all die, in one of those – yes – twelve ways, depending on our species. So the sheet is really rather helpful, you see? It gives you an idea what to expect so it's not too much of a shock when it does."

"Not too much of a shock?" Gff felt his bowels turn to water.

She smiled sweetly, leaned over and pointed at one of the drawings.

"OK, *Sir*, you're a Temeron, so your nearest equivalent species is this one, Picture Number Six. As you can see from this handy, fun cartoon, in an emergency, it's highly likely your eyes will be sucked backwards into your head at the speed of bullets, wiping out your brain. And the really fun bit is that you'll be able to see it happening."

"Fun bit?" whispered Gff.

"Then you'll die, quite painfully. On a Space Shifter there's literally no point in any safety measures. This technology is right out there, at the very limits. We don't really understand it ourselves, but we did lots of testing and yep, that's the twelve ways most species go tits up. Those with tits, naturally. Ha."

"Ha. Question. Is there another way to Area 62? One that's not quite so death-y?"

"Of course. You could take a standard Prophet Five Hyper Transporter."

"Well, I'd rather fly on that, if it's all the same."

"The only drawback with that method, Sir, is that it would take eighty thousand chromo-years, give or take, by which time you'd

definitely be dead. Anything else I can help you with?" she asked.
"Apart from death?"

"No thank you, Flight Lieutenant," smiled Vaag. "You've been a
great comfort."

"Well, one tries," she shrugged. "Have fun."

Gff watched her go and tried not to think of his own eyes
ricocheting around his brilliant brain.

"So, Vaag." He attempted not to appear terrified. "Now we're on
our way, can you tell me what this is all about? What my Big
Responsibility is?"

"Naaah," said Vaag, who tore open a bag of nuts and tipped them
all into his mouth. "It's easier to show you. Also, I get to watch your
expression change, which is always the really fun bit."

Group Captain Mazura's voice burst from the speakers.

"Okey dokey, crew, guests, listen up, this is your Captain
speaking," she purred. "Tower have given us Go across the board and
our superluminal contact matrix with Area 62 confirms we have a set-
to position of SH.A-M69 to ACDC, local time B52. I'm told the
weather at our set-to position is a balmy minus one hundred and
seventy eight, with a twenty five percent chance of some acid snow, so
do wrap up and wear some kind of hat on departure. Please ensure
your trays and seats are in the upright position. Engaging Dimension
Generators in ten Pro-secs. As I always like to say at this moment,
Ladies and Gentlemen, we're on an express elevator to hell."

Gff squeezed his eyes shut. Annoyingly, Vaag just giggled.

Gff expected Mazura to relish continuing the countdown, but the
speakers were silent.

That was worse.

At least if she'd given the classic ten to one launch routine he'd
could have squeezed his backside shut, but this was more like being
blindfolded and waiting for a firing squad to get busy.

Suddenly, the speaker crashed back into life and squealed with
feedback.

"Red! Red! RED!" shouted Group Captain Mazura. "RED ONE situation! Generators Hyper-Oscillating, repeat, Generators Hyper-Oscillating! I'm losing her. Power to main internal shields! I'm losing her, oh God, oh God, no, no, no, no! Mother, no!"

Gff screamed like a schoolgirl. His tentacles went up to his face and he wailed, unable to form words. He emitted a stream of gurgling, spluttering gulps and burps that surely sounded exactly what his backside was doing at the other end. Then, even in the depths of his extremity, Gff realised that's exactly what was happening down-doors.

"And that's what you *would* have heard had there been a genuine emergency," Mazura calmly added, and Gff could hear she was barely able to stop herself dissolving into hysterics. "But it's always good to be prepared, isn't it? Anyway, engaging Dimension Generators...n... n...n...now? No, *now*. No...NOW? *Now? Is* it now? No. Now! Just kidding. Now."

Afterwards, Gff couldn't quite remember exactly what the "flight" had been like. When your senses have no reference points, they simply process what they're given as best they can.

It happened faster than light, but seemed to take infinity.

As Mazura said the word *"now"*, pure white splashed over existence itself, washed out time and space, then melted everything it touched. The entire universe had become this molten, dripping, painful white. But then, that bleached new reality had been sucked down a giant galactic plughole. Gff had felt not only his body, but also his *mind* and *soul* twist and pour down that infinite hole. He'd looked at his tentacles and they'd become the size of the solar system. Gff had stared, astonished, as they writhed amongst planets and stars – he could have held the galaxy in his grasp. Then he exploded and felt his constituent parts fly to every corner of every time at once. Finally, before Gff could register that he was all and all was him and the secret of the universe was simply *be here now*, those parts rushed together again and he was back in his seat.

"Whoah, that was a rush, wasn't it?" whooped Vaag.

Gff threw up all over his suit. Vaag raised his eyes to the ceiling and pressed a comms button on his armrest.

"Anyone got some tissues?" he asked. "The Supreme Miasma's had a bit of an accident."

"It was something I ate," gurgled Gff.

"Yeah." Vaag wrinkled his face in disgust. "You ate the universe. Don't beat yourself up. Everyone pukes, the first time. After that, it becomes strangely addictive. Did you see God?"

"No," moaned Mr Miasma, sat in his own lunch. "I just saw myself explode and become everything."

"Mm, well zen," replied Vaag, sightly disappointed. "You had the basic ride, then. You wait till you see God. Well, no-one knows if it's actually God. It's just this bloke with massive sideburns, wearing a top hat with mirrors all over it. Really weird. Anyway, get yourself wiped up, we're here."

Another female operative had appeared from nowhere. She held a spare suit on a hanger.

"We took the liberty of assuming you'd blow your stomach," she was obviously trying not laugh. "There's a cupboard up front. You could go in there and change. Here are some wet wipes, too."

"Is *anyone* going to show me some respect?" Gff grumbled at Vaag.

"Not really. They've seen them come, they've seen them go. As I say, you're just the guy who happens to be wearing the 'I'm In Charge', badge today. Don't take it personally. Now, please, go and get changed. You look like a pavement at closing time."

*

Gff changed into a less-stinking suit, then gingerly emerged from the cupboard. He smiled knowingly at the Guards as if he'd just stepped in there to do some important Miasma things. No-one paid him the slightest bit of notice.

Group Captain Mazura waited at the hatch.

"I see you did the traditional CS80 burp." She looked down at his new suit. "Don't worry. Everyone does. I imagine you're going to feel much sicker when we go back."

"What?" he asked. "It gets worse?"

"No, no." She waved a paw and dismissed the question. "Nothing to do with the CS80. I mean after what you're going to have to do. Leaders usually feel really sick after that. Well, the ones with a conscience do. So you may be totally fine, on that score."

"Enough, Group Captain," warned Vaag from the hatchway. "Let the Supreme Miasma take things one step at a time. Sir? Welcome to Area 62."

Gff stepped through the hatchway and onto the steps he'd only just climbed minutes before. He gasped and had to steady himself against the hull of the CS80. Usually, when one travels, one has sensory proof of the journey. You see your starting destination recede, then clouds, landmasses, even planets pass by your window, all going in the opposite direction. Finally your destination approaches, tiny at first, then slowly bigger until it becomes your new position in time and space.

None of that had happened today. The CS80 had sat on one runway. Now it stood on another, except the sky was all purple and the previous buildings were gone. It was like a magician had waved his cloak over the whole area, then pulled it away to reveal totally different, crazy structures.

Soldiers, technicians and engineers were all over the craft. Other vehicles whizzed past in the sky and on the ground. Lights blinked, antenna whirled and the whole place seemed to be in frantic movement. At the foot of the steps, another Hover-Limo waited.

"Shall we?" asked Vaag, who gestured to the vehicle.

"Perhaps you can finally tell me what's happening once we're in the car," said Gff.

"No time. We're only going from here…to just over there." He indicated a building not two hundred yards away. "But in our experience, Supreme Misasmas don't like walking anywhere, so we dust off the old limo. Is that OK? Does it make you feel important enough?"

It did, but Gff was reluctant to say so.

"Yippedy dip, skip. Let's go."

Vaag held open the rear door of the Limo. Gff climbed in, but no-one else joined him.

"Aren't you…?" he asked as Vaag shut the door.

"Naah, we'll walk. It's, like, literally a few steps."

So, Gff sat like some kind of infirm auntie as the Hover-Limo slowly glided the full two hundred yards over to another door, while the rest of the party laughed alongside.

Thirty seconds later Vaag re-opened the door. "Nice trip? Not too exhausting?"

Gff scowled and got out.

"I.D.," barked an armed Guard.

Everyone produced identification cards, which were meticulously checked.

"You?" said the Guard, who waved an M41A pulse rifle at Gff.

"Me? You seriously don't…? This is outrageous! I'm Supreme Miasma!"

"I.D.," repeated the Guard.

"Oh come on," said Gff, who looked around the group for support. Everyone had found something incredibly interesting on the floor to examine. "It's me! You know, 'Make The Entire Universe Really Great Again'?" He performed his trademark circular tentacle wave. "It's me!" He pulled one of his pouting "Leader" faces. "Right. What's your name and number? I'm going to give you a court martial. What do you say to that?"

"I.D."

Vaag leaned into the Guard and whispered but clearly wasn't trying too hard, as everyone could hear exactly what he was saying.

"Look. I have security AA-AAA, this man is genuinely the Supreme Miasma. I *know!* I know it looks mad, but he is."

The Guard also whispered, loudly.

"Wait. Isn't he the guy off the TV? The stupid business guy?"

"Aha. I know, I know. What the *fack* and all that."

"I admit we're kept out of the loop here, but seriously, he's Supreme Miasma now? How did that happen?"

"We don't know. But hey-ho, it did, so we have to let him in on all the Area 62 stuff now."

"That is seriously screwed up. That guy's a total shit-for-brains," non-whispered the Guard.

"I can hear you," said Gff. "I'm right here. I'm, like, a foot away. You're not even trying to whisper."

"I am whispering," whispered the Guard, badly.

"OK, so it's all good," said Vaag, turning to Gff. "The Guard has agreed to give you ingress."

"That's not what he said. I heard. He said I had shit for brains."

"I didn't, I said, er, '*it* looks like *rain*'," replied the Guard. Gff tried to give him a furious stare as he passed, but the guy wore mirror shades and was sniggering, so the Supreme Miasma had to concede he probably wasn't that intimidated.

The party stepped into a hangar. It was huge, silent and almost empty, except for an odd cone-shaped object in the centre, illuminated by spotlights. Two Guards stood either side of this curious, silver item. A few plastic seats had been provided.

"Sit, sit," said Vaag. The party of six sat. Gff looked over at the little metal object that dominated the area. Something bothered him about it. Despite what he'd already seen today, this object had just taken first prize as the strangest.

"Right. To business. Quick history lesson. Oy, Miasma, oy, pay attention, over here," Vaag clicked his odd fingers together in Gff's face. "We'll come to that object in a bit. That is why you're here. OK, so as you've realised, Area 62 is no myth. At present there are over forty thousand people here, representing every system, every planet, every backwater mini-roid. We're very equal opportunities. Area 62 is the secret heart of the entire universe, where things really get done.

You can sit in your Dodecahedronal Office, believing you can wave a tentacle and things happen, but they don't, not really."

Gff waved a tentacle to interrupt. Vaag held up one of his hands.

"Shut up. So. If you remember your schooldays, you'll know originally the universe was just a bunch of unconnected planets, all thinking they were extremely important. Back in the dark ages, Instant Dimensional Communications hadn't been invented, so everyone thought they were alone. Slowly, though, as the Superluminal craft made contact, technology spread from the end of nowhere to the middle of absolutely nothing, so planets and civilisations got hooked up. There were some little bumps, of course. The First, Second and Third Intergalactic Wars, for example, in which seven hundred and sixty Quadpra-Tetra Google billions died – they were very unfortunate. But generally, all the different species realised there was money to be made. Once we all agreed on the Galactic Dollar Exchange Rate system, of course…"

"I do know all this," humphed Gff.

"Well, I can't assume that, can I? You're you, so anything's possible, like not knowing basic history."

"Well, I do. My Uncle went to Ha'vaaard University, which proves I'm clever."

At that, one general stared down at his shoes and made an odd sniffing sound.

"Is he OK?"

"He's fine. But the universe is massive. It's infinite. 'Infinite' means massive. So it took quite a while to invite everyone to join the Confederation and then get them all to agree with the idea of twelve Interplanetary Overwatch Systems. In other words, to bunch different groups up into, I suppose you'd call them galactic "continents", each with their own takes on laws, trading etc, etc. Occasionally, however, we'd discover another civilisation that wasn't so…amenable to joining up. In fact, once in a while, some of these civilisations could get a bit bullish about the whole idea. A bit fighty. So that's where Area 62 came in. General Geddy?"

One of the generals – the one not laughing – sat up straight and
began to shout as if he were addressing a parade ground.

"Area 62 began as a testing ground for Solar Bombs, that was all!
But slowly, we added more departments, more R&D! We had an entire
planet to play with, so there was plenty of room for everyone! We're
mainly in the business of defence but defence can become offence if
you add enough power! So here's where all our great military ideas
were developed. The CS80, the Great Fortress Encirclements, the
Target Fleet, Death Stars, Battlestars, Star Destroyers…actually, a lot
of ships with 'star' in their name, now I think about it…anyway,
they're all built and tested here, away from sight. Our job is to keep
everyone in the universe safe from any outside danger!"

"Outside danger?" asked Gff, more confused than ever. "Outside
the universe? But we know every planet, every species now. There's
nothing else!"

The Chief of Staff shook his head and chuckled as the general
bellowed on.

"Well, yes, that's what you're told! Everyone's told that from the
first day of school, that our universe is all there is! You're told we
know everything out there and we are all one happy, peaceful family!
Well, we are now, because we have the means to wipe out whole
systems, should we wish! So everyone gets on just fine!"

Vaag took over. "But that's not true. It's the official line that lets
everyone sleep tight and prevents chaos, panic and brown trousers.
Because, Mr Miasma, if people knew the truth, this whole thing…"
He waved his hands about the room. "…not the hangar, I mean
everything would descend into anarchy. Our cosy, all-together-now
universe is an illusion and Area 62 is the magician's cabinet. This
place protects every citizen of the Overwatch from the truth. That is its
real function. The weapons we develop are just a by-product. We keep
the truth here, Mr Miasma. We keep it, hold it, then surround it with
an asteroid field and gun emplacements, and of the quadra-padra quin-
zill-billions who make up this universe of ours, only forty thousand

people know what is really happening. Make that forty thousand and one, now you are here."

"So what is the truth?" asked Gff, totally lost.

"The truth is out there." Vaag pointed to the strange cone-shaped object in the middle of the hangar. "*That* is the truth. And it is unpalatable. Come."

Everyone walked over to the object. The two Guards stood to one side.

Gff raised a tentacle and looked over at Vaag, who nodded.

The Miasma gently touched the surface of this…thing. It was almost smooth, but many rivets protruded and held together a series of metal panels. This object wasn't much taller than himself, maybe around fifteen feet in height. It had been placed on top of a metal frame, so one could see underneath. Gff bent down to examine the underside, which looked like the bottom of a bowl, curved outward. But it wasn't perfect – a large crack zig-zagged from one side to another. Gff reached up and felt the crack, which was an inch or so deep. The tip of his tentacle disappeared inside. He stood again and walked around the object, as Vaag and the others watched him.

Gff realised this thing had two circular portals on either side and a hatchway between them. He peered through one of the windows, but couldn't make out what was inside.

"What is this? It looks…primitive, like a relic, or something?"

"Like a relic, yes," said Vaag, quietly. He turned a wheel on the hatch, which opened outward. Gff looked inside. There were dials, switches, pipes and wires above a bench which was only big enough for…something…around Vaag's size. There was a simple joystick to one side.

"Wait." Gff's brain tried to process the information. "Is this some kind of ship?"

Vaag slapped his thigh, then pointed at Mr Miasma. "Give the big man a prize from the top shelf! He's only got it, and quicker than we thought!"

Vaag held out his hand. One of the generals reluctantly pulled out a wallet and handed over a five dollar bill.

"General Hutter thought you wouldn't work it out for at least half an hour. I had a little more faith."

"You bet on how long I'd take?" roared Gff, dumbfounded.

"Well, got to have a bit of fun somehow round here," shrugged Vaag. "But yes, it's a ship. Primitive, as you say, in fact it barely qualifies as a ship, per se, it's more of a...pod. A capsule. Barely any propulsion, just these little jets round here..." He pointed at small cone-shaped thrusters around the circumference of the 'craft'. "...and they are definitely not superluminal. These little thrusters couldn't even get this thing into orbit around a very low-density planet, let alone into hyperspace. So we theorise it was once attached to a much bigger kind of propulsor. But even then, look at it. Totally thrown together. No computer, no dimension tracking, no shield generators, nothing. This machine is an equivalent of the knitted woollen rafts of the Sylvian tribes of Genexx. I'm amazed it even got to us in one piece, but yet, here it is."

"So where did it come from?"

"Well, that's the whole point, really. As I say, we tell everyone the entire universe has been mapped, but that's not true. In fact, that's the great big, nasty, smelly lie that keeps everyone calm. The truth is, we keep finding other species and not all of them are nice. Some, in fact, are bloody awful. Here in the Overwatch Systems, we've had our wars and their genocides. We're over that. It helps everyone to believe nastiness is all in the past, but as you can see, there *are* others out there we know virtually nothing about. And that, my dear Miasma, is a very scary thought. Which is why we need Area 62."

Gff had slithered around to the other side of the object. Painted on the side was a square image, made up of three colours, mixed together in various shapes; red lines and blue triangles with thinner white lines bordering them. "What's that?" he asked.

"The experts think it's possibly some kind of identification marking, to show others what kind of ship this is. Some believe it may be a flag called a 'Union Jack', but that's just a theory."

"And here? What are these markings?" Gff indicated three more odd shapes; **B**, **S** and **N**. They meant nothing to him.

"Hm, well, we'll come on to that. But don't get hung up on the details quite yet. It is this ship's existence that's our main worry, the fact it has come here from a place previously unknown to us. Remember, we tell everyone the universe has no further mysteries, but it does and those puzzles are here, at Area 62. Would you like to see what was inside?"

"Inside? But I've seen inside."

"What *was* inside. What once lay on that bench. Would you like to see what it was? That's rhetorical, by the way. You are going to see. Chop chop. Things to do, someone to meet."

The party of six walked toward another door on the far side of the hangar. Gff looked back over his shoulder at the silver object. He felt oddly scared.

*

Vaag opened another door which led into an airlock. There was a hissing sound and Gff felt air shift about him, accompanied by an unpleasant antiseptic smell.

"Just cleaning us up, so we don't contaminate our guest," said Vaag. "You see, that strange capsule has come from a very, very long way away. Like, go to the end of the universe, turn left, carry on for infinity, head to the second star, straight on 'til morning, carry on for another infinity and there you are. A system its inhabitants call Sol. We think that capsule, pod, ship, whatever, must have fallen into a mindem-strength wormhole, purely by accident. There are a few time-breach whorls on the outer surface, which suggest wormhole activity. There was simply no other way it could have got here in the timescale, not with those pathetic engines. No, it had help from Mother Nature. A journey that would have taken forever only took around seventy of *their* years. They measure a year by how long their planet takes to go round its sun."

"That's ridiculous," sniffed Gff.

"Well, we shall see. So yes, somehow, even before that little craft had left its home system, it ran into a wormhole, no bigger than itself. That zapped it right across the universe. The odds are literally astronomical, but it happened. It entered our zone two par-years ago and, since then, we've learned a lot about where it came from. Not all of it good. Actually, most of it very bad."

There was a clanking sound as the far door of the airlock opened.

"Come, come," said Vaag, who gestured for Gff to follow. "Don't be shy, don't be scared. Well, don't be scared *yet*. Come."

The group stepped into another room, much smaller and brightly lit, with every surface a blinding white. In the middle, flanked by yet more guards and scientists, was a white table. Something was lying there, but another light above bleached it out.

"That little capsule you just saw was occupied. It wasn't the first alien object we've picked up and it won't be the last. Every now and then we get an unpleasant reminder that We Are Not Alone and any evidence is brought here for study. Then, once we believe we know everything about the new species and their planet, we act. Or rather, you act."

"Act how?" Gff was reluctant to get nearer to the figure on the table. He'd seen and met many different species, of course, so wasn't squeamish about this one. But the fact it was so unknown gave him pause.

"Patience, Mr Miasma, patience."

The party of six reached the table and the people around it stepped to one side to let them through.

"Supreme Leader, meet D. Jones. D. Jones, meet the Supreme Leader," said Vaag, who did a stupid little theatrical flourish with his hands.

Gff looked down at the figure. It had white skin, made yet paler by the bright lights. In terms of its anatomy, it resembled Vaag. Two arms, two legs, one head. The creature had blonde hair, a little like Gff's own. Gff was very proud of his thatch. Most Temerons lost their hair by middle age, but Gff's was just as thick and lustrous as it had been when he was young. Yes, he had to comb it certain ways to disguise slightly thinner parts of his scalp, and yes, he had to use a lot of Spray-On Hair Glue to keep it from waving about in a light breeze, but he was pretty sure not one single person in the universe had noticed these little tricks of the trade. No, everyone admired his wonderful head of hair. He often saw people stare at it, mouths open, literally in awe. So they should.

Unconsciously, Gff reached up with one tentacle and smoothed his impressive mane. Whatever this creature was, it had an enviable collection of follicles. The blonde was much brighter than Gff's, so it had obviously been using a far superior colourant. He looked up and down the figure. Between its legs was some kind of fleshy tube, flanked by yet more blonde hair. Perhaps this was some kind of feeding pipe. He knew some species had something similar for reproduction, but theirs were much smaller. Maybe this one was for breathing. The figure's eyes were open and stared upward into the light. They were bright blue and Gff could swear they sparkled. It had but one mouth, which gave the impression of a little smile that played across those odd lips. It – whatever *it* was – gave off the feeling of peace, perhaps even quiet happiness.

Gff didn't know what to do next, so gave the creature a little wave with his tentacle. He liked waving. The thing did not respond.

"Hello," tried Gff. "I am Gff, er…" He thought he'd better do the whole bells-and-whistles introduction. "I am Supreme Miasma of the Confederation of the Majestic Twelve Interplanetary Overwatch Systems. Welcome to Area 62."

Rudely, the figure continued to stare upward. Gff was getting extremely annoyed with this. All day he'd been treated with zero respect and now even a totally alien life-form was in on the act.

"Well, that's charming," he said. "So you're just going to lie there, are you? Do you know who I am?"

"It's dead, you twonk," said Vaag. "Surely you can see that?"

He picked up one of the creature's hands and waved it at Gff.

"Hello, Mr Miasma, thanks for having me on your top-secret research planet. Couldn't get me a bathrobe or something, could you? I'm freezing my bits off, here."

"Oh. I thought it was just being ignorant." Gff pouted again.

"No, it's just being dead. Perfectly preserved in its little craft, no bio-organisms to break it down, just *D. JONES* and forever, spinning through space with a smile on its face."

"It looks like you. Is it a Quadra-Terran?"

"No. Pure biological coincidence. Internally it's totally different. But as design goes, the Quadra-Terran is probably the most adaptable configuration. I mean, I can pretty much deal with most planetary surfaces. I have opposable thumbs, like D. Jones here, so tool-making probably kicked in fairly quickly in his evolution. Stereoscopic sight, good for hunting. Yeah, we're similar, but not the same. I don't have one of those, for example..." He pointed at the peculiar fleshy hose between the thing's legs. "But we're pretty sure it's for reproduction. As you know, my reproductive organs are kept behind my ears, which is way more modest."

"How did it die?"

"Like most species, it's an oxygen breather, the most efficient use of available gases. Makes sense. But its pod, capsule, ship, *whatever*, didn't have enough, clearly. Why its species launched D. JONES out here without enough air is another mystery. We know a lot about them now, this species – they call themselves humans, by the way..."

"Hooomanz," repeated Gff.

"Humans," corrected Vaag. "It was wearing this when we found it."

Vaag walked over to a stand. Hung there was what appeared to be a very basic silver flight suit. Another one of those strange red, white and blue squares was fixed to the breast area and again, those symbols, B.S.N. Beneath those, more symbols, which read, *D. JONES.*

"We can read and understand their language now. Took a while. The Universal Translators were running night and day to crack the code, mainly because these 'humans' have so many different kinds of languages. Loads of them. It's a mess there, I tell you. They can't make up their minds what to do with verbs, for starters. They shove poor verbs all over the place. Do they go in the middle? Do they go at the end? Who knows. What about a simple word like, 'the'? Oh, you'd think 'the' would be easy, but no. Some of them make 'the' female or male depending on the object! Seriously."

"They do what?"

"I know. It's messed up. So we got through quite a lot of translators, I can tell you. They kept blowing up, because we didn't know the human language is the *opposite* of language. It divides them rather than unites. The machines got used to one set of rules, but then we'd unknowingly put in another language, like, 'French', it would totally confuse the machines and – bang, goodnight, another few million Universal Dollars up in smoke. But eventually we got the hang of it, separated out all the different tongues. Our dead alien friend here once spoke something called 'English'. The language of a country called England, and, to a lesser extent, a place called 'America', which we believe is what they call a 'Third World Country'. His name is D. JONES. He is the first and almost certainly last emissary of his home planet, which the humans call 'Earth'."

"Earth?" said Gff, still unable to take his eye off the creature. That odd smile transfixed him. Why would something that had died of oxygen starvation, millions of miles from home, be smiling? "They call it 'Earth'? As in soil? Mud? Grime, grit?"

"They weren't exactly aiming high, were they?" agreed Vaag. "We're pretty sure he wasn't sent here deliberately. He just pointed his ship out to space, fired his engines and smiled his way all the way here, dying *en route*. And that puts us in a quandary. Because now we have to deal with 'Earth'."

"We do?"

"Oh, we do. Well, you do. Come on, I have more to show you. D. JONES can wait. He can wait forever. From that smile, I think he probably found what he was looking for, but that certainly wasn't us. Come."

Gff allowed himself to be led away from that creature – an infinity away from his own kind – that lay cold and dead on a table, prodded and examined for eternity, smiling. There was something about D. JONES that made Gff slightly sad, which was odd, as Gff didn't do 'sad'. It was his enemies and detractors who were, 'sad'! Never him.

Vaag led the Supreme Miasma to another door, but stopped before he opened it.

"Sir, once we step into this room, we cannot leave again until you have made a decision. You are the only person in the entire universe who can make it. But you must decide. However long it takes, we will not walk back through this door until you have chosen, like so many of your predecessors. Do you understand?"

For the first time, Vaag actually looked respectful, maybe even slightly sad, too.

But sad for who? Gff wondered.

Vaag put his hand on the handle, an ordinary, anonymous handle on an ordinary, anonymous door. There were no security checks or signs here, simply an entrance leading to who-knew-what.

Vaag must have seen Gff pause. "Yes, it's just a door, Sir. But whatever happens, you will never forget it or the choice you must now make. Are you ready?"

Gff tried to look assured and strong, but his backside was threatening to revolt, again.

"I am," he said.

He wasn't.

"Then, Sir, may you have the strength to do what you have to do." Vaag turned the handle.

Gff didn't know what he was expecting. Some kind of colossal super-weapon. A giant alien. God, in a top hat made of mirrors.

Something, anything, that would deserve the dramatic build up he'd just been given.

But there were no gods, weapons or aliens, just six more ordinary chairs. They weren't on gravity-repulsing field generators. They didn't spin on gyrator ducts, have plasma cannon, or even a little handle that would make them go up and down. They were simply six coloured plastic chairs.

"Bags I have the red one," Gff pushed forward. The red one looked important.

"Help yourself," shrugged Vaag. The chairs were arranged in a rough semi-circle around a computer monitor. Again, nothing fancy, more like one a kid would use for homework. Vaag stood in front of the monitor and pushed a few keys. The screen flickered and came to life.

"Right. So, we find a capsule and inside, a dead alien, species and origin unknown. That always makes us twitchy, because if we have an unknown species with unknown origin, what does that mean? Are they friendly, or are they nutters? Can we do business with them, or will they come steaming our way, shooting first and asking questions afterwards? How advanced are they? In terms of these 'humans', all we had at first was a capsule and a body, and neither suggested they were a top-drawer, wow-lookee-here, blimey-that's-impressive species. But you never know. So we started extrapolating the craft's possible point of origin…"

Vaag pushed a few more keys and the screen lit up with a 4-D map of the known universe.

"The universe is pretty big, as we all know. If the ship had come through a wormhole – and all evidence points to that possibility – it gets bigger still because we could be dealing with multi-dimensional co-ordinates and they are an absolute bugger."

"Bloody dreadful," muttered a general.

"They are. But we cast our net wide and then, after many false starts, started picking up transmissions. Faint, weird, senseless – at first – but transmissions, none the less. Not stars or pulsars, doing their tricksy little radio greetings, but actual, intelligent – well, I *say* intelligent, ha – transmissions. Coming from way, way, over…here."

The screen expanded. Constellations and galaxies rushed past, distant dots became larger and larger until they and their attendant galaxies filled the picture, before all became lost in the infinite blackness of eternity. On and on, they wheeled, these blocks of the galaxy, the camera plunging and swooping through clouds, suns and nebulae. This journey was made of always and forever.

Vaag looked at his watch and yawned.

"Get on with it. Aha. Yes, Mr Miasma, they come from here, the system which these 'humans' call 'Sol'. It has eight planets – it was nine, but like their stupid languages, they can't make their minds up, so, for now, it's eight."

"Wait. You can't have nine planets one day and eight the next," said Gff.

"They can. Oh, believe me, this lot can. So at first we listened and broke our translators trying to make sense of this…babble…of noise. And then we heard this."

Vaag hit another key and a crazed voice filled the room, talking about 'playlists' and 'requests'.

"We've translated it from the original English, so it's probably not what the composers intended, but we think it's close enough," shouted Vaag over the noise. Then the strange voices faded and sweet, stately music began.

"Music?" Gff was dumbfounded. "These humans have discovered music?"

"Aha. Can't be all bad, then, right?" Van paused the recording.

"This is a song by a human duo called 'The Carpenters'. Bit of background. 'Carpenters' are those who work with wood on earth. Creators, not destroyers. Well, they cut the trees down, but then they turn them into something else. But here's the thing; these 'humans' have lots of deity myths. They love them, their deities. They hate, fight, kill each other for them, get rather cross when others don't believe in their chosen illusion – oh, it's a right old party of deities down there. But one of their gods, right, Jesus Christ, came down to earth – apparently – as the *son of a carpenter*. So we started thinking that perhaps this transmission was an official communication from the powers that rule Earth. Well, the ones that like Christ. Then we translated the rest as best we could and, well. You're not going to believe it, but this song is called '*Calling Occupants Of Interplanetary Craft*'."

Gff 's mouth fell open in amazement.

"I know, right?" said Vaag. "That's us. We are occupants of interplanetary craft. This is a message for the Overwatch Systems. They sent D. JONES in person and then they followed him up with this song. Just listen to this…"

Vaag re-started the playback and Gff listened with amazement to the translated lyrics, which were, approximately:

Your minds can do things.
You are telepathic and can communicate through space.
So listen to this song.
And listen well.
Those that ride interplanetary craft, we are calling out to you.
Yes, bizarre, amazing star ships, we are calling to you.
We know you're watching Earth.
And we'd love to speak with you.
Don't be scared, we are friendly, yes we are.
Do not come with war, please.
We are loving and our planet will die without you.
You are space lawmakers, so let us know you've got our message.
All you pilots of interplanetary craft.
Astonishing, wow, great, interplanetary craft.

"Yep, it's a message to us. A message of peace, telling the Overwatch to pick up the Dimensional Phone and give them a call."

"So have you? Got in touch?"

"Of course not. They may be insane. This message might be the work of two total idiots. So we amped up the power, re-calibrated our interstellar eyes and ears and pointed them directly at Earth. Now –

obviously, we picked up a LOT of transmissions, but mainly, well, it doesn't look good..."

Vaag punched another key and images flashed across the screen. Even though Gff had never seen a human until ten minutes ago, he could tell that he wasn't seeing particularly happy members of this species. Their expressions, so close to Quadra-Terrans, looked scared and desperate.

Gff saw wars on that screen – they didn't need translating. Wars are the same wherever you were in the universe. Things blew up, buildings fell down, people fell down. Lots of people fell down.

People screamed, cried, then fell as fire rained from above and death reigned everywhere you looked. On the human faces there were other familiar expressions that didn't need an anthropologist to explain. Hate, rage, intolerance, disdain, fanaticism...while Gff had never seen this particular species before, he'd seen others like it many times. You just changed the number of legs or heads, but the expressions stayed the same. There were always a few doing the hating and lots doing the dying.

"Aha. Yep, these humans, they do love killing. I don't want to tar them all with the same nano-brush, because from what we've seen, some are capable of immense kindness, creativity and what they call 'humanity' – an empathy for their fellow species. Some can be loving and caring, just like any of us. They can be funny, capable of supreme heroism and sacrifice. They are dignified and honourable. Unfortunately..." Vaag held his thumb and forefinger together, closely, "...only this many ever display those qualities. Most of them are, frankly, a total shower."

"Oh," said Gff. "I was just starting to like them. All that stuff about honour and dignity. You made them sound like people we should be dealing with."

"Well, that's the whole problem whenever we come across a new species. It's the big question, the only question, really. What are they really like? We can watch their transmissions, but are those pictures the truth or a bunch of edited highlights – or rather lowlights? Who controls the transmissions? What's their agenda, their bias? Is their news real, or fake?"

"Mmph, fake news," muttered Gff darkly, since he considered any story that wasn't gushingly complimentary about him as clearly fake.

Vaag carried on. "You see, we can't trust any pictures because we don't know the motivations behind them. Are we dealing with a planet full of maniacs? So, Mr Miasma. This is your choice today. What do we do about Earth?"

"Do? In what way?"

"I'll hold the answer to that for a moment, if I may. Our problem has always been this; how do you judge an entire planet? By their leaders? Nooooo. I mean, if humans judged the Overwatch by you, what would they think?"

They'd think it was intelligent, super sexy and had great hair, thought Gff, but didn't say it out loud.

Vaag pushed another key. A series of human faces appeared.

"Look. These are just a few of their leaders throughout human history. Generally, you wouldn't find a more snivelling, self-serving, hypocritical, lying, bullying, dumb-ass bunch of creatures outside a prison. But despite that, the humans always rally behind them, march to their drums, wave their flags and carry out their destructive orders over and over again."

"Ooh, wait, stop!" said Gff, whose eye had been caught by one particular face. "Who's that?"

"That…" Vaag consulted a data stream at the side of the picture. "…he is, was – not sure if he's still alive – a leader called Trump."

"Stupid name," sniffed Gff. "What's that on his head? Is it some kind of hat?"

"It's his hair, apparently," Vaag studiously didn't look at Gff as he said it.

"Good heavens." Gff got closer to the picture. "And he was a leader?"

"Ahmm. He ran that place 'America', where all the guns come from, apparently. Then there was another place called Russia, owned by gangsters, but nominally led by this horror, called 'Putin'."

Another face flashed up and Gff gave little squawk of displeasure. "Urgh, I think I preferred the Trump guy. What happened to this one's face?"

"We don't know. Particle disruption? He lost a bet? Not a clue. But apparently both this Putin and that Trump thought they were just ohmygod, super good-looking, total gravitational pull on every female."

"How deluded. Trump looks like he played Ugly Bingo and all his numbers came in. Mind you, Putin's obviously caught his face in a lift door, which is hardly his fault. Trust me, I know what makes a leader charismatic and attractive."

"*Riiggghhht...*" said Vaag, ending the cavalcade of horrendous images. "So – we can't judge a planet by its transmissions or leaders. They're simply not representative. That's the problem here at Area 62. Do we annihilate an entire civilisation just because a few members of their species happen to be utter fools?"

"Well, it's a good question," said Gff, who tried to sound knowledgable and statesmanlike, again. "Does the goodness of one soul counteract the evil in many? It's a philosophical debate, really, since...wait, what? Hold on, what did you just say?"

"Er, we can't judge a planet by its leaders?" offered Vaag.

"No, no, the other bit. The bit where you mentioned... annihilation?"

"Oh yes, that bit. I said, 'Do we annihilate an entire civilisation because a few of them are idiots?'"

"Yes, that bit. Now, forgive me if I'm misreading you, but that sounded like you intend to blow up this Earth and everyone on it. I got that wrong didn't I?"

"No, for once, you're right," replied Vaag. "That's the deal. Yep. Here at Area 62, we discover new planets and new people. Then, whoever's Supreme Miasma that term has the sole decision on whether to wipe them out. Today, that's you."

"Destroy an entire planet? I can't make that kind of choice!" moaned Gff, who waved his tentacles about his head in a panicky way.

"You can and you will. You wanted this job. Deal with it."

"But I can't judge every person on Earth! It's impossible! What if only thirty percent of them are totally worthless and the other seventy percent are just great?"

"Ah, but what if seventy percent are grade A awful and only thirty percent are worth saving? What about those numbers?"

"But you can't tell! There's no way of knowing! It's not possible!"

"That's where you're wrong," said Vaag and his expression changed. He looked sly, even slightly feral, like a predator waiting to jump its prey. "Because now, we can judge virtually every person on Earth."

He switched the picture again. A deluge of human faces washed by. Gff thought they all looked pretty similar. "That has always been our big problem…" Vaag continued, as the faces flickered on and on, "… somehow, we need to test every *individual* member of a species, to find their *general* worth. But how could we do that without alerting them to our existence and to the fact they're being tested? People cheat in exams, always will, so if they knew their very existence depended on good grades, oh, they'd cheat alright. They'd all pretend to be intelligent, kind, honourable, empathic, brave…whatever it took to save their worthless skins. But now we can test them all, without a single human knowing. And we have."

Gff wasn't convinced. "I'm not convinced," he pouted, because he was someone who Said It Like It Was.

"Let me convince you. Here at Area 62, we developed a way to beam ideas into people's heads. One day, somebody wakes up with a brilliant idea. This person totally thinks they came up with it, but they didn't, *we* did. We can beam our ideas straight into people's minds, so they'll do whatever we want. We used this Idea Transmission technique on a few Earth people, to invent our way of testing humanity. So, first we put an idea for a new kind of smart telephone in the head of a guy called Steve Jobs."

"Ha, jobs," tittered Gff.

"Ha. So Steve Jobs 'invents' our smart phone and then, after that, we created something to put inside those phones, which we called 'Social Media'. We used a kid called, er, Fuckerberg, was it? Something like that, anyway, to really ramp that one up."

The picture changed again.

A series of logos appeared. First was a single blue 'F' symbol, next, a cartoon of a bird-type creature. More logos appeared and even though Gff didn't know their meaning, he was a businessman and could spot corporate trademarks a mile off – they all had a kind of psychopathic WE ARE YOUR FRIENDS aura about them.

"Social Media," said Gff. "Sounds fun. Sounds social."

"Well, that was the idea. OK, now these Earth people all have our 'Smart Phones'. Yeah, smart, right. Humans have become addicted to them. They're never off their precious Smart Phones! They go out with friends and then spend all night lost in their screens, not talking to each other. They have children, then stick them in a corner with a *Smart* Phone, so no-one has to communicate. Whole families, sitting round a restaurant table, all on their phones and none of them know each other at all. The only time they stop looking at their screens is when one of them takes a photo, to show everyone else what a 'fun, happy family time' they're having. Humans walk down the street, not looking where they're going, expecting everyone else to get out of their way because they're busy checking their existence. It's facking madness, honestly. Our Evolutionary Department think in a few hundred thousand years, humans will just have one thumb for 'texting' and their necks will be permanently at a 75-degree angle, to make it easier to stare blankly downwards at their own lives. So – here's the thing; why did we invent these Smart Phones? To test the human race. They all have one. They're attached to them twenty four hours of their day. It's perfect. *The phone takes our test to human beings, all day, every day.* And that test is Social Media."

"Social Media is…an exam?"

"Got it. So, we give humans the most efficient way to communicate with each other, ever. We gave them a little box and an application that lets them be as creative, humane, kind, giving, honourable and yes, *smart* as they want to be. They can learn, talk, better themselves, become one joyful species, transcend hate, fear, war and stupidity, all through this one little screen. It's all there for the taking. That was the exam, to see what the "ordinary" human did with such an invention. Would they use it to become more than the sum of their parts? Do you know what they mainly did with it?"

"Make phone calls?" offered Gff, who privately thought that was a very funny answer.

"Oh, if only. No, they mainly took pictures of themselves and then posted them online so other humans could tell them how good they looked."

"They what? Took pictures of *themselves*? So other people could compliment them?" Even Gff, who was no stranger to narcissism, was slightly appalled by that.

Vaag hit a key and the human faces began to flash by again. Now Gff saw they all had the same expression – that's why they'd looked so similar. He wasn't being species-ist; they genuinely looked the same. Skin colour, gender and age changed, but they were all pulling this bizarre pouting face, as if inviting you to come and sit on it.

These faces were all wearing an identical expression that said, *I'm gorgeous, tell me I'm gorgeous, go on. Tell me. I need to hear it. Love me. Give me your attention. Tell me.*

"Oh, take them off." Gff waved a tentacle at the screen.

"Ugly, aren't they?" said Vaag. "Oh, I'm sure they're considered beautiful back on Earth, but they are amongst the ugliest creatures I've ever seen. Think about it. Their egos are planet sized, but made of glass. Every day, they need the approbation of strangers to make them feel they have worth. It's a shame really, because each and every one of them does have worth. Some just don't know where to find it. There's more, by the way."

"That's not all? There's more?" gasped Gff, who thought that was plenty enough, thank you.

"Oh yes, lots more. But first, don't get me wrong; Social Media, like its users, can be - and is - creative, loving, compassionate, empathic, inclusive. It can be beautiful, wonderful, giving and caring. It really can. It's a lifeline for the lonely, scared, the outcasts and the confused. It saves lives. It can be art. Yes, being human can be an art and Social Media is its gallery."

"But?" Gaff felt a "but," coming on, so had jumped in first.

"Ha, 'but.' But, even the greatest Art Galleries have sewers running under them. And in Earth's case, the sewer is overflowing. They use our Social Media invention to talk about themselves. All day, every day. They take pictures of themselves, then they talk about themselves. We've given them the chance to connect with the entire world, and all they do is tell the world what they think, what they're up to, what they're eating, wearing or facking. On and on, second after second, these billions of one-story news channels, pumping out their twenty four hour updates. You know, they even film themselves watching stuff, so everyone else can see their reactions to it. Seriously. "Kids React To seventies Rock Bands". "Me Reacting To A Horror Film". "Me And My Wife React To Funny Memes". *I* react to those by vomiting. The biggest offenders are the famous, who obviously don't seem to have enough attention already, so their massive thumbs are constantly busy, informing the planet of their every moment."

Gff understood.

Of course, what *he* thought, did and ate was of supreme importance to the universe. He was smart, he mattered. But the idea of every non-entity in the Overwatch insisting the entire galaxy shut up and pay attention was a truly terrifying idea. He also realised the normally calm Vaag was displaying a new emotion.

"You're angry," said Gff, slightly awed.

"I'm angry, but mainly I'm tired," hissed Vaag. "You try living with this for longer than five minutes."

A succession of new images followed. They showed barely and totally undressed humans, taking pictures of themselves in mirrors. "They really love themselves, don't they? They honestly think every other human is dribblingly aroused by their very existence. Yes, their self obsession knows no bounds. So much so, that they'll share even their most private thoughts, feelings and moments with the collective in a bid to get a spurious thrill called a 'like'. A picture of a beautiful sunset might get a handful of likes. A 'Selfie" gets hundreds. Take that as you wish. So that was our test and they are failing."

"But…no…You can't just lump them all in…with…that…" said Gff, trying to find the words, ashen faced.

"No, of course not. But how about this? From the translations, we gather their planet is currently in a transition phase."

"Transition from what?"

"Transition to mildly facked up to totally facked up beyond all recognition. Climate problems, political shit, religious nutbags, over population, you name it, it's happening. So what are they doing?"

"Well, I'd imagine as an intelligent species they'd be working together to rectify the situation."

"Mm." Vaag shook his head. "The crucial word there is 'intelligent'. At this point, at this very point, when they should be looking up and out at what's happening around them, many are looking down at their phones, at themselves and as long as they get 'likes' then forget everything else."

"I feel sick."

"You should. That's not all. We also gave them a Social Media platform called YouTube. It lets them all think they're famous, if that's their priority. I find one of the best ways to judge a species is their attitude to fame. My favourites are the Khardyasheen species of Altair-Five. If a Khardyasheen wants to be famous, their planet gives them TV shows, magazine covers, screaming fans and then, at the peak of their fame, they tear them limb from limb and hang their twitching corpse over the stage as a warning to everyone else not to want to be famous. But *now* just look at what these hairless monkeys do…"

Gff almost wanted to watch through his tentacles, it was too painful.

A young, perma-smiling human appeared on screen. The picture cut quickly between various shots of the human pulling stupid faces. Music pumped. Not even five seconds into the clip, Gff found himself with a headache.

"Why does he need to cut the pictures up so much, so fast?" he asked.

"Because his viewers no longer have an attention span. If you don't give their eyes something new every second, they think it's boring. It gets worse."

"Hey guys!" said the grinning creature. "Diddy-Do-Whoa-Man here, wassup?"

"Guys?" asked Gff from the corner of one mouth.

"We think it's the collective noun for 'my fellow idiots'," clarified Vaag.

"Hey, so, like, so, me and my dogs were out at the mall, just hanging, you know," continued the human, who'd obviously circumvented his need for oxygen. "But you know, we thought, 'whoah, all Diddy Do's eighteen million subscribers would want to see that' right? See what we do at the mall, me and my dogs? So check. *This*. OW WOW WOW OUUTTT!" The picture cut to Diddy Do with similarly dressed others, standing about in a shop, pulling faces and shouting about what Gff could only assume was nothing at all.

"Humans actually watch this?" he genuinely felt like he needed a planet-sized bucket.

"Yep. But not all of them, obviously. It's harmless, though, right? Just a bit of fun. But oh, in the words of Diddy Do-Whoa-Man there, check *this* out."

Vaag took a deep breath and looked up at the ceiling. "Alright, think of a subject, any subject. The more harmless the better."

Gff thought. "Music. Music's innocuous isn't it? Music makes everyone feel good, doesn't it?"

"You'd have thought so, but no. Thanks to Social Media, some humans can turn anything, but *anything* into a shouting match. They have to have their say, you see. Their opinion counts, whether it's informed or not. Generally not. It's got so bad, even their news is dominated by Social Media. Their news! They report a story, and then, inevitably, the reporter says, 'and on Twitter…' and quotes a bunch of people who are neither experts *on* nor connected *to* that story. Just anyone with an opinion. Opinions are fine, of course, but they are neither facts nor news. This has been somewhat forgotten on Earth. Alright, so – music."

He fiddled with the keyboard.

"I'm going to look up a popular Earth band, called 'Coldplay'. Aha, here we go…"

On screen, a pasty-faced man sat at a piano making lots of *whoah whoa whoa oh, whoa whoa whoah* sounds.

"Mmm, catchy," said Gff, approvingly. "I could imagine joining in with that, waving a laser lighter at a Hyper Stadium somewhere."

"Yes, that's the idea. It's pretty much always Coldplay's idea actually. But they write good songs, they're good musicians, it's inoffensive, right? Wrong. Look at the 'Comments' section. When we invented Social Media, we knew it was very important to let humans comment on everything. We thought it would give us a pretty fair representation of how they think. Alas, however, they think like this. Read."

Gff read. Underneath the musical clip, some humans had left their thoughts.

Pat234: I love this one. So emotional!
GITBIT14: Me too. Chris Martin is such a talent.
Pat234: At 2 minutes 12 it always makes my hair stand on end. Brilliant.
S42: coldplay are shit

Pat234: that's your opinion.
S42: your shit to.
GITBIT14: get lost, you sad troll.
Braddestroyer: I'm with S42. coldplay should die.
S42: you coldplay queers.
Pat234: homafobe!.
S42: yeah what you gonna do about it?
GITBIT14: must be sad being you
Sorryass: must be sad being you.
GITBIT14; why can't we all get on?
Sorryass: Coldplay should be hung alive.

"Make it stop," moaned Gff.

"I can't though," said Vaag. "It just goes on and on. Whatever the subject, whatever the film, whatever the Social Media platform, it always just descends into this vicious circle of name calling. Honestly, we did an experiment and put up a clip of an earth-dog playing with a ball. Within three comments it was like a fight had broken out in a secure wing. Carnage."

Gff sat down heavily and stared at the floor.

"We tested them, Mr Miasma. We tested nearly all of them and these were the results. But it's your call. You could let them carry on as they are, then maybe they'll develop hyper and superluminal star-drives to spread that," he gestured to the screen with its never-ending insults, refreshing every few seconds, "...across the universe. Or we take pre-emptive action."

"But surely there are good humans?" asked Gff, who still couldn't look up from the floor.

"There are. But for how long? How long before that becomes the default position for the human species? Maybe it already is. They've only had our Social Media for around a decade, and look at them. The children of the smart phone are already lost in their own importance, copying their idiot parents, pulling 'selfie' faces, eyes down, mind closed...What will the species be like in another ten of their years? We gave them the tools to be most magnificent. They used them to become post-pubescent. I told you, Mr Miasma. I told you back in your office, not even a few par-hours ago. I said I would never want your responsibility and this is why. I'm afraid you can't win, can you? Leave them be and you risk spreading their disease. End it now and you annihilate an entire species. It's your call and you *will* make it."

Gff sat for a while lost in thought. He looked at the screen for a long time. He needed guidance. Just one hint, one moment from the ghastliness he'd just witnessed to help him decide.

Then he had it. Any species that let a creature called "Trump" lead them with *that* hair could only have one possible future.

"Kill the fackers," he sighed. "Kill them all. Then can we please have tea? I'm starving."

"Very well, Sir. If that is your choice, " smiled Vaag. Deep inside Vaag's mind, a dark presence whispered, "I've helped destroy cities, countries, individuals and races. But an entire planet? That's new. No bunkers deep enough for them to hide in, either. Whoo whoo!"

Vaag was unaware of this voice, oblivious to how he'd been controlled by an ancient evil that had stalked the universe since it had first woken on Earth, in a pre-historical hurricane.

He entered a code on the keyboard and a drawer slid out of its unit. Inside was a single bright red button, that flashed, ominously.

"That's all?" asked Gff. "Just a big red button? Bit doomsday-weapony, isn't it?"

"Well yes," shrugged Vaag. "That is kind of the point. When you're ready, Mr Miasma. Press the button, and we can forget all about the human race."

Vaag watched eagerly, unaware a sly grin had spread across his mouth.

Gff raised a tentacle, which hovered over the death of a world.

But then, unbidden, the face of that creature outside flashed into his mind. D. JONES. He remembered the curious smile frozen on it, in death.

What was it smiling for? Gff suddenly wondered. *That was the smile of a creature that was looking for something, or somebody, and has found it. That human* chose *to die, and in dying, found the object of its journey. And what of the other humans I saw? Not the ones Vaag wanted me to concentrate on, but the others, whose faces flashed past, too fast to register. The humans who were also just searching for their own smiles. The ones for whom this "Social Media," was exactly that. Social. Empathic. Unselfish. A lifeline for themselves and to others. What of* them?

Gff's tentacle remained still above the planet - killer. Then he withdrew it.

"Let them live." He sighed. "Everybody deserves a chance to find their smile."

Everyone turned to the Supreme Miasma in shock. Vaag's feral grin slid from his face.

"Even me." he smiled, and slid from the room.

"HEY JOE"

(Billy Roberts, 1962, although authorship disputed, covered by
The Jimi Hendrix Experience, 1966, from the album,
Are You Experienced *)*

December 1973

I promised not to tell anyone. But I can tell you, can't I? I could
always tell you everything.

So, I'm in a place called Bordnersville. I'd never even heard of it
until a few hours ago and didn't choose to stop here. I guess no-one
really chooses to stop in Bordnersville.

So I'm in a ROOM, in a BAR, off the freeway, it's just after 11pm,
I'm a little drunk and I need to write this down, so I'm writing it for
you. I guess this is finally a reply to your letter, even though I'll never
put it in the mail. Wherever you are now, I'm imagining you're
reading this, with no stamp required.

Here's how I happened to end up here.

I was on Route 78, just past Harrisburg, when I just couldn't drive
any more.

The next exit was 89 and my lights picked out a sign,
"Bordnersville." It sounded quaint I suppose, old fashioned,
somewhere we might have taken our circus to when we were kids.
Yeah, of course I remember our circus dreams.

I imagined this place would have a little football team called *The*
Bordnersville Furies and a town parade once a year. Well, that's the
image I had in my head as I took the exit. I was so tired, I could barely
keep my eyes open so it was either bed down or crash.

Here I am, driving for you all the way from Santa Barbara to New
York, but I'm four months too late. It's over 3,000 miles, one side of

the country to the other, and takes the best part of two days by car getting to NY. You took a plane. I wish you hadn't.

I managed to get this far on my last tank of sleep, but had nothing left.

I was drained emotionally, too. This wasn't a journey I wanted to make. I would rather be anywhere but traveling East, to lay flowers on a shitty sidewalk in New York. But I had to, it was the only thing I could do. So as the sign for Bordnersville appeared, I didn't even think, I just turned left and headed here.

I borrowed Dad's car. You always liked my Dad and he liked you too. He was cool with it. He understood. He never said, but I think he was a little proud I wanted to take this trip, alone. Everyone back home felt guilty. Your funeral was the worst thing.

I hadn't seen you for two years and when they brought your body back, the service had an open coffin. Apparently, according to Mom, you still looked beautiful, but I didn't want that memory in my head. I wanted to remember you as you were, before you left. My memories of you mainly come from when we were much younger anyway, when we played together like brother and sister. I thought they were happy times. I had no idea.

As we hit our teens, we grew apart a little, didn't we, but you always seemed to be the same girl. A little more make-up, a little more sass, but the same smile, same curiosity. If there was a door open on a street, you'd always have to go and take a peek inside and who cared if you got caught? If there were two pathways, one well worn and one less traveled, yeah, you'd head straight for the long grass. You were fearless like that. It was only later, back in July this year, that I understood why. You were fearless because nothing could scare you any more. You'd seen it all, been through it all even before you jumped on your one-way flight to NY. Of course you'd always take the overgrown, dark path. You'd been walking on it for years, I know that now.

Your Mom was at the service, naturally. Crying, wailing, playing the heartbroken parent. She did it so well, even I believed her, but only for a moment. Now I know what your Mom really is. You told me in your letter. It was hard to take in, but you had no reason to lie, no, not at that point, and then it all made sense. But I'm getting ahead of myself. This isn't about me, or even you, not really. This letter is about a man called Joe.

*

I'm writing this now, in my ROOM, in BAR, so I don't forget. I promised not to tell anyone, but I can tell you. You always liked a story and I know you'll like this one.

So, I came off the freeway and the road to Bordnersville was so dark! I could hardly see the ground, even with my lights. I felt my eyes closing. It was only 8 in the evening, but it's December and dark as coal out there. I just needed to shut my eyes for an hour or so and everything would be OK.

I never made it to actual Bordnersville so I can't tell you what the town is really like. Maybe it does have a Furies Football Team, parade, clock tower and everything. Maybe it doesn't. I'm not coming back. Bordnersville is someone else's story, but it's become mine too, now, by default.

Suddenly, out of the dark, I saw something every traveler prays for. Shining on the left were two signs on top of each other. ROOMS said the top, BAR said the bottom. Have there ever been two words so gratefully received? If so, I can't think of them. I pulled over with no further thought.

The BAR didn't have a name, other than, it appeared, BAR. I liked that. No frills.

BAR is set in a little parking lot, no filling station, but I could see there were houses nearby and a couple of stores. This place, I guessed, was the furthest outpost of Bordnersville, the last chance to stop before the locals hit Route 78.

I'd been in the car for about 6 hours since my last rest stop. It's only when you move again after a long period you realize how fixed your limbs have become – my legs were like broomsticks so I had to steady myself on the hood of the car. It was cold. I'd been running the heater without even realizing but as I stepped into BAR's parking lot, my breath misted and the chill hit me hard. The door to BAR and ROOMS was only 30 yards away, so I coped.

I grabbed my little bag and headed over.

*

As I stood at the door, I imagined what BAR might look like inside. You taught me how to imagine. So here goes – this is what I pictured:

1/ Pool table on one side, occupied by a couple of greasy guys. They'd probably stare at me as I walked in. You know how sensibly I dress. Yeah, I'm still square, my hair's neat, I never grew it out. I'm "quite a catch," as Mom likes to tease. But clearly I'm no biker or beatnik.

2/ BAR would have booths made of red leather or, more likely, plastic. There would be a guy and a girl furtively meeting up here on the outskirts. In my mind I also saw an older guy and woman, arranging a "business" transaction before they disappeared to ROOMS.

3/ The actual BAR itself would be along one end. Plenty of spirits, not too many beers. Wood. Yeah, lots of wood everywhere.

4/ Neon signs advertising the few beers they do sell. Posters of cigarettes and girls, maybe a black Stratocaster hanging on a wall above a jukebox that blasted Duane Eddy's "Peter Gunn," Wilson Pickett, Sam Cooke, Isley Brothers, hell yeah.

5/ Oh and there would definitely be an old guy at the bar, reminiscing.

Yes, I did it. I made a list, again. Why do I do that? Lists always creep into whatever I write. You always laughed at my lists, but I can't help them. Maybe I just like a little order. Things have got out of control everywhere these days, so perhaps I like to stamp some discipline where I can.

But anyway, those were the images I had in my head as I pushed the door open.

You know, I was almost totally correct. There <u>was</u> a pool table (but empty), the booths (yes, older guy and woman; younger sweethearts) wood everywhere, neon, posters…No old guy at the bar, but if Hollywood built a set based on the direction, "SMALL TOWN JOINT JUST OFF THE FREEWAY," this is what the designer would have dreamed up.

I'd just pulled out every cliché I could think of, but this BAR had it all, even the part I missed: a girl behind the taps, chewing gum, cleaning a glass, looking gorgeously bored.

She wasn't much older than me and I was relieved. Legal age is 21 round here, but this girl didn't look like she'd be scoping for ID. I'm almost 21, for heaven's sake. What difference would three months make? What, I'd be loaded at age 20 and 9 months, but absolutely fine by *21*? It doesn't make sense, but then again, what does?

The girl had blonde hair up in a ponytail and – I swear I'm not making this up – she was wearing a short-sleeved red checked shirt tied up above her midriff. I almost expected to turn and see cameras rolling.

Even though this is Pennsylvania, BAR is so authentically Southern in appearance I'd expected a Texan drawl. But she spoke with a light, almost New England twang. That took me by surprise. I'm going to paraphrase what we said, OK? You always knew how to tell a tale, so I'm going to follow your example.

"You look like a man who needs a beer."

"Aha," I replied, relieved. She called me a "man," so wasn't looking for ID tonight.

Then she'd looked down at my little bag and asked if I wanted a room.

"I knew it," she said, pleased. "People are pretty regular round here. If someone new walks in, they're either lost, tired, on the run, or all three. We have three rooms, $3 a night."

"Which one is best?" I asked.

"Well, Room One has a wonderful view of the parking lot, from Room Two you can see right up the road, and Room Three has both.

They all have a single bed, but there's a shared bathroom, no TV. Sorry it's not the Waldorf, but when you're this far from what's happening, you take what you can get."

"OK," I said and fumbled in my pocket for some cash. She looked down at my right hand and I saw her expression change, just for a moment. People's expressions always change and even if it's subtle, I always notice.

"What happened to your fingers?" she asked. No preamble, straight to it.

It was OK, I've answered that question enough, I'm used to it.

"I was 10, helping my Dad cut wood with his circular saw. He likes working with wood, or, at least, he did. He doesn't any more. The wood bucked, it slipped, I slipped and goodbye fingers."

Her curiosity didn't bother me. So I held up my hand so she could see better. As you know, my little finger's gone, as is the one next door.

"Ouch," she said and winced.

"It was a little more than ouch at the time. I'm just grateful it wasn't the first three fingers, thumb, index, ring…" I held them up one by one. "Then I'd have been really screwed. But you'd be surprised what you can do with just three fingers. But one thing I can't do is handle a gun, according to my doctor. I can shoot just fine with my left hand, but they never asked. Hence, I never got out to Hanoi."

She nodded with a serious expression. We've been losing the war out there for years now, but the people in charge still haven't realized. I remember what you said to me years ago:

A stupid accident in your basement may have lost your fingers, but it probably saved your life. No trigger finger, no Vietnam." Too right, hallelujah and praise the saw.

"I'm sorry, it just came out," she said, a little embarrassed. Then she'd rooted around in a drawer and pulled out three keys.

"So what's it to be? 1, 2 or 3? Oh, that rhymes! I'll remember that, do it for all our *many* guests. Ha."

"I'll take 1. That way I can keep an eye on my car."

"Good idea. You never know, a stray dog might try and steal it. So, beer? We have Coors, Bud or Pabst. That's all, sorry. Our drinkers aren't very adventurous."

I told her I was whacked and needed to go up to my room for a bit of shut eye, then maybe I'd come back for that beer.

"Oh, OK, shame." I was pleased to see she looked a little disappointed, maimed hand or not. She told me she got off work at nine o'clock.

I think – I hope – she was gunning for me to stick around, but my eyelids were protesting.

It would have been nice to talk to her, but I wasn't making this trip to meet a girl. She asked if there would be anything else.

"That will be all Madam," I said, and bowed. Old habits die hard and flirting was one of them. You know how it is, I can't help myself.

She bowed too, giggled, then pointed to a door on the far right, with a hand-written sign on it – ROOMS.

"Your chamber awaits, sir," she said in a terrible English accent. "I *do* 'ope it will be to your liking." I laughed. Then I felt guilty. I haven't laughed a lot, you know, since.

*

It's now 11 at night and I'm writing this in my ROOM which is, as advertised, a room.

It has the standard four walls, floor and ceiling. A single bed is pushed up against one wall, with a window above. Yes, I can see the parking lot, so won't be asking for a refund. The bathroom is directly opposite. The only decoration (if you could call it that) is a Coors clock on the opposite wall and when I first entered, it read 8:45pm.

There's a little dressing table, but no closet. It has a dirty brown carpet and bed, which, as far as I can see isn't infested with any insects or small mammals. What did I expect for $3?

So when I first walked in I decided to just lie down and see what happened. If I woke up and it was morning, so be it. But if my body only needed a little break, I'd go and get that beer.

I lay down and slept almost immediately.

*

When I opened my eyes I expected to see daylight, but it was still black out there. I'd obviously dropped into a deep sleep since my body felt like concrete. The Coors clock now read 9:45pm.

So – my brain had allowed me just one hour of sleep before it rang an alarm bell and started shouting, "Beer! Tony! Beer! Time for beer!"

Yes, I was thirsty. Some say beer dries them out. But you know I'm not like that.

No, I guzzle that stuff down. If I'm parched, give me beer over water any time. I shut my eyes for one moment, then decided, *no, forget sleep. Let's have a beer.*

I wish I hadn't. But to be honest, I really needed that drink. After your letter arrived, I read it through four times. Four times, exactly, word for word, from "Dear Tony" to "fly." I couldn't take it in. I didn't cry until the third read. By the fourth, I was weeping, I couldn't stop. I drank a lot that day. I didn't show Mom and Dad the letter. They knew better than to ask to see it. They know I'll tell them, eventually.

Have you noticed I haven't written your name? I'm barely able to say it out loud and I certainly can't write it, yet. I don't know why that is. Guilt, I guess. Why didn't you write to me before? I could have come, I'd have taken you away. Why did you only write to me when it was too late? Were you so far gone down that path, you didn't think you could find your way back? I'll never know, will I? I only know what you told me and what happened next.

I wish you'd have written before. But what is, *is* and I'll never be able to make any list that puts order or sense on it.

So there I was, in ROOM, above BAR, sliding out of the bed, to go and have a beer. I'd drink, I'd sleep, then I'd drive to lay some flowers on a street that wouldn't even notice them, to try and make it up to you.

But as I say, this isn't my story, or yours. This is the story of Joe.

*

So I went down to BAR, where the music still played and the neon still glowed. The pool table was busy, but not with long-haired bikers, as I'd imagined. Just a couple of ordinary forgettable men in bad suits. They didn't speak the whole time I was down there. BAR's like that. People didn't talk, but Nick did. Nick talked just fine and told me the story of Joe. I'll try and tell it how it was told to me. It won't be the exact words, of course, but I'll do my best to make it come alive, like you always made your stories come to life.

The girl was gone and there was no-one behind the bar. Just an old guy, sitting on a stool, as I'd pictured when I first walked in.

It was like he'd only just got the message, you know? *Cliché old man required at middle-of-nowhere bar. Come quick!*

I wandered over and leaned by the taps, looking for someone to serve me. But it turned out the old guy *was* the barkeep.

I stood there for what seemed like ages and then he spoke up. "Beer?"

I nodded and looked around for someone to serve me.

He nodded back and slowly stood, hip listing downwards. His hands were twisted with arthritis and I could only begin to imagine what was going on inside his pelvis. He slid and staggered round the bar, then grabbed it, like he was hanging on for dear life. In retrospect I think that's exactly what he was doing.

He was – how old was he? Sometimes, when people drink a lot, they can be forty, going on sixty. Then, there are those who are ninety who do a good impression of seventy.

Our lives etch themselves on our bodies, I know that now. Most of my friends don't get it, we're all so young, we think we're invulnerable. Now I understand I'm barely out of diapers. We only really notice the calendar when one of our own generation dies.

Age happens to the old, not us. I've tried to explain to my friends what happened to you, but they just stare, hearing but not listening. It's cause and effect. You left Santa Barbara because of a cause; the effect was; you died. We are all that close, no matter how young we are. I get it now, you taught me.

As this guy hobbled round to the other side of the bar he looked ancient. His skin, even in this low light, was folded and yellow. Everything about him was yellow, actually. Hair, eyes, teeth, nails, wow, this man was *made* of yellow.

It's funny; we associate yellow with the sun, with beaches, fruit, life. But when yellow happens to a human being, it's the complete opposite. So he was maybe a very old sixty or a very young ninety. Whatever his age, he was dying, that was obvious.

"Pabst, please," I said. He nodded, pleased, as if that was the right choice.

"How old are you?" he asked and narrowed those milky yellow eyes.

"Twenty-one," I replied.

He looked me up and down.

"Aha, oh yeah, sure you are. Not far off, don't doubt it, but not quite there yet, neither. I believe you. Twenty-one it is. Pabst? Had you down as a Bud man."

"First beer I ever tried was Pabst. I suppose I'm loyal."

"Loyal's good," he laughed drily as he pulled a glass. "No loyalty these days, no loyalty anywhere. I drink Pabst, too. Fact, I think I'll join you."

He finished pouring mine, then set about his own.

"So." He eyed me again. "I'm Nick. Nicholas."

"Tony. Anthony." I stuck out my hand and as he shook it, his arthritic fingers nipped me like a claw.

"Enjoy your beer, Anthony, Tony." He pushed it over with his other twisted hand.

"Is this your place?" I asked.

He chuckled. "No, noooo. Ha, really? Belongs to my good friend Martin. Has a couple bars round this way. I live over there." He gestured outwards to one of the houses I'd seen, hunkered down close. "I enjoy a beer now and again. Mainly again. Martin has me come in

and look after the place. Not busy, is it? Pays me OK and I can have
the occasional beer. Well, now and again. Mainly again."

He spluttered and I couldn't tell if he was laughing or not. He
magicked up a tissue from somewhere and hawked into it.

"Don't mind the coughing," he coughed. "So how about you, Tony,
Anthony?" Every time he used my name, he said it both ways. "Never
seen ya, so you don't live round here. Or if you do, you've been living
in your basement for…21 years, ha. Saw a car out there. That yours?
Got to be. From the East, saw the plates, aha."

He left his side of the bar and came to join me.

"Mind if I sit with you?" I knew it didn't matter what I said. "Even
though I work here, can't ever get the hang of working here. Prefer
this side. Can't enjoy a beer that side. Feels like I'm on show…"

He turned and waved to the almost empty bar. "Even though
nobody cares. I sit this side most nights, because that side is too much
like I have to perform. Play the bartender."

"Aha," I said, because that felt right.

"Ah-fucking ha, he gets it. The *21-year-old* gets it, just fine." He
sat down heavily on the stool next to mine. Internally, I cursed myself
for wishing up an old guy at the bar, painting the cliché, because now
the cliché was sitting next to me and I'd become his audience. He
asked why I was there and then guessed maybe I was visiting a
relative.

I went to answer, but he held up one of his mangled hands. I felt
closer to him because of that. We both had hands that didn't work any
more, mine through an accident, his through life.

"No, nooo. You're not here for a relative." He played detective.
"Because if it was a relative, you'd be staying there, with them, right.
Noooo, you came off the freeway and this was the first place you
found. Am I right? No-one ever makes a point of coming here, to
Bordnersville. Don't get me wrong. It's a good village. Good people.
It's pretty. But it don't sell no postcards, you know what I mean? We
don't have an influx of tourists every summer. Nearest beach is over
one hundred miles away, nearest falls, what, forty? This is a way

point, Anthony, Tony. It's a place you pass through and don't even notice."

He squinted at me as his mind put a few facts together.

"And why aren't you in Hanoi, or wherever the hell it's all FUBAR this month?"

I got it, then. Nick, Nicholas, was a vet. The right age, whatever that age was.

Sixty years, ninety years, somewhere in-between, he was a vet of some kind. WWI, WWII, Korea…somewhere, sometime, how many times? This man had pulled on a uniform and killed different men in different countries.

I held up my right hand and three fingers as an answer.

He regarded it, turned his head this way and that. "Aha," he said. "Oh, sorry. I get it. Bad hand. Happened a while back, aha? All healed up, nice and smooth. But it's enough to stop you picking up a gun and shooting at people because some fucker tells you to. Aha." He saluted me, then, as if I'd actually fought somewhere.

"Good for you. I shot people. Aha, I shot lots. Once you've watched your first die it gets easier, but it helps to have a motive, uh-huh. So why are you here?" he asked again, back to the only question that counted.

I had a choice at that point. I could have invented something harmless that would have left him satisfied and let him wander away from this dull 21-year-old. But I felt he didn't deserve a lie. I knew I would never see him again. He was dying, so even if I did come back in six months 'for old time's sake', he would be long gone. So I decided to tell him the truth.

And, God save me, he told me his truth, too.

"I'm going to lay flowers in New York, for a friend," I couldn't look at him. Saying it out loud made my eyes wet.

He saluted again. Nice touch, you know, fallen comrade. I told him I was from Santa Barbara.

"Heard of it. Never been. So you come all the way from way, way over there…to go way over there? Must have been a hell of a friend."

I told him you were. I told him you were just 20, too.

"Shit. That's nothing. Look at me. How am I still here? I'm always here. Round and round, going nowhere. Was she pretty?"

I nodded. He looked sad as if your good looks somehow made it worse.

"What was she doing in New York if you come from Santa Barbara?"

"Long story," I replied. It is a long story, but you'd summed it all up in your letter, said all there was to say.

"Got all night," he shrugged. "You tell me, I tell you. How about that?"

I didn't register his answer at first, didn't realize he was going to share something he hadn't told a soul about until I walked in, with my ruined hand and your story. He had a tale too, but couldn't tell anyone from round here. It was like he'd been waiting for this moment. No, waiting for me.

I told him you'd run away to New York to be a dancer, which was close enough to the truth.

He chuckled and I shot him a hard look. I didn't want chuckling. I hadn't talked about you to anyone except friends and even then, in a roundabout way. I didn't want a stranger to laugh, but he held up his cracked hands again in surrender.

"I'm not laughing at your friend. It's going to New York to be a *dancer*. I laughed because it's sweet. It's cute. It's deluded. She was an innocent, then?"

I changed the subject.

"I got a letter. After. She'd mailed it and then…" I felt myself crumbling. I don't think I'll ever cry enough over you. He put a hand on my shoulder.

"She mailed it and then, yeah, *then* happened, it's OK, I get it. Look, don't worry. You're laying flowers, your friend is gone. You're here and that's that and you're doing the right thing. You don't have to tell me. I'm just an old man at a bar and why don't we just have our beers and talk about the Jets, Lakers, or whatever it is guys talk about when they don't want to jaw about anything real."

But I couldn't help it. I'd started and maybe it was because I didn't know this man, maybe because I was closer to where you flew, I just slumped and talked. I knew I'd never see him again. I couldn't tell anyone the whole truth back home. It feels like your letter was for me alone.

I told him about your Mom. I explained how you grew up thinking bad things were normal until one day you realized bad was bad was bad, end of story. I told him how you stole your Mom's money and flitted away to New York in the night.

He held up his drink again. Without thinking, I clinked my glass with his.

"She thought it would be different there. Nobody knew what had happened. Two years, it was." I cried a little more then. You deserve my tears. He waited. "I didn't ask, I didn't look for her. It's difficult, you know? I just accepted it, because that was the easy option. I hate myself for that."

"Don't," he said and that started me off again. Part of me was thinking *this is crazy*. But another part was glad, happy for the release. Sometimes we all need a stranger to listen without judgement.

It turned out that was exactly what Nick was thinking, too.

He sat while I rambled on about how you described New York as being a person – he liked that. "Yeah, New York's a bitch. I've been to plenty of other cities that have been bitches, too."

Then I told him about Frank and his expression changed. I still can't believe you had a pimp. I can't tolerate how I let you go to a city that ate you up, introduced you to a pimp called Frank, then threw you off a building. But then again, I only know that in hindsight, don't I?

"Lot of Franks everywhere," he growled. "Ah yeah, we got Franks in Bordnersville. There are Franks in every street in every town in every country on earth, maybe even the whole so-la system. Franks everywhere."

Then he asked me something that made me choke on my beer.

"So, Anthony, Tony, are you going to kill this Frank, or what?"
That's how Nick, Nicholas, thought. When he was my age, he was
given a gun and told to go off and put a wrong right by firing bullets
into people on the wrong side. That was Nick's idea of solving a
problem. It wasn't his fault, he'd been made that way by history.

"No, no, that's murder, no," I told him and meant it. The thought
had never entered my mind. I was coming to New York to lay flowers,
not to drop a man dead.

He smiled and nodded then, as if I was just like him and we both
knew damn well I was lying.

"Let me get you another beer," he said and hobbled back to the
pumps before I could say no.

We were both silent while he poured two more glasses. I went to
offer money, but he waved it away. I now know that was the moment
he'd made up his mind to tell me the story of a man named Joe.

Joe, you see, was another Frank, in many ways.

Nick had kept the story of Joe to himself until this one moment
when I arrived. I was from out of town, never returning, no threat. I
was the perfect audience.

He sat down next to me and held out his hand.

"I'm going to tell you something that might help you make sense
of what happened to your friend." He stared into my eyes. "But you
have to promise you'll never tell one soul. Not one. Not even when
you ascend to Heaven or fall to Hell, if God or, ha, Satan themselves
beg you to tell, keep your mouth shut. That OK with you?"

I wondered what you would have done in a situation like that. I
decided you would have gleefully shaken that man's mangled hand,
just to hear. It was another dark track and you'd have taken it without
hesitation.

So I did what you would have done and shook. He seemed
satisfied.

You might wonder how I remember everything he said, even with a
few beers in me, but I think my mind was put in "record" that
moment, like my Dad's reel-to-reel. It was as if my brain knew it had

to store every second. I could almost feel it whirring. So I'll tell this story as I remember it. I'll paraphrase, but I'll stick to the essence. That's what you would do, after after all.

So.

"Bordnersville's a tiny place." He continued to look me direct in the eye. I tried to hold that gaze as long as I could, but it was difficult. "So there isn't much crime. Burglaries, mainly. Kids acting up. Fights, muggings, but, you know, they're rare. People just do their thing and let everyone else do *their* thing. Nobody rocks the boat too much. Some might call that dull and boring. I suppose in somewhere like New York, it's the bad stuff that makes the city fizz as much as the showgirls and the spotlights, you know what I mean?"

I did, but kept my mouth shut. I now know I didn't say a word during that whole time, I just nodded and pulled the right expressions. He was giving a performance and you don't talk during the soliloquy. You don't even rustle your bag. You shut the fuck up and let Hamlet do his thing.

"Aha, you do. You know just fine. In the last 30 years, you know how many murders there've been in Bordnersville?" He wasn't asking for an answer, just held up one bent finger. "One. Just one murder in three decades. The previous murder was 20 years before that. Man stabbed another man over money. It's always about money, or women, women or money. Never nothing but. So, I suppose since the last one was over money, the next had to be about a woman and it was, except the woman didn't come off too well. So let me tell you about Joe…"

I could see he was still weighing up whether he was going to do this or not. He took a big glug of his beer and began.

"Joe lived out Fort Swatara Road. A few miles that-a-way. He ran a garage further out, past the Swatara State Park, you know, to get the trade from the walkers, tourists and all. He wasn't born here, like I was. Moved up from Dover, Delaware in '49. So he came from the Big City as far as we was concerned. You know, all sophisticated. But he wasn't sophisticated, no, not at all. Joe was a good-looking man, had a bit of Elvis Presley about him, that kind of slight Cherokee look, but not enough for people to take racial against him. Just enough to give him an upright burning expression. Thick black hair, like Elvis, big lips, doe eyes. He was tall, too. Well, the moment he arrived, the young ladies from round here were fluttering around him like a pervert round school gates and he knew it. The good lookers, they all know it don't they? You're a good- looking fella. Bet you know it too, huh?"

I tried to look surprised, humble and confused all at once but it just came out as a shrug.

"Yeah, you know it just fine. Bet you gave young Mary a few looks when you came in, right? She told me there was a nice-looking fella upstairs. If she weren't off at nine I'd lay money you'd be sitting here hitting on her right now."

I wish I had been. As I write this to you, I dearly wish I had.

"So Joe comes walking into town as if he's King of it All and the other men round here don't like it. Well, who would? We think it's women who get jealous when a looker comes a-clicky-clacking onto their patch, but us men, we're the same. They're a threat, right? But us men, we didn't know the half of it. Turns out Joe was the real jealous type, more than anyone round here could possibly begin to imagine.

"Joe must have been about 25 when he came here in '49. His Mom and Dad died and he was the only child. So he got their money, home, possessions. Sold off the home and possessions, used the money to start up that garage out at Swatara. Smart move. I often wonder whether that was Joe's idea or someone else suggested it, because Joe wasn't known for smart moves. As long as he kept his mouth shut and his doe eyes all big, he did just fine, but the moment he spoke up, he ruined everything. Joe was not an intelligent man. He'd mumble his way through a conversation, hardly make any sense. He'd use as few words as possible to get his point across. Perfect for a mechanic! 'Need gas?' 'Want a clean?' 'Tires?' Yeah, he hardly needed to be a master of conversation for that job, right? Just stick his hat on and stand there with a big grin and oily rag until some car came along, then he could mumble one of his few words and that would do just fine. He kept himself to himself and that suited everyone else just fine, too. As I say, that's how this town operates. But then, in '59, ten years after he arrived here, he attacked a man called Peter May with a wrench.

"Peter had got some gas from Joe's place, but hadn't paid at the time. Joe was OK with that, as long as you paid within a day or so, but May was tight. I honestly believe May thought Joe was so stupid, he'd forget about the debt. Now, Joe didn't have much grey matter up there, but when it came to his stuff, he was sharp. That money was Joe's, you see, and as far as he was concerned, Peter May had stolen it. So for every moment Peter never paid back what he owed, it was like he'd kept going into Joe's wallet and taking out bank notes. Yes, Joe had his things and they were his and if anyone else messed around with them, there'd be hell to pay.

"So four days after Joe'd filled up May's tank, he came into town. May used to drink in a place called Harvey's on the Bordnersville Road. Ha, pretty much everything's on the Bordnersville Road round here. I don't know how Joe knew Peter would be there, I have suspicions that Joe used a few adoring female eyes and ears about the place. But from what I heard, Joe gets out of his truck holding a big old wrench, walks into Harvey's and – no warning – smashes Peter over the back of the head with it. Just one blow, no more. He doesn't lose his temper, say a word. The other customers are shocked, of course, they stand and shout and rush over, but Joe just stands stock still like a wooden Indian until he finally says, 'Don't mess around with my money, Peter', who's in no position to hand over the money or say anything, since he's knocked out and his head is bleeding. Then Joe just climbs back into his truck and drives off.

"So Peter's taken to the hospital where he's stitched up and given whatever tests they do on people who get a hat made of a wrench. The police take statements and it's cut and dried, Joe's guilty of assault. He's arrested, charged and doesn't deny it, just tells them Peter had messed around with his money and had it coming. Funny phrase isn't it? '*Messed around with my money*'? Like money's a person or something. Joe liked that phrase. So anyway, he does six months in jail, which suggests to me he had some previous crimes to his name that were taken into consideration, but I don't know that for sure. But back then I thought anyone who can stick a wrench into another man's skull as cool as if he were chopping onions is probably capable of a lot more and worse. Turned out I was right on that score."

I sipped at my beer and you know, this night was feeling more and more like a movie with every passing moment. First there was BAR, then the expertly cast girl and now Nick, the old man with a beer in his hand and a secret to tell. If it was the other way around and you'd told me this story, that's exactly what I'd have thought it was – a tall tale – but I was right inside it and now there was just me, Nick and Joe.

"As you can imagine, the ladies went off Joe after that. A man who sends his best wishes with a wrench wasn't exactly marrying material, you'd think. But Lisa Rooney thought otherwise.

"To this day, I don't know what Lisa saw in Joe at first. She knew all about the wrench – everyone did, it was a big deal – but she was one of those girls who's attracted to danger. They happen. Go visit a prison and you'll see all the danger girls, sitting with their jumpsuited partners, looking at them as if their shit doesn't stink. They happen. Lisa liked to live on the edge, push things. Maybe Lisa was a little like your friend in New York?"

I shrugged again, conceding she could be. I also noticed he talked about Lisa in the past tense, which was worrying.

"Yeah, they happen. As I say, Joe was a good-looking man and there are some girls who'll forgive anything for a handsome face. 'Course, there are some men who'll walk a mile over broken glass to get to an ass, even if it belongs to the biggest Queen Bitch you ever saw. Funny how that happens, isn't it? You don't marry a painting, you marry a person and no matter what they look like on the outside, you spend your days with what's inside, right? Paintings are nice to look at for a while, yeah, but I wouldn't want to live in an art gallery, you know what I'm saying? Lisa Rooney could have done better. She could have been with a man who may not have had the looks, but the heart. Lisa was ravishing and there, that's not a word someone like me uses more than once in a lifetime. Yes, ravishing. Tall, blonde, movie star, big smile, big everything else that counts, quick to laugh, I don't know why she wasn't on the first bus out of here straight to Hollywood, your neck of the woods, without looking back. But those kinds of girls happen, too. Girls like Lisa, they stick around, find a man and stay with him. That's what she did. After the wrench incident, most people gave Joe more space. We were polite to him, sure, I think we were all worried if we weren't, he'd be back with another tool to beat some manners into us. So we walked softly when Joe was around. Polite, aha, but just enough. So I think that's why so many of us turned up to their wedding.

Not for him, but for her and fear that Joe would come a-knocking on anyone who didn't RSVP the invitation."

I wondered where this was all going. Nowhere good, I thought.

"So Lisa and Joe set up home together in his place on Fort Swatara. She worked as a secretary over in Fredericksburg just down the way. Joe didn't like that, he was a jealous man and even though she was only up the road, he'd drive over to her office a few times each week, just to check. I think he did that so the men there could see him, get the measure of the man, be warned off getting too friendly with Lisa. If you were a man, getting friendly with Lisa was like petting a lion cub. You knew any moment the lion could jump out and rip you to pieces. So Lisa was given a wide berth, too.

Oh, she had lots of girlfriends, but men were careful not to look her way if she was out with Joe. It was difficult, because she looked like she'd just stepped clean out of a centerfold, but there you go.

They never had any kids. Joe didn't want them, so Lisa didn't, either. That was how it worked. Thank the Lord they never did – I sometimes wonder what growing up in Joe's house would have been like. If he takes a wrench to someone over a few dollars, what would he do to a child who *messed around with his things* day in, day out? Doesn't bear thinking about. Yeah, those unborn kids of his had a lucky escape. Lisa wasn't so fortunate."

He sat for a while and I felt he was getting to the center of the story. He'd given me the set dressing, now the real performance was about to begin.

"It was 1963. 24th November. Two days after Lee Harvey Oswald stuck a few bullets into Kennedy's head. Or maybe he didn't, if you believe the rumors. Anyway, I truly believe everyone was so busy with Kennedy, Joe's crime kind of got lost in the hysteria. Not completely, but enough to allow him to do what he did. Are you old enough to remember that? Guess you must be, you'd have been around ten, right?"

I nodded. I remember shock, mainly, gentle sobbing coming from the kitchen. Mom at the table, Dad by her side. Yes, that was my memory of November '63, shock and disbelief. Powerlessness. The exact same feeling I had when I got your letter.

"Aha. Terrible thing. But Joe's crime was just as terrible. I often wonder why people add more grief to a death because the victim is well known. Perhaps it's a mortality thing. We think the famous are somehow protected from life. So when a celebrity dies, we think, 'Woah, if it can happen to them...' But we forget it'll happen to all of us, one way or another. So I was out, ha, guess where, on the *Bordnersville Road* of course. I used to deliver stuff back then. Didn't pay much, but meant I had myself to myself, wasn't in an office and had the wind in my hair..."

He laughed then, and rubbed a liver-spotted hand over his bald head.

"I never had hair, not even back then. But I had my admirers, I'll have you know," he added primly. It was difficult not to smile. "I'd stopped my pickup off by the side of the road. It was a Sunday, and I did extra time on Sundays, you know, every dollar makes a difference. I had a load of boxes and stuff in the back still to deliver, but I was hungry, so I stopped to have my packed lunch, think about Kennedy and my own life. But then Joe walked past, heading towards his house in Fort Swatara Road. That was unusual, because Joe drove everywhere, but now I think he had gone out walking to mull over things, too. It was a cold day, but he was only wearing a thin jacket. So yeah, now I think he'd gone for a walk to consider his options, yes, that's the phrase. *Consider his options.* Makes it sound harmless, doesn't it? Like a business deal. Maybe that's how Joe saw it, a business deal. He had damaged goods, wanted to get rid of them. I don't know. But he looked dark and determined, with places to go. He was striding back in the direction of his house that cold Sunday, two days after Kennedy met his maker.

"So Joe came striding past, I looked at him, he looked at me and that's when I saw the gun in his hand. I wanted to say, 'Hey Joe! Where you going, with a gun?' But when someone's carrying a weapon, it's probably not a good idea to draw attention to it. If somebody's packing for all to see, they have a reason for it and you don't want to know what that reason could be, in case they find a reason to make *you* part of the reason, know what I'm saying?"

I did, even though he'd jumped through a few verbal hoops getting there.

"So I just said, 'Hey Joe,' casual, like as if this was an ordinary Sunday and we were two guys on an ordinary road, just shooting the shit. He stopped then, and tucked the gun in the waistband of his pants like it was nothing. 'The damnedest thing about Kennedy, huh?' he laughed. He actually laughed. 'Wonder what happened there?' We hadn't heard about Oswald at that point, how Jack Ruby carried out a bit of street justice on Lee Harvey. Yeah, just as we were talking, Oswald was getting himself shot to death down in Dallas. But Joe, he looked normal, just a guy with a gun in his pants, out for a November stroll. He looked up at the birds flying by and said, as cool and calm as you like, smile on his face, 'Nick, it's a fine day. Been at work this morning. Dropped back at home. Sheets all crumpled, Lisa in her underwear. She was dressed when I left. Not dressed now. In her underwear!' He laughed again and I laughed with him, because that's what you do, especially when you're talking to a man with a trigger. He scratched his head, like he was considering his options. He chuckled again and said, 'So I guess she's been messing around, don't

you think? Messing around. Got another man, maybe more. So I guess
I gotta shoot her down, right?'

"Now God forgive me, he said it like it was one big joke, in the
same tone of voice you'd use for, 'I guess I'd better put the potatoes in
the oven,' you know. Not a big thing. I should have known. This was a
man who took a wrench to a guy over a debt, but I swear his eyes
twinkled, as if it was just a thing, two guys on a road, joking around.
He gave me a little salute and walked off, whistling. I guess I didn't
want to believe he was serious. We all do that, look away from the bad
stuff, right?"

"So Joe's house is only five minutes from where I'd stopped. I
should've, could've driven off then, got about my business, but
something stopped me. So I just sat with the door open, eating my
packed lunch. I guess something kept me there, to see what happened
next."

He went quiet again. It felt like he was weighing up each part of his
story as he got to it, to decide if he should carry on. Then he nodded,
as if he was giving himself permission to tell the rest.

"Must have only been ten minutes later, Joe came back round the
bend. He didn't have the gun any more. He looked normal. He looked
like just a guy again, a normal guy out for a walk on a normal road,
two days after his president was gunned down. I sometimes wonder if
Kennedy's murder had something to do with it. Maybe the fact that a
president could be shot made what Joe did easier for him. If a
president can be taken down so easy, a two-bit whore would be no
problem, right? I saw his shirt and face was flecked with little spots of
red, like freckles. I didn't want to believe it, but when reality shivers
like that, you just hang on to normality for dear life, right?

"'Hey Joe,' I said, like if I just kept everything on an even keel,
perhaps it would be OK. He looked me up and down with two blank
eyes. I got scared then for the first time, because there was just me,
him and this empty road, not a soul around for miles. And our
president had died not two days before, so death was in the air. 'I shot
her down,' he said. No inflection to his voice, as emotionless as an

engine running. 'Aha, yes, I shot her down. She was messing around, aha. So I shot her down.' What would you do in that situation? What would you say? Uh?"

Nick wasn't asking for an answer, he was asking himself to justify himself.

"So I just sat there and nodded, as if Joe had told me he'd put potatoes in the oven, as if it was just a thing. I couldn't say a word. I was frozen to the spot, couldn't see his gun, but this was a man who turned a tool into a weapon, so I had no doubt he could find a way to send me to the same place as Lisa. 'Aha,' he said, and looked back up at the sky. 'I shot her down. Guess that's it for Bordnersville for me. No-one gonna put a rope on me. She was messing around. A man can't have his woman messing around, right?' I nodded. God help me, I agreed. 'Guess I'll head Mexico way.' He patted his coat pocket. 'Got my savings, got cash, aha. Guess I'll go Mexico way. She was messing around, so I shot her. No-one gonna hang me up, no way. I had to do it. She needed to learn, right?'

"He was totally convinced of his own righteousness. People like Joe, like that guy Frank you told me about, they're so right, aren't they? They walk through the mud and don't get dirty. They do all kinds of terrible things, because they're always right. So I sat there and I shook, but not from the cold.

"'See you around,' Joe said and just walked away, hands in his pockets, off to Mexico like he was going on vacation. That was the last anyone saw of him. No suitcase, no nothing, just a coat full of money and his own sweet self. They found Joe's gun at the house, his fingerprints on it, cut-and-dried case, not least 'cos he confessed to me, straight out. You know, he shot Lisa in the face? Aha. I guess he didn't want anyone ogling her, even when she was dead. Can you believe that? A man who can look his wife in the eye and shoot her in the face? I didn't know that at the time, of course, but it all came out at the inquest, that was hard. The police tried to find him, of course. They went down all the usual avenues, Greyhounds, airports, full APB, the whole Dragnet, but Joe, he was just – poof! – gone, turned to

smoke. No-one saw him again. I was the last. Walking off, down the
Bordnersville Road, hands in his pockets, off Mexico way."

We both sat there for a while, pondering the past. But something
about the whole story was bothering me. Mentally, I'd started
twitching half-way through, wondering where this was going. But
then, when Nick started talking about inquests, investigations, and
APBs I really started to think.

You see, he took so long to get to the point. First there was all that
stuff about Joe's history, but then the actual meat of the tale – the
murder – was wrapped up in a couple of minutes. But that wasn't what
made me feel a little weird about the whole thing. It was how he'd
started the story, how he'd made me shake his hand and promise not to
tell a soul about it.

Now that made no sense whatsoever, because this tale of his was
out there, in the open. Everyone in Bordnersville would have known
about it. The first murder in thirty years? This place isn't New York,
where lives are snuffed out like candles; here, that event would have
been seismic. It wasn't a secret for God's sake. So why the big drama?
Why the handshake and the 'til death and beyond pledge?

So I asked, of course.

"It's a hell of a story, but why make me shake on it, promise never
to tell another soul? It's not exactly confidential, is it?"

Then Nick looked at me with a curious smile on his face.

"Oh, Anthony, Tony, the 21-year-old is sharp, isn't he?" He thought
for a moment, then clapped me on the back. "If you hadn't picked up
on it, maybe I'd have stopped there. But you got some brains on you.
You promised not to tell anyone, you did do that, right?"

"I did, but since everyone knows…" I started, but he held up a
hand to silence me.

"That's what everyone knows, uh-huh, yes, that's right. That's the
story everyone talks about, nothing secret about that, no. It's all there
in the records. You could go to Harrisburg County Hall and get the
transcripts of the inquest, read all the evidence, uh-huh, it's all there.
Joe's fingerprints on the gun, his history of violence, his jail term.

They even concluded that it was likely Lisa had been messing around, but they didn't know who with and would it have made any difference if they did? Yeah, adultery is a crime in some states, but not here, but I reckon murder is a bigger crime, right? So what if she was 'messing around'? She didn't deserve a bullet in the face. Yeah, that's what everyone knows…"

He gave me a slow wink and for some reason, it sent chills down my spine.

"But now I'm going to tell you what they don't know. That's why I made you make that promise. I don't have long left, I'm no fool, I know that. I got no way of knowing if you'll tell anyone, but I have to tell someone before Jesus makes the call. There's no-one round here I can tell. I may be dying, but they can still take a dying man's freedom.

I'm like Joe in that respect. No-one's going to make me die a prisoner. But I got to get this out of my head and you're perfect, Tony, Anthony. You're passing through, you'll be gone tomorrow and it seems like you have your own version of Joe with Frank in New York. So you're just the right guy, turning up here, for one night only. You promised, right?"

I agreed, but I was scared. I wasn't sure I wanted to know what could be worse than Joe shooting his wife in the face.

"Ah-huh, right." Nick took a big lug of beer and a deep breath.

"I loved her. I truly loved Lisa and I think she loved me. Why she went with Joe, I'll still never know, not really. I asked her about it once, but she just said, 'It's a woman's prerogative to change her mind,' and that was that. I think maybe she was attracted to Joe at first because he was the strong and silent type and girls like Lisa, well, as I say, she was attracted to the edge. That's why she started messing around. But only with me. That was dangerous enough as it was – she couldn't afford to have a few men on the burner, one was enough. One was too many, as it happened.

I delivered stuff, as you know. That was how I really got to know her. I'd do groceries and she was just far enough out on Fort Swatara for the supermarket to be inconvenient. Plenty of people like that

around here. So for 50 cents a week, I'd pick up the groceries and
deliver them. Halfabuck's not much, but it adds up when you have
enough groceries to deliver. Easy work. Joe was at his garage most
days – people need gas 24 / 7, right? Lisa was at work during the
week, but I'd drop her groceries off in the evenings and at weekends.
God, she was beautiful! Now, I was fifteen years older than her, but
when she was 40, I was 55, that's not so much of a difference. I made
her laugh. Do you make girls laugh, Tony, Anthony?"

"Sometimes," I replied.

"Well do it more times," he waggled a finger at me like a teacher.
"Get a girl laughing and it's more impressive than what you have
behind your fly, every single time. I made her laugh a lot and that's
something Joe never did. Boy, that guy couldn't tell a joke if you put
gun to his head. So I knew her from deliveries, like I knew a lot of
people.

But the first time I knew her, er, intimately, was in Fredericksburg.
I had a delivery out there and saw Lisa waiting for a bus in the rain, so
of course, I offered her a lift, like any gentleman would do for a
gorgeous blonde, right? It's only a short drive back here, but she was
flirting, full throttle.

I'm not exactly an oil painting now, but a few years ago, I can
safely say I was still distinguished. I've had my admirers, as I may
have mentioned. She put her hand on my knee as I drove and she was
giggling, throwing her head back and making me feel like Cary Grant.
If Joe had seen it, he'd have shot the both of us, right there. So I pull
up outside of her house and you know what she does? She leans back
into the cab and says, 'I think a knight in shining armour deserves a
kiss.' I thought it would be a peck on the cheek, but no, she comes at
me like a lover and next thing I know, we're in the pickup and who-
knows-what is happening. Part of me is thinking if Joe comes back,
we're dead, but another part of me doesn't want it to stop. What guy
would? That would have been 1959. We never spent much time
together, it was impossible. If anyone had seen, the cat would have
been out of the bag like greased lightning. Maybe two or three times a

year we got intimate. I'd go by Joe's to check he was there and then straight to Fort Swatara. I was the delivery guy. My truck was always outside some place or other, there were plenty of women at home alone, no-one paid any mind. And since Lisa's house was off the beaten track, no-one saw a thing anyway. Most of the time, we just jawed on her doorstep and laughed. I fell in love with her. At nights, by myself, I fantasised that Joe would fall under a train, or that we'd just midnight-flit away and start a new life somewhere else, but yeah, it was just a fantasy. I think she loved me. I hope she did. She looked at me in that way, you know?"

I did.

"But I never asked and she never said. So maybe I just kept that hope alive in my head. We talked on her doorstep and we did whatever else in my pickup or sometimes in her home, but that was rare. So that's where I'd been that morning, 24th November, 1963. God forgive me, that's where I'd been. At her house. Joe's truck wasn't there, I had the perfect cover, I was after all, just the old delivery guy.

I went on the off-chance, because Joe worked on Sundays. I knew it was always risky, but as I say, she liked the risk. We found out – once the inquest came in – that he'd taken his truck out and left it by the side of the road, further up toward the park. I think he'd done that so Lisa wouldn't hear him coming. He must have missed us by only 10 minutes or so, otherwise I'd have been dead right next to her. No-one knows exactly what happened that day, but here's what I think, for what it's worth.

"I reckon Joe took his truck out and he's thinking about stuff. He was a jealous enough guy at the best of times, so I'll bet he went out, parked up and walked back. He lets himself in the house and there's Lisa, in her underwear. The bedsheets are crumpled and Joe wants to know why. Lisa was smart, she would have found an excuse. Maybe she had a headache and had to go back to bed. Maybe she was going to take a bath, who knows what she said, but whatever it was, it was enough to waylay Joe's suspicions, but not for long. So Joe takes his gun and he goes for a walk, to consider his options. And he's walking,

thinking and becoming angrier and angrier. Maybe he already knew, in
his heart, that his wife was messing around. So he takes a walk down
the Bordnersville Road and what do you know, the only soul he sees is
me, who's just been to bed with his wife. That was why I got so
scared, not the fact he was holding that gun, but if somehow he could
see straight into my mind and see the truth. But I swear, when he
laughed and talked about shooting Lisa, I didn't think he'd do it. I
swear, I'll swear on a mountain of Bibles, I thought he was joking. But
I should have known better – as I say, Joe didn't joke. If Joe says he's
going to shoot his woman, he's going to do it, uh-huh. It never crossed
his mind she was messing around with me, why would it? Old, bald,
ugly Nicholas and Lisa? Nope, that idea was literally unthinkable, so
he never thought it.

"I sat there and watched him go. Why didn't I stop him? Because I
was scared for myself, too. God forgive me, I let him go and I was
relieved. I should have driven there, overtaken him, put Lisa in the
pickup and put my foot down and driven till I got to the coast. Then
kept on driving all the way into the sea, over to Europe. I should have
done, but I didn't. I just sat there with my lunch and watched him go.

What was I thinking? I let her die. That's what I did. Now I think
part of me knew just fine what he was going to do, but – ha – big man
that I am, I saved my own skin. From that very first kiss in the pickup,
I knew where it would end."

His eyes went to tears. He had loved her. At that moment, I knew
he'd loved her with all his heart.

It took a while for him to come back from wherever he'd gone in
his head.

"So Joe comes walking back. He'd left his gun by her body. She
was in the hall. I think he just opened the door and shot her where she
stood. I don't reckon he said anything to her, no big 'why?' no
emotion, like a butcher in the slaughterhouse, just a job to be done. He
shot her in the f-f-face."

He just crumpled then. I didn't know what to do. I couldn't put an
arm round him, there was nothing I could say. I knew that image

haunted him every single night. The idea that the woman he loved would have been executed like that – not just killed, destroyed.

"I knew what he'd done even before he said a word, before I saw the flecks of red on his face and shirt. I knew. And he stood there and talked about going to Mexico, like it was a little jaunt, nothing special. He stood there with his coat stuffed with money and his wife's blood on his face and talked about it as if he'd just, I don't know, put some potatoes in the oven. Then he walked off and no-one saw him ever again."

He sat and thought quietly for a while, then his shoulders slumped and he whispered, *"except, ah, that's not true."*

Then *h*e exhaled, blew out his breath like he'd been holding it all his life.

"Uh-huh. That's what I told the police, that's what I told the inquest. I almost believe it myself, I can see Joe, walking away, hands in his pockets, off to Mexico. They never found any trace of him on the bus, or at the airport, or anywhere for that matter, because it never happened. He never walked away.

"'I'm not gonna get no rope,' Joe had said and I knew it. I knew people like Joe, the mud doesn't make them dirty, not ever. I knew what was going to happen – he was going to disappear to Mexico and there'd be no justice for Lisa. She'd be in that hallway forever, with her ruined face and Joe would never pay. He'd live it up down there, with more women, drinking, dancing, loving as if she never existed.

"I didn't think about what happened next. It was more like a reflex action. I reached into my glove compartment, where I always kept my gun and I shot him. I shot him like I believe he shot her. Not a word, no emotion. He didn't react in any way, no shocked expression, no noise, he just fell. I shot him through the heart so he was dead before his head hit the road. I was like a robot, Tony, Anthony. A machine. I picked him up – I remember he was heavy – and pulled him into the back of the pickup. I had some tarp in there to cover the deliveries from the rain and put that over him. I didn't think about it, no, not at all. He was meat. I drove him out to the park, weighed him down with rocks and then sent him to the bottom of the lake, money and all. I didn't want his money.

"Then I went home, cleaned out the truck and waited for the storm to break.

"When news of Lisa's murder came out, I went straight to the police, like I was the concerned citizen. I told them I'd seen Joe, but never mentioned how he'd had a gun in his hand. They would have asked all kinds of questions, you know, '*Why didn't you call us? Why didn't you stop him? Surely you knew?*' all that. I never told them how Joe said he was going to shoot Lisa down, for the same reasons.

"I just described how I'd seen him heading toward his house, how we'd said hello and that was that.

It all tied up anyway – his gun was on the floor, covered with his fingerprints, there were no other suspects. My evidence put him at the scene, at the time. I told them I'd seen him again 10 minutes later, how he seemed a little freaked out and was talking about going to Mexico, but he wouldn't say why.

So they had a murderer with previous known violence on the run, a witness – me – the weapon, the whole nine yards. It all made sense. But of course, only you and I know Joe didn't go anywhere but the bottom of a lake. And that's why I made you promise, Tony, Anthony."

I just stared at him. I've never met a murderer before. I'd just shared beers with a killer. Nick shrugged.

"I'm not proud. But he would have walked away and I couldn't let him do that. I loved her."

He stood up painfully and lurched round to the other side of the bar. "Sometimes, you have to do the right thing, even if it's the wrong thing. People like Joe, like your guy Frank, they don't deserve to breathe. They have to know that justice will come."

He opened a safe underneath the spirits and pulled out a small black velvet bag which he put in front of me.

"No-one knows you're here. No-one knows your friend wrote you, 'cos you never showed anyone the letter, right?"

I nodded, unsure where this was going. No-where good, I felt.

"No-one knows who you are in New York, no-one knows what you know. And Frank, he wouldn't have a clue, would he? You're an invisible man to someone like Frank. To Frank, you're no threat, because you don't exist."

He pushed the bag toward me.

"All you have to do is find him. Say, 'Hey, Frank,' then the name of your friend , so he knows and then do what I did to Joe. It only takes a second. 'Hey, Frank,' he smiled, and mimed shooting a gun.

So now I'm sitting in ROOM, writing this letter, with a pistol in a velvet bag on the bed.

I started this journey wanting to lay flowers for you, but I think I may end it laying something else down, too.

I love you, Caroline.

"THE A TEAM"

(Ed Sheeran, 2011, from the album, +)

The snowflake woke her up.

It tumbled from wherever snowflakes are born, straight from heaven to her bottom lip. One cold kiss, then it was gone.

She opened her eyes. The snowflake wasn't alone, more twisted down from the white-out sky above.

The girl lay there for a while as her face became dotted with snow. She realised her mind was like the sky; blank, white, and empty. She scrunched her eyes shut and willed a memory to come, any context to who and where she was.

Nothing.

She opened her eyes again and risked looking sidewards.

She wasn't in a bed, that much was obvious. To her right was a concrete pathway and beyond that, bushes, dusted with snow. A litter bin's contents spilled out onto the pavement below. The litter was frosted and she thought, dully: *This weather makes everything beautiful, even stuff nobody wants anymore.*

The girl began to suspect she was something nobody wanted any more.

She pushed herself up a little.

So, here she was, on a park bench. She crossed her eyes, looked up at her fringe and registered it was blonde.

OK, that's a start, she thought. *I'm blonde and I'm...*she held up her hands.

She was wearing gloves, but they were torn and her skin could be seen through the rips.

*I'm white. God, I'm so white. I'm almost as pale as the sky today. I'm blonde, white, lying on a park bench and I'm...*she looked down at her clothes. *I'm wearing dirty jeans, scuffed trainers and a ripped raincoat. I'm blonde, white, scruffy and...*she stretched and her arm emerged from the raincoat's sleeve.

There on her wrist was a tattoo of angel wings. She stared at the ink for a while and it sparked off blurred memories.

Where was I last night? She wondered. *Who was I with, what did I take, that I would wake up, alone, with no memory on a bench today?* She felt empty, but it wasn't hunger for food so much as a physical ache for another sustenance. She felt about in her pockets and pulled out a few random items.

There was a comb, a single key and a bubble pack of pills marked "Trazodone".

She turned the medication over in her hand, thoughtfully. It definitely brought back memories. She recalled waiting...in a pharmacy, a hospital? Somewhere bright and clean, anyway. There were people in white coats—well, they'd looked like white coats, although she wasn't sure. But she had waited.

Waited for what? And where had she waited for something to happen?

She knew the pills were supposed to help get her through the day. They could stop her mind whirling, but where had she been given them? Her brain felt fried. Whatever happened last night had fallen over her memory, just like snow lay across the litter and made it disappear.

She felt around in another pocket and her fingers closed on something cylindrical.

She pulled that "something" out and stared in amazement at banknotes, rolled up and held together with an elastic band. She counted the money, £100, in tens.

She looked at the cash thoughtfully, rolled it up and carefully returned it to her pocket.

I am blonde and I am scruffy, I have pills in my pocket and £100. I am young, but not too young, and I have a tattoo of angel's wings on my wrist, she thought. *Wait. I have a tattoo of* angel's wings *on my wrist?*

She examined it again. Memories circled. Were they real, or just stories someone had told her, a long time ago? She didn't know. The stories felt authentic, but also fantastical, fairy tales that made dreadful realities fade away.

I've been told stories and taken drugs. Both have helped to make this world slide. Oh yes, I had to take those drugs, didn't I? There was no choice.

So who am I? Where am I?

Jesus. I'm cold.

I really need to do something about that.

Without thought, she held up her hand flat against the sky. The angel wings tattoo on her wrist slid into view again.

The snow stopped.

Her eyes widened, mouth opened, and she looked at her hand, now surrounded by impossible snow that was suspended about her like frozen static on a screen.

Oh my God, she thought. *I just stopped the snow. How did I do that?*

She reached up and plucked one single flake from the air. It was real and started to melt in her fingers. She placed it back, where it hung, then, slowly, impossibly, turned.

I am blonde, scruffy, with a pocket full of pills and angel's wings on my wrist and I just stopped the snow. That *is very cool.*

There wasn't much else she could think after that.

A jogger came round the bend and puffed his way toward her through the snowfall.

"Hey! Hey, mate! Did you see that?" she excitedly asked the runner as he slowed. He was a middle-aged man with a red face and a too-big belly.

"See what?" he peered about, confused.

"That. See? What just happened. I did that. I did that! Cool, wasn't it?" She bounced on the bench and grinned at him.

The man looked slightly worried. "Sorry, what? Do you want some money or something? I don't have much change…"

She waved his offer away. "No, no, I don't want change, I mean the snow. The snow just stopped, didn't it? See? I did that."

"The snow just stopped?" He said in disbelief. "No it didn't. It's getting heavier."

She glanced about herself and the man was right. The snow fell, as normal.

As the jogger started to move away he cast a fearful look back at her, as if he'd just run straight into a mad person. She recognised his confused and scared expression. It felt like she'd seen those emotions on people's faces for years.

"I did stop the snow," she said to herself. "I did." She held up her hand flat to the sky again, but the snow simply fell onto her palm, just as it should.

As the girl stood, she noticed a bright red piece of litter and bent to pick it up.

It was a flyer and the headline read, "HAVE YOU BEEN SAVED?" Underneath was a picture of Jesus, with his arms round two grateful sinners, who looked up at him adoringly. The Messiah resembled a football manager with two of his favourite players. Underneath Christ was another line, "COME AND MEET JESUS AT ST JOHN'S, MARKET ROAD."

"Come and meet Jesus," she said softly and stared up at the sky. Her expression became confrontational. "Oh, ha, yes. Right. Yes, I see. I see now. NOW I get it. Thanks for this." She waved the flyer up at the clouds. "Aha, yeah. I see. It's coming back, some of it. Got some memories, finally. Just a few, cheers. Right. Yeah. The stopping snow thing. Right. Yep, got you."

The sky remained silent and dismissively shed its frozen self about her.

"Keeping schtum, ha? Listen," she went on, more confidently. "I'm going to need a bit more guidance than this…I mean, thanks for the hint and everything." She held up the flyer again. "But I really hope that jogger wasn't my guide. I think I scared him off. Yeah, right. Aha."

She cackled and turned her face to the clouds. "Yeah, aha. Do your worst. I know who I am."

The girl pulled back her sleeve and revealed the angel tattoo. "Yeah, see? I know who I am."

She looked up and down the path and made a decision. She went right, in the jogger's direction, and sang a little song to herself. She scuffed her trainers through the snow, hands in her pockets, as her blonde hair shone against the white.

*

Soon, the girl found herself at a gate. A clock tower stood on top of what must have once been the park keeper's house, now boarded up and graffitied. It was 11 in the morning.

I lay there on that bench for how long? She wondered. *How long before the snow kissed me awake? And nobody thought to shake me, wake me, check if I was OK? What kind of place is this?*

But she knew exactly what kind of place this was. The snow made it look peaceful and still, but it was noisy and angry. Yes, there was a fury and violence here, where people would knock you to the ground and take everything you had. Perhaps they'd even take *you.* She remembered love was a commodity in the streets she walked. Images were coming back to her. *No, it's not* love *where I live.* She shook her head. *It's got nothing to do with love. People hook up so they're not alone, that's all. People like me. But no, not like me. I'm bulletproof. I get through it all. I can take it. Whatever they throw at me,* in *me, I can take it.*

That need, that hunger, rose and gnawed at her again. She reached into her pocket, pulled out the bubble pack of pills marked "Trazodone", and held them up. There was no other information on the silver packaging, no dosage or clues. She tried to remember what they were for, but nothing came. That part of her remained hidden.

Alright, the girl thought. *I need to find St John's Church, apparently. Which way?*

Outside the park was a row of shops. She stopped outside one and peered at her reflection. Inside, mannequins stared back at her blankly, dressed in party frocks and mini skirts. She looked a mess in comparison.

OK, so my clothes could do with a bit of work. She went closer to her reflection. *But the hair's good. I like the hair. Ooh, quite pretty, actually. But then, we usually are, aren't we? It helps. We do what we need to better when we're pretty. We're traps. Girls like me, we attract the bad.*

Those odd, jumbled souvenirs turned inside her mind. It was like watching a Rubik's cube being solved. Sometimes, the memories locked together and made sense, at others, they were a random collection of colours and patterns. Parts of her past rose then sunk again and she wasn't sure if any of them were real or make believe.

The girl noticed she wore just a little make-up and that was strange, because there was none in her pockets. She had a hint of mascara, a faint trace of eyeliner, but nothing else. This face didn't need much. Her lips were full and naturally red, cheekbones high and defined.

Someone made me up, but who? she wondered. She touched her face, pulled expressions and stuck her tongue out. Inside the shop, a little girl saw, laughed and stuck out her tongue in return. Her mother spotted the silent exchange and pulled her daughter from the strange blonde outside.

The girl turned from the window. *Yes, I must look awful,* she mused. *I wouldn't let my little girl play faces with me. Except I don't have a daughter, do I? I know that much, too. It wouldn't do to have a child, noooo, this world gives no special dispensation to mothers.*

She looked up and down the street. A rat-faced teenager in a hoodie and tracksuit leaned against a wall. He chewed at a sausage roll and stared at her with dead eyes. Two old ladies chattered away at a bus stop, oblivious to everyone and everything around them. Shoppers went about their business with straight ahead determination.

A man approached, and studiously avoided her attention.

"Excuse me?" she asked, as politely as she could.

"No." The man strode past.

She watched his back.

"Ah, ah," she whispered to herself, then louder, "I've been polite. Turn around. You. Turn. Around."

She bent her forefinger into a little hook and mimed jabbing it into the man's back. He suddenly stopped in the street, turned back and stared.

For a moment, his face was blank, but then his eyes narrowed and he hissed, "Whatever it is, no? OK, no." He gave her one last look of pity and disdain, then marched off.

"Wasn't that how it worked?" She muttered to herself, then looked at her hooked finger and shook it, like a broken machine that needed a good rattle to get the inner workings operational again.

"That probably did look a bit mad," she conceded. "I'm sure that's how it worked."

She noticed the passers-by were doing exactly that, passing by. Clearly they all hoped she wouldn't stop them. This pavement-traffic was very busy. Everyone had places to go and were all late, by the looks of things. She was the only rock in the river of people that rushed by.

A homeless man lay on the floor in an alleyway. As she passed, he mumbled, "Serrrjoawn".

His eyes were closed, so he either slept or didn't want to see the world any more. She stopped in front of him and tilted her head like a dog.

"I'm sorry?" she asked.

He didn't open his eyes.

"Sanjohn," he spluttered.

"Sanjohn?" she repeated. "SanJohn? St John? Is that what you're saying? St John? Are you my messenger? My guide? St John? Is that it?"

People walked around them and she knew what they were thinking: *That's typical. See how their type gravitate to each other. He's probably her dealer. He's probably her <u>boyfriend</u>. What do they talk about, the nowhere people? Ignore them, they speak in another language, one we don't want to hear.*

"Sern John." In his sleep, he raised a hand and pointed a finger *that* way, down the street. "Snnnnjjjnnn," he snored.

Hmm, she thought, *perhaps he's been snoring all this time and I heard what I wanted to.*

"Sssssjnnnn."

She smiled sadly at him. He looked fifty-something but was probably only in his thirties. The street did that; it leeched you away. It wasn't something you saw happen overnight; the erosion was gradual, but unless you escaped, inevitable.

How have you ended up here, she wondered, *with dirty slush soaking through your clothes? How can you even* sleep?

But she knew. It was how they all slept. Their method came from an old song she'd heard a long time ago, "Whatever Gets You Through The Night".

Yeah, she thought, *whatever gets you through the night, whatever it takes, just do it, take it, screw it, just to close your eyes and escape, for that brief time. Whatever gets you through the night, drink, powder, needle or pipe. Or lying down with anyone, men, women, old, predatory, just to feel a proper bed beneath you again.* She'd done it all, taken it all, because she'd had to.

The snow fluttered about her and landed on the sleeping man. *Perhaps,* she thought, *if he's lucky, the snow might take him away from all this, just carry on falling until he isn't here any more.* It was a harsh way to think, she knew, but sometimes there was nothing else to pray for.

She reached into a pocket and pulled out the roll of £10 notes.

What would £10 do? she wondered. *£20? £30? £100? I can't save you with this. I could stuff the whole roll in your pocket and it would buy you a little time, but wouldn't buy you freedom. There's not much I* *can do for you. You're lost now and money won't point you in the right direction.*

She considered the cash again and held the roll up to her face.

After that, things happened very fast.

Suddenly, the roll of money wasn't there any more. Like a magician's trick, a hand flashed in front of her, and – poof! – the cash was gone. A figure in black barged her out of the way and she fell backwards.

She saw the back of a track-suited teenager jet away up the street. She knew his type, had met them every day. That rat-faced little vermin boy had spotted an opportunity and taken it. People like him lived in the moment, where little concepts like consequences and responsibilities were alien. He simply did what he wanted, when he wanted and fuck everyone else – they were just in his way.

He'd seen the money, wanted it, taken it. He ran on instinct alone.

"I don't think so," she snarled at the running boy, gathered herself, and gave chase.

A few shoppers watched her go, but mostly, the pursuit was ignored – that's the rule – if you don't see, it's none of your business. *The girl chasing the teenager through the snow? I don't see them. The man collapsed in an alleyway? I don't see him. The bullies, rapists, abusers, refugees, hungry and homeless, lost and broken? No, can't see a thing. Keep my curtains closed, my phone on and my head down and for God's sake, don't look, because if you do, you cannot un-look.*

She didn't yell after the boy, there was no point. Clearly he'd been yelled at all his life, so shouting would make no difference. Her expression became emotionless. Some feral sixth sense made the thief look over his shoulder and shock spread over his pinched, pasty face. He obviously wasn't used to being chased, not these days, when every pocket contained a knife and nobody thought twice about pulling it.

He darted into the traffic, and she knew the cars would stop for him – they always did.

People like this boy just walked into the road and parted the vehicles like Moses in trainers. A few skidded to a halt and furiously sounded their horns, but this *boy* knew no drivers would confront him. His clothes, his uniform, sent out the message, loud and clear: *I am tooled up and I do not care. I am gangsta, I am chav, I am top boy, I am roadman, I deal, I steal, I do not feel.*

She followed him, but didn't bother to zig-zag around the cars. She followed a straight line and leapt, sure footed over the bonnets, eyes fixed ahead. There were a few shouts from inside, but more of shock. First, that boy and now this pretty blonde? It didn't make any sense.

The teenager risked another glance over his shoulder, and she was still behind him, not ten feet away. He darted into another alleyway, but his footing was not so confident. He slid and crunched into a large metal bin, then crumpled to the ground.

She ran into the alley and stood before him. She hadn't even broken a sweat.

He looked up at the girl and curled his top lip. Then he stood and sucked air through his teeth, a curious challenge. They were alone with only one option left.

He knew it, she knew it.

So, inevitably, he pulled a knife. It was only a few inches long, but it doesn't take much to end a life, just a little metal, the right spot and it's done. Most of the time, there was no thought involved and the girl knew this boy really had no thought involved.

She looked at the knife and raised an eyebrow.

"Alright, you worthless little shit," she sighed and stared into his shark eyes. "Here's what's going to happen. You give me my money, then you walk out of this alley back to whatever putrid nest you've scuttled from today. Or you don't. I'm not bothered either way."

Those empty eyes flickered for a moment, but that was all.

"Fuck you," he said, then completed the script with some more classic lines, dredged from his ghastly bag of reference points.

"Fuck you, bitch. Fuck you, you get dis, bitch, you get dis. You want dis, huh?"

She laughed in his face, then started to speak faster than he could keep up. His expression changed from a snarl to confusion.

"'Dis? Dis'? Oh, we're the proper little 'gangsta' aren't we, white boy? Have you heard of 'cultural appropriation'? No? Too many syllables, I guess. Ever heard of Black Panthers? Ah-ah, no, not the Marvel film, silly. Do try and expand your reference points. Don't know what that means? Well, now's the time to finally be clever and give me back my money. 1...," she counted, "I'm going all the way up to three, OK? You can count, right? Who knows? 1...2..."

She didn't get to three. Faster than the boy could react, she rushed forward and in one movement, grabbed the knife, then head butted him. His nose exploded.

He dropped the weapon, then clutched his bloodied nose and slid down to the floor.

She pocketed the blade.

"I'll be getting rid of *dis*, thank you." She smiled sweetly at the broken boy on the ground, then held out a hand to him.

"My money?"

"Fuck you, bitch"

"Oh, change da rekkid." She kicked him full in the stomach and he bent double. She reached into his pocket and pulled out her roll.

"There. We could have avoided all that nastiness, couldn't we? But ooooh no, Mr Gangsta, Mr Dis and Dat here, had to play the big man."

She bent again and gently touched his bloody nose. "You need to start behaving yourself. I'm serious. Because if you keep this up, compared to where you're going, that will feel like a kiss."

She stood, curtsied and left.

*

Father Liam Watson of St John's Catholic Church, Hackney Road, slowly walked through his place of worship and reverentially lit each candle as he passed.

He'd been in this parish for just over a year and the job had come with its own blessings and curses.

One blessing was this building. He looked with pride up at the vault, back to the golden altar and around the statues, all with their own stories to tell and lessons to give. If he ever found himself stuck for a sermon (it happened more than he'd like to admit) then all the inspiration he needed was here. He could find Christ's wisdom built into the very walls. The people were a blessing too, although there weren't many regular worshippers. That was par for the course these days.

One curse was the area, which had so many problems. Poverty, gangs, drugs, prostitution and a multitude of other sins were just outside the walls. Father Watson often kept the doors locked, which went against everything he believed. The church was supposed to be open to all, but he knew there were some who would ransack the place for no other reason than it was there.

He did what he could to give the strays some kind of path, but many of them didn't seek the light, they wanted to get lost, to stay in their darkness.

Father Watson lit the candles. He tried to obliterate the shadows.

"I am the way and the truth and the life," Jesus had said. Liam felt it was one of the Saviour's most simple and effective statements, just ten words. But as a child he'd always misheard it as "I am the way and the truth and the *light*."

Blasphemously, he preferred his misheard version. Jesus was the life, yes, but also the light. He flickered in even the blackest night. So every day, Liam lit the candles and let their glow draw the lost to him.

He carefully raised his taper to the last wick. It spluttered then caught, strong and bright. Father Watson looked up and smiled.

At that moment, the door flew open, snow rushed in, and the flame died.

The snow was accompanied by a girl dressed in a dirty raincoat, torn gloves and scuffed trainers.

He recognised her type immediately. The strange mix of clothes screamed Charity Shop, but while the dirt on them told him she'd slept rough, her hair was clean, shining blonde and her pale face was pretty.

He knew eventually that face would crumble.

Unless the doorway-dwellers got off the streets, even the prettiest profile would dry out and collapse, but for now, hers was intact. "Sorry." She dusted off her clothes. "Did I do that? The candle?"

"It's OK." Father Watson smiled. "Candles have a habit of going out. They're fragile that way."

"Yeah, but you can always light them again. I think light is always looking for a way in. Candles give it somewhere to stop, you know, just for a bit."

"Yes, yes, true, er, come in, come in. We have plenty of room, as you can see."

Only a few parishioners sat quietly in prayer and contemplation.

She ran a finger over the top of one of the pews, then held it up to her face.

"Oooh, this place needs a clean. Look at that." She held her forefinger to him, the tip dirty and black.

"Dust to dust, ashes to ashes…," he offered and she sniggered.

"Are you here to pray? Or…"

"Well, it's the 'or', actually." She looked about the church. "Lovely," the girl whispered, but it came out, "*laaavely*", pure East London, like a real-life Eliza Doolittle.

"So which St John is it?" She asked. That took Watson by surprise as no one had ever framed the question before. "Naaah, don't tell me. Cassian? Ephesus? Merciful? Fisher?"

Liam's mouth fell open in shock. "I've never met anyone who's ever even heard of Cassian. Well, not from the laity, obviously."

"'Not from the laity'," she snorted. "Get *you*. '*Not from the laity*', Well obviously no one would have heard of Cassian round here. He's not exactly East End, more Eastern Orthodox, right?"

Watson struggled to find something to say. She burst into giggles.

"I'm mucking about. It's John the Baptist, isn't it? It's always John the bloody Baptist."

She waved a fist at the ceiling of the church, like a bus conductor from a '70s sitcom. "I'll get you, John the Baptist!" she groaned in a silly voice. "Give another saint a go, whydoncha?!"

Father Watson looked at this odd girl with something that approached awe and thought, *Who* are *you*?

She sat down on the nearest pew and patted a spot next to her.

She's just walked in and acting like she owns the place. Liam thought, now slightly affronted. *Coming in here, patting* my *pew, giving* me *permission to sit! No, wait, hold on. It's* God's *pew and we're both just passing through.*

He sat.

The girl was silent as she stared about the church. As Father Watson watched, he realised she wasn't just looking but studying. "Aha. Got it. Victorian Gothic, yeah," she concluded, satisfied. "I think about 1850?"

"1852," he answered, quietly astonished.

She snapped her fingers in annoyance. "Damn. So close. Two years out. No cigar. Just look at that font. Look at the base! It's... monumental. I do like Gothic, but it can get a bit fiddly, you know, frills over content?"

"It does, it does," he agreed.

"Anyway..." The girl rummaged through her pockets and took out the mugger's knife. The priest stared at it.

Oh, he thought. *So this is how it's going to go. She's like that, is she? A religious obsessive with a knife.*

He'd seen knives before, of course, but never had one pulled on him. He held up one hand in supplication and spoke calmly.

"Now, we don't need to have that in here, do we?"

The girl looked up at him in confusion, then down at the knife. She smiled, turned it in her hand and offered it to him, handle first.

"Don't panic, Father. I "liberated" this from a sinner earlier. I thought you may have access to some kind of knife amnesty project or something. Anyway, take it if you like, or I'll throw it in a pond or something. Rather not though, in case it hurts the ducks. Mind you, no

ponds round here. Plenty of pond life, but no ponds. Do Hackney
Marshes count?"

He gingerly took the knife. "I don't think the Marshes count. Is that
why you're here? The knife? Why are you here?" he asked, the only
question on his mind since she'd blundered through the door.

"Ah, no. Not the knife." The girl pulled out the flyer of Jesus and
his two sinning fans, then began to gabble at a velocity that
approached the speed of sound. "OK, right. Here's the deal, right?
OK. I found this earlier. It says, 'COME AND MEET JESUS.' I don't
think it needs quite the strident capitals, but I suppose it gets the
message across. Ooh, Jesus looks a bit white, doesn't he? Bit too
Caucasian. Did the artist clock many pasty white people in Judea,
circa AD30? Nice bridgework. Teeth like a Kardashian, that man.
Look at his *laaavely* hair, too, what conditioner did he use? Pantene
for messiahs? Ah, and I don't think Big J wore a robe like that, either.
Sparkling clean, ain't it? Couldn't move for laundrettes in Galilee. The
whole thing's just riddled with historical inaccuracies. Bit like the
Bible, then. But anyway, I took this flyer as a message, an order,
whatever, so here I am. At St John the Baptist's place, grrr!" She
waved her fist at the roof again. "I don't know why after that, though,
so is He here? Jesus? Do I have to make an appointment?"

Father Watson didn't know what to make of her. First she'd shown
stunning insights into Church history and architecture, but was now
off on a tangent. *Drugs*, he thought. *That's it. I've seen this mania
before. She's on something. Not weed; she's too sparky. Coke? No, too
expensive. Speed? Spice? No, too catatonic.* Something, *anyway.*

"Well, Jesus *is* here, He's everywhere."

She waved her hand at him, impatiently. "Yeah, yeah, I know, I
know. Omnipresence. Good trick if you can do it. But look, it
explicitly says, 'COME AND MEET JESUS.'" She boomed it in a
God-like way and a few people looked around. One coughed,
pointedly.

"Yes, but He's not *here*, here," said Watson patiently. "That flyer means you can find Him here, in yourself. You meet Jesus within yourself. Is that what you want to do? I can help."

"No, I want to meet Jesus properly, actually," she folded her arms, like a petulant toddler. "If I see a poster saying 'Come and see Santa Claus in his grotto', I damn well expect to meet the beardy red guy. Not be fobbed off with some existential shit like 'Santa is in all of us if you just know how to look'."

She didn't seem angry; her eyes twinkled with amusement.

"Well, er..."

"I'm fucking with you." She punched him on the arm, then put on a "gangsta" voice. "Yo. I'm fuckin' wit yoo, fadder! Whoops, sorry. Swearing." She slapped herself on the wrist and tutted. "But look, I found this flyer. I've come here because I think you are going to send me to the next place I need to go. That's how it works. You know, stations of the cross and all that. You have to go to here to get to there. No passing go, no collecting £200. Station to station. So where am I headed, Father? Any ideas?"

Drugs, he thought again. *She's a pretty girl, on drugs and probably homeless. That all makes her a target, a victim-to-be. Yes, I know exactly where you need to go.*

"Right." He took a deep breath. "I need to ask you a question. Please don't be offended. Are you taking anything?"

"Anything?" she rooted around in her pocket again. "Well, there's these. Although I haven't taken one today. But I feel a need coming on."

Father Watson took the pack of pills marked "Trazodone". He'd never heard of them before, but then, he wasn't a pharmacist.

"Have I taken anything?" she asked herself. "Oh yeah. Everything. Anything. That's what I do, Father. I take stuff from everyone. I take it all. I don't have any choice. I take everything that comes my way."

He looked at her sadly and saw that truth in her eyes.

"You need help."

"Well, I'm not sure about that." She spread her hands to say *it's no big deal*.

"You do. Do you have support? Someone to give you guidance?"

"I think so. Well, yes, but…"

"OK, OK. I think this is why you came here…" He picked up the flyer from the pew. "Alright. You saw this flyer, it sent you here and that *was* Jesus, OK? Of all the bits of paper, you chose this one. Or rather, Jesus chose it for you. So you see, you did meet Jesus, but didn't realise. He gave you this, to bring you here, so I could send you on to where you need to be. Yes?"

She bit her lip. "OK. Makes sense."

"There's a cafe up the road, 'Benny's'. Go in and ask for Mark."

"I thought you said it was, 'Benny's'."

"It is, but that was the old owner. It's Mark now. He does outreach for the community with a group of volunteers who know what you're going through. They'll get you where you need to be, off the stuff, off the streets, in somewhere safe, do you understand?"

"That's where I need to go? A cafe? Really?" she asked, confused.

"Aha. Tell him Father Watson sent you. That's me."

"Nah! Never. You're a man of the cloth? I'd have never guessed," she laughed and he joined in.

"He'll give you some hot food and you can have a chat, see how he can help. I'll call ahead, let him know you're on the way."

"I don't need an appointment? He's like Jesus, just there?"

"He's just there. What's your name? So I can tell him?"

She sat and thought for a while.

"Well, let's not get too formal. Just tell him the blonde girl's coming. That should do."

"OK." He understood. When you have nothing, your name is precious, sometimes the only piece of you left. "You'll definitely go?"

"The flyer told me to come here. You told me to go there. That's how it works. I'll definitely go. Does he do bacon sandwiches?

"He definitely does bacon sandwiches."

"Bonus result." She stood and held out her hand. Father Watson shook it. They looked at each other earnestly, like employer and candidate at the end of a job interview.

"Take care," he said.

"Oh I do," she replied. "That's what I always do. I take care."

*

A handsome, silver-haired woman in her early 60s stood in the park where the girl had woken up.

She held a briefcase and was dressed in a smart black trouser suit and white macintosh. A black hat sat on the back of her head.

She looked left and right, concerned. She'd already stopped several people who hadn't been able to offer any help.

No, nope, sorry, no. Nobody had seen her. A blonde girl, in a dirty raincoat? They'd have remembered *her,* for sure.

She'd walked here for 30 minutes already, but her teeth chattered and her hands were frozen. A jogger approached and his large belly bumped up and down with every step.

"Excuse me, excuse me." She waved a hand at him like someone hailing a cab.

The jogger slowed. He didn't look impressed, but she knew joggers never did when they had to stop. Even when waiting to cross a busy road, they carried on jogging, as if stopping for one moment would undo all their hard work.

"Sorry to bother you…" She looked suitably pained that she'd dared to interrupt his oh-so-important run. He continued to jog on the spot impatiently, as expected – the exercise equivalent of looking at one's watch. She reached into her coat and pulled out an identity card. "I work for the council, social care…"

He squinted down at the card. On it was her photo, name – Angela Dawson – and job title: MANAGER, SOCIAL CARE UNIT, HACKNEY E1. He continued to jog. Clearly he had important places to go.

"Sorry, I won't take a moment." She showed him a passport-sized photograph of the blonde girl, bleached by the flash. Her wide blue eyes stared straight ahead.

"Have you seen this girl? She was last spotted coming this way. She's, er, vulnerable, right now. I need to find her, get her, er, sorted out, you understand?"

The jogger finally stopped. He took the photo from Angela's hand and peered at it.

"Yeah, she was here when I came through earlier. I do 8k every morning," he added proudly and handed back the picture. "I come down Hackney Road, right, then I head up and over Hoxton way…"

"That's great," said Angela. "I wish I could be that fit, but alas… You saw her?"

"Aha. She was sitting on a bench back up that way. Just sitting there, in the snow. I thought she was odd."

"Odd?"

"Social Care?" he asked. "Is that the druggies and that?"

"We do help people who are struggling with addiction, yes. Now, this girl…" She attempted to gee him on.

"'Struggling with addiction'," he scoffed. "Serves 'em right. They get on it, why should I pay to get them off it? My daughter, right? She can't afford a flat, but they just hand the druggies out houses and that."

"It's very complex," Angela replied as politely as she could, then held up the photo again. "You saw this girl?"

"Druggie, is she?"

"She has certain…You said she was on a bench?"

"Aha. Just sat in the snow, like she didn't even notice it. Oh, oh – you know what she said?"

Angela waited. Ironically, the jogger didn't seem to be in a rush.

"Totally mental. She said she'd stopped the snow. How mad is that? Of course, I ran straight past that one, I can tell you, before she knifed me and that. She said she'd stopped the snow. Barking mad. It was falling all about her and she said she'd stopped it. She was all big eyed. Oh yes, I see it now. Drugs. How bonkers was that, eh?"

Angela closed her eyes for a moment and thought, *Oh dear God, no. If she's talking about stopping snow, she's out of control. I need to find her. Now, this moment.*

"She has certain…" Angela tried to find a description this man could empathise with. "She's young. Like your daughter. She needs help."

"We all need help, love."

"True, but she's…she's, ah…" Angela gave up. "Listen. Did you see which way she went?"

"Nah. But she was facing this way when I looked back. That don't mean anything though. The shops are this way, through the gate. Yeah, I bet she's gone there. You know, to beg and that."

"I doubt it." Angela had become sorely tired of this man. "She isn't a beggar. That I can assure you."

"Oh, they all end up beggars eventually." He started to run off again. "Hope you find her."

"Thank you. I'll try the shops. You've been most helpful."

The jogger disappeared without another word. Angela watched him go, then turned back to the path.

Please, please take your pills before you do anything you'll regret. Anything I'll *regret.* She felt panic start to set in. *You should have come to me, first. You know the rules. I'm responsible and now you're out there, out of control and if anything happens I will never forgive myself. You suffer enough.*

With purpose, she began to stride toward the clock tower, gate and shops.

*

Angela continued to ask almost everyone she passed on the way through the park.

A woman with a young daughter had seen a scruffy blonde pulling faces on the street. Some old dears had seen the same girl talking with a tramp – they thought she'd been talking – but then, oh, the *hullaballoo*! The girl had furiously *chased* some young man, heaven *knows* what he'd done, but she pursued him into the road and off! It had been quite exciting, what had he done? Who *was* she?

A few other people had seen this bizarre chase, and all pointed in the same direction: up the street, westwards. A couple even described how the same teenage boy had emerged from an alleyway with blood dripping down his face.

Angela was more worried than before. If she'd chased someone, possibly assaulted them, what else was she doing? How confused was she? Had she taken her Trazodone? She knew she must, otherwise it could lead to 'episodes'. That lesson had been drilled into her, but for whatever reason, it seemed that she'd passed on the medication.

The flakes still drifted down. The girl was somewhere out there, as chaotic as the snowfall.

Angela looked at all the people as they went about their business. The truth of the world was right there, in front of their faces, but they looked straight through it. Most people had a filter that blocked out anything unpalatable.

Empathy is in short supply these days, but, well, that's solipsism, right there, she thought. *What do I care about? I care about what is important to me. I can't judge everyone just because people have priorities, even though those priorities are generally selfish and screwed up. People are just animals and life is out for what it can get. The flower tries to block others from getting the light. The lamprey fixes onto the shark. There are a lot of lampreys out there,* she mused, and looked about for a flash of blonde amongst the white, *and they will fix on to whoever they can steal scraps from. And they will fix on to* her, *wherever she may be. They always do.*

She had no idea where the girl could have gone. They'd arranged to meet, as always, so Angela could offer help and advice – again – but something had gone wrong. The girl had wandered by mistake and was now loose in the world with no tether. And if she hadn't taken her medication, who knew what she was capable of?

Angela stood silently in the middle of the pavement and tried to think. She wouldn't have gone far. Instinct, if nothing else, would keep her in this area. It was a place the girl knew all too horribly well.

But where would she go? She wouldn't just stand out in the snow, she'd find somewhere…appropriate. Yes.

Angela looked over the road at a library. *Aha, maybe.* She was amazed libraries still existed. Books seemed like quaint novelties from a bygone era, like magic lanterns. If Angela saw someone actually reading, she'd catch herself watching them, fascinated, as if they were an exotic exhibit in a zoo. A person, with an actual book, actually reading? The girl often had her nose in a book. She read, paid attention. She liked to learn. A library seemed the obvious choice.

She was about to cross the road when a sign caught her eye. It read 'ST JOHN'S PARISH CHURCH' and pointed in a westerly direction down MARKET STREET.

"Oh yes, that's it." Angela said under her breath. "Not the library, no. There you are. At St John's, of all places. Of course you are."

*

Things had started to come together for the girl.

This was how it worked, she knew that now. Signs, symbols, clues and directions could all be found if you knew where to look.

So – the flyer took her to the church. The church sent her toward "Benny's café", where she'd meet a man called Mark – good Biblical name – and he'd give her the next piece of the puzzle. *Yes, this is how it works.*

More memories had returned. Stronger, clearer, they'd made their way through the blizzard in her mind. She knew she had to take her pills, but worried the medication might scare off those emerging memories again.

She now remembered Trazodone was supposed to centre her and smooth her out, but she already felt centred, smoothed, in control. She was just fine.

What if the pills sent her off course again? She had places to go, people to meet and those people would understand.

Father Watson had been helpful, but still, she hadn't told him the truth and wasn't that ironic?

She wouldn't confess all to a holy man, but was about tell some guy in a cafe everything.

Ah well, she thought. *The Lord Moves In Mysterious Ways. If I have to confess in a cafe rather than a church, so be it. I have been led down this road and so I must take it. That's what I do.*

She'd been walking for a few minutes now, but still there was no sign of Benny's Cafe. Oh, there'd been *The Big Sandwich, Laskas, Tea 'N' That*, but either Benny's was a stealth establishment or she'd gone the wrong way.

She took a deep breath and walked toward a mother with twin babies in a pram.

"Excuse me," she'd planned to say. "Do you happen to know where Benny's Cafe is?"

Yes, she would say that, just like an ordinary peckish girl, desperate for a bacon sandwich.

I can do that. I am a consummate actress.

She stood up a little straighter, then looked down at her dirty raincoat and scuffed trainers.

Who am I trying to fool? She thought. *Maybe I should just tie a sign round my neck saying, "GOT ANY DRUGS?"*

The new mother, totally shattered, was blankly looking in a shop window.

She approached the mum from behind, but just as she was about to say, "Excuse me," both babies' eyes flew open and stared at her.

"Secrets must be kept," said one, in a creaking, ancient voice. The girl took a step back, put a hand to her mouth and tried to hold in a scream. The mother heard nothing, saw nothing, just continued to stare into the shop window.

"You know why you are here," sighed the other child, who regarded her sternly. "Why are you asking? Why have you not kept to your path, as was agreed?"

The girl gazed at the two infants, who held her stare.

"You have not taken the pills." The first baby pointed its tiny finger at her, accusingly.

"The pills focus you. They aid the transfer. You know this. Why have you allowed yourself to become lost?"

"I didn't…" she whispered.

"You are being sought."

"Sought? By who?"

"You know. The one who cares. Go to the Cafe. Wait. Be silent. Be still. Wait. Only speak to the one who cares."

As the mother looked back at her babies, they both shut their eyes simultaneously. She smiled down, then finally noticed this blonde who stared, wide eyed into her pram.

She didn't see that, the girl thought. *She didn't hear. Just me. No one else in this street saw anything. Like the jogger didn't see the snow had stopped.*

That idea scared her.

The mother scowled. "What are you looking at?"

The girl shook her head and tried to form the correct expression. She didn't meet many children, thank heavens, and very few babies. She tried a shy little grin and lied. "They're adorable, just like my sister's twins."

The mother softened, just a little.

"Sorry. I haven't slept in years." She smiled and looked down at her children. "Well, it feels like years. Boys or girls?"

"Sorry, what?"

"Your sister."

"My sister? Oh, my sister." The girl felt her mind judder.

"Does your sister have boys or girls?" The woman's smile had melted away.

"Girls. Two of them. Look, sorry, uh, do you know where Benny's Cafe is? I'm supposed to be meeting someone there."

The mother pursed her lips. "Up there." She pointed, politeness gone. "It's behind the bus stop. There."

"Oh, thank you." The girl risked a look back into the pram.

The babies' eyes had opened again and bored into her. She realised her hands shook, and not from the cold.

*

Benny's Cafe looked like all the others she'd passed. Plastic tables, till and serving area at the far end, hot plate and grill.

She smelled the frying from outside and her stomach turned. No more play acting, she really was an ordinary girl, a bit peckish and desperate for a bacon sandwich.

The cafe was busy enough but there were still a few tables at the sides. An older woman stood behind the counter and a large man in his 30s took an order. He laughed with a customer and, the girl saw with delight, wore a standard-issue blue-and-white striped apron, just like a proper cafe owner should.

At that moment, he looked out of the window. For a second his face was blank, but then he smiled and gestured for her to come in.

There was a bell on the door – of course there was – and as she stepped out of the cold and into the steamy warmth of Benny's, the man came over and gave a crooked smile.

"Now." He turned the apron in his hands nervously. "I've either just invited a random passer-by into my cafe – in which case welcome, thanks – or you're the blonde girl Father Watson sent my way?"

"I'm the blonde girl you're expecting." She gave another silly little curtsey and stuck out her hand.

"Mark." He formally shook it. "I know, I know, it says Benny's Cafe, but that was the guy I bought it off. Everyone knows it as Benny's so it seemed silly to change, just for ego's sake." He waited, still holding her hand. "You are? Father Watson didn't give a name, just 'the blonde girl'."

"Yep, that's me, the blonde girl, see?" She took a lock of her hair and waggled it at him.

"Oh, OK, that's fine. I understand. Listen, take a seat. You want something? A bacon sandwich?"

"You read my mind."

"No mind reading involved. There are very few problems that can't be, not solved, no, but put aside, just for a moment, when you have a bacon sandwich."

"Totally. Oh, er, unless you're veggie." She sat down at a side table and glanced around at the haphazard collection of posters that passed for interior decor at Benny's Cafe. One asked you to "COME TO GREECE." Another advised "NOW WASH YOUR HANDS." David Bowie stared out at a photo of a red Lamborghini on the opposite wall. Mark saw her look and smiled. "They've been here since I took over. Benny hadn't changed them since 1985, I think. Again, I don't have the ego to take them down. Sometimes, things just go round and round and you don't even notice them after a while, huh? Mum!" he shouted over to the woman behind the counter. "Bacon sandwich please." He looked down at the girl. "On white? Brown? Red sauce? Brown?"

"White, always, red, always."

"An excellent choice, madam," he said approvingly and sat down opposite her.

"OK, so since Father Watson sent you, I'm guessing you could do with a little help or advice, or both." He became suddenly businesslike. "I was like you once – well, I don't know who you are or what you're like, but what I mean is, I needed help. I fell in with bad people in my twenties, doing stuff I shouldn't. Benny helped me, gave me a job, had faith. So I'm passing it on. I have volunteers here, people like me, who've got away from the shit and started again. We kind of pick up the slack the council doesn't have the time, money or manpower to do, which is a lot. Do you have a Care Worker?"

"I have someone I...they're supposed to sort me out, but I don't remember who they are."

"From Hackney Council? Another? Are you passing through?"

"They're local, yes. They work round here."

"Number? Contact?"

"I can't remember. I was supposed to meet them but I got lost. It happens. Maybe it's you I'm supposed to meet. I dunno. Other things are coming back, though."

"That's good. Listen, have your bacon sandwich. Do you want a cup of tea?"

"Ooh yes, white, three sugars."

"Three?"

"Too much sugar is the least of my problems."

He laughed. "Well, at least you're honest. Get yourself warmed up and then we'll talk. You can tell me your story."

"Yes, I will," she smiled. "It's a good one."

*

Once again, Father Watson held a taper and made his way to the front of St John's Church.

A beeping sound came from inside his robes. He made a mental note to turn down his phone's volume whenever he was in "uniform". He retrieved it and saw a text:

BLONDE GIRL HERE :) WILL CHAT & LET YOU KNOW. THNX FOR SENDING HOPE I CAN HELP. MARK

He wrote a quick reply – BLESS YOU – muted the phone and raised the taper.

At that moment, Father Watson experienced a frustrating sense of déjà vu, as once again, the door opened, snow rushed in, and the candle was extinguished.

He raised his eyes to the vault. "Oh come *on*," he whispered.

This time the blizzard had entered with an older woman in a stylish coat and trouser suit.

"Oh, I'm sorry." The woman took in the taper, candle and Father Watson's slightly vexed expression. "Ooops. You just lit that, didn't you? And I put it out again."

"Right on both counts," he replied and thought, *This is clearly a day for interesting new female visitors.*

The woman scrabbled about in her coat then pulled out her ID card, "ANGELA DAWSON. SOCIAL CARE UNIT, HACKNEY, E1".

"I'm, er, yes, I'm Angela and, er, yes, what it says on the tin, I'm Social Care. I wonder if…"

Father Watson held up a hand and took a chance. First the blonde girl, now this silver-haired woman? They had to be connected. "Let me guess. Blonde? So high? Possibly high in other ways? She was here. Is that what you were going to ask? If not, I've totally got the wrong end of the stick."

"No. Wow. Yes. That was exactly what I was going to ask. Blonde girl, so high. Probably in a raincoat? She was here?"

"Aha, about, what, only fifteen minutes or so ago."

Angela Dawson put a hand to her forehead in frustration.

"Damn. Do you know where she's gone? She was supposed to meet me. I'm her…I guess I'm her…point of contact. But she didn't turn up today and, well, here I am."

"I sent her to Benny's Cafe. You know Mark at Benny's? Halfway house? He works alongside you lot. Social Care."

Angela looked blank for a moment then smiled in recognition. "Oh yes, Mark. Benny's. Aha. Threw me for a second there. Oh, remind me, where…?"

"Turn right out of the church, five minutes. On the left. I'll call him and let him know you're on the way, shall I?"

"That would be very helpful."

She looked about the church just as the girl had, with the same expression of recognition and reverence. "It's beautiful," she said, softly.

"That's what your blonde said. She seemed quite enamoured with the place."

Angela sat down on the same pew the girl had used earlier. "She would. Mind if I sit down? I need to stop. I've been marching all over the place in that…" she hooked a thumb over her shoulder, back at the snow. Then she patted the seat next to her, just as the girl had done.

So Father Watson internally sighed, then sat again.

"Do you mind if I ask a few questions? Before I go and find her? I wouldn't normally, but well…" She fluttered her hand up and down, at his robes. "I can trust you, naturally. Think of this as confession, just not in the box."

"I understand." It happened a lot. Just as a doctor is a doctor whether at surgery or not, a priest is always a priest, wherever, whenever.

"How did she seem?"

"Well…wait, it feels odd just saying, 'her'. She wouldn't tell me her name. What is it?"

"Ooh, no, nooo," Angela shook her head and put a finger to her lips. "Don't ask, don't tell. If she didn't want you to know her name, I must respect that wish. This is confession, remember, Father. No names. I just want a heads-up on how she was."

"How did you know she'd been here?"

"I took a punt. She is extremely religious. It defines who she is. It gives her light and believe me she needs a lot of light; Heaven only knows how dark her life can be. She is quite the scholar. You might not think it, but she is."

"Oh, I saw. She guessed the age of the church almost to the year."

Angela seemed unsurprised. "I bet."

"She also knew rather a lot about St John. Or rather, the lesser known St Johns."

"Oh well, St John – the Baptist, naturally – is her Guardian Saint. So when I saw the sign, I thought, *Aha, yep, she'll be headed there*. Back to St John's. Makes perfect sense. How did she seem?"

"A little wired. Jittery. She had a knife."

"A knife?"

"No, no, not hers. She gave it to me to get rid of. It's safely back in the office."

"A knife would have gone against everything she is. Anything else?"

"She seemed to think she'd been led here. Maybe she was. She'd found a leaflet for the church, thought it was a message to come and meet Christ, but seemed put out that He wasn't *here*, here, you know what I mean?"

"She said she wanted to come and meet Christ?" Angela frowned. "Like, actually meet him, or pray?"

"Actually meet him, like he had an office here. Yeah. So I called Mark and sent her to him, instead."

"Yes, of course. Thank you, Father. I'd better get going, in case she moves on."

Angela went to rise, but Father Watson stayed seated.

"Will she be OK? She wasn't like a lot of the others I see from the streets. She was a bit manic, but I felt a tranquility off her, if that makes sense."

Angela looked a little sad. "She's like that. As I say, I can't talk in specifics, but…Her delusional universe is very complex. I'm surprised she didn't mention it, being here in a church. Churches normally set her off."

"What kind of delusions, if you don't mind me asking."

Angela thought for a moment, then pushed on. "I think you're the perfect person to tell, actually. Ironically, I think the delusions keep her sane. They build a private reality she can deal with. Let's face it, this world is crazy enough – what harm would more of the same do? Her belief doesn't hurt her or anyone else, but sometimes she freaks people out. Because she believes it, Father, totally."

"Believes what?"

"It's a classic delusion of grandeur. Amazing she never said. You see, she has utter, unshakable belief that…"

Angela sighed and shook her head.

"…Well, Father, she believes she's an angel."

*

"An angel?" Mark Arnold repeated, as calmly as he could.

"Mmm-mm," the girl replied through a mouthful of bacon sandwich. "Yep, an angel. Not a metaphor. Not, 'ooh, I'm such an angel'. The real deal. This sarnie's really good by the way. Crispy, just how I like it. You're not surprised? Good. You shouldn't be, since I was sent here. I get it now. You're who I'm supposed to be meeting, right?"

Mark Arnold, the owner of Benny's Cafe, waypoint for the lost and lonely of Hackney, thought he'd seen and heard it all. He'd lived on the streets, mixed with crackheads and dopers. He'd spent hours in broken flats as drunk, intense men had lectured him on the Moon Landings, or lack of them. He'd been out there on the very edge of reason himself, imagined all kinds of paranoid fantasies. The street could send you to very strange places, but this was new.

Mark had taken courses in managing the vulnerable. What you didn't do was laugh in their face, or try to talk them out of their carefully constructed reality. That could be very dangerous.

You had to take things slowly. If this girl claimed to be an angel, chances were that belief wasn't something she woke up with this morning. Her delusion had been built from the ground up over many years.

It had probably started when she'd prayed for some kind of higher power to get her out of an awful situation. With no parents or authority figure, her brain would have conjured up something she could always rely on, whatever hellish situation life threw at her.

To survive, she had to believe someone looked out for her, so why shouldn't that protector have wings and a halo? This special angel would have been at her side even in the darkest hours. No matter how cold it ever got, her angel would always come flying.

But then, perhaps, that fantasy had come unstuck. Maybe something really bad had happened and the angel hadn't saved her. It had failed to fly and stop something terrible.

At that point, the girl would have had a choice; either accept her heavenly bodyguard didn't exist, or find a new one, an angel that would always be with her.

It made total sense. If no angel had come to help, she'd become one, then guard herself.

She'd never have to plead for divine intervention because she *was* the intervention. Her wings were always there, folded. She could use them to soar away any time, even if that meant flying into her mind, where nothing could reach her.

He'd seen how these fantasies could start innocuously. He knew one guy who started making "Magic Marks" on the walls in chalk, just for a laugh. He believed his weird little symbols would confuse passers-by, a silly game. But as time, the street and whatever he put in his veins tore him away, his Magic Marks became real. He started to thank them whenever things went right. In the end, his body was covered with a spider's web of curls and lines, marked there by a needle dipped in ink. They'd found him dead in a derelict house, where the walls crawled with chalk, and his skin was lined with a roadmap of insanity.

But however the girl's delusion had started, this was the end result. Right here, right now, in her reality, she was an angel.

He had to take this very carefully.

Mark's phone beeped. He glanced down at the screen.

SOCIAL CARE CAME TO CHURCH ON HER WAY KEEP GIRL THERE? Asked the priest.

Mark texted back without looking. YES THX CALL SOON.

"Well, I'm not sure if I'm exactly who you're supposed to be meeting, but Father Watson sent you here, so let's see if we can sort out what you need and how I can help," he offered, and wisely avoided the "angel" angle.

The girl didn't want to leave that particular subject though. "I got the flyer, which took me to the church, and then the priest led me to you. So you must be my contact. That's how it works, right? Now, obviously, the transfer has left me with some holes in my memory, but that is how it works. I do know."

"The transfer? What's the transfer?" Mark hoped the social worker would rush through the door very soon.

"Oh, I get it." She waved her sandwich at him. "Feed me up, then test me out. This is a test. I see. You want to find out how much I remember, see how capable I am. Yeah, I was told that could happen. Get me oriented. The transfer. From heaven to earth, right?" She sighed, as if this was all totally obvious. "OK, OK, you're playing dumb, I get it. Let the girl do the work. Fine. Couldn't get a top up on me tea, could I?"

"In a moment. Just…tell me what you can."

If she was in this hysterical state, it was best to let her carry on until the cavalry arrived. She didn't seem dangerous. In fact, she seemed totally reasonable, even if she *was* talking about the impossible.

"Angels get transferred to earth during snowstorms, obviously. They're good camouflage for when we just pop into existence on this plane. We merge with the snow, become one with it, then split away. It's like we've just walked out of the snowfall. No one sees a thing. Have you never realised more snow falls when really bad things are happening? More angels required, see? World War II, for example, was covered in snow. But if we're needed somewhere hotter, sandstorms have the same function. Snow, or sand. We come in under cover and we leave under cover. Do I pass?"

"So you arrived…today?" He knew she shouldn't be indulged, but couldn't help himself. This was already one of the most rational insane scenarios he'd ever heard.

"This morning, yep. But something went wrong. It happens. Look, we jaunt between dimensions. It's not a trip on the 86 bus, you know. I was supposed to arrive at my contact's address, but I woke up on a park bench…embarrassing, really."

Of course you did, thought Mark. *You came to on a park bench in the snow after a night of getting wasted and then your delusion stepped in to save the day. Oh no, noooo, you haven't been doing drugs in some den somewhere, no.* You've *been in heaven and they just screwed up the co-ordinates.*

Of course, he said none of that, just nodded in a noncommittal way.

"So I stopped the snow, right, because I was cold."

Mark must have somehow given away his surprise, because she pursed her lips.

"Of course I can stop the snow!" she said, a little too loudly. "I came here made of snow! We control it! Of course *I* can control it too. What kind of test is this?"

He held up a hand, to neither agree nor disagree. "Sorry, go on."

"Now, I know, I know…" She pulled out the bubble pack of pills marked "Trazodone" and put them on the table. Mark didn't recognise the name, but that was hardly a surprise, since new mood-control drugs came on the market every day.

"I know the rule," she said, impatiently. "As soon as I land, I take the Trazodone. It's like a kind of anti air-sickness thing. Helps you get your head together when you get here. Brings back your memories which obviously have a bit of lag. Dimension-shifting isn't instantaneous, your physical self arrives before your mind, your soul. We're working on that. Why am I telling *you* this? OK, OK, the medication focuses the job in hand. But I just didn't feel like it. I felt alright. I was in no rush. So I didn't take them. Boo to me. I'm fine."

"Job in hand? What job?" Mark asked.

The girl didn't seem to hear and ploughed on, lost in her reverie. "Then I found the flyer for the church. Some kid tried to steal my money. I'm afraid I beat him up. I may be an angel, but I'm not, like, all feathers and serenity."

She pulled up her sleeve and held up the angel wing tattoo proudly. "Guardian, see?"

"Guardian?" Mark prayed the social worker would ride in, quick. He was way out of his depth.

"I really do have to spell it out, don't I? Are you that worried I don't remember? I do. I'm OK. There are five types of angel.

Guardians, like me. This is my fifth tour of duty. Then there are
Instigators, who are more like air traffic control – they try and get
humanity on the right flight path, you know. Warriors – they're
badass, the ultimate badasses. They'll kick Satan's arse to Hell and
back, uh-huh. Then there are Teachers, who whisper the right ideas in
people's minds. Healers – well, they're more concerned with healing
the soul rather than the body – and finally, Hairdressers."

"Hairdressers?"

"I'm fucking with you."

"So...you're a... Guardian. What does that entail?"

"You want me to read from the instruction manual? I don't have it.
Alright, Guardians...we have the worst job. But that's why we're most
in demand. We get in the way."

"Get in the way?" Mark was transfixed. Someday, this girl was
going to make one lucky psychotherapist very, very rich.

"Aha. That's what we do. We get in the way. So, to prevent
someone getting hurt, we're like bodyguards for the soul. We throw
ourselves in front of what's coming. So instead of Susan, Paul, David
or Caroline taking the drugs, we do it. As many as we can. Because if
we're taking them, that's one less line or pill on the street, right? We
take them to stop someone else doing so. We can't do them all, but if
we weren't here, much more would get through. We take as many as
we can, leaving as few as possible. It's a dirty job. But... " she didn't
need to complete the quote, just spread her hands wide and shrugged,
sadly.

"So yes. I take it, whatever it is. I get in the way of all kinds of shit.
I'm the eternal victim. Better that I get assaulted, raped, beaten,
drugged than one of you lot. I'm immortal. Look, I'm not saying it's
easy. It's horrible, but what's the choice? It's what we do. We take it,
whatever it is. I've been knifed. Overdosed, messed up in all kinds of
ways. I've taken it all. I take it all because then, it means I've got in
the way of someone else taking it."

Mark sat silently. Here was the truth of who she really was,
wrapped up in this incredible unbreakable angel story. If she believed

she couldn't be hurt, perhaps she wouldn't be hurt. Somehow, deep down inside her, this "angel" had kept part of her safe. But for how long?

"I'm sorry." He didn't know what else to say. He looked into her eyes and saw the frightened girl within. Not an "angel" sitting here as if life was a "tour of duty" that would end whenever she got back up to heaven, just a scarred human who'd found a reason to take everything. She'd created a reality to explain her toxic, dead-end life. This delusion was as powerful as any drug. Perhaps it even worked, in a roundabout way.

"So now I'm here again. Back on earth, reporting for duty. Ready to do it all one more time. Because that's my job. Maybe one day I'll take a career side step, try being a Healer or Teacher or..." She smirked. "A Hairdresser. But now, I'm a Guardian. So. Do I pass? Remember enough for you, boss? So where do I go? What do I do? Who shall I be tonight?"

Her expression changed, then, from open faced to hard and cocksure. "A *don't mess with me* crack head?" Then she pulled a wide-eyed, blinking expression. "How about little girl lost, needs help?" Lascivious, then, hooded lids, parted lips. "Come and do it to me, whatever you want. I'll take it." She sat back and took a sip of her tea. "I've done them all and more. So what's it to be?"

Mark had nothing to say. He was saved by the bell.

The cafe door opened and Angela Dawson rushed in. She spotted the girl and came over, concern on her face. She didn't look at Mark, just stared down at the girl and held up her I.D.

"I'm Angela Dawson," she said, firmly, but gently. "Angela Dawson. You know me, right? I'm the one who looks after you. From the council. Remember?"

As Angela spoke to Mark she kept her eyes on the the girl. "Hi. Sorry. You're Mark, right? Father Dawson told me she'd be here."

"You? *You're* my...?" The girl looked between Angela and Mark. "But I thought he..."

Angela picked up the Trazodone. "You haven't taken any today, have you? No need to answer, I know you haven't. You don't remember me, do you?" She waved her I.D. at the girl's face again. "You must take your Trazodone, or we lose you. You know that, don't you? Come on, remember."

"You…look after me? But I thought…the Priest…?"

"You know what happens if you don't take your medication. I have to sort out your housing, your benefits, all over again. But I can't do it if you're like this."

Angela popped a pill from the bubble wrap and held it out. "I'm sorry," the girl said. She looked like a child who'd been caught out.

"Mark, may I have a glass of water for her pill, please?"

"Of course, of course."

Angela walked with Mark to the counter and whispered to him.

"I'm so sorry you had to deal with her. How is she? She was supposed to be with me, but went missing this morning…Thank you for looking after her."

"She said she was an angel," he whispered back. Angela rolled her eyes and sighed.

"That happens. As soon as she comes off the Trazodone, she lapses. As you've probably gathered, that's her coping mechanism. She's harmless. Well, for now she's harmless, but it spins out of control. It could get worse unless….well, she's wound herself up to a complex state, obviously. Going to the church didn't help. It never does. You weren't in harm's way, but it must have been a little scary. I apologise."

"I've seen worse. Honest, I really have."

Angela smiled and looked him up and down. "I imagine you have. You're the real angel around here."

He took a bottle of water from the fridge and handed it to her.

"So what now?"

"I take over. It's what I do. I'll get her back to the housing unit, have her examined. It's cold today. Once the Trazodone kicks in, she'll be less…out there. Calmer."

They walked back to the table. The girl took the water and downed two pills.

"Thank you for the sandwich and tea," she said, weakly.

"That's fine, anytime," he replied. "I hope you get, you know, sorted."

The girl nodded and looked back at Angela for approval or permission to leave. She'd lost her angelic spark.

Delusions aren't always bad, Mark thought. *While she believes she's an angel, she's untouchable. I saw it in her eyes. When she's human, that's when the problems start. That's when it all falls down and she's vulnerable.*

He watched the girl leave. Angela had a protective arm around her shoulder.

Don't lose those wings, Mark thought. *You keep them folded up. You never know when you might need them.*

*

The social worker and the girl stepped out into that whirling London snow. Angela looked up into the clouds.

"Not stopping, is it?"

"Not stopping," agreed the girl. "I'm sorry, I'm so sorry. I thought *he* was the one who looked after me. I got confused. I should have taken the pills. I'm sorry."

"Sssh, ssh" said Angela, like a mother to a child. "It's not the first time and it won't be the last. Please don't forget. You need the medication or this happens."

The girl nodded, chastened.

"But Uriel…" Angela said and there was a hardness in her voice. "You really do have to stop telling people you're an angel."

"I know."

"Because one day, someone might actually believe you." Just for a moment, Angela's eyes glowed halo-gold. "And *then* where would we be?"

"STATION TO STATION"

(David Bowie, 1975, from the album Station To Station)

June 1976, London.

"Stop the train."

That's all David had to say, just three words. David never had to ask twice.

He was on his private *'Station To Station'* tour train just outside Victoria Station. Laid out on his table were two fat lines of cocaine, all that was left of the original six.

"Oh, and get me some more of this." He waved at the white powder and rubbed his nose. "I hardly got any sleep last night, I'm knackered."

Arms behind her back, his P.A. stood to attention at the end of the carriage and waited for any more insane, random instructions that might come from her boss. She nodded, turned and disappeared into the vestibule. The train, which had barely been going over ten miles an hour, shuddered to a halt.

David's P.A. returned to the carriage, eyebrows raised, ready for her next command.

"Now, listen, 'ere's the thing, right," David said, in his most South London of accents. "I'm not being funny or nothing. I'm not being funny at all, actually, I am, in fact, being deadly serious. But look at that. Just look at it."

He angrily gestured toward the window.

There, painted on a wall, in whitewash letters three feet high, were the words, "THE THIN WHITE DUKE RETURNS!" Painted next to them was a crude but effective cartoon of David himself, hair slicked back, eyes crossed, tongue out, lightning flash over his chest.

"I don't look like that," he whined. "Makes me look like a right tit."

David tapped his manicured nails on the table and stared at his P.A. as if she was somehow responsible.

"It's taking the piss, that's what it is, but you, know, I'm not that bothered," he sighed, stretched and tried to look nonchalant when it was clear he was seething.

"It's just…I mean, who's doing this? Everywhere we go on this tour, some arsehole has written that on a wall somewhere I can see it. It can't be the same geezer, can it? Unless one bloke's going all over the country with a bucket of white paint just to wind me up. It shows no respect."

He smoothed down his waistcoat. David was wearing his "stage uniform". White shirt, black slacks, black waistcoat, blonde hair oiled back. It looked very striking in the spotlights, "*very Caligari*" as David often reminded his road crew, who wouldn't know Caligari from California.

"I mean, alright, yes, I am white, I'll give the idiot that much," he began to speak ten to the dozen, nostrils filled with powdered Columbian rocket fuel. "And I could have a bit more weight on me. I'm a bit thin. Not as thin as I was two years ago, that was just stupid. I looked like a broom that had learned to talk. I haven't weighed myself for a bit, but alright, yes, I'm probably about nine stone, which isn't great. Maybe less, now I think about it." He rubbed his nose again. "Good stuff this, actually. Where did you get it? It should be legalised, really. Make a note!" His P.A. pulled out a little notebook and tried to look interested. "Put 'LEGALISE COCAINE' down. That's a great idea. Imagine how much work people would get done. Anyway, *Thin White Duke*. So yes, OK, good, fine, I get it, I'm thin and I'm white, that's accurate – it's just the bloody rudeness of it. And the picture! It shows no respect for me. And what's with the 'Duke' bit? What does that even mean? 'Duke'? That's not even, like, a

proper big title. It's a bit above 'Lord' isn't it? Is it? I don't know. Why
are you asking me? 'King' that would have been good, I could maybe
cope with 'The Thin White King' but maybe not even that. We haven't
had a king in this country for years now, have we? 'The Thin White
Duke'," he snorted.

"It's a liberty. People can be so rude." He sniffed and a blob of
white appeared in one nostril. David inhaled and it disappeared, like a
druggy magic trick.

His P.A. attempted to look both sympathetic and angry. David had
already snuffled up a sizeable amount of today's supply and it wasn't
even lunchtime, not that lunchtime was much of a concept on the
Station To Station tour. David could live off a simple diet of red
peppers and milk, with a few side orders of cocaine, naturally. Lots of
the old jabber-jabber powder. Once he'd stuck most of South
America's GDP up his nose, he flew off on these angry stream-of-
consciousness rants. It was best just to let him get on with it.

David grimaced out of the window and waved his thin white hands
in the air like a paranoid muppet. "Everywhere I go, some saucy swine
paints that shit on a wall. I don't like it one little bit. Everywhere. On
the walls in Edinburgh, Manchester, Liverpool, Stoke...STOKE, I
mean can anyone in Stoke even write? Wherever we've been on this
tour, there it is, '*The Thin White Duke Returns!*'" He sat down again
and ran his hands through his blonde, greased-back hair.

There was something about that particular, peculiar choice of
words which had really got to David. It wasn't even an insult, there
was no profanity involved, so why had that strange graffiti wound him
up so much? He had bigger fish to fry.

"We should get into Victoria," his P.A. offered. "We're just sitting
here, holding up the traffic, the trains, I mean. We're due at
Paddington."

"I know, I know," David replied. "But I can do what I want. If I
want to sit here, in my train, in my country, on my tour, looking at a
frankly insulting piece of graffiti, aimed at me, painted there, where
whoever did it knew I would see it..." He stood up again, than sat

down just as quickly, which resembled an anorexic jack in the box. "Yes! That's it! They know! Whoever's writing this, they know exactly where I'm going to be on this tour! Exactly! See?"

He waved his hand at the writing again. "That wasn't there when we left Victoria three days ago, was it? But now it is. They knew, the despicable graffiti artist knew! They knew I'd be coming back this way! They have my itinerary! Is it the French?"

"Well, your movements aren't exactly classified," offered his P.A. "Everyone knows where you're going, they have done for months. I don't think it's an inside job," she added, well used to David's frothing chemical paranoia.

"Oh really? Well explain this, then. It was on a wall coming into Edinburgh, wasn't it, the stupid picture and the same phrase, 'THE THIN WHITE DUKE RETURNS!' I hate the exclamation mark, too. It's really sarcastic, don't you think? It's like, 'Oh, goody goody, the fool's back in town'."

The P.A. nodded, but couldn't really get her head round how an exclamation mark could be sarcastic.

If only he'd fly, there'd be none of this nonsense. But David was phobic of flying, always had been. So he travelled to his appearances by train, chugged up and down the country, hours upon hours, station to station. His entourage had to go the same way, which was such a pain. She wished they could fly and meet their boss at the venues, but the Chief insisted they all go by rail. So there they were, stuck on a puff-puff with a cocaine-fuelled ego monster, who'd whipped himself up into a frenzy over a stupid piece of graffiti.

"Get Mick," ordered David, darkly.

"Can't we just get into Victoria and deal with it there? We'll miss our connection."

"No we won't. It's me. The next train won't be going anywhere until I'm on it. Get Mick."

The P.A. nodded, turned from the Man in Charge and rolled her eyes. He was really on one today and it had started the moment he'd woken up and asked for "a quick snifter". Then hey-ho, off we go on a journey of staggering boredom with a man who'd had his mental pedal to the metal the whole way, Edinburgh to London.

"Get Mick, he'll sort this out. *'The Thin White Duke Returns'*," he mewled. "Exclamation mark. It's a liberty."

He stared back at those whitewashed words. It was such an odd turn of phrase, but strangely familiar and unnerving, although he had no idea why.

David Jones, leader of the British Union (formerly the *British Union of Fascists*) and currently prime minister of Great Britain, sat, crossed his arms and sulked.

"I should have been a fucking rock star," he growled to himself. "Not a politician. Rock stars have it easy. Just turn up, sing a few stupid songs, go home. Look at me. Pop stars get respect. I'm the bloody prime minister!" He pointed at a lightning flash badge on his waistcoat, the symbol of the British Union. "I'm the second youngest prime minister since Pitt the Younger! And I have much better dress sense. And look at the respect I don't get." He pointed at the graffiti again. "That Mick Jagger and His Beatles get buckets of respect, just for jumping up and down like big bender pogo sticks on a stage."

"Mick Jagger and His Beatles are total shit, though," said his P.A. helpfully. What she didn't say out loud was, *But then again, thanks to you, Boss, all music is total shit these days. God, I miss good music.*

*

Eventually, Mick Ronson appeared.

Mick was effectively David's deputy prime minister, but no one ever used that term. Britain had been run as a benevolent dictatorship for decades now, so there was no pyramid structure of power, just the Leader and then everyone else, who constantly tried to second guess what he wanted.

David felt like Mick had deliberately taken ages, but it had probably only been two minutes. That was another side effect of the cocaine – the clock didn't behave as it should. Sometimes it slowed down and melted, others, the second hand whizzed around like it was, well, like it was on coke. David Jones needed that drug. He was in charge, for God's sake. There were meetings to hold, rallies to speak at, big responsibilities. How was he supposed to cope as prime minister without some kind of chemical crutch?

His team always advised against the white lines, said stupid things like, "It is illegal you know," and, "It's quite habit forming, I hear," but let them try and run the country; they wouldn't know where to start.

He so wished he hadn't taken on this *Station To Station* speaking tour. Despite all the lovely drugs, it had been as boring as a box of sloths.

The idea of Station To Station had been simple. As the new prime minister, he'd tour all the UK's major cities and at each destination, remind the faithful what a great job he was doing. His predecessor, the B.U.F.'s founder, Oswald Mosley, had been prime minister since 1939, *37* years in the job! They were massive shoes to fill, so night after night, David had to prove his feet were big enough.

But it was all so, so dull.

"Alright, Dave? Problem, sunshine?" asked Ronson in his thick Hull accent.

Mick Ronson wore the standard uniform of the British Union, a collarless black shirt buttoned at the back, drawn in by a thick belt with a big camp silver buckle. On one arm, he wore a red armband with the party's striking lightning flash logo. But Ronson's hair was a little too long and, somehow, he seemed to wear the outfit in a deprecating way.

Mick had joined the Party in the '60s, when David had been promoted to Minister for Truth. But David had always felt Ronson treated the job as a bit of a laugh, nothing more. It got him beer, VIP passes and women – lots of women – and that seemed to be his real motive for sticking around. Mick Ronson wasn't a born fascist, but he was a great side man. He took care of business.

"Hello, ooh, train seems to have stopped," Mick cheerfully surveyed the remains of his boss's white powder party. "Decent of you to clean that messy cocaine off the table. Most people would use a napkin, but you go the extra mile. We're due at Paddington, you know. Got a big gig in Cardiff, remember?"

"It's not a gig," sighed David. "It's a rally."

"Nah, it's a gig. It's all showbiz, isn't it?"

"It is NOT showbiz, it's politics."

Mick played a little guitar on the side and was clearly a frustrated rock star. If he hadn't been wearing the uniform of the British Union, David thought he'd probably be strutting about like Mick Jagger and His Beatles, or the children's pop entertainer Gary Glitter. Mick treated the whole enterprise like it was some kind of rock and roll adventure. He even had groupies, for heaven's sake. He called them his "Ronsonettes". Secretly, David wished *he* had groupies.

"Yeah, come on, it's rock and roll, man. Fascism is pure rock. But instead of a guitar solo, you do a speech. Come on Dave…"

"Don't call me Dave. Or 'man'."

"But that's your name, man."

"My name, Mick, is David."

"Yeah, but Dave is so much more personable. It's modern. Modern Prime Ministerial. We had an 'Oswald' for decades – I mean, what kind of name is that? You're Dave, a man of the people. You're giving the British Union a new, funky, cool image. You're in your late 20s. The birds love you. You rock that look, you know. The waistcoat and shirt, slicked back hair. The birds can't get enough of you. It's rock and roll, man."

"Stop saying 'man', we're not American hippies. If you want to go and sing pop songs to little girls, be my guest."

"Yeah, that's all there is these days, isn't there? Pop songs for little girls. Sometimes I pray I'll stick the radio on and hear something good out of America. Jimi Hendrix. Creedence. That bloke Lou Reed. The guy in make up, Jobriath. He's amazing. He's really shaking music up out there."

"Make up," sniffed Jones. "Make up on a man. That's how low America has sunk. The last man to openly wear make up here was that Quentin Crisp geezer and we know what happened there. He made himself up right to the gallows. Mick, you know all those acts are subversive and banned. You know the law regarding contraband music that has been identified as, 'Contrary To The Creative Health Of The British Nation'."

"Cocaine was illegal last time I checked and yet, unless that's flour and you've been trying to make a very, very tiny loaf of bread, you seem to be using it quite enthusiastically."

"I'm going to have it legalised for certain situations," David said, haughtily.

"Which situations? 'Whenever the PM Fancies A Toot?' Look around you, boss. Cocaine? A tour train? Cheering fans? Rock and roll, man."

"They are not fans, they are politically tuned supporters."

"They're fans. And why are they fans? Because you, my friend, are making fascism sexy again. Just accept it. You love it when the ladies scream. When you do the salute, they wet themselves. You do look ever so manly when you do the salute. Ooh, you really should do the salute at Victoria when we get into the Mercedes."

"For starters, Mick, must we go into this again? The British Union is *not* a fascist organisation."

"Yeah, it is. Come on, we had Oswald Mosley as prime minister for over three decades. There are no elections any more, haven't been since the '30s. We're aligned with Speer's Third Reich. Come on, you even said 'Britain needs a fascist dictator', a couple of years ago. You can dress it up however you want, but it's good old fascism."

"I am not a fascist."

"Course you're not. You just flirt with it. You pinch fascism's bum. You compliment fascism on its shapely legs. You flutter your eyelashes at it and buy fascism drinks. Offer to show it your etchings. That's all. But you also happen to be leader of the British Union, which, let us not forget, started as the B.U.F., not the B.U. And what did the F stand for?"

"We got rid of that bit. Look, are we going to do this now? Again?"

Ronson pulled at his black shirt. "It's bloody tight, this. Why does fascism have to be so tight? Can't we get a little baggy?"

David sighed. "The British Union is not baggy."

"Well, look, whatever. What's the problem, why have you stopped the train?"

David twitched his head toward the graffiti.

"Oh. THE THIN WHITE DUKE RETURNS," Ronson yawned. "Oh, that again. It's everywhere, isn't it?"

"Yes, it is. Everywhere we go. The police are still no nearer to finding the perpetrators. It's the resistance. I tell you, it's the resistance."

"The police are pulling out all the stops trying to find who's behind this, you know that. But writing THE THIN WHITE DUKE RETURNS is hardly seditious, Dave."

"It's David. Call me David. Or even better, Prime Minister. And you didn't add the exclamation mark to 'RETURNS!' The exclamation mark tips it over the edge."

"Oh, whoops. 'THE THIN WHITE DUKE RETURNS!'" Mick said brightly and did sarcastic jazz hands. "I mean, you are thin and white. Maybe they mean it in a nice way. You know, ooh good, he's back! Hooray!"

"I don't think so. It's taking the piss. You know, comparing me to part of the old system of Lords and Dukes and all. It makes me look like I'm a hypocrite.Why THIN WHITE DUKE?"

"I don't know. You tell me."

"I know who it is," David sulked. "It's the A.F.L. Which, as you know, is a criminal organisation."

"The Anti Fascist League don't exist any more. You know that. The last lot blew themselves up with that bomb, which was meant for Mosley in '64. Idiots. Britain's happy under our rule. We have full employment, great trade links, don't have to answer to Europe, ha, 'the Common Market', yeah, good try, Europe. The A.F.L. are a myth now. They never did anything apart from a few bombings and kidnaps, they hardly dented us. So why are you so bothered about that?"

"Mosley never had graffiti about him."

"Oh, he did. Lovely stuff on walls like FASCIST SCUM and DIE NAZI. Comparing you to a skinny pale member of the ruling class is nothing. Why are you so upset about it?"

David glared at Ronson. "Don't question me. You answer to me. I am Prime Minister. I am your Leader. So you find out who's doing this, bring them to me and then I have them hung by their scrawny neck."

Mick stroked his chin and thought for a while. "I don't think you can hang someone for graffiti. I can check, if you like."

"I can! I'm in charge! I'll change the law!" David stood again and started to pull some of his 'speech poses'. He banged his fists together, very dramatic, very fascist. "I can do that! I can do whatever I like! I am leader of the British Union!"

"Alright, alright, dial back the *Sturm und Drang* a bit, darling, this isn't Berlin. Oh, you've got a bit of the old charlie coming out of your nose."

David picked some of the compacted powder out of his nostril and turned it in his fingers. He thought about trying to shove it back up but decided that would be rank.

"Graffiti's nothing, Dave. You're only upset because you've hoovered up a few grams this morning. Lay off the marching powder for a bit, you'll get some perspective. So what do you want me to do about it?"

"Well, have it washed off, for starters. Then find who's responsible and have them brought to me, so I can stamp my boot on their face, forever."

"Oooh, she's a queen bitch today. Okey dokey. Now, may we start the train again? We've been sitting here for a while and the rest of the country might need to go about their business."

David pouted and sulked, again.

Mick raised his eyebrows. "Tetchy, isn't she? I'll tell the driver to get a shimmy on, shall I?"

Prime Minister David Jones didn't answer, just stared out of the window at the offending graffiti and wished for terrible retribution.

*

The Station To Station train rolled into Victoria ten minutes behind schedule, which amused Mick Ronson no end.

"I thought fascism was supposed to make the trains run on time," he giggled.

"Oh, get lost, Mick."

"If I did, *you'd* be lost, mate."

As the carriage rolled to a stop, two members of the Prime Minister's Protection Squad were first off, in black and silver uniforms, lightning flash badges on their peaked hats. David watched them snap to attention and thought, *Holy Christmas, they look so cool. Our uniforms are just* better, *aren't they?*

He also noticed two ordinary constables standing with a man in a raincoat who held a briefcase. Raincoat Man produced ID and paperwork for one of David's squad, who turned and stepped back inside the train.

"Excuse me, Sir. Detective Inspector Visconti is on the platform, Sir. He's here from the Subversion Division, Sir. He'd like a word."

"Let them on board, they may have an audience," said David, imperiously.

The police stepped onto the train.

The constables appeared suitably awed in the presence of the Leader, but Visconti simply looked about, uninterested.

"Oooh," said Mick Ronson, excitedly. "A detective from the Joy Division. Should be interesting."

Visconti smiled, then spoke with an American accent. "I'm Detective Inspector Anthony Visconti. Yes, Mr Ronson, we're aware that the word 'subversion', can often be short hand for some of the more interesting crimes out there. Pornography, prostitution, perversions, all manner of fascinating depravities. But they are still crimes and that dismissive nickname 'Joy Division' rather demeans our work, wouldn't you say?"

"Yeah, Mick," said David, who took back his hand and wiped it on the seat. "It's 'Subversion Division'. Now, Detective, if you're here, I assume you must have something of supreme interest for me, otherwise you are wasting your prime minister's time and if that's the case, I'll have you all locked in the Tower."

The constables both gulped simultaneously. David saw their Adam's apples move as one and laughed.

"Not the Tower," he added. "Probably just Pentonville, somewhere like that. You're not British are you, Mr Visconti?"

"You are very perceptive. I moved here from New York, took citizenship. Say what you like about this country, it has the best police force in the world and I wanted to be part of that. I won't waste too much of your precious time, but we've been told to report any developments immediately. We know you're very concerned about the subversive graffiti that's been appearing across the Union."

The cocaine began to talk on David's behalf. "Too right, ooh, yes, right, yes, too right I am." He banged his fist on the table. "This is how revolutions start, you know. First a bit of writing on a wall, the next my head's in a basket and I like my head. I like it here, see, on my shoulders. I would not like it in a basket, no, even if said basket was beautifully woven. I do like baskets, actually. I don't have anything against them, *per se*. I'm not 'basketist', but, look, stop interrupting, first there's writing on a wall, then it's the whole face down in some wicker palaver. I won't have it. Stupid French, inventing the guillotine. And baskets. Did they invent baskets, Mick? Did the French come up with baskets? I bet they did. Just like the French to come up with a receptacle for my lovely head."

As David went off on another coke rampage, Mick attempted to calm him down with a hard stare, but since David was wearing the hardest, most thousand-yard stare in the carriage, Ronson's was somewhat ineffective.

"Yes, indeed," said Visconti, well aware he was with a man gripped in a drugs seizure, but unable to do a thing about it. "No Sir, we'll be having no baskets or guillotines on my watch. But we thought you might want to see this…"

He pulled out a black and white photograph from his briefcase and laid it on the table in front of the prime minister.

"Who's she?" asked Ronson.

"It's a he," replied Visconti.

"Really? Looks like a bird. Do you know him, Dave? Er, prime minister?"

David stared down at the photograph. The subject did appear female at first glance, but was actually an androgynous young man, probably mid twenties.

His hair was a mass of corkscrew curls, completely at odds with the 1966 *Doctrine Of Acceptable British Appearance* introduced as a bulwark against perversive American influence. This girl/man had his head tilted back and a smile flickered around his full lips. His eyes were heavy-lidded and ringed with black. All in all, he looked ready and willing to do extremely dirty things to you.

"No, I don't know him. Her. Him. Who is he? Is he wearing make up? You've got on my train just to show me some kind of sexual insurgent?"

"Yes, he's wearing make up. He's also wearing, see, here," Visconti indicated the man's cheekbone, "what appears to be glitter."

"Glitter? Why would he do that? Is he a pop star? If he is, he should know that make up on a man is an offence unless used for the purposes of legal theatre. But again, I ask, why bother me with this? Arrest the chap and get off my train."

"He's not a pop star. He describes himself as a revolutionary. The name he calls himself is Marc Bolan. Marc with a 'c'"

"The French spelling!" David recoiled as images of head-filled baskets flashed through his mind. "I told you, Mick! The revolution! It's here!"

Visconti waited for his Leader's drug-panic to ebb away a little.

"No, No, we don't have any actual proof that this Marc Bolan is behind the graffiti, but we've had information and built up quite a picture of him. He's vehemently opposed to the British Union – once he gets a few drinks in him, apparently he uses some quite choice words against our government. He's also been buying up whitewash and brushes – not a crime – but we also have witnesses that put him at the scenes of at least three of the graffiti sites, down here, in London. If nothing else, he's guilty of rabble-rousing, illegal public utterances and, er wearing make up."

"Then arrest him! Bring him to me! If he's responsible, put his head on a spike! Yes, put his head on a spike, not mine! I've got a lovely head!"

"We would, but he's nowhere to be seen. He's like some kind of... elf. He magically appears from fairyland or wherever, stirs up some shit, maybe paints some graffiti, then goes back to his wonderful world of clouds and dragons, where clearly people wear stars in their hair and cavort with unicorns."

"He's an elf? From fairyland?" asked David, who was terribly class A-confused.

"No, he's from Stoke Newington. But we have his real name. He calls himself Marc Bolan. But the name he was born with was Mark Feld. F.E.L.D, Mark with a K."

It took David a moment, but his pupils became even wider and he whispered, "Mark Feld. Wait. Hold on. Mark Feld? Wait. Mark Feld? Wait. Oh. Wait. Feld?"

Ronson watched his boss's face go whiter and thinner than normal, but said nothing.

*

David sent Ronson away to another part of the train and then spoke to the police in private. After a few minutes, the constables and detective left, with purposeful expressions on their faces.

Eventually, David stepped down from his carriage. He was a little shaken, but knew it was showtime. He supposed he was a bit of a rock star; he could switch on a performance no matter what happened backstage.

Crowds waited on the concourse. David never knew if they'd turned up because they genuinely loved him, or had been herded there to shout and scream his name. He had to admit he was a nicer looking proposition than Mosley. Back in the day, Oswald had an upright, aquiline appearance which some women found rather attractive, but age hadn't been kind. Mosley had ended up looking like an Italian gangster, which was never a good thing, not even if you *were* Italian and a gangster. The Italians had flirted with fascism too, but had been just too damned lazy and stuffed with pasta to carry it through.

David climbed into his open-topped Mercedes next to Mick and the crowd roared. Mick didn't want to ask his boss what had transpired in the carriage, but had a good idea. This was neither the time nor the place to find out. That would come.

"Do the salute," said Mick over the din. "Go on. They bloody love the salute."

David snapped out his trademark fascist salute and the station erupted.

"Told you. Crazy for it."

"So what happens next?" asked David, through gritted teeth.

Mick leafed through a sheath of papers and muttered, "I'm not your bloody P.A."

"You do what I ask. So at this moment, you are my bloody P.A."

"Keep saluting. OK, aha, yep. So we're on the train at Paddington at 1. On board, that interview I told you about. Straight to Leek-Land, where you have a gig at Cardiff Arms Park. Big one, that. Mind you, it's the only one we're doing in Wales, so you're getting the whole Welsh contingent in one hit."

"It's not a gig."

"Come on, David. You have searchlights. You walk on to Walter Carlos's music. You do an encore. It's a gig."

"It's not a gig. Wait, what, interview? What interview?"

"Keep saluting, the press are over there. See? The dudes with the cameras."

David turned and did a particularly sharp salute for the photographers. He wouldn't want them to get the wrong idea and think he was just *waving*.

"I told you. I've arranged an interview with some guy called Bernstein from the *Washington Post*. Last minute, sorry, but has to be done. The Americans are very interested in Britain's new, charismatic young Leader. Apparently, Bernstein is one of their top boys. Did a lot of pieces on Nixon, got him off the hook with the whole Watergate thing."

"What does he want to know?"

"Oh, the usual. Bit of history, some context, few funnies, you know, let the Yanks know fascism isn't all bad."

"I'm not a fascist."

"Keep saluting, Dave. Arm up, higher. Eyes and teeth, Leader, eyes, tits and teeth." Then he sang, in a stupid Ethel Merman voice, *"Dere's naw business like shaw business, like naw business ah naw..."*

*

Another station, another train. This one was shorter, just the engine and two carriages, an executive train, *most* befitting of the P.M.

Another crowd waited at Paddington, so David did more saluting, signed a few autographs, pulled a few poses. Thankfully, there was no THIN WHITE DUKE graffiti to be seen.

Carl Bernstein, the American reporter, was already on board in another carriage, but David wanted time to himself before the interview. This morning he'd been coke-jittery but now he was just jittery, full stop. Once alone, he treated himself to a couple of strengthening lines.

It was somewhere around Reading when the drugs began to take hold, just as Bernstein sauntered into David's carriage with a look of amusement on his face.

He was around the prime minister's age but looked older. He thrust out his hand.

"Mr Jones! Carl Bernstein. Good to meecha. Fine image, the whole waistcoat thing, the hair, the shirt. Real gouster look you have there." Bernstein sat down without being asked. David instantly took a dislike to the man. He behaved as if they were equals, when he was just some hack. "Y'know, looks kinda rock and roll."

David heard Mick Ronson give out a little snigger from behind him, which he'd attempted to mask as a cough. David turned and shot Mick a look, but Number Two just shrugged as if to say *I told you so, mate.*

"It's not rock and roll," David coated the words with as much disdain as he could. "I am prime minister of Great Britain. If you want rock and roll, you should talk to Alvin Stardust."

Alvin Stardust was currently the UK's biggest pop star. His last album, *Space Oddity,* had gone to number one. David didn't care for the man. His music was borderline subversive and he was dangerously close to being arrested for his risqué performances.

Stardust wore leather gloves like a pervert and held his microphone like a telephone. It was ridiculous behaviour from a grown man.

"Or maybe I should be chatting with the Sex Pistols?" Bernstein's eyes twinkled.

The Sex Pistols were an illegal underground act who did hit-and-run performances. They'd turn up with their equipment, hijack a gig, sing songs about anarchy and 'God Save Oswald!' then disappear into the night again. Soon enough, the police would find them, but they'd gained a worrying amount of notoriety.

"I'm not here to talk about music," sniffed David. "I've had enough of talking about music today. The Sex Pistols are just a fad. The British Union is here to stay."

"Then let's talk about that," Bernstein arranged his notepad and pencils on the table just so. "OK, treat me like I'm stupid…"

That won't be difficult, thought David. *You're American.*

Like most British people, David was condescending to those other English speakers across the Atlantic. He felt threatened by their absolute geo-political superiority. To assuage his feelings of inferiority, he assumed a rather conceited intellectual high ground and dropped into it now.

"I shall do my utmost best," he replied, snootily.

"Oh, thanks. OK, so, talk me through the British Union. The history, your involvement. Sum it all up for our readers. Under your leadership, it's already feeling different. Re-energised."

David could handle this.

"Well." He tapped out a cigarette and lit it. Bernstein waved a hand in front of his face to dispel the smoke, but David wasn't bothered. It was his train and he would have as many Gitanes as he liked. The French propensity for revolution may have scared him, but he did so love their fags.

"Treat you like you're stupid, OK, Mr Bernstein. The British Union was formed in 1932, by Oswald Mosley. Is that basic enough for you?"

"If it's basic enough for you, it's basic enough for me," Bernstein smiled, although it didn't touch his eyes. David blew smoke up into the air so it slowly settled over them both, like a gas attack.

"In the beginning, it was known as the *British Union of Fascists*. Unfortunate name, really."

"But it was and is a fascist party, right?"

"No, it's socialist. A benign socialist dictatorship, if you will. It's for the many, but led by just one. It's much better to have power concentrated in one person, stops all the infighting. Naturally, that person has to have the country's best interests at heart."

"Oh, naturally."

"So at first, Mosley had trouble whipping up much support. It turns out we British aren't particularly disposed to fascism. But then he had his famous Meeting on the Train. A real Road to Damascus moment. It's part of British Union legend."

"This is when he met the *Mysterious Man*?"

David laughed. "Yes. It sounds made up, but to the day he died last year, Mosley swore it was true. He'd alighted a train at Euston one night in 1933, alone. Unusually, he had the carriage to himself. Mosley was heading to Manchester to deliver a speech at the Free Trade Hall. At Crewe, another man got on, who recognised Mosley and they started talking. Our Leader complained the B.U.F. wasn't getting anywhere and this man gave Oswald what turned out to be the best advice he'd ever received. *'Lose the Fascist part of the name, Oswald. Just be the British Union. A union of all British People, strong and stable... Don't pigeonhole your policies as fascist, people won't like it. Be a* Union, *Old Man, just a good old-fashioned* British, *socialist* union.' Oswald took the advice, rebranded the party the British Union and concentrated on the more socialist aspects of policy. That's when he started picking up in the polls. By 1936, the B.U. had the majority in parliament. By '37, Mosley was prime minister. Hitler was making worrying noises and it looked like war was on the horizon. To be fair, Hitler was one of the first rock stars, I suppose, all those searchlights and stagecraft.

But anyway, in '39, Adolf got blown up by a bomb in a Beer Hall and Albert Speer took over. Hooray, no war.

So the Third Reich and the B.U. formed a bond. Speer got rid of Hitler's more, er, *outre* policies on race, rounded up the fanatics – remember, the S.A, the S.S? Dreadful people. Economically, the Reich and Britain tied themselves together and lo, a new era of prosperity. People liked it. Jobs were up, wages were up, it was all hunky dory. Mosley had the rules changed and became prime minister for life. Was that a stupid enough description for you?"

"Oh, very," said Bernstein. "But both the Reich and Britain, they *are* fascist states, aren't they? They're run on fascist lines. Just because you're the British Union now, not Mosley's old B.U.F. All you did was remove one word. The policies are the same. The power structure, too. One man's vision for the whole country's consumption. You have virtually no immigration, not even from your own colonies. Art and culture are controlled from a single state-owned broadcaster.

Books, fashions, music, hell, even haircuts not fitting the Union's guidelines are outlawed. So like it or not, this is a fascist country, with all the lack of freedoms that entails. You can call a dog a cat, but it still barks."

David smiled, tried to marshal his thoughts, and stared deep into Bernstein's eyes. "It's a loaded word, fascism. But fascism's just nationalism." The reporter didn't blink.

"Yeah, it's loaded alright. This country used to be a democracy, Mr Jones. What happened there? How did Britain slide into this…island mentality?"

"Well, being an island probably helps with that," smirked the prime minister.

"You know what I mean. You've pulled up the drawbridges, retreated into yourself, denied the existence of the rest of the world. Come on, Mr Jones. You censor the movies we make, you don't play the music we produce and why? Because of one man's idea of this odd concept called Britishness.

It's an idea from 30 years ago you guys lapped up without thinking of the consequences. You see the red, white and blue and something weird happens to your minds."

"Oh, Mr Bernstein, are you just going to sit there and pull us apart? I don't need to remind you that school kids in your country pledge allegiance to a flag every single day, in class, like German kids did under Hitler. You all carry guns because of a two hundred year old piece of paper. That's like us still burning women at the stake because we never repealed the witchcraft laws. You don't even know who or what you are as a nation, Mr Bernstein. So please don't sit there and tell us you know who *we* are."

The reporter raised his eyebrows and nodded. "Very well, very well. Let's try another tack before we need a referee in here. Let's go back to this meeting Mosley had, when he was told to drop the word 'Fascists' from the British Union of Fascists by some passing passenger. Why was it so mysterious? Sounds pretty straightforward to me."

David breathed an internal sigh of relief. He could control the British press – all two newspapers, Mail and Express, both in the B.U.'s pocket – but frustratingly, the rest of the world's media never toed the party line. They asked questions.

"Well, OK, Carl, here's the weird part. Mosley couldn't remember what the man looked like. Later, Oswald described it like this other traveller had been cloaked in darkness. That's all he could recall, as if the bloke was sitting there with the lights off around him. He was wearing a well-tailored suit and his hands were pale and manicured. Strangely long fingers, apparently. His shoes were expensive, but that's all Oswald could remember. The man's face had somehow disappeared from Mosley's mind the moment he left. The damnedest thing. A man with no name and no face, got off at Stoke-on-Trent, then disappeared. But if he hadn't got on that train and whispered good advice into Oswald's ear, the B.U.F. would have withered on the vine, I'm sure of it. Whoever that geezer was, he changed history just by talking to the right man at the right time. Odd, ain't it?"

"Very." Bernstein didn't seem interested and turned to a fresh page in his notebook. "Let's talk about you, now."

"My favourite subject."

"Before you suddenly dropped into politics, as Minister for Truth, I hear you had a dalliance with being a musician. Considering the B.U.'s position on most music, that seems a bit odd. Did you want to be a pop star?"

"No, a musician. That's a very different thing. I was in my teens, a lot of teenagers want to be musicians. It's a noble calling."

"So were you clandestinely listening to Elvis Presley on Radio Luxembourg after lights out?

"That's an illegal station. I may have heard some Elvis as I turned the dial, but that was all."

"Aha, so you heard but you didn't listen. That's like a pot user saying they didn't inhale. Very convenient. What made you swap music for a career in government?"

"Ultimately music doesn't achieve anything. I wanted to make a difference, to change things, but no one ever does that through music. Oswald thought it made sense for a young person to take care of that side of policy. As Minister for Truth, I was able to guide British music to more refined heights than it was previously headed. Morals needed straightening up. We are not homo *inferior*, we could be homo *superior*. We put controls on the clubs, made bands get state-approved licences, vetted each song that was played on the Light Programme. Yes, I was proud of that. Just look at Mick Jagger and His Beatles! The best of London and Liverpool, selling the blues back to America! That's an achievement."

"Selling plastic blues to little girls. You'll be selling us plastic soul next."

"Success is success."

"I suppose. But you still have an aura of a rock star about you, though. This Station To Station speaking tour has all the hallmarks of a music concert, you have to admit that. At times, I find it's like watching Led Zeppelin."

Led Zeppelin was a band who'd defected to America and were peddling some ghastly noise to easily fooled teenagers out there.

Mick Ronson coughed and it sounded strangely like another giggle again. "The prime minister has better hair than Robert Plant," he said, completely straight. Then Mick yawned and looked out of the window. He mouthed, "just going for a slash" and rushed out of the carriage, clearly someone who needed to void his bladder there and then.

Bernstein wasn't finished. "Why would Mosley anoint someone like you as his chosen one?"

"Mosley liked my attitude. So he pretty much instructed the Union to vote me in as the next prime minister. When the Leader makes his choice clear, it doesn't do to argue. So here I am. If I'd pursued music, I almost certainly would have ended up in some illegal beatnik shared house, strumming an acoustic guitar, writing embarrassing lyrics, maybe wearing a dress, trying whatever it took to get noticed. I would have amounted to nothing."

"But now you're really something."

"Oh, aha, I really am."

"Station To Station still sounds like a rock tour, though."

David pulled a face of exquisite condescension. "Well, it's not. You're just thinking of trains, but this is a journey for me. I'm changing from one David Jones to another. To become Leader, these are like my... stations of the cross, tests if you like, to assume the mantle. These are more than just physical stations, they are waypoints in the development of my soul. From here, I can survey the nation, see its hills, mountains and valleys, try to feel the people in the soil. If I don't do it now, it'll be too late. Too late..." he mused.

"Whoah, wow," said Bernstein. "That was the single most pretentious thing I have ever heard. And I've interviewed Jobriath."

David opened his mouth to argue, but found he couldn't really say anything in return.

At that moment, everything went horribly wrong, horribly quickly.

*

The whole event only took twenty seconds at most. However, during extreme situations, time helpfully stretches itself out, so you can watch everything fall apart at your leisure.

At first, David thought the carriage ceiling had rushed down towards him. One moment, he was facing Bernstein, the next, the ceiling was on his head. That wasn't right, unless a giant had stomped on the train and crushed it like a tin can. But yes, he'd definitely felt the ceiling on his head when it should have been up there, in its rightful place, on the ceiling.

The other peculiar thing was that Carl Bernstein had made the odd decision to fly into the window. It was very strange. Even in the heights of his cocaine mania, David had never entertained the delusion of flight, but here, for real, Bernstein had defied gravity. He'd flown like a rag doll out of his seat and struck the glass with a rather sickening bass thud.

David's legs had been wedged under the table, so he'd remained earthbound, with a ceiling on his head like a bad flat hat.

But no, that wasn't right either. He tried to think, but it was bloody difficult. His brain bounced around his skull then came to rest. So he *had* taken off. That's why he'd felt the ceiling on his head.

But now he was back, sprawled over the table. His nose hurt where it had taken the impact and he still managed to think, with surprising clarity, *It had better not be broken. I do not wish to look like a common pugilist.*

A microsecond before he and Bernstein had done the ejector-seat dance, there had been one hell of a bang. Not an explosion, more a massive crash, metal on metal, like the world's biggest cymbal had been struck by its largest drumstick. Then, David had taken off, Bernstein had flown like a crumpled bird and the whole carriage had shimmied like Carmen Miranda's hips. Then the train had slid, shook and wobbled, but stayed upright.

David's head hurt. The carriage hurt, too, it creaked and moaned. The sides had been twisted into shapes they did not like, *oh no, not one little bit* and complained about it, loudly.

"Awww," David groaned and slowly pushed himself up from the table.

"Awww," echoed Bernstein. "I think I've dislocated my head."

"Awww, fuck!" shouted Ronson from the door. "Are you OK, Dave? I was in the bog. I think the train's derailed. Dave, are you alright?"

"I'm here, too, hello?" said Bernstein, weakly. Ronson ignored him and bent down to his master.

"Anything broken? How's your head? Blurred vision?"

"Nothing broken, I don't think. But I have taken a *lot* of cocaine today, so my head and my vision are somewhat compromised anyway. Ow."

"Stay there," said Ronson.

"Really? I was planning on getting up and going skateboarding."

"Skateboarding's illegal, as you well know. I'll get straight on the radio," Ronson turned and left the carriage.

One of David's Protection Squad staggered in. The bodyguard still managed to salute his Leader then offered up a crappy little first aid box, like a gift.

"What's that?" asked David.

"First Aid," said the bodyguard, proudly. He rooted through the box then pulled out plasters, some TCP and a roll of bandage just about large enough to wrap a thumb. "Sir. Do you need tweezers?"

"No I do not need tweezers," the prime minister growled. "Do I look like I need tweezers? Why would I need tweezers? I haven't got a splinter in my thumb, you…" David was too concussed to think of a creative insult, so just added, "…fucking tweezer bloke."

"Safety pin? Thermometer? Should I take your temperature?"

"I'm still here," moaned Bernstein.

"Oh, if you can't find someone else to do it properly…" David stood, weaved a little and reached into the pocket of his slacks, "… then do it yourself." He grabbed a small bag of something white and powdery then sniffed from it, long and loud. "Thermometer," he gasped. "Why in the world would I need a thermometer?"

"If you have any kind of morphine that would be just great," pleaded Bernstein, who also stood, staggered, then fell over again. No one even seemed to hear him.

"So what was that?" asked David. "What happened? One minute, the Great American Writer here is having a go at me just because I'm a fascist…" he finally looked down at Bernstein who rolled on the ground and tried to stand again. "Which I'm not, as I just explained at some length – the next, it's whoops, where's the floor gone and we've recreated Neil Armstrong's moon disaster."

"Well, Sir, I was up front, in the engine, Sir."

David sat down again, felt his nose and pushed it side to side. Then he looked at the bodyguard, disdainfully.

"Why were you in the front? Please don't tell me you were playing real-life Hornby Train Set up there. What, were you getting your little spade and giving the choo-choo its coal? When you should have been in here, guarding my body, which is, after all, your job title?"

The bodyguard held up a small plaster, which David waved away.

"According to the driver, there was a problem at the points," he said. "They hadn't opened properly, so…something to do with the wheels not locking, or something. Shall I get him back here to give a full report?"

David bashed a palm into his forehead in frustration, then winced with the pain. "Oh yes please, tell you what, let's get some sandwiches made, sit round and discuss what happened. Maybe find a secretary to take notes. Of course I don't want a report now, four eyes."

"I'm…not…wearing…glasses," attempted the bodyguard.

"I. Am. *Concussed.*" David yelled, and fell sideways. From the floor, he shouted, "just get us off this train and find some ambulances, police, you know, the whole dee-daw, dee-daw, fun, flashing light parade which is traditional when the *prime minister* is involved in a train crash."

"Well, it's less of a crash – more a derailment, according to the driver. The wheels didn't lock, you see…"

David held up one finger to his lips. "One more word, I swear. One more and I'll derail your neck."

The bodyguard shut up.

Mick Ronson rushed back into the carriage.

"I've spoken to Central on the radio. We're in the middle of nowhere between Reading and Swindon. Luckily, we're almost right next door to a military barracks. They're sending an ambulance and an escort. Be here any moment."

"Good, some professionals at last. That was lucky. I didn't fancy standing on the sidings like a hitchhiker."

"How do you feel?" asked Mick.

"I feel like I've been in a train crash, oooh, no, sorry, I meant a 'derailment'." He looked back witheringly at the bodyguard.

"Come on then, let's get you out of here and thank our lucky stars no one's hurt."

"I'm hurt," whined Bernstein. "Actually, I'm hurt quite badly."

"Everybody ready then?" said Ronson, who'd neither heard nor would have cared.

*

Sure enough, with military efficiency, an army ambulance and jeep escort arrived within minutes.

Ronson took charge again and dealt with soldiers and medics who'd alighted from the vehicles. David let him get busy. The combination of extremely pure cocaine and a train crash had made him very fragile.

After speaking with various servicemen, Ronson squatted by David and Bernstein, both sat at the side of the road.

"OK, here's the plan. We're heading straight to RAF Aldbourne. From there, they'll airlift you to the nearest hospital, proper. But the medics want to check you over, right now. You are their number one priority. So me, you and the...er... reporter will go in the ambulance. Protection Squad will ride up front with the soldiers as an escort. But since no one even knows we're here – even we didn't know we'd be here – the chances of some kind of attack are nil. But better safe than sorry. The ambulance has two beds, you can take them, I'll be with you all the way, OK?"

"Thank you," whispered Bernstein.

"Not you," replied Mick.

Two soldiers helped David and Carl into the back of the military ambulance. It was dimly lit, with a partition between the driver's cab and the rear. A young medic waited in the back, along with a nurse. They both quietly took their patients' blood pressure, shone lights into their eyes and checked for breakages. David lay back and felt more out of it than ever. Dimly, he realised shock had probably wrapped him in its arms.

At the rear, Ronson hung onto a strap for balance and looked straight forward, intently.

David thought Mick appeared to be both extremely worried and rather nervous, which was understandable. As second in command,

Ronson may have to take responsibility while his boss received treatment and recuperated. That thought probably terrified him.

Ha, thought David, dully. *I hope he* does *get a go. Let* him *see what it's like to run this country. It's a* trifle *more complicated than shagging impressionable young birds.*

The nurse bent down over David. He couldn't really focus but knew she was pretty.

"Have you all sorted out soon enough, prime minister," she said, from a long way away. Her voice was light and playful. "Literally taken care of, I promise."

David peered up at this angel. She had big dark eyes and sensual red lips. Before politics called, he'd only had a couple of girlfriends, but was now married to the nation. He was expected to be single and devote his life to the British Union, but as he looked at this girl, part of him felt he'd made a mistake. A girl like this could turn a man's head from fascism and that was saying something.

Her dark hair spilled over the shoulders of her white uniform and framed her face.

"I may be not quite myself," David grinned, weakly. Quickly, he shut his mouth. It was full of cracked and twisted teeth like crazy paving and certainly not his best feature.

"But can I just say, you are very, awfully, very pretty."

"Aaw, you tease."

"I mean it," he flirted onwards. "You have a lovely barnet, too. So long and curly…"

Something stopped him. Nurses weren't supposed to wear their hair down. It wasn't hygienic. They were supposed to keep it pinned up under their hats. But then again, this was an emergency, so perhaps she hadn't had time for protocol.

Who cared anyway? He could look at that pretty face all day.

The nurse reached up, pulled off her hat and shook out more of that lustrous hair.

She's almost in slow motion, David thought. *Like a Silverkrin advert. God, these drugs are strong.*

"What's your name, darlin', if you don't mind me asking?"

She smiled and demurely looked down at the gun in her hand. The prime minister registered what beautiful eyelashes she had, then did a slow double take at her pistol.

Oh, well, that's suddenly very odd, because, yes, that's a gun and she's pointing it at me.

"My name is Nurse Bolan," she said. "Or rather Mark Feld, as you once briefly knew me. I'm not actually a woman, or even a nurse. Had many I-Spy books as a kid, did you, Dave?"

"You're Mark Feld?" David now recognised "her" from the detective's photograph he'd seen earlier.

Mick Ronson went to rush at the 'nurse', but she raised the gun at him. From the driver's cab, another soldier aimed a rifle his way. Mick stopped, held up his hands and backed off.

"No heroics, Ronson. Stay focused. As you may have guessed, David," said Nurse Bolan. "We aren't the military. Nice flirting, by the way, I'm very flattered. You are now our prisoner. So, prime minister – hey, let's not be formal – Dave me old mucker, you are now a captive of the M.U. Not the B.U, the M.U."

"M.U.?" whispered David.

"Oh, one revelation at a time, Dave. By the way, there's no point wondering if your Protection Squad are suddenly going to swoop in and save the day either, because our guys have taken care of them in the Jeep. We made sure the train jumped its tracks. We were ready with this military charade, to jump into action and get here before any other rescue could, because we knew exactly where your 'accident' would take place, see?"

"What?" wheezed Bernstein, who'd suddenly sharpened up, eyes wide. He'd clearly realised a huge story was unfolding and he had the scoop. "We've been kidnapped? By a nurse?"

Thanks to adrenalin and fear, David also felt a lot sharper. "She's not a nurse, hack. She's not even a she. She's a bloke. He's a bloke."

"Oh, the prime minister's very insightful, ain't he?" said Bolan, who put a hand on his hip and did a cheeky little moue.

"You did the graffiti," said David. "I recognise your face! You!" He attempted to point at Bolan, but realised his hands had somehow been tied without him knowing.

"Don't talk to him, prime minister," shouted Ronson. "Don't say a word. Our own people will have realised we're not on the train by now. They'll be in the air, on the ground, scouring the area, blocking the roads. You won't get away with this, bitch. Bastard. Whatever." He glowered at the nurse.

"Ooh, less of the drama, Ronson. Dial it down a bit, you're not on stage. This is real life, remember. This is happening." Bolan glared at Mick. "Don't ever forget. This is happening. For real." He threw a pair of handcuffs at Ronson. "Pop them old, old chap. I'm sure you know how to put handcuffs on yourself. You've had plenty of practice with all those Ronsonettes, in all those rooms."

"Yes, alright," Mick grumbled. "Not in front of everyone. You'll pay for this. You'll pay for it with your lives."

"Rein in the Oscar performance, Ronson. Don't listen to him, Prime Minister," Bolan/Feld went on. "He's only trying to give you hope. We're easily way way ahead of anyone realising you're gone. We have a huge head start and are going to a very secure location. Oh, and I did some of the graffiti, but not all. Just did my bit, showed some disrespect, knew it would wind you up. It did wind you up, didn't it?"

David tried to pull his haughtiest face and turn away, but Bolan grabbed the PM's chin and turned him back. Marc pouted, then his big red painted lips broke into a massive smile.

"Oh ho, yep, I knew it. I knew it would get to you. THE THIN WHITE DUKE RETURNS, EXCLAMATION MARK! That was my own little act of sedition. Throwing spiteful darts in your eyes. But… " he looked down at the prisoner and realisation dawned, "…you don't really remember me, do you? *Chaaaaarming.*"

"I didn't until this morning, you'd totally slipped my mind."

"Oh, I'm hurt, prime minister. I knew it would all come back eventually. That's why I did the graffiti, why I made damn sure you

got a photo of me, to jog your memory. *I* sent it to the police! Me! *I*
filled in all the extra information, so when we met again, here, in this
ambulance, just as planned, you on a stretcher and me in a skirt, you'd
be up to speed. But you're not fully up to speed, it seems, if you can't
recall why that particular piece of graffiti, THE THIN WHITE DUKE
is pissing you off so very badly."

"Who are you?" asked Bernstein.

"Trust a reporter to ask the right question." Bolan smiled at David
again. "He knows, but doesn't really know, just thinks he does. Let me
tell you about me and Dave…" he looked down at his upside-down
nurse's watch. "…I've got about ten minutes. Are you sitting
comfortably? No? Then I'll begin."

                                    *

"I'm only a few months younger than you, Dave," Bolan/Feld said, as
the ambulance bumped and rumbled to who-knew-where. He turned a
ring of hair around his finger again, a faraway look in his eyes. "But
you thought you were better. Back then, the early '60s, we both
wanted to be musicians, You now claim that 'wanting to be a
musician' meant dreaming of being an oboe player in the Royal
Philharmonic, something respectable, but we both know what you
really wanted back then. You wanted to be a rock star. You had your
beady eye on the drugs, the birds, the sex, the sharp *schmatta*."

David lay on the stretcher and studiously didn't look up at Nurse
Bolan.

Bernstein listened intently and it was clear the reporter had filed
every word.

"It was '64, just before Mosley really stamped down on music and
culture in this country. Remember how the establishment started
getting upset about rock and roll in the '50s? Oh yes, rock and roll, it
was new, there was no precedent. No laws to deal with it. The
Establishment saw it as a threat, because it was unknown. They didn't
really know what R&R was capable of, back then. But soon they got

the idea, oh yeah, they got the idea alright. Quickly, they started making the foreign radio stations illegal, didn't they? Outlawing Teddy Boys, fashions. Cinemas couldn't show rock and roll movies... It was ghastly. It was as if us kids had been given this colourful box full of the future, but then the B.U. shut that box, took it away, threw it in a landfill. Rock and roll was happening everywhere else in the world but Britain. I still can't believe they made fun a crime just because it had 'jungle rhythms' and wore crepe shoes.

"So when *we* met, Dave, it was 1964. The Culture Laws were in force, but not as draconian as they are now. Alvin Stardust, really? Mick Jagger and His Beatles? Did you see The Beatles before whats-their-names, oh yeah, John and Paul blew their minds out in that car? What an odd way to top yourself, but hey-ho. I saw them once, in an illegal Scouse club called The Cavern. Before Jagger took over, they were amazing. Sex on legs, sex in 4/4 time. That's what could have happened, but Mosley shut it all down.

Sure you could form a band, but by '64, you had to be vetted. It wasn't much of a dream for a kid – state-sponsored rock! – but I thought maybe I could subvert it. Get my licence to buy an electric guitar, then start playing around, being naughty, just to see what I could get away with. But to form a band, you needed a government-approved manager – still do – so we both turned up, same day, almost same time, to Les Conn's office in Soho. What a name for a manager, huh, Dave? Conn?"

"Yes, I remember," said David, weakly.

"Yes, you do, but not everything, it seems. We'd both got round the fashion restrictions by being Mods, hadn't we? Remember them? The Mods? The establishment just thought we were all smartly dressed young men, but couldn't see that was the fashion. Cuffs just the right length, a certain cut of the jacket, a nice unconventional lining, the right amount of buttons – it was all secret code, wasn't it? Mosley's fashion police never spotted us because we could only be seen by those in the know, but if you *did* know, you could spot a bell boy from a top boy a mile off.

"So, there we were in Les Conn's office and you thought you were the King fucking Bee, didn't you? Oh, you were Top Mod and I was just some Stoke Newington chancer, wet behind the ears. I introduced myself, 'Hello, I'm Mark Feld' and you didn't even shake my hand, just curled your lip, looked down at my shoes and said, 'They're not proper brogues, mine are the right sort.' What an arsehole, even then. So I bet you never recognised me from the photo, did you?"

"Hmph," managed David.

"No, I looked pretty different. Shorter hair, no make up. I was certainly not wearing a nurse's uniform, ha! Amazing what a few years can do to ya, isn't it? Oh, but you had the attitude, even back then. So we both sat down in Les Conn's gaffe. You're looking at him like he's shit off your shoe and I'm so eager to impress. He was straight off the parade ground. Proper ex-military man. He says…" Bolan put on a crusty old drill sergeant's voice. "'*I need to know if you 'orrible young men have a work ethic before I even hear your songs. The government wants hard workers, even in the music charts. No shilly shally. Hard-working singers for hard-working people. You both look smart, but do you* think *smart?*' Remember that, Dave? I do. Every word."

David remembered the gist of it, but not the detail. Bolan clearly did, though.

"So, Conn handed us a tin of whitewash and a brush each. We looked at our tins and brushes like they were alien objects, didn't we? That was his idea of an audition, to see if these young upstarts could put in a decent day's work before we even picked up a guitar. Very old fashioned, very British Union of Fascists. If you want to be a pop star, let's not bother with the songs, let's see how you cope with a few orders. The antithesis of rock and roll! He wanted us to whitewash his place, give it an undercoat, to prove we had the gumption and elbow grease to write songs for the masses! You were horrified. I thought it was hysterical. He went to his coat stand and there were two boiler suits there, already covered in paint. He must have done a lot of auditions before us, huh? So we pulled on the boiler suits – which you hated – and got to work. Once you'd relaxed, you were a bit friendlier, but so competitive! So there we were, the two wannabe pop stars with no manager, no equipment, desperate to get on the ladder, but literally *on* a ladder, a couple of brushes between us and the charts.

"You said my name out loud, a lot. 'Mark Feld, Maaaaark Feld. *Mark* Feld. Mark *Feld.*' You said it every which way. You told me Mark Feld didn't sound like a star. I told you David Jones was even worse. Since then, I changed my name, you kept yours. That says a lot.

"A couple of hours later, Conn came back from his Soho liquid lunch and inspected our masterpieces. He liked mine. Said I was clearly a grafter, but you... He looked at your walls and lost the plot... Now do you remember what he said as he kicked you out with no contract, no chance, no hope? He ended your pop dreams that very moment."

David felt himself redden with rage. He'd pushed that day deep down into his mind, from where it could never surface again. But Bolan/Feld had just dredged it right back up from that dark lake.

"Remember what he said? '*Who the hell do you think you are?*'" Bolan yelled in the voice of Conn's drill Sergeant. "'You walked in here like you're some kind of *duke*, with your superior attitude! Too good for work, are you, *duke?* You haven't even tried! You treat me with contempt, sir! *This is thin whitewash,* duke! Damn *thin* whitewash, duke! Too thin!'"

Bolan fell about laughing. The soldiers in the front of the ambulance joined in.

"THIN. WHITE. DUKE. Three words that shut the door on you. Oh, it was priceless. So I got the contract, equipment and gigs. You got nothing. But oh, you had your revenge, didn't you? Of course, I never amounted to anything. I was too subversive even then, but kept my hand in. I still play, you know, I'm in a band you've never heard of, under the radar. We're called T-Rex. We were Tyrannosaurus Rex, but that had too many syllables."

"So T- Rex was better? Stupid name," hissed David.

"Maybe. No worse than 'The Lower Third', or, oh God, yes, 'The Beatles'? That is shit. Who puts puns in band names? 'The Beatles'? Jesus. I bet those Scousers were overjoyed with that one. But more to the point, you've never heard of us. There are loads of bands like mine, a resistance if you like. We don't fight with guns and bombs, but with chords, glitter and sex. My guitar kills fascists."

"That is the most pretentious thing I've ever heard," snapped David.

"No, your whole 'Station To Station' justification was the most pretentious thing I've ever heard," piped up Bernstein.

Bolan smiled again. He looked like an indulgent parent watching two of their toddlers arguing.

"So anyway I'm out there now, singing about Hot Love and Get It On in sweaty, illegal clubs to sweaty illegal kids. We'll never have a single hit, but that doesn't matter. We're doing it. You try to stop us, but we're doing it, with glitter on our faces, smiles on our lips and hard-ons in our Y-fronts. We get it on, Dave, we get it on in a big way."

Bolan looked at his watch again. "But time is against us. Oh time, you wanker. Anyway, the next part of the show is about to begin."

The 'nurse' produced a plastic mask and pushed it over David's face. He tried to struggle, but the gas overcame even the cocaine in his system. As he fell unconscious, he looked up at Bolan's pretty mouth, and wondered what it might feel like to kiss it.

*

David woke on the floor of a bare white room with no windows. Ronson was unconscious next to him with Bernstein in another corner, breathing heavily. His head hurt, again. A single bulb illuminated three chairs arranged along a wall.

David pushed himself into a sitting position. Ronson groaned and opened his eyes.

"Where are we?" he croaked.

"How should I know?" the prime minister's voice cracked. He was so thirsty.

"I couldn't stop them, I'm sorry," Ronson slowly pulled himself up.

"They had guns. Thanks for trying, but whoever they are, they mean business."

Bernstein also moaned and his eyes flickered.

"Oh hoo-fucking-ray, the cavalry's awake." David stood and rubbed his forehead.

"You actually know that freak Bolan?" Bernstein asked from his foetal position on the floor.

"I met him one day." David held up a finger. "One bloody day. And he does all this? Because I got to be prime minister and his stupid band never had a hit? Bit extreme, isn't it? What does he even want?"

Bernstein tried to sit up but fell sidewards. He found that position more to his liking, so stayed in it. "Well, he wants you, that's obvious. But I doubt it has anything to do with a day's painting twelve years ago. I've seen his graffiti around, wondered what it was. Now I know."

"Graffiti's one thing, but kidnapping the prime minister is a whole other game. Well, Carl, if you live through whatever-this-is, you'll have a story to tell, huh? Finally get that Pulitzer prize you've been dreaming of."

"I haven't been dreaming of a Pulitzer prize." Bernstein lied.

"You're a journalist," David sniffed. "You've had plenty of wet dreams about that certificate."

Ronson checked the door and felt along the walls.

"Find any hidden escape routes, Biggles?" asked David.

"Nope. But the walls are whitewashed," Ronson answered. "Quite badly, actually."

"Oh, just hilarious," David groaned. "Even this room is a shit visual piss take. I will strangle that Bolan, that Feld with his own hair, I swear."

At that moment, there was the click of a lock and the door opened. The three prisoners all turned to look.

Six of the strangest people David had ever seen trooped in, holding guns. They were all dressed in a different costume of some kind.

Marc Bolan was amongst them, changed out of his nurse's uniform. His cheeks were dappled with glitter and he wasn't smiling.

Marc now wore a tight shiny purple jacket with large lapels. As this ostentatious item fell open, David saw the lining was covered in silk-screened pictures of Bolan's own face. He sported a pink feather boa and on his head sat a massive top hat, like the Mad Hatter's. His trousers were shiny silver that led down to boots with implausibly tall soles.

"Oh, it's the queer nurse," said Bernstein from his prone position. "But looking even weirder, if that's possible."

David's mind was in a whirl – he couldn't tell if these people were boys or girls. One, clearly the leader of this odd collective, imperiously walked in front and stared at each of his captives.

This man (or woman?) looked even stranger than Bolan. He wore a body stocking covered in geometric patterns, but one arm and leg were bare. If that wasn't odd enough, its head made David choke in shock. This thing's barnet was *red hot red* and spiked up as if the scalp had caught fire. The face was painted as white as the walls of the room, but bisected by a curious lightning flash of red and blue. That flash looked very familiar to David. It took a moment, but then he recognised it.

"That's the symbol of the British Union!" he shouted, affronted. "How dare you use our glorious symbol as some perverse mask?"

The man/woman stared at David without emotion. "It is not your glorious symbol. It is an ancient Viking rune, Sol. It represents the sun. For I am the light against your darkness."

David turned to the prostrate Bernstein. "And you call *me* pretentious?"

"OK," wheezed the reporter. "They just trumped you somewhat in that regard."

"Thank you. Finally."

"Excellent work, Marc," said the thing. "You have faced much danger to bring us our nemesis. You shall be rewarded. Your rank is now King of the Rumbling Spires."

Bolan looked thrilled and bowed at the lightning-flashed androgyne.

"Oh, Jesus," whistled David. "We were supposed to be on a train but we've got on the Sunshine Bus by mistake. So, Oh Holy Leotarded Loser, who might you be? Because I'm the fucking prime fucking minister."

The thing waved away David's words like a child would blow away a dandelion.

"I am Aladdin. Although some call me Ziggy. I am Aladdin, because I will let loose the genie from Britain's bottle and it will grant the wishes of the oppressed. I am also Ziggy, which starts with Z, because I am the end, the final letter. The full stop on history."

"You're also a looney. Two names? That's confusing."

"Yes," conceded Aladdin/Ziggy. "Some people *do* get confused between the two personae."

The rest of his curious mob nodded in agreement. "Yeah," said Bolan. "Some think the lightning bolt character is *Ziggy*, but it's *Aladdin*. When he wears the eyepatch, or the gold circle on his forehead, *that's* Ziggy. People don't pay attention, do they, Zig, er, Aladdin, er…Ziggy??"

"I'm currently *Aladdin,* you tosser, try to keep up. Yes, yes, alright, Christ, let's not get tied up with who I am when I'm wearing what, we've got better things to do, haven't we?"

Bolan and the rest looked suitably chastened. This strange creature continued.

"Yes, prime minister, I am your nemesis. In many ways, we are the same, but opposite."

"No, wait, that doesn't work," said David. "It's an oxymoron."

"No it isn't. Shut up. We both know how to unleash Dionysus in the crowd. We are ancient symbols, you and I, of the elemental powers of passion, of derangement…"

"Yeah, this lot have definitely won the pretentious league," muttered Bernstein.

"But I channel those forces for good." Bernstein and David started to giggle and Aladdin/Ziggy tried to ignore them. "As do my Young Dudes, here. For they are the generals in our army. We are not the British Union. We are our Yin to your Yang."

Bolan held up his hand like a schoolboy, "Nooo, excuse me, Sir, nooo. It's our Yang to their Yin isn't it?"

A small muttered debate began amongst the weirdos as to which was more fitting. Aladdin put his hands over his hears. "Shut up! Everybody button it! I'm doing the talking. It's Yin to their Yang, I say so, so it is."

"Ooh, quite the dictator isn't he, boys?" David smirked. "Or is it girls? It's hard to tell these days. Are you a bloke?"

"Yes, yes, of course I'm a bloke," squealed Aladdin, who didn't sound male in the slightest. "But I'm sexually fluid!"

"Eeeoo" squirmed David. "The weirdo said sexual fluid, Mick, eeoo."

"I didn't! I'm messing with gender roles!"

"You're messing with a wardrobe in the dark is what you're messing with."

"Oooooh, shut up," shouted Aladdin. "We are here to dispense justice and usher in a new age for Britain."

"Dressed like that?"

"Yes, dressed like this, yes! Can't you just let me get on with my exposition?"

David shrugged as if to say, *be my guest.*

"This is Eno, my Controller of Oblique Strategies." Aladdin indicated a balding woman next to him. A perplexing arrangement of black feathers emerged from this stick-thin woman's neck, which was encircled with a choker. Her bare chest had no bosom and she wore black trousers that started frighteningly tight at the crotch but then became monstrously flared. The feathers round her shoulders gave her the appearance of a camp, dead ostrich. "It is <u>no</u> pleasure to meet you, Sir," she said, in an obviously male voice.

"Oh, Jesus, you're another bloke?" David groaned. "Bloody hell mate, drop the make up and the clobber. Oh, and cut your hair. Growing it long doesn't make your bald bits any less baldy, you follicular fuck. It looks ridiculous." David ran a hand over his own thick mane, just to rub it in.

"Don't listen, Eno, you have wonderful hair. This is Diamond, my Head of Future Legends." Aladdin pointed at another follower, who looked even worse.

Diamond was also bare chested and sported a copy of his master's rather impressive spiked red barnet, but it was clearly a cheap, dyed wig. From the waist down, he wore what could only be described as badly sewn-together furry trousers. A mangy tail hung sadly between his legs and he'd stuck cardboard claws onto some brown moccasins. Diamond had painted his nose black, with whiskers drawn on alongside. Two furry ears were attached to the top of his head with an Alice band.

"Are you supposed to be a kangaroo?" asked Bernstein.

"Oh come on, not again," whined Diamond and looked to Aladdin for support. "I'm a dog. I'm a dog. I'm clearly a dog. Why doesn't anyone realise I'm a dog? I'm a *dog*." He rubbed at his eyes.

"Don't cry again," said Bolan.

"I'm not crying, I've just got some dust in my eye, or something."

Bolan mouthed the words "*He's crying*," at Aladdin, who gave a gesture that everyone should ignore it.

"Why's he a kangaroo, sorry mate, dog?" asked David, sweetly.

"Because I will lead the pack!" Diamond roared, but his top lip wobbled like a child's. "And our pack will tear yours apart, for we are stronger! We are cats that are bigger than rats! No, rats that are bigger than cats! Balls! I know what I mean!"

The rest of the gang nodded sympathetically at Diamond,

"Rats bigger than cats! And, the death! *Aaaooooooooooo*!" He attempted to howl, but broke off into a nasty cough.

"Do you want some water, Graham?" Eno asked, concerned.

"No, I'm OK, I'm fine and I'm not Graham," sulked Diamond, then erupted into another coughing fit.

Another person stood further back dressed as an astronaut. Except, on closer inspection, that costume also appeared jury-rigged.

"I mmmamamatomn," the spaceman said.

"Sorry, what?" asked David.

"Immamajjrrtom," he repeated.

"It's the helmet, mate, I can't hear you."

The spacemen angrily threw open the visor of his helmet, which, David realised, was plastic, way too small and clearly part of a children's costume from Woolworths.

"For heaven's sake, I said I'm Major Tom!" said the pasty faced starman, who had no eyebrows and looked rather anaemic.

"Major? In which army, exactly?" asked David. "The Royal Fuckuliers?"

"Fuck off," snarled Diamond. "And you can fuck off while you're at it."

"What kind of semantic car crash was that?" David frowned in confusion.

"Can everyone please stop swearing? It's not revolutionary behaviour," Aladdin pleaded as he attempted to regain control. "Major Tom is our Controller of Advanced Technologies."

"Advanced technologies? Oh, let me guess, a Stylophone? And why's he dressed in a kid's plastic space helmet?"

"I'll wallop you one," grunted "Major Tom", who held up his fists, wrapped in silver oven gloves. The whole outfit had been made of Other Things, as if Tom's tailor were a demented Blue Peter presenter. His oxygen tanks were washing-up-liquid bottles, the pipes a garden hose and his boots Wellingtons, all badly sprayed silver. "I will, I'll knock you bandy." Tom skipped up and down on the spot like Muhammad Ali.

"Right, everyone be quiet, please stop, I'm getting a headache," ordered Aladdin. "Finally, the Head of my Goon Squad. They are my personal protection, my bodyguards. He is…Pierrot!"

Seemingly oblivious to everyone else in the room was a man dressed in a flouncy, shiny, blue-and-white costume. Lost in concentration, he pulled odd, angular mime shapes. A white hat that looked like an upturned flower pot sat on his head and his face was painted white, with bright red lips. A cigarette hung from them, insouciantly.

"Why's he dressed as a clown?" whispered David, reasonably.

Pierrot stopped pulling shapes and finally looked round at the captive.

"I ain't a clown!" he said in a South London accent as thick as David's. "I'm a Pierrot! Well, alright, I am a clown, but I'm the external clown! I mean the eternal clown! I represent sadness! Yes, mate, sadness for all who cross us! For you, I am true 'orror! You should 'ave an 'orror of this room, because this is no game, prime minister! This is genocide! Political genocide! For my Goon Squad, my elite band of warriors, will soon be marching down Whitehall, left, right, left right!" He began to strut about, still making strange shapes.

"Calm down just a bit there, Pierrot," sighed Aladdin.

David yawned. "I'm finding it just a little bit difficult to be scared by a man dressed by Billy Smart's Circus. No, dressed by Billy Smart's Shite Circus."

"Scary? You want scary? I can do scary, mate!" said Pierrot, who attempted to roll up his multi-layered, sparkling chiffon sleeves but failed. One ripped and he tried to pretend it hadn't happened.

The rest of the crew pushed and shoved each other as they tried to get at David. Aladdin windmilled his arms effetely at them all, which gave the whole group an appearance of eccentrically dressed kids arguing in a schoolyard.

"Stop! Stop! Everyone stop!" screamed Aladdin/Ziggy.

"Creep," snarled Pierrot at David, who pulled a sarcastic *ooooh-I'm-sooo-terrified* face back at him.

Everyone calmed down reluctantly. "So what do we have here?" Aladdin tried to look like the last five minutes hadn't happened. "The fascist prime minister of Britain. A reporter, all the way here from the New World. And with him, the second-in-command of Britain's evil empire, *Mick Ronson!*"

At that, Mick screamed like a berserker and suddenly ran forward at the motley group of oddities. He went straight for Aladdin, but before he could get close, Bolan produced a club from down his trousers (David hadn't thought it was a club down there) and whacked Ronson round the head with it.

Mick fell to the ground, a dead weight. Bolan bent down and felt the back of Ronson's head. His hand came up bloodied.

"I think I hit him a bit harder than I meant to," he said, apologetically.

"You'd better not," said Aladdin. "Is he alive?"

Bolan felt about Mick's neck. "I did some basic research as a nurse, you know, for the role. I do like to subsume myself in a part. Yes, he's alive and…breathing. Phew. I'll put him in the recovery position. That's what you do, you see. If the patient were to vomit whilst unconscious, the recovery position prevents them from choking on it. Obviously, I'll be monitoring him so…"

"Yes, yes, I get it," squawked Aladdin, furiously. "Eno, Diamond, tie up our two other prisoners. Eno, you tie Bernstein, *watch the knots!* Diamond, you restrain our prime minister."

David and Carl were hauled to their feet by the Dead Ostrich and the Kangaroo/Dog.

"As Head of the Goon Squad," said Pierrot, slightly put out, "actually, any tying and restraining should be under my purview, really."

"Purview?" muttered Eno. "Oh, she's been at the dictionary again."

"If you've killed him…" snarled David. "It won't be long before we're found and then you'll all be facing something way worse than a billy club round the head."

"Oh, I'm sure we will," Aladdin nodded, unruffled. "Now, to business. Is there anything you'd like to ask before we proceed? I have a tendency to waffle, so I'm happy to take guidance, have a bit of structure."

"*You* want *me* to lead my own interrogation?"

"Well, only as much as I lose the thread," Aladdin/Ziggy replied airily. "I'm a creative. We all are. Losing the thread aids the artistic process, but doesn't help dealing with logical progressions. You know, sometimes, I just cut up words and put them together, to see what happens. It creates a chaotic, some might even say pure circumvention of typical thought processes…"

"Oh drop it, Jung. Bloody hell. What a shower. One question. Why are you dressed like…that?"

The group all looked at each other as if they'd seen their outfits for the first time. A couple did silly twirls.

Ziggy/Aladdin rolled his eyes. "Because we're in disguise, dur. We are a revolutionary group. It wouldn't do for us to conduct our business in our day-to-day wear, would it? All the great revolutionaries wore disguises."

"Name one."

There was a long pause as the group looked up and around the room for inspiration.

"Dick Turpin?" offered Major Tom.

"A highwayman, not a revolutionary," David said. "Try again. I'm just curious how much basic research you've done."

"Batman?" tried Eno. David didn't dignify that with a response.

"Oh, oh, I know! The Lone Ranger!" said Bolan. David sighed.

Ziggy/Aladdin took control. "Prime minister, most revolutions take place in disguise at first. They sneak into the popular imagination under cover as something else we can identify with, whether that's an idea, work of art, political stand, even a song. People don't like seismic change, it unsettles them. So it's best to dress revolution up as something they recognise, so they can invite it into their home. Even the B.U.F. did that, right?"

David worked the ropes behind his back, but the knots seemed very tight. He was really worried about Ronson. *Was* Mick breathing? He couldn't tell for sure.

"Aha, yes. At first you were the British Union of Fascists, but then – what an odd story! – Mosley meets a mysterious man on a train who tells him to dump the 'Fascist' bit and hey presto! It worked. You sneaked fascism through people's front doors disguised as socialism. Amazing what the right choice of words can achieve, isn't it? Had you stayed as the B.U.F. you'd have got nowhere."

David could see why this bizarre-looking creature led the group now. At least he made sense.

"So, to the meat of this whole adventure. You represent the B.U. We are part of the M.U. We've worked behind the scenes for years now to undermine the British Union. Not with bombs, but with ideas, little whispers, subversion wrapped up in orthodoxy. We are not the *British* Union. We are the *Musicians' Union*."

David took a moment to think about that statement.

"Musicians' Union? Now I'm really scared. What are you going to do, beat me to death with a theremin?"

"Oh, if only. You think this is about politics? Ha, politics is the sideshow. Politics is the tent at the fair most people pass by, because they're all heading to the Big Tent. The one with the bright lights and dancing girls, the fire-eaters and calliope steaming out a jolly tune. The Big Tent with the huge glowing sign on the top that reads; 'CULTURE'."

"Culture?" hissed David. "Oh here we go, culture, the bolt hole of the elite, the bourgeoisie, the intellectuals, the superior, like you. Oh, how you all invoke culture to show how you're not like the common man, how you're above the sludge. You make me sick."

Ziggy stared at David almost pitifully.

"You haven't understood that word at all, have you, prime minister? Culture isn't highbrow, or lowbrow. It's what's around all of us, all day. We are culture, don't you get it? The Greeks weren't 'highbrow' because they went to see plays by Aeschylus! They went because it was a bit of fun, made them think, something to do, because it was popular. And popular culture doesn't mean stupid culture. It means popular, that's all. Art galleries – well art galleries that aren't censored, like ours – they're full of paintings that were just popular, not clever, elitist or degenerate. Take Shakespeare's plays; they didn't start out to be picked apart by professors, they were just big hits with the public. No one who went to see Macbeth thought they were watching something bourgeois. The groundlings were booing the villains, heckling, paying no attention, walking out... So... Who decides whether culture is highbrow or lowbrow? Well, people like you, prime minister. A country can always be reliably judged through its culture and and here, we have none. You had the agents of the zeitgeist imprisoned, then shot. What is freedom, except the ability to express an idea without let or hindrance, even if that idea offends others? True freedom is the right to sing, sculpt, act, say, dance, write, film anything in any way you wish. But freedom is also the right to object to it. Object, yes, but also accept it."

David tried to meet Aladdin's gaze, but couldn't. The man's anger was hard to stare out.

"Your British Union stamped down anything they considered worthless. But culture is cumulative. A small idea can create a big change. One man, dressed like me, is a freak. But perhaps one day, another man may feel liberated enough to follow my example. To be free from what he thinks he should be, to become what he is. And then another and another, until the freak becomes the norm and thus we win a victory without a shot being fired. Because I dress like this, I start a small revolution. But the British Union doesn't even allow this tiny protest.

David, you once wanted to be a musician. But your music dream was lost in whitewash. So you turned to politics and if you couldn't play with the toys, no one could. Under you, as Minister For Truth, the B.U. Moral Laws became tighter and tighter until culture itself was forced underground. Without culture, this country is dead. It may limp on for a while, unaware it has received a mortal wound, but it is dead.

You are the killer and there will be justice. I will leave you to think about that for a short while, then we must reconvene to do what we must to save Britain."

Eno started clapping, then realised no one else had joined in, so stopped. His face flushed.

"Brown-noser," whispered Bolan out of the side of his mouth.

Aladdin swept from the room as imperiously as he'd entered. The Ostrich, Mad Hatter, Plastic Spaceman, Shit Clown and Kangaroo/ Dog cast dark looks back at the prime minister as they followed.

"Well, that was instructive, wasn't it?" said Bernstein. There wasn't much David could add.

*

So David, Carl and the unconscious Ronson waited in a whitewashed room for help to arrive, but not a single siren or chi-chop-chop of rotor blades could be heard.

Then, Ronson groaned.

"Mick!" whispered David. "Mick, thank God! Are you OK?"

Ronson rolled over, grasped at his head, then moaned when he saw blood on his hands. He tried to push himself up, failed, then tried again.

"Mick, we're tied up," David said, frantically. "You're not. You need to get us out of this. Come on Mick, come on, help."

"Alright, alright." Mick clambered uncertainly to his feet. "What happened?"

"Marc Bolan hit you with what I thought was his penis."

"Sorry, what? He hit me with what you thought was his penis?"

"It doesn't matter, I'm panicking. Listen, the weirdos, they went out, but I don't know for how long. They might be outside, but they might not be. You've got to untie us. I think they're going to do something terrible to me."

"OK, OK, give me a moment, I'm bleeding. So what happened after I was out?"

"Well," said Bernstein. "On the plus side, I've got enough material for three Pulitzers."

"Oh, cheers, how philanthropic of you," snorted David. He turned to Ronson. "I'll explain later. Just get us out of these chairs."

"Alright, let me think," said Ronson. "No point just untying you if they're right outside. Let me go and check the lie of the land. That door might be locked and then we're going nowhere, right?"

"Hurry," David pleaded.

Ronson made his way over to the door and opened it. Mick put one finger to his lips as if this were pantomime and poked his head round the frame. Then, he stepped through.

"Bet he does a runner," whispered Bernstein.

"Shut up," answered David.

Thirty seconds later, Mick returned. "I can hear them at the far end of the corridor," he bent down behind Bernstein's chair to untie the ropes.

"Whoah, stop. Untie me first!" squeaked David. "It's me they're after, untie me first!"

Ronson ignored him and carried on untying the reporter. "Bernstein, listen. Outside the door there's a corridor that goes left to right. *Right*, that's where they are, somewhere. Maybe in a room. I heard them. But *left*, there's a door. It's not locked, I checked. It leads to a gangway and some stairs. Down the stairs is another door; it's open and I could see daylight. So go left, OK, just run, mate, run left as fast as you can."

"Hurry up! Forget him! Untie me!" shouted David as loud as he dared.

"OK, OK," said Ronson. Suddenly, Bernstein's hands were free. He stood unsteadily, but found his balance.

"Go. Go!" Ronson pointed at the door. "Run, get help, quick as you can."

"UNTIE <u>ME</u>," David wailed.

Bernstein ran toward the door then turned back for a moment. "I'm going to run ahead, if you don't mind, er, David, er, prime minister? Love to wait, but every second counts. See you out there, wherever out there may be…Great interview, by the way." Then he was gone.

"*UNTIE ME.*" David stared at Ronson, who simply stood up, stretched and sighed.

"No can do, I'm afraid, Dave. This is where you stay."

"What?" choked the prime minister. "Have you lost your mind? Untie me!" He bounced about on his chair. "They'll be back any moment! Untie me!"

Ronson calmly sat down.

"Relax, sweetie, that won't help."

"Untie me. Untie me, for the love of God untie me, or I will have you executed very slowly and very painfully. Untie *me untie* me *untie me.*"

"So here's what's going down," said Ronson, slowly. "There is no RAF Aldbourne. I never called Control. I just let my friends at the Musicians' Union know that Phase One of the plan had been completed, the train was off the tracks and the package was ready to be picked up. The package, by the way, being you."

David couldn't speak. He felt like his vocal cords had shut down.

"I've been in the Musicians' Union since 1969. I was already working with you by that point, of course, but I saw what you were doing to music, to culture. I couldn't let that happen. My eyes were opened. I play guitar, man! It was bad enough in this country before, but once rock and roll was outlawed, I knew action had to be taken. The M.U. had to be convinced that David Jones' right-hand man was on their side, but once I played the solo from "Johnny B. Goode" on my Les Paul, they knew I was a kindred spirit."

"The Les Paul is contraband," David managed to say.

"I've just confessed to being a traitor and you're more worried about my Les? I've got a stash of gear hidden in Hammersmith. Yeah, I got Leses, Fenders, a Marshall Major Head, whoah, that's a pulveriser, I got a Vox Tone Bender...No? But forget all that, I'm doing the explanation, Dave. You need to shut up for the *explanation*.

"So I joined the M.U. Well, you heard Aladdin talk. The man knows his onions. Glitter, not guns. Excitement, not explosives. So they're out there, doing their things, slowly changing the world, one undercover gig at a time. We've got a whole load of young punks hitting the road, too. Like the Sex Pistols, on tour secretly. Yeah, spreading the word, spreading the idea. The Pistols have just played Manchester, ironically round the back of the Free Trade Hall, where Mosley first announced your new British Union. I bet the Pistols will find some likeminded souls up there, see if they don't. But nothing will change under *you*, Dave. You're a symbol of the old way. You're Mosley's choice, for God's sake, so you need to go, old chap. Think of this as enforced retirement.

"We came up with a plan to put something on the rail tracks, organise a train derailment on a day when you had less security. I sorted that out. Then after the crash I'd 'call control' to organise a rescue, but of course, the rescue was the Musicians' Union, already standing by. Didn't you think it was weird how quickly they turned up? Anyway, Bolan filled you in on that. I like Bolan, he's got some cracking songs. He's just written one called 'Madman', it's great, not that you'll ever hear it.

"I also made sure Carl Bernstein was on the train. That way, we had a respected, American, neutral reporter around to tell the world what happened with this terrible kidnapping. That's why I let him go, so he could go spread the word."

Ronson did a bad American accent. "Gee, Mick Ronson was so brave! He tried to tackle them, but they nearly killed him! Knocked him clean out!"

"Actually," mused Mick and felt the back of his head, "Marc did hit me a bit hard, but the claret is all fake, from a fancy dress shop. Believable enough for the job, though. So Bernstein will get help, lead it back here and you know what they'll find? Me, spark out, covered in bruises. Yeah, they're going to drug me, then kick me around for a bit for authenticity. Not too much though, just enough."

"But what about me?" David asked, although he didn't want to hear the answer. Mick carried on.

"Bernstein will tell the entire world about these weird crazy people who took the prime minister hostage and nearly killed his loyal

Number Two in the process. Meanwhile, me, the brave hero, will become prime minister. I checked the Party rules and that's the deal. I'm second in command, so legally I get bumped to P.M. the minute anything happens to you. Then I'll work under cover, but in plain sight, to start turning things round. Not too much, not too quick, but laws will be relaxed, licences will be easier to obtain, there will be more instruments imported...Les Pauls, Fenders, Moogs, Marshalls, rock and *fucking* roll, You see what I'm saying? There will be a revolution, but it won't be televised, not at first. Eventually, since no one would have realised a coup had even taken place, they'll all be involved. First, it's a revolution of the mind. Maybe only a few minds at first, but give people the tools and they will use them. You can't kill rock and roll. You can't imprison culture. It will come back, stronger than ever. And I'm going to open the door for it."

"But what about me?" David whispered.

The door opened and the odd M.U. freak parade trouped back in. Ziggy, Eno, Diamond, Major Tom, Pierrot and Bolan looked as serious as six men effectively wearing fancy dress *can*.

"Oh, just great." David rolled his eyes, glad of the distraction. "Dozy, Beaky, Mick and Titch have reformed and they've bought Peters and Lee. I was so missing you."

Eno held an acoustic guitar.

"Even better!" laughed the prime minister. "Oh great, lucky me, the lunatics are putting on a gig. Ostrich man's brought his axe. I'm honoured."

"It's Eno," said big bird, darkly.

"Oh no, it's Eno!" David giggled. "Sorry, did I ruffle your feathers?"

"Silence!" shouted Ziggy. "You have heard the charges against you. What do you say in your defence?"

"Ooh, let me think. Give me a moment to consult my legal team, do hang on." David made a big show of thinking. "Well, Lady Leotard, Hatty, Feathery Failure, Skippy the Bush Twat, Space Cadet and Bozo the Dancing Arsehole, I have considered my defence."

"Which is?"

"Fuck right off."

"I thought it may have been that." Aladdin/Ziggy sadly shook his head. "Before we carry out the sentence, we have one last statement to make to you." He nodded at Eno, who raised his guitar. The others then held hands.

"Bloody hell, it's the Osmonds. No, it's worse, the New crapping Seekers," gasped David. "Are you about to teach the world to sing?"

Eno played two plaintive chords. David recognised them as C followed by E. Before he could repeat the refrain, the prime minister spoke up again. "Sorry mate, I think you'll find you're out of tune."

"I'm not." Eno manfully tried to play on.

"Oh come on, Emu. Listen! The E is way out, for starters."

"He's right," agreed Bolan, who produced some plastic pitch pipes out of his jacket pocket and blew on them. "That's my E, play your E again."

Eno plucked at the E string, Bolan blew on the pipes, Ziggy tried not to look to the ceiling in desperation, Mick looked down at his shoes. David couldn't tell if he was laughing or weeping.

Eno tried to tune the E. David helpfully whistled the note for him. Up and down went the pitch of the string as it drifted painfully in and out of tune.

"Yooadittheern," said Major Tom.

"Open your bloody helmet!" Ziggy ordered through gritted teeth.

"I said you had it then, I mean, clearly the *grrhrgggbhhh*" Tom's visor shut again and cut him off.

Eventually after at least five minutes of disastrous tuning, everyone seemed happy. The representatives of the Musicians' Union joined hands beatifically once more. Eno began to strum.

Each participant attempted to provide close harmonies with the others, but since no one knew exactly which notes they were supposed to hit, it was a cacophony.

"*We are who you* could *have been*," droned the weird collective. David winced.

"But your truth was never seen. The path is lit in true neon. We are the Musician's U-ni-on."

"Stop, stop!" shouted David over the din. "Did you really just rhyme 'true neon' with 'union'?"

"We're getting a neon sign made, actually," said Bolan, haughtily. "So factually, it's correct."

"Factually, it's shite," replied the prime minister.

"Our statement has been made." Ziggy tried to ignore his hostage's sniggers. "Any last words, prime minister? And don't say 'fuck off'."

"Oh," said David, disappointed. "Wait. Hold on. What? Last words? Last words? What do you mean, last words?"

"Make a note, Bolan," said Ziggy. "His last words were, '*What do you mean, last words?*'"

"Not the greatest last words, not for the ages," mused Eno.

"They weren't my last words, you cretin! I'm not making any last words! Let me go! Let me go!"

"Scratch those last, last words," said Ziggy. "His new last words were '*let me go!*'"

"What's going to happen?" David looked about his captors wildly.

Ziggy wondered if he should order Bolan to write that down, but decided against it.

"What's going to happen?" repeated Mick. "Well, mate, it's going to hurt, but only for a moment."

David looked Ronson in the eye and growled. "I knew I should have been a fucking rock star."

"That's the last words!" shouted Bolan. "Brilliant!"

David Jones shut his eyes as Aladdin shot him in the forehead. The bullet left a red sunburst and slowly, a thin trickle of blood zig-zagged down his face, like a lightning bolt.

*

David Bowie's eyes snapped open and he came to with a head full of white light and nostrils caked with cocaine.

His P.A. sat on a sofa in David's rented Bel Air home and leafed through *Vanity Fair*. She looked up from the magazine and then down at her boss, sprawled on the floor. David lay on some awful felt-tipped scribble he'd drawn on the carpet during his drug blackout.

"Aaaah." Bowie rubbed his nose with one hand and grabbed his aching forehead with the other. "Aagh, shit, aaah. What happened? Where am I?"

"Well, we'll start with you taking most, if not all of the cocaine in L.A. and take it from there, shall we?" she asked languidly and held up the magazine. Mia Farrow stared out of one page. "I like this dress of hers. Is it me?"

Bowie tried to focus. "I'm not really…In a dress-judging frame of mind."

"No, you haven't been in any frame of mind for the last day or so. OK, you're still in L.A, it's still 1975 and wow, you hoovered that stuff up like it was about to be rationed."

"Was I bad?"

His P.A. turned the pages and considered the question for a while.

"*Welllll*, that depends on your conception of the word 'bad' really. If, by 'bad', you mean ranting like a madman, hallucinating, twitching, running about, screaming, shouting, miming, talking to imaginary people…then yes, you were 'bad'. If, however, you think all those things are perfectly acceptable, then you were just tickety-boo."

"What was I shouting about?" David asked, but didn't really want to know.

"Most of the time, I had no idea. I just bunkered down and enjoyed the show. Well, I say, 'enjoyed', but it was more 'tolerated' if I must be brutally honest, which I must."

"Like what?"

"Oh, well, you know how you love your 'characters' and over the last twenty-four hours I've met a full cocaine-cast of them. So there was…oooh, let me think…" She started to count on her fingers, one by excruciating one.

"So. For starters, you were Major Tom, no surprise there. Then a teenage Essex boy, followed by Eva Braun, but dead."

"Eva Braun?"

"Mm-mm. You were Eva Braun, in some room or other, dead, with Hitler and Satan."

"What?"

"I was just as confused. Then…a stripper, or was it a dancer? Anyway, some tragic girl. God, there were so many people in this room, it was almost a party. Almost, apart from the sweaty paranoia and dribbling. Oh, you were an alien - again - *plus ça change* - but toot is quite a self-congratulatory drug, isn't it? So you weren't just any alien, but President Of The Entire Universe."

"Ow."

"Uh-huh. Then…Some old geezer in a bar, an angel, and, oh, the highlight; in your coke-frazzled mind, you'd become the leader of Great Britain. No, wait, the *fascist* leader of Great Britain. This current Nazi fascination of yours will get you into trouble if you're not careful. People don't really like Nazis very much – do try and remember that. You were giving speeches, saluting, the whole shebang. Then you started screaming about being kidnapped by Ziggy Stardust."

"Kidnapped by Ziggy?"

"Yup. Told you it was bad. You acted the whole thing out. You are quite a good actor, but your method rather relies on expensive and illegal chemicals. You said Eno was there. And Bolan, Ronson. Some others I couldn't make out. Oh, and then Ziggy shot you."

"Ziggy shot me?"

"Quite the switcheroo, isn't it? You killed off Ziggy. Looks like in your subconscious, Zig's still there, trying to get his own back."

"Aargh," moaned David who lay back on the carpet and closed his eyes.

"Side effects," she said. "All drugs have side effects and it seems one of cocaine's is turning you a teensy bit right wing."

"I've got to get out of L.A." He kept his eyes closed. "Somewhere I can't get any drugs."

"Well, I hear West Berlin's lovely, in a bombed out, total-opposite-to-Los-Angeles kind of way. And what with it being walled off by Communists it's the perfect place to wean yourself off both drugs and fascism. Just don't bloody go with anyone who'll get you into trouble."

"I'll bear it in mind," David replied. "God almighty. Who'd be a fucking rock star?"

Cover Stories

Richard Easter, September 2018

RUN OUT GROOVE; SIDE TWO

Taking up a load of 262's on benzedrine in '74. Sounds like a song to me.

Needle…*Up.*

LINER NOTES

"Space Oddity"

Guidance: *Ken Pitt / Angela Jones*
Decibels: *Werner Von Braun / Ralf Hutter*
Management: *Terence Jones*
V2: *Schneider*
Synth: *Professor Eno (EMS Synthi A)*

"Dear Prudence"

Jewellery Rattling: *John Lennon*
Scrambled Eggs: *Paul McCartney*
I Am The Click Track: *Ringo Starr*
The Devil's radio: *George Harrison*
Dry Reverb: *Great Wakering*
Synth: *Nick Rhodes (Roland Jupiter 8)*

"Sympathy For The Devil"

Percussion: *Stalin's Organ*
Lyrics: *Joseph Goebbels*
Jumping: *Jack Flash*
Production: *Beelzebub / Jesus Christ*
Management: *Martin Boorman*
Synth: *Dave Ball (Sequential Circuits Prophet 5)*

"Caroline Says (II)"

Suite: *Jane*
New York: *Andy Warhol*
Air Con: *Alaska*
Metal Machine Music: *Lou.*
Wild Side: *Holly*
Synth: *Vince Clarke (Sequential Circuits Pro One)*

"Calling Occupants of Interplanetary Craft"
Vox: Karen
Song: Richard
Klaatu Barada Nikto: Gort
Hubcap Diamond Star Halo: George Adamski
Oxcart: Area 51
Synth: Vangelis (Yamaha CS80)

"The A Team"
Angel: Interceptor
Hackney: Columbia Road
Guitar: Fender
Uriel: To My Left.
Divide: Minus
Synth: Gillian Gilbert (E/mu Emulator)

"Hey Joe"
Guitar: Hendrix
Stack: Marshall
Haze: Purple
Fire: Monterey
Crossroads: Robert Johnson / Tony Hatch
Synth: Thomas Dolby (PPG Wave)

"Station To Station"
Graphics: Speer
Young Dudes: Ian Hunter
Zinc Alloy: Marc Bolan
Warm Jets: Cherry Vanilla
Trains: Hornby
Fascism: N/A
Synth: David Bowie (Moog Minimoog)

Cover Stories *was recorded at Snow Studios in Chorlton, Manchester, then mixed and mastered at Duvet Sound. Thanks must go to David, Mick, Keith, Charlie, Brian & Bill. Lou, John, Paul George, Ringo, Richard, Karen, Jimi and Ed. Plus for additional instrumentation, Marc Almond, The Mambas, Laibach, Siouxsie & The Banshees, Klaatu and Soft Cell. Sounds and textures courtesy of the Korg Sigma, Roland Jupiter 8, Sequential Circuits Prophet 5 and Hohner Strat copy '86. Love and inspiration goes to and comes from The Regiment Of Fur and of course, my beloved Hil and Wynter xxx.*

hilaryeasterjones.com
(promotions, book production)
addedpixels.com @yannickmcosta
(IT, website design)
drlindsayporter.co.uk *(editing, proofreading)*
@simonpcherry *(cover graphics / design)*
The COVER STORIES (©Richard Easter) Logo is trademarked
thevividpress.co.uk
@thevividpress
email us: hello@thevividpress.co.uk

Oh, and does anyone here like The Human *League?*

Richard Easter *has been a professional writer for 30 years. In that time, he's never been far from music.*
He's had a Top 5 single, performed on Top of the Pops *three times and played drums for the Bee Gees. Richard's co-presented shows on BBC Radio 1 and 2, written for the* NME, *got lost in Broadcasting House with George Michael, watched the KLF burn a wicker man on the Isle of Jura, was first to play the Manic Street Preachers on national daytime radio, wrote* The Voice & Stars in Their Eyes *and managed to track down Joy Division's actual synthesiser, bought it, then broke it, which was very Joy Division of him.*

Also by Richard Easter: The Snow Trilogy

The Snow Trilogy comprises The Gentle Art of Forgetting, The General Theory of Haunting *and* The Littel Tale of Delivering (The Sleigh).

Although the stories can be read independently, in any order, they are all connected.

Minor characters in one book become major protagonists in another. Ideas set up in one story are given further explanations elsewhere. Themes recur in all three, but in different contexts.

The twenty second of December is a crucial date across the trilogy, and events from hundreds of years ago impact on every work, while love, loss, memory and, of course, *snow* weave around all three. Snow is as important a character as the individuals you will meet.

AN EXCERPT FROM "THE GENERAL THEORY OF HAUNTING"

Six work colleagues have managed to battle their way through dense snowfall to reach a New Year's Eve party at a remote mansion in Dorset.

Isolated there with no phone signal or internet, the guests' secrets and personal demons begin to surface. But the Hall itself also has a secret built into its walls. A grand and terrible purpose, kept hidden for over two hundred years.

One by one, the party-goers begin to experience "events," that may or may not be real. In the following excerpt, one of the guests, Anne Barker, is first to realise that - just maybe - *others* were invited and they've waited a *long* time for the festivities to begin...

*

Anne Barker sat on the edge of the bed and watched as the snow pushed and jittered against the window. Her eyes flicked to a bag on the floor. It contained her pills.

No, she managed to think distantly. *No, too early. You just had them. You had the pills when you were supposed to have them and you're not taking them again until eleven. You know that.*

But the pills were such a welcome exit. The medication kept her blurred rather than focused and acted as an antibiotic against herself.

She stood, as she should, and tried to do what was expected of her. But what was that? To join her colleagues downstairs and pretend?

Anne walked slowly over to the desk and mirror, where she stared at an emptiness that stared back at her. She tried a smile and it looked real enough. Anne picked up a brush and pulled it through her hair, as if corralling those stray strands would bring order elsewhere.

She took a small bottle of perfume, sprayed it into the air, then watched as the droplets flew and disappeared. They were another non-existent layer to hide behind.

But then, as Anne sat back on the bed, a small creak came from behind her and the mattress shifted downward, just a little more.

It felt as if someone or *something* had also sat down. Someone or something that wanted to join her this evening.

Anne didn't move.

There was no one else here. She'd seen Dan leave, but the bed had *creaked* and the mattress had rolled, and she'd felt that movement so many times. It was a simple tilting that said, "you are not the only one sitting here. I am behind you. Look around, see, *I am here*."

A sharp aroma came from that place. Another fragrance joined Anne in that room, similar to her own perfume, feminine, but not the same. Similar, yes, but filtered of its gentle bouquet, harder, harsher. If it were music, the scent would be discordant.

Anne closed her eyes. She'd had moments like this before, 'events' she'd never told Dan about, in case he tried to take the pills away. That could not happen. Anne needed the pills, but occasionally they magicked up these little 'performances', where reality wobbled for a moment.

Moments, seconds, yes, but never like this.

The mattress shifted again behind her, as if that somebody or something had changed position.

Anne knew she should just look round and see for herself that her room was empty, that nothing and no one stared at her back, at her vulnerable long white neck, who wanted Anne to sit awhile with them and *see what happened*.

But Anne couldn't. She was frozen. Her chest rose and fell imperceptibly, and she kept her eyes shut. The room was silent, save for her breath and the tiny taps of the snow as it flittered and jumped against the window.

If Anne had opened her eyes and turned her head a little, she could have seen the desk. If she saw the desk, she could see the mirror and, it followed, the reflection of whatever sat behind her. But Anne's mind was more fragile than even she knew, and if something *were* reflected there, it would shatter her.

Slowly, Anne opened her eyes, but couldn't turn her head. It had been fixed in place by fear. She simply stared ahead at the bathroom door in front of her. Anne breathed like her lungs were made of paper, would rip if she gulped air down like a drowner. So she inhaled softly in case the sound made whatever was sat there shuffle forward to investigate.

Don't breathe, she told herself, but simultaneously thought, *this is not real. This is the pills, this is the pills made real, nothing more. I must not look round because if I look round, and there is someone sitting there, grinning, I will never come back. I will be lost, my mind will tear, and I will never return. If I look round, and there is a shape under the sheets, a shape that reaches out, I will stop. I will stop being Anne Barker. I will stop being of this place. Just breathe. Be calm. Breathe.*

Quiet and shallow, Anne took in the barest oxygen she needed and continued to stare, unblinking, at the bathroom door. She prayed her peripheral vision wouldn't register movement in the mirror. If something moved there, Anne suspected she'd simply sit paralysed as whatever it was reached for her.

Anne breathed, then realised she was not the only one who did so here.

Yes, she heard it. Faraway, soft, yes, but she heard it. Something that had no need of oxygen behind her inhaled, exhaled. The breaths became deeper, but rolled, almost mechanical, like a respirator in an operating theatre. Human but inhuman, like the other perfume that had filled the air, not quite right somehow, not quite of *here*.

"Oh," she managed to vocalise, but it was a sound with no emotion, it simply escaped like air, dumb in meaning.

No no no, she thought from afar. *I am broken. The pills have broken me.*

The breath behind her changed. The mechanical in-out-in-out fluttered and shifted, like a broadcast picked up by a dying transistor radio. This new sound weaved and bent, but was recognisable, none the less.

No, no that cannot be, Anne thought. *It is the sound of crying. Who is crying behind me?*

A tiny part of her took control, the ancient centre of her brain responsible for survival.

Anne Barker slowly stood, put one foot in front of the other and walked toward the bedroom door.

If she could reach the door and turn the handle like an ordinary, normal person, the world would return to ordinary and normal, too.

Such a simple thing, to open a door.

Not far now. This 'event' was the pills. The pills that helped her now damned her. The pills had become real.

Anne reached for the handle, but stopped.

She had to look, to know this was just her mind in the throes of a short-circuit. That alone was a terrible enough idea, but preferable to the thought that… something impossible… waited there, just a foot behind her back.

She closed her eyes. She would turn, face the bed, open them, and there would be nothing there apart from what the pills had dreamed up.

Decision taken, Anne turned with her eyes still clamped shut.

Then, from two feet in front, but a billion miles away, from the other side of the universe, but here in the room, a voice suddenly whispered, harshly, "You are *nothing*".

Anne tried to keep her eyes shut but couldn't.

She backed up against the door in terror and looked in the direction of that rasped, hateful statement.

"Do it," that accusing voice grated like metal on metal and went silent.

The bed was empty.

She staggered a little and put her hand out to the wall.

I am lost, she thought and felt faint. She fell against the door, which was still mockingly solid. *I am hearing voices now. I am lost.*

Anne Barker, already buffeted by a storm within her, had become untethered.

COMING SOON

"The Gentle Art Of Forgetting" (part of The Snow Trilogy)

A thirty year old woman named Jane Dawn wakes up in a hut, deep in a snow covered forest.

She has no memory of who she was, where she is and how she got there. She is not alone.

To uncover Jane's truth, and how she's ended up in this strange new frozen place, you'll jump and slide about time and space. Piece by piece, the jigsaw of her life will be revealed .

This is a tale of true love, great loss and how the tiniest decisions can have the greatest consequences.

Here is part of the first chapter, where both you and Jane are thrown into the very deep end of the story.

*

Listen.

For a moment, there was something that sounded like an old fashioned kettle boiling.

Then Jane Dawn woke.

She came to, blinked, and slowly her eyes focussed.

It took an effort for her to see, as everything seemed blurred and white. Then she realised everything *was* blurred and white, because her vision was filled with thick snow.

Her mind was blurred too. Thought itself was an effort.

Distantly, Jane knew she was now *somewhere different*. She faced a window, *somewhere else*, and eventually managed to think, *now where am I?* But putting those words together in the correct order proved difficult.

Wherever she now found herself, it was completely silent. No background rumble of traffic, nor aircraft droned overhead. No ticking of clocks, or conversation in another room. Just Jane, this wood-framed window and the deepest of silences. Against it, even her shallow breathing seemed a cacophony.

She looked through the window and saw a dense line of trees in the distance. Their branches drooped under a thick layer of snow.

There was an empty clearing between wherever she sat and the tree-line. No green shoots, saplings or rocks peeked from that smooth, frozen landscape.

Jane was drawn to the snow that fell outside. She couldn't pull her eyes from it.

In the sky above this frozen clearing, a green Aurora performed aerial origami, folded into shapes; a wave, a sand dune, a sheet drying in a brisk wind. Then it dispersed, like ink in water. The Aurora diluted, faded and was gone.

She never saw it.

But with every flake that fell past her eyes, she felt strangely comforted, as if the snow hadn't just erased the ground, but *her* too, like chalk from a blackboard, ready for the next lesson.

Jane was inexplicably calm, because other than her name, she couldn't remember anything. Her memory, like the ground outside, had whited out, become smooth and featureless.

So she watched as both the snow and her mind drifted.

She had no desire to look away from this window. Jane knew there was something she should think, but it was just out of reach, a lifebelt that floated one way while the drowner chose to flail in the other.

*What should I. Be thinking? I don't. Know. I am…*and then, oh-so slowly, words came with difficulty, fetched from part of her mind she no longer knew.

I am numb. Dumb. I am. Strung. Out. Inert. Yes.

She reached up and placed her hand flat on the window.

It was solid.

Aha, oh, take note. This is. Solid.

That was important. The window was solid. The window was real. So it followed that all this was real, too.

Outside, the Snow chased its shadows to ground, thicker and thicker.

Part of her, inside - only a small part, a tiny, sensible, aware Jane, many hundreds of miles away, shouted, ran in circles and tried to attract her attention.

Listen! What's happening? This tiny Jane deep in her mind screamed. *What is happening to you? What is happening? What is happening Jane? What is happening you were not here you were somewhere else not here* before*, ask yourself what is happening?* Ask ask *ask.*

Oh be quiet, she thought, still oddly tranquil, in emotional slow motion. *I'm just Watching The Snow.*

And even as Jane thought that phrase, she realised the words had capitals, like a heading in an instruction manual. *I am Watching The*

Snow, she thought again, and there they were, the capitals, **W.T.S**. Watching The Snow, in bold, capitalised in her mind. Curious.

*You don't give a capital to a word...*she tried to remember. *Oh no, you do NOT give capitals to words...unless...the beginning...sentence of a noun...proper noun?* She stopped, confused, and stared back at the flakes.

"I think that's enough, Jane," someone spoke from behind her, and she felt a rough, dry hand gently touch her face and pull it softly away from the window.

*

"The Gentle Art Of Forgetting" will be available December 2019 from The Vivid Press, as an Ebook download, or at your favourite bookshop.